GHOST ARCHIPELAGO

DESTINY'S CALL

OSPREY
GAMES

FROSTGRAVE
GHOST ARCHIPELAGO

DESTINY'S CALL

MARK A. LATHAM

OSPREY GAMES
Bloomsbury Publishing Plc
PO Box 883, Oxford, OX1 9PL, UK
1385 Broadway, 5th Floor, New York, NY 10018, USA
E-mail: info@ospreygames.co.uk
www.ospreygames.co.uk

OSPREY GAMES is a trademark of Osprey Publishing Ltd
First published in Great Britain in 2018
© Osprey Publishing Ltd

ISBN:
PB 9781472832702
eBook 9781472832733
ePDF 9781472832740
XML 9781472832757

18 19 20 21 22 10 9 8 7 6 5 4 3 2 1

Originated by PDQ Digital Media Solutions, Bungay, UK
Printed and bound in Great Britain by
CPI (Group) UK Ltd, Croydon CR0 4YY

Osprey Games supports the Woodland Trust, the UK's leading woodland
conservation charity. Between 2014 and 2018 our donations are being
spent on their Centenary Woods project in the UK.

To find out more about our authors and books visit **www.
ospreypublishing.com**. Here you will find extracts, author interviews,
details of forthcoming events and the option to sign up for our newsletter.

CHAPTER 1

Yana Selishe marched through the broad Avenue of Ancestors, as the sun's first light chased away the shadows, transforming the city behind her into a glittering, golden wonder of domes and spires. Yet her destination was, as always, the darkness.

Yana's men flanked her, their footsteps accompanying the sounds of chains as they dragged along their prisoner. Ahead, the golden-masked guards – the *Bidajah* – watched silently as the towering doors of the Temple of Birrahd swung slowly open. The citizens of Yad-Sha'Rib whispered dark tales into their cups of what took place in the temple – if they dared whisper it at all. Few knew the truth better than Yana. She was once an assassin, now bound by ties of blood to serve the Merchant-King, So'Kurrah, as captain of the city's Manhunters. But to serve her king meant to serve his right-hand man, the Grand Vizier, Zhar-Mharrad. And it was to the vizier that she now went, dragging along the captives, doing her duty as always, without question.

She crossed the threshold of the temple without pause. The light of dawn appeared to falter as it kissed the shadow of that cursed earth, the darkness seeming to hiss defiantly as it retreated. One by one her men passed through the portal, some forty cubits high, with doors of polished black stone guarded by Zhar-Mharrad's faceless men. Yana suppressed a shudder of disgust at what the temple had become. She vaguely remembered the days when the doors were chased with gold, and pilgrims came from leagues around to make offerings to Birrahd. Those days had waned as Zhar-Mharrad's fortunes had waxed, and now there was only the black.

The great doors closed softly behind them. Ahead, rows of braziers fizzed to life of their own accord, marking the way through the silent temple. The Manhunters followed the path of fire, skirting the dimly lit prayer chamber where hooded cultists knelt in silent supplication to the God of Many Forms. Yana led her men down the winding stair shod in obsidian scales like the back of a twisting serpent, down into the belly of the great temple; down, down into the pits, where fires always burned and screams always echoed.

The screams today were different.

Yana had known something was amiss as soon as she had stepped into the unnatural darkness of the temple. Her prisoner had felt it even more acutely, and now as they descended to the lowest level of the black pits, he writhed as though in great pain. Like all the tortured souls in this place, the prisoner was a Heritor – a strange breed, imbued with uncanny powers from birth. The so-called 'gifts' of the Heritors made them the very devil to hunt. Some were fast as lightning, others strong as giants. Some communed with spirits, others could transform their very bodies to shadow. They would be powerful indeed but for the curse they bore – the 'Blood Burn' that wracked them with pain should they overstretch their abilities. The dog that Yana's hunters dragged along now had almost escaped them by fleeing through a solid wall! That was a new one, even for Yana Selishe, and tracking him had been like hunting a ghost. But Yana had not established herself by giving up easily, nor did she fear the cursed creatures she hunted. She had pursued the man doggedly through the night, until he could flee no more. Now he was her prisoner. His fate would not be pleasant, but better that than that such a creature be allowed to roam free in the Golden City.

Finally, they reached their destination. Firelight gleamed from the floor of a polished, black stone dais, upon which stood the Grand Vizier himself, his back to his huntress, gazing into a brazier of flickering green flame. His crimson cloak, trimmed with intricate cloth-of-gold serpents, trailed down the dais steps. His arms were outstretched, bony fingers, tipped with gold claws, curled as he concentrated on the flames. Beside him, on an ornate silver perch, sat his favourite pet, a large, two-headed raven, the feathers of its head missing with age, its beady eyes staring at Yana, reflecting the fire from the brazier. It always looked as though it knew what was going on. Sometimes, the vizier spoke to it as though it possessed true intelligence.

Yana craned her neck, trying despite herself to catch a glimpse of whatever Zhar-Mharrad could see in the fire. But just then, with a sudden flare and a plume of silver-green smoke, the flame was extinguished, and the vizier turned to face her with a theatrical flourish. The raven squawked.

'It is always an honour when Yana Selishe visits the temple.' Zhar-Mharrad's voice was deep and earthy. His thin, dark lips enounced each word with cold precision. 'You bring me another prize.' His piercing, painted eyes gleamed even in darkness, fixing Yana with a look of cruel mockery. For her, or her prisoner, she could not tell.

'I do, Grand Vizier,' she said, bowing low and despising herself for doing so. 'A Heritor, found in the Al'Sarifal district.'

'Ah!' Zhar-Mharrad smiled, his moustaches twitching. 'And tell me, what was he doing in the docklands? Eking a living from crumbs, like a gutter-rat, perhaps? Or was he... trying to find a ship?'

Yana frowned. 'My lord vizier is astute, as ever. He was looking for a ship,' she replied.

Another scream echoed from some far-off chamber. It didn't sound entirely human. And there was something disconcerting about the vizier's manner. More so than usual.

'Of course he was,' the vizier said. 'Your men may deposit the prisoner in the east dungeon, and take their leave. You, *Ku* Selishe, shall come with me. I have something to show you.'

Despite her reservations, Yana nodded to her second-in-command, her *jemadar*, Faizil. She saw in his eyes both relief to be dismissed from this fell place, and yet concern for his captain. His worries were misplaced: Yana Selishe was known by her enemies as the 'Shadow-Viper'. Zhar-Mharrad might make her skin crawl, but she did not fear him. She feared no one. Faizil obeyed Yana nonetheless, giving a signal to the others, and marching from the chamber.

Zhar-Mharrad descended the steps from his dais, and walked past Yana towards a corridor she had never before noticed. She suppressed a shudder, not at the fell wind that blew from that corridor, nor at the sinister howls that reverberated in the very rock, but merely at the prospect of spending any time alone in the company of Zhar-Mharrad. She was cruel, yes – she had to be, in her line of work – but the Grand Vizier was something else. He was soulless. Some said he was in league with demons, and Yana did not doubt it.

Yana followed the vizier along the passage. It twisted and turned for what seemed like an age, the way lit only by ominous green glowstones set into polished walls. They ascended a winding stair, and at last came to another black chamber, altogether more sinister than those Yana had seen before. It was circular, with a domed ceiling painted like constellations, glowstones sparkling in place of stars. It might have been beautiful, but for the horrifying carvings on the walls, of inhuman creatures and twisted beasts – the one-thousand-and-one forms of the god Birrahd. By flickering green light, myriad pairs of beady black-stone eyes stared into Yana's being; never had she felt so vulnerable than here, under the inquisitorial gaze of Zhar-Mharrad's patron deity.

The Grand Vizier's eyes joined those of the carvings, and Yana realised he had been staring at her, a twitching smile beneath his black moustache suggesting that he enjoyed her discomfort. What's more, he stood before a strange pedestal, which Yana had not noticed when she had entered the room. It grew almost organically from the smooth stone floor, terminating at a broad bowl, filled with some dark, oily liquid. Zhar-Mharrad stood with one bony hand outstretched over the bowl. With a single golden claw, he pierced his palm, and a bead of dark red blood fell into the pool, causing a perfectly circular ripple upon the liquid within. For the briefest moment, Yana felt sure the shadows at the vizier's back had twisted, and hungry eyes now thirsted for blood.

'Tell me, Ku Selishe,' the vizier said, again using the formal address that he surely knew Yana hated, 'do you know how the Heritors came to be?'

'I have heard the stories, oh wise Vizier,' she replied, caring not if he sensed her tone of mockery. 'Stories of the Lost Isles.'

'Yes, the fabled "Ghost Archipelago". The place that changed the Heritors' ancestors, granting them extraordinary gifts, which they have passed down to their progeny for generations since. Now these lesser creatures thrive across the world, trading upon the reputation of their more illustrious forebears, enjoying power that they never earned.'

'That may be so in other cities, but not in Yad-Sha'Rib. The man we found today is the first Heritor seen here in nearly thirteen moons.'

'There may be others, but they have long learned to stay hidden, never to use their gifts, for fear of attracting your attention, Ku Selishe. Truly, you are a blessing to us. King So'Kurrah himself said those very words to me just recently.'

'Your words flatter me,' Yana said, bowing. She no longer fooled herself that So'Kurrah held power in the city. His vizier had long since inveigled his way into every facet of government. His golden-faced soldiers patrolled the streets at night; stood watch over the king's family; guarded the king's treasure. Or, rather, they ensured that the king could do nothing without Zhar-Mharrad's say-so.

'Do you know why your prisoner today was looking for a ship so brazenly?' Zhar-Mharrad went on.

This gave Yana pause. It was true that the man she had caught had not been taking the precautions usually displayed by his kind. Indeed, he had been showing off his powers in a bid to attract a daring captain to take him from the city – a rash course of action that had led to his downfall. Yana said only, 'Desperation, I suppose.'

'In a manner, but not just that. No, he was stirred to activity after a long time in hiding, because he felt the pull of magic in his blood. He felt the call of the Lost Isles.'

'What do you mean, Lord Vizier?'

'Those screams you heard from my dungeons. I could see they bothered you. They had about them the edge of agitation, of frustration, not just at their confinement, but at their inability to heed that which calls them. The Ghost Archipelago has appeared, Ku Selishe.'

'Then the stories… they are not just stories.'

'Indeed not. After two hundred years, the Lost Isles have returned to the world, and the Heritors can sense it. The source of the Heritors' power – the Crystal Pool – calls to them, in their dreams, in their every sense, in their blood. It calls home its wayward spawn, to complete whatever it is they started all those years ago. But we shall not let them achieve their goals!'

'What do you mean, Vizier?'

'I mean the wastrels who call themselves Heritors do not deserve this power. They are arrogant fools, vagabonds, dilettantes! They misuse power that they have not earned, passed down from far worthier adventurers than they. Imagine if even a handful of them were to drink from the pool. Imagine what might happen if their powers were increased. Who knows what gifts they would gain: power over men? Life everlasting? And what then? Would you, our most fierce Manhunter, bow to a Heritor? Would they even let you live, knowing that you have enslaved so many of their vile ilk?'

Yana felt anger rise in her craw. 'I would never bow to those… freaks of nature,' she growled. She knew the vizier was playing to her own pride, but his words made sense all the same. She had too long witnessed what the Heritors could do, for good and for ill. She remembered her predecessor in the ranks of the city's hunters – her father. She remembered how he had met his end, and the Heritor who had brought it about.

'Good…' the vizier smiled. 'Then you must redouble your efforts, for I have heard whispers on the wind of another Heritor at large. Their identity is concealed even from my power, for reasons I cannot ascertain. But they are out there, and they will be looking for a ship, mark my words. That man you brought in just now – he had the right idea. If he was searching for a captain, it is because word is out upon the streets of our city. Word that treasure-seekers and fortune-hunters need a Heritor to guide them across the sea to the Lost Isles. You shall find any such captain, and deal with them. Do I make myself clear?'

'Perfectly. But, Lord Vizier… if I may…?'

'Yes?'

'You said we must stop the Heritors from reaching the Crystal Pool. How can we do that? They will surely be setting sail as we speak, from every city in the world.'

Zhar-Mharrad smiled wickedly. 'Their numbers are perhaps not so great as you imagine, Ku Selishe, and the voyage is perilous. But you are correct that we need an advantage of our own, which is why I have selected a Heritor from the dungeons to act as our guide.'

'My lord!' Yana gasped. To treat with the Heritors was long forbidden, under pain of death. Not that it truly surprised her that Zhar-Mharrad might stoop so low.

'Fear not, child. I have taken precautions. Behold!' Zhar-Mharrad now flicked the dark liquid beneath his hand, and the strange bowl reverberated with a deep hum. The surface of the liquid began to dance; spikes of oleaginous water stabbed upwards, before once more being absorbed into their mass, and then, as one, were perfectly still.

Zhar-Mharrad beckoned Yana forward. She stepped to the pedestal, peering cautiously at the liquid. The bowl still resonated, but the liquid was now unmoving, like a polished slab of obsidian. But upon that dark mirror, an image began to form: hazy at first, but now clearer. At once, Yana recognised the dungeons below. In the centre of a filthy cell, a man hung by his wrists from chains. His face was covered by matted hair, but from the sallow skin that hung from his skeletal frame, Yana could tell that he had seen too many summers.

'He is one of yours,' the vizier purred. 'One of the first you brought to me. You captured this man when your father could not.'

Despite herself, Yana glared at the vizier. 'I thought he was dead!'

'King So'Kurrah himself ordered the stay of execution, for this man's value to us could yet be immeasurable.'

'I was not told. Why was I not told?'

'Because you are a soldier!' Zhar-Mharrad snapped,

and at once a sharp edge came to his words. A chill breeze blew about the room, and the shadows themselves seemed to shrink in upon them.

Yana bowed. She had forgotten herself in her anger. And she had forgotten the dark forces with which Zhar-Mharrad communed. 'Forgive me,' she said, the words sticking in her throat.

The chill subsided, the shadows retreated; the vizier had made his point. 'You hate this man, it is natural. But is it not the way of your order to set aside such feelings for the greater good? This Heritor will be my guide when I set sail for the Ghost Archipelago.'

'But... his power. Any man he looks upon is held in his sway. Perhaps it would be better to take another... – '

'I have chosen him,' Zhar-Mharrad snapped. 'Birrahd wills it, and so shall it be. Besides, I have taken precautions. Look.'

Yana gazed again into the pool. She saw the man more clearly now, as he raised his head. His hair fell from his face; Yana recognised him fully as the man who had killed her father. But his uncanny powers were no more a threat.

The man had no eyes.

Yana looked to Zhar-Mharrad, whose ever-present smirk was now a broad grin, full of menace.

'Now, Ku Selishe,' he said. 'If you are satisfied, I believe you have a job to do.'

CHAPTER 2

Every night, the dream was the same.

Samir tossed and turned, plagued by visions of lush jungle and skull-carved mountains; of screeching, reptilian creatures, and bottomless pools of rich blue water hidden in lost valleys. He ran through undergrowth, through caves, through long-forgotten coves, running endlessly from some unseen pursuer, to the ominous thrumming of distant drums. It should have been frightening, but the dream was not a nightmare. It filled Samir with a thrill the likes of which he had never known in his young life. Every nerve in his body jangled in heightened elation. Every noise of the jungle reached his ears; every strange smell carried by foreign winds reached his nostrils. He ran faster, jumped higher, shouted louder and felt more alive than at any other time he remembered.

He entered a cave. A vast cavern, whose limits could not be seen in the enfolding darkness. From some distant crack in the upper reaches, a crepuscular ray of silver moonlight shone upon the mirror-smooth surface of a strange pool. Sam stood upon its shore, and he was not alone. One by one, torches were lit, illuminating the faces of men and women of every creed, from every far-off land

Sam had ever read about in storybooks. They muttered words Sam could not understand, and then, solemnly, one by one, they stepped forward to kneel by the pool. As they dipped their hands into the water, the cavern reverberated, a vibration that rumbled through Sam's very bones. The distant drumming echoed all around, growing louder, more rhythmic. And a light, white and pure, shone from beneath the water's surface. Men turned, inviting Sam to join them, to kneel by the pool and bask in its glow.

He stepped forward, his limbs almost failing in strength as the vibrations grew stronger, and the drums grew louder. It took an age to take just a few steps, and the light seeped over the water's edge, and began to consume him. Something within Sam burned. He tried to cry out, but could not. He felt every fibre of his being pulled apart and clashed together again. He felt as if he might die, but knew he would be reborn, somehow different. But still, he could not stand it. The light seared, the drums boomed, and Sam roared with pain, with elation and ecstasy, with grief for the life he had known, and now left behind.

Sam fair leapt from his bed, crying out despite himself, and then stopping in his tracks as the familiar walls of his tiny bedroom swam into view. His heart pounded; sweat-drenched nightclothes stuck to him. He clutched at the amulet that he always wore around his neck; a jagged, crescent-shaped chunk of oxidised bronze. It felt like ice against his skin, yet its familiar presence brought him comfort.

Through holes in the ragged sackcloth hanging over his window, the dawn sun glowed, casting his room in an orange hue.

CHAPTER 2

The door opened, and Sam jumped, as if for a moment he believed that some predatory creature from his dream had followed him back to the real world.

'Samir! What is wrong?' Sam's mother stood in the doorway, wringing her hands with concern for her only son.

'Nothing, mother,' Sam lied. 'It was just a bad dream, that is all.'

'Again? Do not think I am a fool, Samir Lahij. I see what is happening.'

'You do?'

'Your father always said this day would come.' Her eyes were large and full of worry. 'You feel something, don't you? Like... something calling you away from here?'

'Not calling. More... pulling at me. I cannot explain it, Mother. I dream of places I have never seen, yet I am certain they are real. My blood rushes like the tide – like I am meant to be at sea. I don't know where I am supposed to go, but still I know the way, like I have made the journey before, long ago. But... it is stupid of me. I have never left Yad-Sha'Rib.'

'Do not ever think you are stupid, Samir. You are far from that! That place you dream of is real, I think, although I have never seen it. Your father spoke of it many times. Jungles, steaming and hot, and filled with strange creatures. Mountains taller than the highest temple spire, carved with faces of monsters and gods. A mysterious pool in a moonlit cave...'

'Yes! My father really spoke of these things?' Sam leaned forward eagerly, his heart skipping a beat.

'He did. It was something to do with his gift – that very gift that you share. And there was something else...' Her face became very grave.

17

'Tell me!'

'He said a time would come when all of your kind would feel this call to a faraway land, to the place where your ancestors found their power. The "Crystal Pool". And he said this would be the most dangerous time of all, for your kind – the Heritors – would strive to set sail no matter the risk, while ambitious men would go to any lengths to gain the secrets of the pool for themselves. Wicked, dishonourable men; and unspeakable tyrants. You know the kinds of people I mean. I have warned you.'

Sam knew all too well, even though his mother would not speak the name of the Grand Vizier, lest spies be inexplicably lurking outside their hovel. 'Yes, mother. I stay away from the guards. I never show anyone what I can do... what I am. I wear the amulet always.' He untucked it from his nightshirt as proof, its greenish surface shining dully in the brightening morning sun. It was heavy – almost the size of Sam's palm – but he never removed it, as his mother insisted.

'Then put it back,' she said. 'You know it must be worn near your heart. You may hide from mortal eyes, but the amulet protects you from... unnatural sight. Your father was careless, but he left me with that gift, for you.'

'I know,' Sam said, sadly. He had heard the story of his father's death many times. How he had tried to find more of his kind within Yad-Sha'Rib before the vizier could capture them. How he tried to lead an uprising against Zhar-Mharrad's regime, but had instead been slain by the Manhunters. Or, rather, by the most legendary of the Manhunters, the 'Shadow-Viper', whose true face had never been seen, whose name was whispered in fear. Yes, Asim Lahij had been a so-called Heritor, blessed with magical powers, as was Sam. An idealist – a revolutionary. A brave man. And, as Sam's mother was always quick to remind him, it was his bravery that had got him killed.

'Sam, I must ask you to make me a promise.'

Sam knew what she was about to say. 'If I can,' he said.

'Promise me that you will resist these foolish notions. Promise me that this... magic... in your blood shall not control you. You will not try to leave the city. You will not... leave me.'

Frustration, sorrow, pity and anger clashed within Sam's breast. 'But what if father's cause was right? What if it is my... my destiny?'

'Swear it, Samir!' she insisted. 'You are fifteen years old, and this is not a game. I lost your father to this curse. I will not lose my son.'

Sam hung his head. 'I swear,' he muttered.

'Then we shall say no more about it,' she said. 'Now get dressed – it is a little early, but we may as well begin our chores. I will make breakfast. Your favourite.'

She smiled brightly, as though nothing had been said at all, then shuffled from the room with a song on her lips.

Sam pulled back the sackcloth curtain, and gazed out of the little window, across the pitted roofs of the shanty town, to the distant horizon where a sliver of shimmering sea glittered tantalisingly out of reach. It was rare that he considered just how little he had, or just how unfair his lot was. His mother had raised him better than that. But now, as he stared out towards the docks, the press of hundreds of dilapidated hovels, all teeming with life, felt stifling. He imagined what it might be like to run to the harbour, find a ship, and sail across the sea.

He squeezed the amulet tight, so that the irregular points dug into his palm. These feelings did not come from within him. They came from without, as though some unseen force was controlling him. And in the face of such magic, what power did a promise made by a mere boy hold?

* * *

'Run, Sam. Run!'

Hassan barged into Samir in his haste to get away. Sam snapped out of his daydreaming only to stop himself falling, and snatched a glance back down the market aisle. Angry shouts reached his ears. Black turbans bobbed closer over the heads of the crowd. Hassan had attracted the attention of the guards.

'Come on, Sam!' Hassan called back, voice filled with elation at the thrill of the chase.

Sam turned after his friend, and ran.

Hassan was off to a head-start, and sprinted so quickly through the narrow market streets that Sam almost lost sight of him. He was a year older than Sam, and a head taller, although scrawny with it. He'd lost some of his skill at thievery as he had grown, but his pace and agility usually made up for it.

Sam risked another look back, and his heart leapt to his throat as he met the eyes of a town guard, glowering brows bunching together beneath a black turban, a great scimitar swinging at his belt. He was almost upon Sam, a broad hand reaching out, straining to grab the scruff of Sam's neck. Sam dived low, scrabbling through the legs of a spice merchant, sending the trader staggering in surprise into the path of the guard. The curses that reached Sam's ears were evidence enough that the guard had collided with the trader, and Sam picked up the pace.

Sellers and customers alike grabbed at the boys. Sam saw Hassan shake off one such do-gooder, and himself ducked beneath the thick arms of a labourer. Sam swiped at a stack of baskets, sending the goods toppling into the street behind him to slow his pursuers. He saw Hassan make a sharp right turn, and followed suit, leaping up onto a livestock wagon, upending several cages and sending a pair of chickens flapping and squawking into the faces of the onrushing guards. Some men shouted after them, others laughed. Most ignored the spectacle – it was just another day in the market district, and Sam was just another thief chancing his luck with the law.

He squeezed between a fat, silk-wearing merchant and his wife, darted under the feet of a troop of servants laden with baggage, and followed Hassan. The guards had not yet given up the chase, but now Hassan was dashing up a steep, winding alley, where the ground ran with a torrent of filthy water and the seedier taverns of the Al'Sarifal district birthed odours of indescribable unpleasantness.

Sam caught up with Hassan as the older boy sprang onto a pile of wine-crates, and shimmied monkey-like up a clay drainpipe. Sam followed, and knew from the shout behind him that they had been seen. He reached the flat roof, where Hassan took his hand and hauled him up, beaming broadly. Sam cast a look down into the alley; one guard shook his fist at the boys, while another turned about and rushed back to the market to head off any chance of escape. It was futile – Sam and Hassan had played this game many times before.

They set off immediately, this time dashing across the rooftops of gleaming stucco shops, taverns and storehouses. They leapt across gaps that less nimble lads might have shied from, barely missing a stride as they scrambled ever onwards, ever upwards, the sun on their faces and the salty sea air in their nostrils.

Finally they slowed, the sounds of the crowd dying away far behind them, and the open sea stretching out in front of them. Dozens of ships bobbed about in the docks at the throat of the Mangnahim Bay. Hundreds of sailors and labourers scurried back and forth like worker ants, loading and unloading goods from all over the known world. The scent of herbs and spices, fish, tea, tobacco and wine drifted on the air, speaking to Sam as it always did of distant places and the promise of adventure.

The boys bent double, panting to catch their breath. Hassan slapped Sam on the back.

'That was close,' he laughed.

'You're getting too big and clumsy to steal from the upper market,' Sam said, playfully. 'What did you get that was worth all this trouble?'

Hassan gave a toothy grin, reached into his tunic, and pulled out three oranges.

'Is that it?' Sam laughed.

'What do you mean?' Hassan affected a wounded look. 'If you're not careful you won't get any.' He at once began juggling the fruit, launching them higher and higher, until finally he fumbled them and dropped all three.

Sam darted, eel-quick, and snatched one up. 'You never were good at juggling.'

Hassan shrugged, and retrieved the other two oranges. 'Keep that one. I'll have one, and take the other back for my sister. She'll appreciate an orange even if you don't.'

'Not if she knew how you'd come by it. Seriously though, Hassan, you must be more careful. I don't want to lose a hand for the sake of an orange.'

'Don't be serious,' Hassan frowned. 'What's the point of being friends otherwise? I can stay at home to be lectured. Say, look over there!' Hassan's mood lifted at once, and he pointed along the row of ships. 'The one with the striped sails. You see that flag?'

Sam saw. The ship was long and clumsy-looking, and its prow tapered into a tall, carved figurehead. A green pennant fluttered in the morning breeze from a single mast, and upon it was emblazoned a golden dragon, its body drawn in long, interlocking threads, like knots. It was a sigil of the Northmen. And there was only one captain who ever came to Yad-Sha'Rib flying such a flag.

'The Pirate Prince has returned!' Hassan said, and at once began to climb down from the roof.

Dagomir, the Pirate Prince, a reaver from frozen lands. He was one of the few of his folk ever to ply his trade along the Swahal'shar Coast, and one of the few pirates who would dare make anchorage in the city of Yad-Sha'Rib.

These facts alone were enough to seal his reputation. It could only mean that Dagomir had gold aplenty to pay the guards, and a good reason to take the risk.

'Hurry up!' Hassan shouted from somewhere below. 'I want to see the ship!'

Sam felt something strange; some sense of foreboding that he could not explain. But despite his reservations, he followed.

* * *

The reality of the teeming dockside from the ground was somewhat different from the glittering illusion of romance from on high. Sam and Hassan very rarely ventured down to the Al'Sarifal docks, for despite their rich pickings, they were not fertile ground for opportunistic young thieves looking for a thrill. They were dangerous, full of pirates, spies, mercenaries and cutthroats. Stealing an orange from the market just three streets away frequently led to a half-hearted chase from guards fat from the profits of bribes. Here at the docks, where the guards rarely ventured, petty theft might earn a dagger in the back and a watery grave.

Not that the docks were entirely devoid of security, beyond simply the hired swords paid by ships' captains to defend their precious cargoes. Upon every wall stood a single man in red and black robes, statue-like, distinctive only for his golden mask gleaming in the early sun. The Bidajah, personal army of the Grand Vizier Zhar-Mharrad, were an unwelcome sight at the best of times. Why they would take a personal interest in the comings and goings at the docks was a mystery – or, at least, it would have been had Sam not known of the Heritors. He suddenly felt very vulnerable.

Samir and Hassan stuck close together. The older boy's confidence had visibly diminished now that they found themselves pushing through the press of burly sailors who stank of strong liquor and musky sweat. The forest of masts ahead, the sea wall, the press of harbour storehouses, all conspired to block out the sun. It was a pleasant morning elsewhere in Yad-Sha'Rib, but not here. The docks did not respect the clock, and the business of the colourful, seafaring visitors to the city never ended. It could just as easily be dusk. The taverns, which made a roaring trade in beverages prohibited in other parts of the city, were already open, and packed to the rafters. Outside, men gambled on dice and cock-fights, or brawled in the gutter filth. Labourers went back and forth on legitimate business, while merchants haggled with captains for their goods. Every stripe of life from every corner of the globe could be found in Al'Sarifal, the most notorious – and wealthiest – port in the Mangnahim Bay, and the marriage was not always felicitous.

'We shouldn't linger here,' Sam whispered, pulling on Hassan's sleeve. It was not merely the sly glances from thieves and pirates that disconcerted him. The closer he was to the water, the more he felt that strange sensation swelling within: the call of the ocean, of the mysterious isles across the sea.

'We're almost there,' Hassan replied, although his attempt at nonchalance was unconvincing. Hassan was an experienced thief, for his age. He must have noticed the local street urchins shadowing their every move, wondering why these two upstarts had ventured into their territory.

But he was right. The dragon figurehead loomed over them now like some great beast of wood and copper. Its eyes were red glass, glaring down at the boys fiercely. It was bigger in the flesh than it had appeared from the rooftops. The ship from which it sprouted was broad-beamed and shallow-draughted. Round, painted shields lined the gunwales, from behind which ballistae pointed in formidable broadsides.

Sam reached out, touching the smooth wood of the figurehead. The ship bobbed slightly upon the swell, and with it Sam felt tangled emotions surge through him. Energy seemed to course through the grain of the wood, into his hand, filling him with a deep longing to leave this city. He had the overwhelming urge to jump aboard, to stow away. He closed his eyes for a moment to quieten these rash thoughts. He tried to think of the promise he had made to his mother.

'What does it say?' Hassan asked.

Sam opened his eyes. Hassan pointed to the ornate gold and green lettering at the prow, spelling out the name of the vessel in the trader's tongue. He had never learned to read.

Sam mouthed the sounds of the unfamiliar language carefully to himself, and then said aloud, 'Something "Wrath". I don't understand that first word. *Va-nee-ah*,' he enounced.

'It says *Vanya's Wrath*,' came a loud, thickly accented voice behind them, making the boys fair jump out of their skin.

As one, they turned. Behind them stood a tall man, broad of shoulder, skin white as jasmine and tousled hair like spun gold. His eyes shone emerald green, like the bay in winter. It would have been a kind face, were it not for the scar that ran the length of the left side, and the mouth that sneered rather than smiled. Behind the man was a press of sailors, of every creed and colour, looking to their golden-haired master with deference.

'Vanya is a goddess among my people,' the stranger said. 'She is mistress of the storm, who drags ships to the bottom of the sea. Some wonder why I court the attentions of such a goddess. But in truth, after all we have been through, it is clear that she is in love with me, otherwise I would have long gone to a watery grave.'

'The Pirate Prince...' Sam gasped.

'The same. Now, would you care to explain why two thieves are loitering about my ship?'

Sam felt a rough hand upon his shoulder. Two men had flanked the boys. They were cornered by Dagomir's pirates.

'Perhaps you've come to join the crew?' Dagomir grinned, drawing mocking laughter from his men. 'There's not much call for skinny street urchins at sea. Although some of the men were recruited in distant lands where lads like you make hearty meals.'

One of the men leered forward from the crowd. Every visible part of his flesh was tattooed with some outlandish design. The man smiled, revealing two rows of teeth filed down to points. Hassan cried out, and struggled in vain against his captor. The laughs and shouts grew louder as the men revelled in their sport.

'This one is different.'

The voice came from the ship, and at the words, the commotion ceased. Everyone turned to the speaker, and Sam craned his neck to see.

There, sitting cross-legged near the figurehead, was a man, still as a statue, eyes closed. If he had been there all along, Sam had not seen him. He was a wild-looking fellow. His skin was dark as jujube bark, with rows of bright white dots painted across his face from cheek to cheek. His complexion was youthful and smooth, but the grey streaks running through his shock of black hair hinted at his true age. He wore simple robes of grey, and would have easily passed for a beggar with his garb and demeanour. Yet there was something unnerving about him: something powerful.

'Which?' Dagomir said.

The strange man's eyes flicked open, and settled firmly on Samir. 'This one. He is, perhaps, the one you seek.'

Sam's blood ran cold. He felt Hassan's questioning gaze boring into the side of his head. The amulet at Sam's breast, always ice-cold against his skin, for the very first time felt warm. Uncomfortably so, and it seemed only to increase as the wild-haired man's eyes remained upon Sam.

Dagomir, the Pirate Prince, leaned forward, so that his stubbled face almost touched Sam's own. His breath smelt of rum, even at this hour.

'This is Makeno,' he said quietly. 'He is a warden. A sorcerer. Some say his magic is dark indeed. Perhaps he has chosen you to be his next... blood sacrifice.'

Sam knew the man mocked him, but there was a very real threat in the words; a threat of some sinister fate that Sam had no wish to meet. The grinning men all about had eyes that had seen much cruelty, and Sam had no doubt they would deliver him to a violent end if their master willed it. Hassan struggled harder. Sam looked about, desperate to find some avenue of escape.

From the corner of his eye, he saw movement. One of the Bidajah leapt from his post, to much consternation from the bustling dock crowds. Sam could not see over the heads of the pirates that surrounded him, but there was at once a hue and cry. Shouts of anger, of excitement, and of outrage. Dagomir was not immune to the commotion, and looked about with what was surely worry upon his face. But surely the Pirate Prince was not afraid of the Bidajah?

The noise came closer. Someone shoved one of Dagomir's men out of the way, and he bundled into Sam and Hassan. Sam felt the grip of his captor loosen upon his shoulder, and knew his chance had come. He stamped down hard on the foot of the man who held him. The men let go with a cry. Sam shouted to Hassan, and slipped between the pirates, into the crowd.

'Emilio! After them!'

It was Dagomir's voice. Sam did not wait to see who Emilio was, or whether he was close. Instead, he ran, following in the wake of the imposing Bidajah, who now numbered five, and who parted the crowds with ease.

Moments later, Hassan was at Sam's side, laughing with sheer relief. Encouraged and exhilarated by their lucky escape, the boys picked up speed, racing as fast as they could away from the *Vanya's Wrath*.

CHAPTER 3

For a time, the two boys were carried along with the mob, which surged away from the docks, into narrow slums and warrens of Al'Sarifal that rarely saw a breath of wind or beam of sunlight. Sam felt fear rise within him again, and this time it was more immediate, more visceral, than anything posed by the pirates at the docks. This was not some adventure from which wiles and the speed of youth would carry Samir and Hassan. If the vizier's golden-masked men were chasing someone down, their quarry must be dangerous indeed.

Sam thought of his father or, rather, the scene that he had imagined from his mother's descriptions. He knew he could not draw any closer to the Bidajah.

He looked about, and saw a means of escape. A way up to the rooftops of the low dwellings, and then higher perhaps, to the ruinous buildings that neighboured them.

'Hassan!' he cried. He pointed. 'Up. Up!'

Sam's friend cut across him, using his superior size to forge a path, and soon the boys were away, leaping onto a pile of junk, up onto a wall, and then scrambling up a sloping roof that was more holes than tiles.

Breathless, they followed the progress of the guards from their vantage point.

'There,' Hassan said, pointing.

Ahead, where the crowd thinned, four black-clad soldiers dashed across the street, their faces masked not by gold, but by black scarves.

'Hunters!' Sam gasped. He had seen them only once before, and not in broad daylight. Every cutpurse, beggar and petty thief in Yad-Sha'Rib told stories of the Manhunters. Agile as monkeys, quick and deadly as snakes, they tracked down the most dangerous criminals in the city, and took them to the great Temple of Birrahd, where they were never seen again. Their favourite quarry was said to be unlicensed wizards, although to hear the stories one would think even the lowliest cripple risked being snatched away if they stayed too late on the streets after dark. The merest glimpse of them set Sam's teeth on edge. It was the Manhunters who had killed his father. The Manhunters who had consigned Sam and his mother to a life in the slums.

His fear subsided. And it was replaced by something he did not remember ever feeling before. Anger. Ice-cold, vengeful anger. More than that, he felt strong. Power flowed, from deep within.

Sam's mother had always warned him of the hunters. She had spoken of them as if they were *Yoggac'chi* – capricious spirits known for stealing children from their parents in the dead of night. She'd told him that if ever he saw a hunter, he must flee, like his life depended on it.

Hassan was already running, leaping to the next roof, following the course of the Bidajah, who even now moved to intercept the hunters. Sam paused, remembering the warnings of his mother.

'Come on, Sam,' Hassan called. 'We'll never get another chance to see the hunters catch someone. What are you? Scared?'

Sam hesitated. He knew that whatever secret power he possessed, it was surely not enough to take on the hunters. He could not risk discovery and capture by giving in to anger. So what could be gained by following Hassan?

'Samir!' Hassan hissed.

And before he knew what was happening, Sam was leaping the gap, and he and Hassan were running once more into certain danger.

* * *

Sam peered over the ledge at the scene unfolding below. An old man, dressed in rags, stood in the centre of a fork in the dirt road. He turned about confusedly, sensing that he was trapped. But he did not know the full extent of his predicament – could not – for he was blind. A filthy rag was tied about his head, covering his eyes. His mouth was contorted into a snarl. He reached about, arms outstretched, striking at shadows.

The poor commoners who lived here scattered in all directions, slamming shut their doors so that the hunted man could not embroil them in whatever crime he had committed. Three of the Bidajah advanced slowly along one fork; the other two had manoeuvred around behind the man, blocking the second road. The third and final way out of the meagre square had at first been clear, but now two shadowy figures leapt silently down from a rooftop opposite

Sam and Hassan. Sam had not seen them, but now the hunters stalked towards their prey. On a rooftop above stood their commander. A woman, Sam thought, though she was entirely disguised by her black uniform, which covered all but her eyes. Her turban and sash were deepest crimson, braided with cloth of gold – the only ostentation on any of the hunters, and doubtless indicative of rank. If she noticed the two boys on the roof across the street – or even cared about their presence – she gave no sign.

Sam winced. His stomach cramped, and nausea swept over him.

'What's the matter?' Hassan whispered. 'You have been acting strangely all day. Are you sick?'

'It's nothing,' Sam said. In truth, he had no idea what the matter was. He was sure he wasn't ill, but this sensation was entirely new. 'That man,' he whispered. 'He is a Heritor.'

Hassan's eyes widened, and he looked down at the blind man. 'That beggar? One of the forbidden magi? Don't be stupid.'

'Heritors are not magi,' Sam corrected his friend. 'A magi would not become so trapped. But he is a Heritor. I feel it.'

'Feel it…?' Hassan looked confused, but had no time to question Sam further.

One of the Bidajah who had circled behind the old man now advanced, a cudgel in his hand. He towered over the blind man, who at first did not seem to hear the approach of his enemy. The cultist brought down the cudgel, aimed squarely at the back of the old man's head; and at the last moment, the man spun about, raising a forearm, upon which the cudgel cracked like a mere twig against stone.

Sam's heart leapt to his throat. The blind man hit out at the Bidajah with a single, controlled strike to the chest. The larger man flew away from the old man, landing in a heap by the feet of his companion. Sam had never before seen a Bidajah bested in combat; he had never even heard of anyone so much as challenging the personal guard of Zhar-Mharrad. Sam knew his instinct had been right – the old man was surely a Heritor.

Another Bidajah leapt forward, pouncing bodily on the old man. The Heritor flung himself backwards, slamming the guard into a wall with a sickening crunch, but the cultist did not let go. It was said that the Bidajah underwent terrifying trials that inured them to pain, and struck them dumb. Sam could well believe it.

As the Heritor tried to free himself, the other Bidajah advanced slowly, in unison. But the hunters came too, dashing in front of the golden-masked guards. One of them took out a slender, silver cord, glittering with enchantments. He swung and loosed it. It looped about the wrist of the Heritor, and the old man's prodigious strength was at once sapped. The hunter tugged at the cord, and the Heritor was yanked along with it, falling face-first into the dirt with the Bidajah on his back, pinning him to the ground.

As the hunters darted forward to their quarry, Sam felt the rage rise within him again like bile. He remembered the story of how his father had been similarly outnumbered, slain for no crime other than trying to escape an unjust king. It was a story that he could tell no one, but that he kept within him like a talisman. He looked down; he had unconsciously taken his amulet from beneath his shirt, and held it tightly in his hand. Again, it grew hot to the touch, as though it were guiding him. Or warning him.

Hassan looked to Sam, frowning. 'What are you... ?'

Before his friend could finish the question, Sam tore the amulet from his neck, and pressed it into Hassan's hand. 'Look after this,' he said. 'Please.' Without further pause or thought, he leapt from the rooftop.

Sam touched down onto a ledge, sprang from it, and rolled across the ground, righting himself just a few cubits from the blind man. He had no plan, but for now he was free of the restrictive properties of his amulet. His heightened senses and cat-like agility, so long repressed, would now have to save his life. But Sam had never practised his skills and now, on the ground surrounded by soldiers, he knew he had risked his life for a chance at revenge.

He dashed forward to the old man, who wrestled feebly with the Bidajah on his back. Sam landed a kick at the guard's throat, right below the golden mask. It was like kicking a rock, but it had the desired effect. The Bidajah rolled away, but began to clamber to his feet almost immediately.

Sam ducked, instincts screaming, and the cudgel of another guard swung harmlessly over his head. He threw himself to his back onto the ground, and kicked upwards with both feet, slamming them into a Bidajah's groin. The huge guard barely grunted, but staggered backwards a few steps, and Sam scrabbled to his feet again.

The Heritor was up now, too, staggering weakly, lashing out all around in confusion. The hunter with the silver cord pulled the Heritor about like a marionette.

Sam darted between the oncoming Bidajah. His nerves jangled, his very skin seemed to burn with a warning of danger, and Sam darted aside immediately. A crossbow bolt stroked his cheek, its flight almost cutting him as it flashed by, thudding into the door of a hovel behind him. Sam looked up to see a hunter reloading.

He did not pause. Sam dodged and weaved around his assailants, their strikes and grasps appearing cumbersome to him, as though they were moving through quicksand. He barged with all his might into the cord-wielding hunter. Sam was not particularly big or strong, but he had momentum, and it was enough to unbalance the black-clad soldier.

The Heritor was alongside Sam in a heartbeat, landing a blow to the face of the hunter. It rattled the foe, but the old man had little of the strength he had displayed previously. Sam grabbed at the man's wrist, trying his best to loosen the cord, which bit cruelly into the old man's flesh. At Sam's touch, something changed in the Heritor; some feeling was exchanged between Sam and the old man, deeper than words. Sam sensed the resistance sapping away from the man. He touched Sam's face with a trembling hand, and with a hoarse whisper said, 'You fool. Run!'

He pushed Sam away in desperation, but only into the path of a Bidajah. Sam felt two strong hands upon him, pinning his arms to his side. The hunters and the Bidajah were regrouping after the confusion of Sam's interference. Sam struggled, but to no avail – the golden-faced guard was possessed of unholy strength.

'Enough!' shouted the old man, with a rasping voice. 'This boy need not be harmed on my account – no one does. Be merciful; I shall come quietly.'

The woman on the rooftop cocked her head thoughtfully at the offer.

Something whistled through the air, too fast for anyone but Sam to see until it was too late. A rock struck the hunter on the side of the head, sending him sprawling. It was Hassan. He clambered down to ground level, yelling taunts and curses at the guards, trying to goad them into a chase. Sam sensed a chance at freedom, and pulled against the grip of the Bidajah with all his might, but to no avail.

The blind man sprang into action, breaking his promise almost as soon as it was made. He strained against the enchanted cord until pain was etched across his face, and at last he reached the staggering hunter, jerking a dagger from the soldier's belt and launching it towards Sam in one fluid movement.

Sam again saw the dagger flying towards him, time appearing to slow for all but him. He stopped struggling against the Bidajah, and flung himself in the opposite direction. The guard grunted as the dagger thudded into the side of his ribs. No blood flowed from the wound. In a heartbeat, Sam was free. He turned on his heels, and ran towards Hassan. But one of the Manhunters had had the same idea.

Sam skidded to a halt. The hunter grabbed Hassan's wrist, staring intently at the amulet in his hand. He jerked Hassan's hand upwards, showing the amulet to the woman on the roof.

'Kill the boy!' the woman shouted from on high. 'Bring me that amulet. Spare the old man.'

Sam threw himself at Hassan, sending both of them crashing to the ground, away from the hunter. Sam wanted to keep running, to urge Hassan up and on, but at once he was wracked with pain, exploding through his body as though his blood had ignited. His vision swam. He felt Hassan push at him; he heard words imploring him to get up, but the sensation was incapacitating. Sam curled up on the ground and cried out in agony.

Two Bidajah loomed large over the boys. Sam felt Hassan dragging him away from them, and finally he managed to move, scrabbling back on his elbows as the hulking men brought up their cudgels, impassive golden faces staring down ominously.

With a great shout, a figure darted between the boys and the guards. A narrow blade flashed. One of the Bidajah staggered away, clutching his ribs. The other came on unperturbed, and the mysterious swordsman thrust at him. The guard parried the blow with his cudgel, and swung at Sam's saviour with a mailed fist. The swordsman leapt away, and snatched Sam by the scruff of his neck.

Sam looked up into the eyes of a dark-haired man, undoubtedly a sailor for the gold in his ears and the flamboyant cut of his beard.

'Time to go,' he said, his accent foreign. He shoved Sam along the road. The pain subsided but a little, and Sam followed blindly, clutching at his guts that still felt like he'd swallowed a flaming torch. The sound of footsteps pounded behind them. Hunters shouted. The city guard were summoned.

Sam looked back to see the number of pursuers growing, and gaining.

Hassan picked up another rock and threw it at an onrushing guard, catching the man square between the eyes. He always was a good shot. His audacity was answered by the twang of a crossbow. Hassan dived low as the quarrel hit a barrel behind him. The amulet skidded from his grasp, across the street.

As the swordsman gave Sam another hard shove, Hassan jumped up, winked in their direction, and disappeared down a narrow alley, barely big enough to squeeze through. One of the hunters and the newly arrived city guard peeled off after him. The others stayed with Sam and his rescuer.

They ran like the very *djinn* were on their heels. They took every twist and turn, ploughed through hovels unbidden to the chagrin of their residents, raced across foul-smelling yards, and leapt rickety fences. The clamour did not die down – Sam had been singled out for death by a commander of the city's hunters, and that was enough to inspire every guard in the district to give chase. But which district? Sam had become so turned about that he no longer recognised the environs. Did the foreigner know where he was going? There was no time to draw breath to ask.

They squeezed through a winding alley, emerging into sudden, blinding daylight. Sam could hear ships' bells, and the cry of gulls. They must have circled back to the docks. The swordsman dragged Sam down a steep hill, towards a row of towering warehouses. He put two fingers into his mouth and gave a shrill whistle.

At this command, the streets were flooded with urchins. They poured from every door and alleyway, every cellar hatch and stockpile, rushing past Sam, clogging the street. The guards came ever onwards, stumbling over the children, even succumbing to the sheer tide of them, falling to the ground into the sea of diminutive gutter-thieves.

Sam was yanked away once more, losing sight of the urchins and his pursuers. He followed the swordsman into a darkened storeroom, out the other side, down into a cellar, up again into a dingy yard, in and out of so many rooms and along so many lanes that his head spun, and his lungs were fit to burst.

'In here,' the man said. He pulled the lid from a large basket, and bundled Sam headfirst into it before he could protest.

Sam could barely think, or speak, or move. The pain had lessened, but had been replaced by exhaustion. He thought he might pass out.

The swordsman's bearded face loomed over the basket for just a moment.

'Stay quiet. Do not move until I come for you. If you do, you're as good as dead.'

And with that, the lid was placed over the basket, and all was dark.

* * *

Hassan squeezed along the narrow passage, and out into a yard. He pushed past a group of washer-women busy at their tubs and mangles, ignoring their cries of indignation as he hopped over a fence, through a chicken coup, and out the other side. A fat, red-faced guard blocked the path one way – a familiar face, as it happened, from the market earlier. The guard's expression darkened as he recognised the thief who had escaped him.

Hassan laughed, and skipped away in the opposite direction, thumbing his nose at the ponderous guard as he went.

Pain bit sharply at Hassan's ankles. He yelped. His legs snapped together, and before he knew what was happening he was on the ground, mouth full of dirt. He looked down to his ankles, desperation gripping him as he saw a thin cord wrapped tightly around them, small lead weights interlocking, holding the cord in place. He tried to untangle the cord. He could feel it cutting off his circulation.

A shadow enveloped him. A hunter stood over him, back to the sun, a dark figure whose mere presence chilled Hassan to the bone. He tried to crawl away, but too late, he felt hands upon him, a rope tied about his wrists, and a hood placed over his head. In darkness, confused, Hassan was hoisted upwards, and carried away, to who knew where?

CHAPTER 4

'Your Majesty, I would ask only for a moment of your time, alone.' Yana leant forward, as close as she dared, towards her king.

So'Kurrah turned to her, his expression vague on his doughy face. He blinked twice, and then seemed to behold his faithful Manhunter afresh. 'I... uh... What is it, my child?'

He called her that, from time to time. It reminded Yana of days past, after the death of her father, when she had been as good as raised by the Merchant-King. It seemed a lifetime ago, when his face had been square and strong, and his vitality boundless. That was before Zhar-Mharrad had taken control of all the king's business. Yana gritted her teeth.

'You know that the vizier plans an expedition to the Lost Isles?' she ventured.

'Wh – what of it?' So'Kurrah's eyes dashed nervously from side to side at the very mention of the Lost Isles and all they represented.

'It is just... Well, I mean to say that it is a dangerous quest, Your Majesty. I wonder if the proper plans have been put in place in the event that the vizier... *does not return*.' She stressed these words carefully.

So'Kurrah's dull eyes flickered, as though he struggled to take Yana's meaning. His expression changed first to one of mild panic, and then to something else entirely. Something akin to eagerness.

'Do you really think that could be so?' So'Kurrah hissed, eyes widening.

Yana held his gaze, and nodded slowly. She could say little aloud, for fear of the vizier's spies within the palace, even here in the throneroom. But with that look she conveyed her meaning: *It could be so, if you will it. I could make it so.*

Panic returned to the king's eyes. 'But... but... who would oversee the armies? The defences? The temple? Who would protect me from the Heritors?' He became shrill.

Yana's heart sank just a little. Was So'Kurrah now so befuddled that he embraced his subjugation? She would free him from Zhar-Mharrad's influence if she could, but her oaths were as binding as chains of steel. No Manhunter would lift a hand against the Grand Vizier without So'Kurrah's express order; and that, it seemed, would never be forthcoming.

'Fear not, my king!' a deep, cultured voice intoned. The throneroom seemed to grow a little darker, and a little colder, as Zhar-Mharrad entered. 'I have no intention of failing in my quest. You shall never be without me, I swear it.'

So'Kurrah smiled weakly as the vizier swept through the throneroom, taking his place at Yana's side.

'You have done well, Ku Selishe,' Zhar-Mharrad purred.

'Yes, yes. We know we can always rely on the hunters,' the king added, almost bitterly, slumping back into his seat.

The capacious royal behind sat upon a pile of velvet cushions. A slave fanned him with a palm-branch. Yana wondered, not for the first time, if she were any different from a slave herself.

'To be an obedient servant is its own reward,' Zhar-Mharrad said, as though reading Yana's thoughts. 'But to be so effective in the execution of one's duties... well, that brings rewards of a more material kind. Don't you agree, your most profitable Highness?'

The Merchant-King looked mildly confused for a moment, before blinking, saying hurriedly, 'Of course, of course. Yana Selishe, you shall be showered with gold for this most excellent work.'

'Your Majesty is too kind.' Yana bowed.

The king looked at her somewhat sheepishly for a moment. Unusual – So'Kurrah had long been bereft of the courage and guile that had won him the throne as a young man, but he had never before appeared so nervous when addressing Yana. Perhaps there was something more at play between the king and Zhar-Mharrad. Though the thought of the Grand Vizier exerting even more control over the king irked Yana greatly, she would still rather be ignorant of their affairs. In Yad-Sha'Rib, it was said that a little knowledge was a dangerous thing. Yana was herself the blade in the darkness that proved the rule.

'The man returned to the dungeons was a dangerous Heritor, Your Majesty,' Zhar-Mharrad explained to the king. 'Not only that, but despite the inherent threat he posed both to the Manhunters and to your adoring subjects, he was captured alive, in accordance with our instructions.'

'Yes, yes,' said So'Kurrah. 'But I do not understand why he was taken alive. That is to say, if such a wretch poses so great a threat to my city, why has he not been executed?'

'Because, most Affluent Majesty, we have spent considerable resources preparing this particular wretch for a pivotal role in our great plan. He is to be my navigator to the Ghost Archipelago – the Lost Isles.'

'Preparing? Then why did he escape?'

A look of anger flashed across Zhar-Mharrad's features for but a moment. His great black brows furrowed. In that same moment, the king noticeably cowered. And then the Grand Vizier's expression quickly returned to one of deference, and the king's relief was palpable. That So'Kurrah the Wise had come to this beggared belief.

'It was an unfortunate oversight,' Zhar-Mharrad said, his deferential tone clearly disingenuous. The So'Kurrah Yana's father had told of would have had the vizier decapitated for the slight. Those days were gone. Zhar-Mharrad went on, 'I relied too heavily on the city guard to keep watch over the prisoners. But they have grown fat and indolent, Your Majesty. I would recommend recruiting more Bidajah to prevent such a situation arising again. Say the word, and I shall make it so.'

The vizier held the king's gaze for just a moment too long. The king turned his eyes away and nodded. 'Do what you must, Vizier,' he said.

Zhar-Mharrad's cult had already spread far beyond their humble beginnings. Now, their ranks threatened the supremacy of the king's own soldiery, which was doubtless what the vizier wanted. Yana knew as well as the king that the

Bidajah were not recruited. They were *made*. The devout of Birrahd would clamour for the honour to join the ranks of the golden masks, to become faceless soldiers in Zhar-Mharrad's growing cult, blessed by their dark god. And yet those blessings came at a terrible price. Few knew the true cost; few had heard the screams emanating from the bowels of the great temple. That the faithful suspected the horrors that lay in store for them in Zhar-Mharrad's laboratories, and still volunteered, spoke volumes to the vizier's power of persuasion. No one had ever seen the faces beneath the golden masks of the Bidajah. Yana doubted there would be faces to see.

'Your Most Propitious Majesty is wise indeed,' Zhar-Mharrad fawned. 'As to our plans: work is complete upon the ship. I shall set sail within days – as soon as the current Heritor threat has been eradicated from our fair city.'

'You think there are others?' the king frowned.

'Oh, certainly!' said Zhar-Mharrad. 'Even as the Manhunters captured the escaped prisoner, another Heritor was seen assisting him. A boy. He has escaped us, for now, but my spies are already abroad. And there was another prisoner – a friend of this mysterious boy. I have already begun interrogating him, and he will talk before the day is done, if he values his life.'

So'Kurrah dabbed at his brow with a silk handkerchief. 'It is an epidemic!' he cried. 'My city is overrun. Who knows what dangers lurk in the shadows, even in my own palace. These... "Heritors"... they say they can walk through walls. Breathe fire!'

Zhar-Mharrad looked to Yana for support, and she had little choice but to comply. It was, after all, the truth.

'They can, Your Majesty,' she said. 'I have seen this and more. But fear not... while we draw breath, you are safe.' Perhaps Zhar-Mharrad had not wanted her to reassure the king, but he was not her master. Not yet.

'My magic protects this palace from those vermin, Your Majesty,' Zhar-Mharrad interjected, with a barbed look at Yana. 'But this boy is particularly intriguing. He carried something – an artefact – of a type not seen in the city for a long time. The twin, in fact, of this.' The vizier held out his ebony staff, atop which was a jagged lump of bronze, engraved with strange sigils.

'What is it?' asked the king.

'This was captured many moons ago, by a certain Jarra Selishe, father of our favoured huntress. My endeavours lead me to believe it is a magical charm, linked somehow to the Heritors. It hides them from my scrying, but it also prevents them from using their powers to their fullest potential. The carvings are strange indeed, perhaps originating from the Lost Isles themselves. I believe it enables its bearer to walk abroad in our city undetected.'

'Are there... others like it?'

'One can never be certain of these things, Your Majesty. This is a fragment of a larger piece. The boy seen by Ku Selishe had another fragment... I wonder what secrets might be unlocked were the piece to be reconstructed. This is all the more reason to find this upstart – a boy who dared attack the city guard, and who even bested a Manhunter!'

So'Kurrah looked to Yana. 'Is this true?'

'I would not say... "bested"... Your Majesty. But he evaded my men, yes. His whereabouts are at present unknown.'

'Then he must be found!' The king's voice raised several pitches. 'Captain Selishe, what is being done about this Heritor?'

Yana hadn't expected that. The king's paranoia on all matters relating to the Heritors had grown of late. Zhar-Mharrad's influence was surely behind it. 'We are exploring every avenue,' she said. 'He will be found.'

'I think you have both tarried too long,' the king said, his agitation getting the better of him. He held up his podgy hands, and two slaves rushed to take them, hoisting So'Kurrah from his cushions. 'Use every resource at your disposal. Spare no expense. I cannot sleep knowing there is a Heritor at large, especially one as dangerous as this boy! Find him. Kill him!' So'Kurrah's voice reached a girlish pitch.

Yana wanted to offer some reassurance; the boy she had seen had been little more than a grubby-faced slum-dweller. But already in the king's mind the lad had become akin to a Yoggac'chi.

'At once, Your Most Remunerative Majesty,' Zhar-Mharrad interrupted. 'The boy shall be in the dungeon before the moon rises. Come, Ku Selishe – I would walk with you.'

The pair bowed as they retreated from the presence of the tremulous king. So'Kurrah, who had led the merchant uprising that had liberated the city from the corrupt Caliphate. So'Kurrah the Wise, who had negotiated Yad-Sha'Rib's independence from the Dar'Shur Empire, making the Golden City the wealthiest and most envied settlement for a thousand leagues. Yana remembered this from when she was a little girl living in the palace grounds. She remembered the arrival of Zhar-Mharrad the Ageless, and the first public executions of Heritors. Now, So'Kurrah was a bilious river-hog, afraid of shadows.

Moments later, Yana walked across the palace terrace, Zhar-Mharrad by her side. The vizier, dressed as always in his sweeping robes and tall black turban, looked singularly out of place in the airy palace halls, with their gleaming marble walls and gossamer drapes that diffused the afternoon sunlight into a golden glow.

The two unlikely companions walked in silence for a while, the nervous glances of the occasional servant indicative of the fell reputation of both – Yana, the chief Manhunter of Yad-Sha'Rib, and Zhar-Mharrad, a dark sorcerer in league with the demons of the underworld. Neither servant nor palace guard lingered in their presence. Yana could not remember the last time anyone had spoken to her like a normal human being, rather than with fawning deference born of fear.

The vizier's presence was becoming interminable, when finally he said, 'Ku Selishe, I can trust you, can I not?'

'Of course.' Did he know what she had said to So'Kurrah, and why? Yana knew she had to be careful.

'Good, good. There is a matter that has been weighing heavily on my mind of late, and there are few I can confide in. Few whose counsel I can trust. How ironic! That the most trusted advisor of the Merchant-King has no one to turn to himself. And who could relate to a man like me, who has gazed so long into the abyss?'

'Soon, my work will be done. The mysteries of the Ghost Archipelago will be revealed to me, for good or for ill. My great work is the discovery of the Crystal Pool – the source of unbidden power, that birthed upon an unsuspecting world the thrice-cursed race of Heritors. Soon, I shall set sail personally to the Ghost Archipelago. Soon, I shall find the pool and learn its secrets for myself. With my skill at magic, and the power of those legendary waters, my power shall be unrivalled. I shall destroy the Heritors utterly, and return to Yad-Sha'Rib immortal. I shall use my power to make this city the greatest in all the known world.'

'In the name of our king, So'Kurrah,' Yana said, in a more accusatory tone than she had intended.

'Of course,' Zhar-Mharrad smiled devilishly. 'So'Kurrah shall ever be lord of all he surveys. I shall see to that. But you must understand what this means? Without the Heritors, there will be no need for the Manhunters. You shall be released from your obligations at last.'

'My oath is to protect the king, come what may,' Yana said, trying hard to mask her suspicions. 'After the death of my father, gods praise him, I was inducted into the order by So'Kurrah himself. It was a singular honour, and it means that technically I am his ward, and his servant, until my life ends.'

Zhar-Mharrad waved a hand dismissively, golden claws gleaming in sunlight. 'What if I told you that the king has already granted permission for you to leave his service, a free woman? Free to enter my service. To be inducted into the mysteries of Birrahd, and to serve the temple as its protector, just as you now serve So'Kurrah.'

'Permission?' Yana almost spluttered.

'Yes. On the condition that I return victorious from the Ghost Archipelago, and the Heritors are eradicated. It is a condition that will surely be met. And that being so, I will have more need of your services than King So'Kurrah. After all, what will he need protecting from? Surely you would gladly transfer your oaths of fealty to the... true power in the land.'

Yana stopped. That was as close to a tacit admission of treason as she had ever heard, and yet she did not cut Zhar-Mharrad down where he stood. She did not even know if it was possible to slay the black-hearted sorcerer. And looking at him now, self-satisfied and leering, she felt the strangest sensation that she was trapped. Trapped as surely as So'Kurrah's slaves.

There was no refusing Zhar-Mharrad; if she did, she knew she would meet a black fate indeed. The glimmer in the man's dark eyes confirmed as much. The lascivious curl of his thin lips made her shiver. All she could hope for was that Zhar-Mharrad failed in his bid to master the Crystal Pool – but what then? Would the Heritors ascend to dominance over the world, as the vizier had for so long prophesied? She surely could not brook that eventuality. By wishing for Zhar-Mharrad's failure, was she putting her personal feelings ahead of the greater good?

And so she bowed, and said, 'You do me the greatest honour, my lord vizier.'

'Excellent!' Zhar-Mharrad beamed. 'I know that I presume too much to give you a command while you still serve So'Kurrah, but there are matters that are vital to our success, and thus by extension are the will of the king. I would have you find that boy.'

'I do not understand. Is the boy so important to our plans? You have chosen your Heritor already.'

'I care not about the boy. But his amulet... now that *is* integral to our plans. Thankfully, it took mere moments for his little friend to confide in me all of his secrets.'

Yana frowned. 'But you said...'

'Do not question me,' he snapped. The vizier seemed to grow several inches taller, and the golden hall darkened around them. His glower again dissipated quickly. 'My apologies, Ku Selishe. It is a... trying time. I could not be entirely forthcoming with our glorious ruler. You saw how agitated he became at the mere mention of the amulet... I fear increasingly for his health. And so I confide in you, that together we might make the city a safer place for our lord. I have managed to translate a small part of the inscription on this amulet. I believe it to be part of a compass of some kind, and it pertains almost certainly to the Crystal Pool. With the fragments united, the way to the pool shall be clear to me.'

'I understand. But what has this to do with the boy in the dungeon?'

'Ah. That boy has merely told me the last known movements of his friend, the Heritor. They were at the docks, talking with a Northman. A captain by the name of "Dagomir"?'

'I have heard of him. A braggart who calls himself the "Pirate Prince". He is long overdue finding his head on a spike, my lord vizier.'

'That will not be necessary. Not yet. Instead, I want you to ingratiate yourself with this pirate. Use whatever guile you must – or wiles, if there is no other way. Find out if the pirate really does wish to find the Lost Isles. And if so, I want you on that ship when it sets sail.'

'Sets sail, my lord?' Yana was confused. 'You mean to let them go?'

'No. I mean to let them lead the way to the island, for two Heritors are surely better than one. Once there, we shall kill the boy and all who side with him, and take the amulet. Our victory will then be assured.'

'I see.'

'Not a word of this to the king,' Zhar-Mharrad whispered. 'If he knew that a Heritor was loose with a means to find the Crystal Pool, I am not sure his nerves could take it. We must end this threat ourselves, you and I, for the good of the king.'

'For the good of the king,' Yana repeated, bowing again.

'Excellent. Now go, prepare yourself. I have already dispatched spies to the Al'Sarifal district. I shall send a message to you presently. Do not fail me… Yana.'

CHAPTER 5

The light from the pool was warm, all-consuming. Sam felt it flood into him, glowing within his veins, in his lungs, his belly. He drowned in the light. He opened his eyes, blinded at first by the sheer brilliance of it, but above him now was not the vast, endless whiteness, but some shimmering veil. The surface of water, seen from below. A circle of moonlight, shining down from the roof of a cavern. The silhouettes of men and women leaned over around the edges of the circle, looking down into the depths of the dark pool, in which Sam was sinking deeper and deeper.

It was not light that filled his lungs now, but water. He tried to call out, and the last bubbles of air escaped him. He was drowning in the Crystal Pool. There was no escape. He belonged to it.

* * *

Sam leapt to his feet, gasping for breath, spluttering water all over himself. Hearty laughter erupted from the tavern patrons. Sam blinked, confused, wiping water from his face, shaking like a soaked dog.

Before him, backed up by a motley band of pirates, stood Dagomir, an emptied bucket in his hands, and a broad grin on his square features.

'Welcome back to the land of the living, lad,' he said. 'Thought you'd never wake up.'

'Wh… where am I?' Sam asked. He didn't like the way the pirates were looking at him one bit.

'You, my lad, are in the cellar of the Dancing Leopard, the most disreputable tavern in all of Al'Sarifal. There is no more secret place in the city.'

'Secret?'

'Unless you wish to be found by the hunters?' More laughter followed this suggestion. 'It can, of course, be arranged.'

Sam looked about the dingy confines of the cellar that smelled of torch-smoke and mead. There was no way out. 'What do you want with me?' he asked.

'Straight to the point. I like that. What I want, lad, is for you to join my crew, and come with us on a voyage. A long and very dangerous voyage.'

Sam felt his pulse quicken, just a little. Not with fear, but with anticipation. 'A voyage to where?'

'No one knows,' Dagomir grinned. Sam noticed for the first time a gold tooth in the Pirate Prince's mouth, gleaming in the torchlight. 'We go in search of a chain of islands, which are often called the Lost Isles. Because… well, no one knows where they are. Except for you, of course.'

'Me?' Sam gasped. 'How would I know? I have never left Yad-Sha'Rib.'

'I believe you, boy. But you know it all the same, because you're one of them. A *Heritor*.'

Sam tensed. 'I don't know what you are... – '

'Don't bother lying to me,' Dagomir snapped. 'There's magic in you, that much is clear. But we have magic of our own. Isn't that right, Makeno?'

At this, Dagomir's crew parted, making way for the wild-haired man from the ship. He looked even more fearsome now, in this fire-lit room, with his painted face and necklace of bones. Yet now that he was standing close, he was smaller than Sam had imagined. He leaned upon a gnarled staff, adorned with trinkets, and fixed Sam with such a stare that he felt the wild man was looking into his soul.

'He is the one we seek,' the man – Makeno – said.

'Then we have an agreement,' the Pirate Prince replied.

Makeno turned to Dagomir and nodded. 'If the boy goes with you, I go with you.'

'Makeno here is a wise man,' Dagomir explained. 'He has many gifts, not least of which is power over storms – appropriate, considering our goddess likes to send them our way from time to time, for her own amusement. I suppose you've never put out to sea before, lad? No? So you won't know what it's like to be battered by wind and rain, to have your mast struck by lightning, and your ship tossed about on waves high as mountains. You're in for a rare treat.'

This brought peals of laughter from the men.

Sam glowered. Every part of his being wanted to go. He felt like he belonged on the ocean, though he did not understand how he could guide Dagomir anywhere. But this pirate already talked as though Sam had agreed; like there was no choice.

'No,' Sam said.

The laughter stopped. Curiosity became animosity. Dagomir took a threatening step forward.

'Say again?' he said.

'I will not go with you,' Sam said, defiantly. 'I cannot leave my friends, and my family. What if the hunters find out? What then shall happen to my mother?'

That seemed to have some effect on the pirate. He sucked at his teeth thoughtfully. 'The best thing you can do for your mother now is stay away from her. You have been seen, lad. The hunters will be looking for you. Whether you come with us or not, things cannot be the same for you again, or for your mother. If you are far away from her, then they cannot use her against you, or you against her. There will be no profit in harming her.'

Dagomir's words sounded wise, but Sam could not trust him. The man was a reaver, a notorious rogue, and his ever-present smirk was, in Sam's short experience, an indication of a treacherous nature. 'And Hassan?' Sam asked at last. 'What became of him?'

'Who?'

'He means the other boy,' came a voice from the crew. Another man stepped forward, darker-skinned than his Northman captain, slender of build, with a black bandana tied about his head and an affectatious little beard. At his waist, a thin-bladed sword hung from an ornate belt. Sam recognised the swordsman who had rescued him back at the slums. The man winked at Sam. 'We have not been introduced. I am Emilio Villa-Lobos, first mate of *Vanya's Wrath*. Your friend is a brave lad, but I lost sight of him in the square. Last I saw, he was leading the guards a merry dance. I have no doubt he slipped away.'

'There you have it!' Dagomir beamed, arms outstretched. 'Your mother is better off without you, and your friend Hathfor...'

'Hassan!' Sam snapped.

'...Hassan, my apologies, has escaped to fight another day. Now listen to me, I am not forcing you to do anything. You are not my prisoner, you are an honoured guest! How many boys your age get to join the crew of the Pirate Prince, eh? And I know you want to find the Lost Isles as much as I do. I've heard stories, lad. Stories of how the Heritors feel the call of the islands in their blood. You dream about it. You yearn for it, like Emilio here yearns for a harlot's warm caress every night. And you can join us, on the most famous fighting ship for a thousand leagues around, and find fortune and glory!'

'I have never wanted fortune, or glory,' Sam said, warily. He could not trust his own feelings on the matter, for the fight within himself was too great. And he surely could not trust the word of this smiling 'prince'.

'Then do it for your city,' Dagomir said. 'Emilio tells me you leapt in to battle recklessly today. He says you were possessed by rage. Why was that? Have you seen the injustice that the Bidajah inflict on this city? Have you known people snatched away by So'Kurrah's hunters?'

Sam glared daggers at the pirate.

'Ah!' Dagomir said. 'You have. Someone close to you. A brother? Father? That's it, I can see it in your eyes. They took your father. That must mean he is a Heritor too. When we find the Lost Isles, and the fabled Crystal Pool, it is said that great powers await us all. A mere mortal like me might hope for longer life, or unnatural good luck. But for a Heritor like you... who knows what powers you might unlock? You can come back to this city as a conqueror if you wish it. You can storm the dungeons and rescue your poor father, and...'

'He's dead!' Sam shouted, feeling the first swell of tears stinging his eyes. 'The hunters killed my father, and took everything from my family. And that's why I don't want to leave my mother. She has no one else.'

There came an awkward silence. Most of the pirates remained stony faced, staring at this boy – this freak – before them. But Dagomir's features softened. Some humanity crept into his eyes for the first time since Sam had met him.

'Right, you rabble!' he said to his crew. 'Make preparations. Check the coast is clear. You, and you, back to the ship. Look lively!' At once the crew jumped to the captain's orders, and made themselves look busy, if only to give Dagomir a little privacy. Only Emilio and Makeno remained, and the three strange companions crowded a little closer to Sam. Dagomir placed a firm hand on Sam's shoulder. 'I know what it's like to lose a father, lad,' he said. 'In my land, fortune and title are not always passed down through royal bloodlines, but are taken at the point of a sword. I really was a prince, and I would have been king, but for a blade that buried itself in my father's ribs one dark night. So now I am an outcast. A wanderer far from home. But I have made something of myself after all, eh? And you can do the same. Come with us, boy. Makeno will teach you how to use your gifts. I will teach you how to sail, and how to fight. We'll find this Crystal Pool, and drink deep of its bounty. And then we will return to Yad-Sha'Rib not to conquer the city, but to liberate it. Take vengeance upon the Merchant-King and that black-hearted vizier of his. Drive out the gold-faced guards. Kill the hunters and empty their dungeons of captives. All this you can do, and I will help you do it. But first, you must take a chance. Does it sound worth the risk?'

Sam pondered this. Dagomir looked sincere, but his words sounded practised and honeyed. Sam instead looked to Makeno, who did not appear to be one of Dagomir's lackeys. The sorcerer's eyes bore an expression Sam was unused to seeing. Respect. The man nodded slightly, encouragingly.

'When do we leave?' Sam asked.

'Ha!' roared Dagomir, his great mirth returning in a heartbeat. He slapped a hand on Sam's shoulder so exuberantly Sam almost fell to the floor. 'You hear that, men?' the Pirate Prince shouted. 'We have our guide, and time's a-wasting! We make sail at sundown. Step to it!'

* * *

The shadows had begun to lengthen across the dockyards, and the frenetic industry of the early morning had subsided. Sam pulled the hood of his borrowed cloak down over his face. The guards were out in force, and Dagomir's pirates had begun their return to the *Vanya's Wrath* in small groups, so as not to arouse suspicion. Dagomir had gone on ahead. Sam was entrusted to the care of Emilio, Makeno, and two rather brutish crewmen who looked more suited to brawling than sailing.

Sam rubbed at his chest. It was the first time in as long as he could remember that he had not worn his amulet. He felt naked without it.

'Looking for this?' Emilio whispered, leaning in close. He pressed the bronze amulet into Sam's hand. Sam breathed a sigh of relief, and slipped it around his neck immediately. 'Where did you find it?'

'Your friend dropped it. In all the excitement, I forgot I'd picked it up.'

'You should have remembered sooner,' Sam said.

'Oh?'

'Because it hides me from the vizier's magic.'

'Then we'd better hope he hasn't been using his magic to find you,' Emilio said. 'Or maybe I'll live to regret the mistake.'

'I would not worry,' Makeno said, his accent rolling and evasive. 'It is Samir's power that gives him away. If he does not call upon it, then the black sorcerer won't see him.'

'It has always kept me hidden,' Sam said, indignantly. He had put his faith in the weighty amulet his whole life. He believed in its protective powers.

'It has kept you hidden by weakening you,' Makeno said, matter-of-factly. 'Without it, your power burns bright, and your enemy is drawn to you, like a moth to a candle flame. With it, you lead a normal life, more or less, but it comes at a price.'

'What price?'

'You cannot lead a whole life in hiding. You cannot be true to yourself. And you cannot fulfil your destiny.'

Sam pondered this. 'Earlier, in the square… I felt more powerful than ever before. But afterwards I felt pain like never before. Like I was on fire. Was that because of the amulet?' He touched at its bronze surface. Suddenly it was not so reassuring.

'No, young one,' Makeno said. 'That was the Blood Burn. The more you use your abilities, the worse it gets. I think today was the first time you ever truly tested yourself. You pushed at the limits of your powers, and your blood resisted. As you grow more confident – more powerful – you will be able to resist the Blood Burn for longer. But you shall never be free of it. It is doubtless why that old man gave up the fight, for one as strong as he would surely not need to surrender to mere mortals.'

'I don't think that was it,' Sam replied. 'I think he was trying to save me.'

Makeno paused. 'Interesting. In the city of Yad-Sha'Rib, Heritors are not known for their selflessness. Such virtues can only get a man killed; or worse. It seems you found an unusually virtuous man in a city of scoundrels.'

'So the Blood Burn…' Sam said. 'Why does it happen? Is it like… a curse?'

'Yes, boy, it is precisely that. It is the curse of all Heritors passed down from their illustrious forebears, for drinking the forbidden waters of the Crystal Pool.'

'Forbidden…' Sam said, wide-eyed. 'But isn't that what we're trying to find?'

Makeno laughed. 'You have much to learn about the world,' he said. 'The acquisition of power is never without risk. Some men are willing to risk more than others. See?' He nodded ahead.

The little group approached the *Vanya's Wrath*, and standing at the prow, looking across the docks towards them, was Dagomir. Seeing him there, cutting an imposing figure in the orange evening light, it was easy to imagine that all the stories of the Pirate Prince were true.

'Act naturally,' Emilio whispered to Sam as they reached the gangplank. 'You are just another member of the crew. Do nothing to attract attention.'

As casually as he could, Sam boarded the *Vanya's Wrath*. Dagomir did not move a muscle, but said quietly, 'Emilio, to my cabin with the new arrivals.' Sam felt Emilio's hand on his shoulder steering him away from the captain, towards the rear of the ship.

Emilio swung open a small door and bade Samir enter. Sam stepped within, Makeno followed, and Emilio closed the door behind them. The cabin was completely dark. Sam blinked against the gloom. Emilio struck up a tinderbox to light a lantern. In the flare, a pair of eyes gleamed from the rear of the cabin. Sam jumped. The lantern burned, casting its yellow light into the cabin, and there, sitting across from Sam and Emilio, was a Manhunter, face covered in black save for the eyes, feline and cold.

Emilio leapt in front of Sam, jerking his sword from its scabbard, pointing it menacingly at the black-clad warrior, who made no movement.

'I'd put the sword away if I were you,' the hunter said. A woman's voice. Sam's eyes adjusted slowly, and he noticed now the slender form, the gold-trimmed sash at her waist. 'I'd hate to have to kill you before we've been properly introduced.'

Emilio looked about the cabin nervously. There was a dining table, a few scraps of furniture, a single window, shuttered. Behind the woman was an open door, leading to another dark room, in which Sam could make out the outline of the captain's bunk. He half expected more assassins to be hiding in there.

'Where are the others?' Emilio said. 'Hunters rarely work alone.'

'This one does.' The door swung open and Dagomir stooped to enter, flashing a grin to his mate. 'And it's very rude of you to point a sword at my guest.'

Emilio looked every bit as confused as Sam. 'Captain?' he said.

'You planned this all along!' Sam cried. 'You're going to turn me over to her, for a reward!'

'You do me an injustice, lad,' Dagomir said, adopting a wounded expression. 'I only just met her. This Manhunter has come to us as a friend, at a most fortuitous time. For pity's sake, Emilio, put the sword away. Have I not always steered you true?'

Emilio scowled at the woman, who still had not moved. Slowly, he sheathed his sword, and with that action Sam felt the weight of the world come crashing down. He would be taken to the black temple and spend the rest of his days in the dungeons. There could be no other explanation for the presence of the woman. Why was Dagomir drawing out the inevitable?

'Will you please say something?' Dagomir said to the woman, looking increasingly exasperated.

She sighed, and stood. She was tall. Her stance was commanding, as it had been on the rooftop in the square earlier. She was a warrior – that was obvious, even to Sam. She was festooned with weapons. Sam counted at least a dozen throwing knives. A pair of wickedly curved daggers with gleaming silver hilts sat at her hips. There was a sword at her back. Sam only now noticed a crossbow on the bench beside her. His instincts told him to run. His reflexes and speed had helped him back in the square, but here in this confined space, he feared she could kill them all.

The huntress reached behind her head. Was she reaching for her sword? Sam tensed; he saw Emilio do likewise. Instead, she unwrapped her headscarf, revealing perhaps the most beautiful face Sam had ever seen. Her skin was golden-brown, eyes large and dark, full of mystery. She unpinned her raven-black hair and shook it loose. That a thrice-cursed hunter could wear the face of a storybook princess seemed somehow an affront to all Sam held dear.

'My name is Yana Selishe,' the woman said. 'Captain of the Royal Hunters, first among equals, killer of killers. And I am at your service.'

CHAPTER 6

Sam glared the woman, his heart thudding in his chest, hatred for her rising like bile to his throat. She beheld him only for a moment, utterly impassive, barely acknowledging his existence. She spoke directly to Dagomir and Emilio.

'We don't have much time,' the huntress said. 'Zhar-Mharrad knows about the boy, and what he is. The Bidajah are already on their way.'

'And your hunters?' Sam interrupted, furious that she spoke about him like he wasn't there, yet terrified still of what might befall him. 'Where are they?'

'They will not come, for I have ordered them not to.'

'And do men always do your bidding?' Captain Dagomir smirked.

'So far.'

'Wait, Captain,' Emilio said. 'I must take the boy's part in this. We have all heard the tales of the hunters. They are loyal to So'Kurrah – it is said that each would rather take their own life than betray him. Even by your word, my captain, I cannot simply trust this woman.'

'Your mate is right,' the woman said. 'I am loyal to So'Kurrah. Indeed, I am the most loyal of his Royal Hunters, for I was raised in the palace grounds, and after the death of my own father I was made a ward of the Merchant-King. I am sworn to his service by the strongest oaths. But even if he might see my presence here a betrayal, I cannot. For it is my belief that So'Kurrah himself is a slave, and it is my solemn duty to free him.'

'A slave?' Sam scoffed. 'What would the king know of servitude?'

'Of servitude? Nothing. Of fear for his life? A great deal.'

Emilio stepped forward. 'And who would so frighten the most powerful man in Yad-Sha'Rib?'

'So'Kurrah, may his name be praised, is no longer the most powerful man in the city, and has not been these fifteen years or more. Not since the arrival of the black sorcerer into the Golden Palace.'

'Zhar-Mharrad…' Sam whispered nervously, as though saying the name might conjure the man himself to the cabin.

'Indeed. I have followed the Grand Vizier's orders diligently for too long. I have seen the dungeons beneath the Temple of Birrahd. I have seen the laboratories in which Zhar-Mharrad practises blood magic, and communes with demons.'

At this, Makeno, who had said nothing since entering the cabin, spat on the ground, his craggy, painted face twisting into an expression of disgust.

'Listen to me,' Yana Selishe said. 'I shall tell you what I have only briefly explained to your captain. Zhar-Mharrad even now prepares his own expedition to the Lost Isles, with an enslaved Heritor as his guide – the man I captured this morning not far from here. The vizier has convinced the Merchant-King that the Heritors pose a threat to the city, and that only by discovering the Crystal Pool can he – Zhar-Mharrad – end the menace of their kind once and for all. But I believe Zhar-Mharrad to be a traitor. He plans to drink from the Crystal Pool and multiply his power tenfold. He shall return to Yad-Sha'Rib a conqueror, and none will be able to stand in his way. The dungeons beneath the black temple will be full to bursting with sacrifices to Birrahd.'

'If this is true,' Sam said, 'why not kill him yourself? You are an assassin, aren't you?'

'Kill a man protected by demons? If only it were so simple. This one knows.' The woman nodded to Makeno.

'It is true,' Makeno said, his voice a low rumble. 'If he is protected by demons, it is likely that no mortal hand can slay him. Not easily, at least. I hope you do not think this Heritor will do the deed for you, Miss Selishe. He is just a boy.'

'No, I do not think that,' the huntress replied. 'I would ask no one to take a risk that I would not take myself. What I ask is to go with you to the Lost Isles, to see this fabled "Ghost Archipelago" for myself. If I can help you find the Crystal Pool before Zhar-Mharrad, then so be it. Then perhaps we shall have the power to defeat him.'

'You wish to drink from the pool yourself,' Sam said. 'Captain Dagomir, you cannot trust her! Imagine if the power of the Heritors falls into the wrong hands.'

Dagomir stroked his chin. 'Lad, dozens of ships have already set sail for the Lost Isles. I imagine dozens more will follow in the coming months. Do you suppose all of those captains have as honourable intentions as I? This is a race, and I say may the best man – or woman – win.'

'You should listen to this man,' the woman said to Samir. 'He speaks sense.'

'Not so fast,' Dagomir said. 'I appreciate the warning, but it will take more than that to persuade me to help you. When you came here, it was to seek passage to the Lost Isles. Now, it seems that, by helping you, I'll become the most wanted man in Yad-Sha'Rib. I depend on these waters for my living, and that of my crew.'

'You can hardly turn me over to the Grand Vizier,' the huntress smiled. 'Not while you are harbouring a Heritor.' She fluttered her long, dark lashes at Dagomir, and Sam sighed as he saw the Pirate Prince grin like a smitten fool. 'But it is fair that you seek compensation. I will work my fair share during the voyage, and I'll pay my way with this.'

With a quick movement, the woman unhooked a pouch from her belt and slid it across the table. It came to a halt a few feet from Dagomir, and out spilled a small fortune in gold *darics* and blood-red rubies. Dagomir's eyes lit up, and Sam felt his own do the same. It was more money than he had ever seen in his life, contained in just one small purse.

'I told you, I am a ward of the Merchant-King, and my resources are not insubstantial. If we are successful, and we return to Yad-Sha'Rib free of Zhar-Mharrad's vile influence, you will be paid five times this amount by my grateful king.'

'You make a compelling argument,' Dagomir mused.

'Wait,' Sam said. 'What of my friend, Hassan? What became of him?'

The woman shrugged. 'I don't know who you speak of.'

'The other boy from the square – the one who helped me.'

'If he was not a Heritor, I have no business with him. May he die in his own time, in whatever manner seems fit.'

Something about that reply chilled Sam to the bone. He looked to Dagomir one more time, desperate to have this woman thrown from the ship. 'Captain, we travel to the Lost Isles, and that is dangerous enough – you said it yourself. But now, because of her, we may have to fight the greatest sorcerer in all Dar'Shur.'

'True, lad. But I've made worse bargains, and with less attractive passengers. The crew of *Vanya's Wrath* can fight when called upon, don't worry about that.'

'Do we even have enough men for this task?' When Sam had been surrounded by pirates back at the tavern, the odds against him had seemed insurmountable. Since then, he had counted perhaps twenty crew; as he half expected the ship to be stormed by soldiers at any moment, that seemed fewer than sufficient.

'We have too many men, if anything,' Dagomir said. 'Makeno, tell the lad what you told me.'

Makeno nodded. 'The Lost Isles are protected by means both natural and magical. To navigate the routes to the central islands is to court the attentions of sea-creatures; to pass through the Mists of Concealment; and then to wind our way through narrow corridors of jagged rocks and treacherous shallows. Small vessels are best, but they run the risk of sinking in the Southern Ocean before even reaching the Lost Isles. This is a good ship, strong and fast... but can it pass through the maze of rocks? I have my doubts.'

'Thankfully for all of us,' Dagomir grinned, 'my people have forgotten more about seamanship than Makeno here has ever known. Long have the Northmen crossed the open seas on shallow draught vessels like this. She is strong, aye, and broad abeam, but her hull is half the depth of a Dar'Shuri *dhow*, with a keel strong enough to crack an iceberg.' He looked to a puzzled Sam. 'An iceberg is a big floating block of ice that can sink a ship, and... Never mind. The point is this: the *Vanya's Wrath* is legend because of the remarkable things she has done. She will add to that legend by becoming the largest vessel ever to reach the Ghost Archipelago intact.'

Emilio laughed. 'There are wizards in Brythos who would pay handsomely to bottle some of Captain Dagomir's confidence for their potions!'

'Besides,' Dagomir added, 'the goddess Vanya is the jealous sort. She'll not let foreign gods toy with us. She'll part your Mists of Concealment easily. She's saving me for herself, you understand.'

More laughter. Sam couldn't stand it.

He did not have to suffer it for long. At that moment, the door flew open, and a red-faced crewman almost fell into the cabin.

'Guards!' he cried. 'The guards are coming.'

A thin smile crossed the huntress's lips. 'It seems the time to make your decision is up, oh Prince of Pirates. What shall it be?'

Dagomir gave no answer. Instead, he sprang from the cabin, pushing past the crewman and bounded across the deck.

'Every man to his station!' he roared. 'Man the oars. Push away!'

Most of the men were already in motion, but those who weren't now leapt to action at Dagomir's command.

Sam rushed out onto the deck as most of the crew vanished below. Two men helped Dagomir crank up the anchor. Emilio ran aft to the tiller, and with a pained groan of timbers the ship began to move away from its moorings. All too slowly.

Any pirates, labourers or beggars still milling about the harbour front now made themselves scarce as iron-shod boots shook the ground. The gleaming masks of the Bidajah descended the steps to the docks, like liquid gold spilling down pale stone. From the streets east and west came the city watch, some with spears, others with bows. Sam could not breathe. If the ship did not get underway quickly, they would surely be boarded.

He glanced behind him. Yana Selishe stood in the shadow of the cabin. Her crossbow was now in her hand, a quarrel nocked and the string drawn.

Oars dipped. The ship rocked. For a moment Sam was taken by the illusion that the neighbouring vessels in dock were lurching forwards, but quickly realised the *Vanya's Wrath* was going backwards, sliding away from the harbour wall even as the archers began to rank up.

'Faster, you dogs!' Dagomir shouted down the stairs.

The ship began to glide to starboard, wheeling outwards as the oarsmen coordinated themselves to manoeuvre in the tight space.

'Shields!' Dagomir and his companions hoisted shields from the bulwarks and held them aloft as they scattered across the deck.

Arrows loosed. One thudded into the mainmast. The others whistled harmlessly over to starboard.

'A warning volley,' Selishe muttered. 'They're showing us that we're well in range.'

Dagomir punched the nearest man on the arm. 'You – man a ballista. Return fire.' He called to the second man. 'You, with me. Set the sail.'

The bow of the ship swung perilously close to a docked vessel, the dragon figurehead missing it by a hair's breadth. At the other ship's stern appeared two soldiers, seizing their opportunity, leaping aboard the *Vanya's Wrath* with scimitars drawn.

Dagomir urged the crewman to the ropes, while he himself scraped his heavy, straight blade from its scabbard. Spurred to action, he now looked less the dashing rogue and every inch the tall, fair-haired warrior of legend. He swatted the first soldier aside with his shield, and thrust his blade into the onrushing second, skewering the man like a boar on a spit. Dagomir freed his sword and struck down at the other soldier, slaying him while he still struggled to his feet.

While Dagomir's back was turned, a third soldier leapt onto the deck, creeping up on Dagomir, sword readied.

Before he could even shout a warning, Sam felt the air part beside his head, and a black-fletched quarrel tore past him. The soldier screamed as the missile struck him in the eye. Dagomir spun about, surprised at the sight of a third assailant, who writhed in agony on the deck before breathing his last.

The crewman at the ballista finally loosed a great bolt towards the soldiers arrayed on the harbour wall. Shields and armour clattered. The ranks parted; men screamed and fell. Under direction from their captains, more soldiers filled the ranks, and bows were again drawn. The crewman had no time to reload the ballista before a storm of arrows flew towards the *Vanya's Wrath*. Dagomir and his men threw themselves to the deck. Sam felt a hand on his shoulder, pulling him sharply back into the cabin as an arrow thudded into the doorframe where he'd been standing.

'We need to see some of that speed you showed back at the square,' the huntress said. 'Or I'll spend the rest of this voyage saving your life.'

Sam reddened. He looked out again at the forest of arrow shafts that littered the deck. Dagomir was on his feet, already pulling on a thick rope. The bows swung fully clear of the nearest vessel, and the open mouth of the harbour lay ahead at last. The sail dropped fully, fluttering as Dagomir angled it to catch every breath of wind. But wind was hard to come by in the sheltered bay. Someone below deck called 'Heave,' spurring on the rowers.

'We're away,' Sam gasped.

'Not yet,' said the huntress. Look.

She pointed fore, to the point where the two outer walls of the harbour almost met, like the pincers of some great scorpion.

Sam was not at first sure what he was supposed to be looking at, but then he saw it: the water between the two great walls was dancing unnaturally, forming a barrier of white foam. Moments later, something erupted from the waves – a huge, rusting chain, draped with seaweed. Beneath it, a criss-cross of smaller chains emerged, a net of metal. Dagomir had seen it, too, and was already at the portside bows, calling men from the oars – calling them to arms.

'What is it?' Sam asked.

'Harbour defences,' the huntress replied. 'Booms, attached to winches on the walls. You see there?' She pointed to the left of the chains, where men in city livery huddled behind a buttressed wall. 'We need to release the winch, or we're dead in the water.'

'We?'

'I'd rather not been seen, but needs must. Come.' Yana Selishe sprang from the shadows. 'Captain!' she cried to Dagomir. 'Hard to port. Take us as close to that harbour wall as you can.'

'Are you mad, wench?' Dagomir said. 'We'll be boarded.'

'No, we go on the attack. I count six guards. I'll take care of them, and the boy will release the winch and lower the booms.'

'Him? No, we're better served manning the ballistae and holding position.'

'Then you'll soon be dead, Captain. I've seen what the boy can do. Trust me.'

'I've trusted you too much already...' Dagomir grumbled. And yet he bellowed, 'Emilio! Hard to port! I want us scraping that harbour wall.'

The huntress nodded. 'We'll be back aboard before the other guards arrive.'

'No one has asked my opinion of this plan,' Sam said, trepidation overcoming him.

'That's because it is irrelevant,' said the woman. 'This is our best chance of success, and you will play your part.'

Sam shook with anger. This huntress… this vile woman was of the same caste who had killed his father, and now deigned to give him orders like he was one of her soldiers.

'I like this one,' laughed Dagomir. 'Shields!' he roared, and as one the men hoisted their wooden shields and took a knee. Selishe pulled Sam down to the deck as arrows clattered and thudded around them.

'They're losing range,' the huntress said.

Sam looked up, and saw the archers hustling from their position, coming around towards the harbour wall, to intercept the ship. 'They're on the move,' he said.

'Aye. But we're almost there,' said Dagomir. 'Woman, this is your chance. Don't fail. And don't betray us.'

'Captain, if I wanted you dead, I'd have killed you already.' She gave Dagomir a sultry smirk. Dagomir flashed a winning smile. Sam rolled his eyes.

And then they were racing along the deck, Selishe just ahead, keeping low behind the bulwarks. As they reached the figurehead, one of Dagomir's crew popped up from a hiding place with a shortbow at hand, loosing an arrow at the men on the harbour wall. A moment later the ship shook all along its keel, and the hull scraped the stone of the harbour wall, making a noise like a wounded elephant.

'Fools,' Selishe hissed.

'You said the closer the better,' Sam reminded her.

The woman glared at him, as though she did not at all appreciate his opinion, and then jerked her head towards the bulwark. 'Let's go.'

With that, she was up and over the wooden walls of the ship, sword in hand, silent and nimble. A man's gargled death-rattle followed. Sam removed his amulet, afraid it would slow him down, but more afraid of what sorceries would follow him without it. But from nowhere, an outstretched hand was before him, a dark-skinned hand, and a wrist adorned with bracelets made of bone and bronze. Sam looked up into the face of Makeno, who nodded at him sagely.

Sam pressed the amulet into Makeno's hand, and, his heart in his throat, raced forward and leapt to join the huntress.

*   *   *

Yana hadn't been sure if the boy would follow. It was hard to believe he was a Heritor, even after what she'd witnessed in the square. She'd never met one so young. So... weak. She imagined he might well freeze in fear, and if he did, no matter. She could easily perform this duty alone; but she needed to put the boy to the test first.

She pulled her scimitar from the guard's chest, slicing off the ear of a second with an effortless backswing. She took one step, widening her stance, spinning on the ball of her right foot, and swung her sword in a silver arc, opening up a third adversary from belly to chin.

Sam darted beneath the clumsy flailing of a guard, who Yana decapitated with her fourth clinical stroke. A fifth backed away along the flagstone walkway, already spattered in his comrade's blood and having no heart for the fight.

More guards were coming, but they were minutes away. They tarried; they should have been waiting here from the start, but instead had left the position lightly defended.

Samir ran behind the low fortification that housed the great winch. Yana sprang after him. The boy ducked beneath the final guard's attack, stamped on his toe, drawing a yelp. Yana hesitated for a moment; she wanted to see how the boy acquitted himself in battle. The guard jabbed at Sam with a gauntleted hand. Sam hardly seemed to move, but avoided the blow effortlessly. It was like he was several seconds ahead of the guard, anticipating his every movement. Remarkable. She wondered what his weakness might be; she wondered how dangerous he might become if he matured and his powers grew.

Another sword-swing. This time Samir stepped aside, and kicked the guard's hand. The sword left the man's grasp, popping into the air, and Samir snatched it away. He spun about, using the blade to hack at the thick rope of the winch. It frayed; another blow would do it, but the guard was slowing down proceedings too much. Enough.

Yana snatched a throwing knife from her sash and hurled it into the back of the guard's neck, between helmet and stiff leather collar. He staggered backwards, allowing her to retrieve the blade from his spine before he crashed to the ground.

'You didn't have to kill him,' Sam shouted angrily.

'Stop showing off and cut the rope,' Yana commanded. 'Company is arriving.'

The imminent arrival of more soldiers, whose feet could already be heard stomping along the walkway, sparked Samir to action. He hacked again at the rope, and for a third time, finally slicing through. The great winch spun about, and Sam had to dance away from the whipping rope as it rapidly unspooled.

'Time to leave,' she said.

She ran to the end of the harbour wall, where even now the *Vanya's Wrath* was drawing level, its shallow draught proving its worth as it scraped over the remnants of the drooping boom chain.

Dagomir waved at them to hurry; he didn't have to tell them twice. Yana took a short run up, and leapt nimbly from the wall, grabbing at the ratlines to break her fall. The boy was beside her in an instant, and slipped down the ropes like a monkey. She remembered how he had leapt effortlessly from a rooftop in the slum square. He'd make a fine sailor if he lived long enough.

From her vantage point, she saw a dhow coming up behind, its fan-shaped lateen sails not fully set. Yad-Sha'Rib's navy was used primarily for defence. Its ships were slow and strong, and heavily armed. If they managed a volley from their ballistae and catapults, the *Vanya's Wrath* would be reduced to so much kindling.

An arrow tore through the sail by Yana's head. She cursed, and shimmied swiftly down the ropes to join Sam on deck.

'We can't let that ship gain on us,' she said.

'Fear not, sweet maiden,' Dagomir mocked. 'Makeno is preparing something special.'

At the bow, Makeno sat cross-legged, his gnarled staff across his lap. His eyes were closed, and he muttered some strange incantation in a guttural, rolling tongue. As he chanted, wind whipped about them, catching Yana's hair, and filling the sail. She looked around; the rest of the sheltered harbour was still. The waves lapped gently at the harbour wall, and the dhow behind them struggled to catch a breath of wind. And yet the great green-and-red sails of the *Vanya's Wrath* filled, billowing outwards, and the dragon pennant at the topmast flew outwards, arrow straight. The ship picked up speed so suddenly that Yana almost lost her balance.

'What is this?' she gasped.

'Your Grand Vizier thinks he is the only sorcerer in Yad-Sha'Rib?' Dagomir laughed. 'Well, maybe he is now, because the only other is here with us. They call him Makeno Storm-Caller. I travelled far to find him, and with his magic he repays us a thousand-fold.'

It had seemed at first impossible that they would get away, but they had. The *Vanya's Wrath*, true to the boasts of Dagomir, cut effortlessly through the water, and as the red rind of the sun set over the Mangnahim Bay, the ship had put a great amount of open water between itself and the golden city. Yad-Sha'Rib was soon little more than a daub of yellow painted on a dark canvas, and for the first time in his life Sam smelt sea air free of the stink of the slums. To the port side, flying fish leapt in the ship's wake, dancing upon water cast with hues of purple and orange. To starboard, the ship's shadow made the water appear cold and green. Sam looked one last time across the bay, at the sight that the bards often sang of. Yad-Sha'Rib, city of endless wealth and a thousand dangers.

Samir went to find Dagomir, who was standing at the bow, deep in conversation with his quartermaster. He sent the man away when he saw Sam approach.

'A lucky escape!' Dagomir beamed. 'We'll not be caught now; not by any ship of this city. The *Vanya's Wrath* is too fast. Get used to her, lad, she'll be your home now.'

'For how long?' Sam asked. 'How long until we reach the Lost Isles?'

'Well, assuming the dusty old tomes I've read are correct, and assuming that you're able to steer us true… a month, at the very least.'

'A month! Impossible. I have to send word to my mother.'

'Don't be soft, lad. There was but one chance for that and I'm afraid we missed it. Remember, she's better off not knowing where you are – that way, if anyone does find her, she can't be held accountable, can she?'

'You mean she cannot give us away,' Sam said, sullenly.

Dagomir shrugged. 'That too.'

'Wait… How can we sail for a month? This ship cannot hold enough food and water for such a journey.'

'Lucky we have wine, then,' Dagomir said, with a grin. He saw Sam's face unmoving, and sighed. 'The island of Caldega is ten days' sail. We put in there for resupply. After that, you will be our navigator.'

'Caldega,' Sam said with awe, remembering stories he'd heard. 'It is a pirate island. The most dangerous and treacherous place in the world.'

'I've seen worse. I was born to worse.' Dagomir looked wistful for a fleeting moment, but quickly enough the roguish twinkle returned to his eye. 'I'm the prince of pirates. We'll be all right.'

'But beyond Caldega... I have heard there is nothing, until the lands of monsters are found. Places ruled by headless men, and beasts who crawled from the sea long ago and refused to go back. Places where demons live, and gods toy with men like pieces in a game of *pachisi*. What if we reach those by mistake?'

'There will be no mistake, Master Samir. If we reach such a land, it is fair to say we have found our destination. Now, no more questions, I have a ship to command.'

CHAPTER 7

Whatever Samir had imagined a sea-voyage to entail, he had been wrong. By the end of the third day, when the last sliver of land had vanished over the horizon, Sam felt sick from the constant tossing of the ship, and spent most of his time getting in the way of the men going about their business. The *Vanya's Wrath*, too, which had seemed so imposing at the docks, now seemed very much smaller. All the smaller considering Sam's main ambition was to avoid the Manhunter, Yana Selishe. And yet, the woman in black appeared everywhere he turned; each time he was forced to acknowledge her, he managed barely more than a surly grunt, which made him feel very foolish and childish. He hated her.

Sam found some solace in the few friendly faces aboard the ship. Emilio was a pleasant fellow, always ready with a joke or story, or a whistle on his lips. Although to hear the other men talk he was twice the rogue that his captain purported to be. Sam spent most of his time in the presence of the ship's carpenter, Bardo, who when not attending to some serious matter could be found whittling the most intricate ornaments, talismans and friezes from wood, or carving strange figures from the bones of massive sea-creatures, his massive, paw-like hands surprisingly dextrous.

'This was once a hydra's toe,' he'd say with a wink. 'And now it is the likeness of Dorak, a god among my people, who guards the gates of the Dreamlands against the unworthy.'

Sam though this Dorak sounded somewhat like Birrahd, only not as cruel. And so he had asked, 'Do you think they are one and the same? Birrahd and Dorak? Just called different names by men of faraway lands?'

Bardo had thought hard on this, so that his tattooed brows wrinkled into great furrows. 'Maybe so,' he'd said at last. 'Only, I don't think Dorak would imprison men within his temple. He wishes all men to be free to make their own decisions, for good or ill. He weighs the good they do against the bad, and if he finds more bad than good… well, they'll pay the balance in the afterlife.'

'Aren't you worried? Being a… a pirate, I mean?'

'Still time to make amends, lad,' he'd said. 'I plan to die with my slate wiped clean, which is about the best a man can do.'

The only time Sam felt truly at ease aboard ship was when Dagomir gave him a job to do. And the job to which he was most suited was lookout, for he was the best climber of all the crew, and despite his sea-sickness he could ascend the ratline to the tops in mere seconds. He'd taken to wearing the amulet again, for the time being, but still his uncanny abilities were evident in his sure-footedness and cat-like balance.

On the fourth day, Emilio took pity on Sam, and handed him some welcome distraction from gazing nauseously at a horizon that stubbornly refused to stay still.

'Before we reach Caldega,' he said, 'there is one very important thing you need to know – how to fight.'

'I can fight,' Sam said.

'Really? From what I have seen, you are very good at not getting killed. But that is not the same thing. Here, take this.' He tossed a sword to Sam, who snatched it out of the air easily.

Sam examined the blade. It was similar to the one Emilio even now brandished, only shorter. The hilt was ornate, with a domed guard. The blade was thin and pointed. Sam tested it, surprised at how much it flexed. 'Are you sure this is a sword?' he asked. 'It looks like something my mother would use to knit.'

This drew laughs from the few men working nearby, and an affected scowl from Emilio. 'This, my young friend, is the favoured weapon of my people,' he said. 'It is an elegant blade – not like the clumsy scimitars of Dar'Shur. It is the weapon of an artist.'

More laughter. 'Maybe you should use it to write with, then,' a fat Dar'Shuri crewman scoffed. 'It looks more like a stylus anyway.'

Emilio cleared his throat indignantly. Ignoring the men, he said to Samir, 'First, adjust your stance. Put your feet like so.' He turned sideways, adopted a wide stance, and pointed his right foot outwards, directly at Sam. 'Now, raise your sword in salute, so.' Emilio held his sword in front of his face, blade pointing to the sky, and then swished it down and outwards towards Sam.

Sam copied this strange procedure, and the points of their blades touched.

'Now, when I step forward, you step back. Keep your weight on your back foot when I strike. If I slash, you must parry, understand? If I thrust, you must step back. When I have made three strikes, it is your turn. We'll go slowly at first. Go!'

Emilio did not go slowly at all. He tapped Sam's sword away, then sprang forward. Sam saw it coming easily, and leapt away as instructed, but too far. His back foot twisted on a guide rope, and Sam tumbled backwards into a pile of fishnets. Sam wiped seaweed from his face as the men laughed at his misfortune. To his credit, Emilio scratched at his neck, and shrugged apologetically.

'Come on, lad. Get up and we'll try again.'

'Maybe he should learn some real fighting,' a voice interrupted. Hush descended on deck as Yana Selishe appeared from below.

'Come now, miss, I'm instructing the boy. It could save his life.'

'Do you think he can defeat his enemies by dancing them to exhaustion?'

Sam got to his feet, slowly. The huntress was not looking at him. She was walking silently, gracefully, in a wide circle. Her eyes were fixed on Emilio. Not a man spoke, but all looked at the woman suspiciously – she was a stranger, and more than one pirate had whispered that her presence aboard the ship would bring bad luck. One who has been so close to the presence of evil sorcery couldn't fail to be tainted by it, they said.

'I wouldn't challenge Emilio,' Dagomir's booming voice broke the silence. He leaned against the starboard bulwark, green eyes twinkling. 'He is the best fighter among all my crew. Almost as good as me.'

'Better,' Emilio said, his tone light but his eyes following the huntress warily. 'Mainly on account of you always being drunk.'

'I'll drink to that!' Now the laughter returned.

'A glowing endorsement,' Selishe said. 'Perhaps we should put on a demonstration for the boy, so he can see how real warriors fight. That is... unless you are afraid of being beaten by a woman.'

'Madam, you would not say that if you had seen my last visit to Caldega,' Emilio laughed. 'But you intrigue me. I always thought the Manhunters of Yad-Sha'Rib preferred to stab men in the back, not fight them honourably.'

Yana Selishe slowly, and with great show, drew the curved scimitar from her back. It was shorter and narrower than the ones hefted by the city guard. Sam did not think that was because Selishe was weaker; rather that she favoured speed over power. 'You talk too much,' she said. 'Defend yourself!'

So swift was the woman's strike that Emilio almost ended up the same way as Sam. He rapidly adjusted his footing, hopping backwards, weight on his heels, using the thin blade only to redirect the woman's strikes away from his body.

Emilio rolled his shoulders, turning as though he really were dancing. Yana Selishe overstepped, and now Emilio slashed downwards, causing her to jump and twist. His blows came in a dazzling flurry, the flexible blade singing as it scraped the side of the huntress's scimitar. Dozens of slashes and thrusts seemed to blur into one formidable attack, and yet the woman remained calm, her face barely showing any sign of worry or exertion. She tapped aside the sword, hopped agilely over low sweeps, and stepped nimbly aside powerful thrusts without even bothering to parry. Emilio grinned the whole time, like a man who rarely exercised his skill-at-arms, and relished the thrill of the duel. His blows became more ostentatious, his swings more powerful, his dance more vigorous. At last, when the woman had run out of deck, he cried 'A-ha!' and leapt forward with a piercing thrust.

His sword hit only wood, point thudding into a bulwark like an arrow, the blade flexing upwards. The woman leapt higher than Sam thought possible, tumbling in mid-air, landing with consummate balance on the swaying deck. Even as Emilio jerked his blade free, he found the edge of a scimitar at his neck, and the dark eyes of Yana Selishe beholding him like a mere plaything.

Mutters circled through the crew. Dagomir offered slow applause.

The huntress sheathed her sword. 'What was it you were saying about scimitars?' she asked.

'I concede they can be useful in the right hands,' Emilio said. 'But I wonder how many other tricks you have. Perhaps we should find out – after I finish the boy's instruction.'

'Another time,' Sam said. 'It's my turn on watch.'

'It can wait,' Emilio said.

'No, I can work my fair share.' And with that, Sam leapt up to the ratline, and scurried up to the tops to relieve the dozing man on lookout. At least climbing was one thing he could do better than anyone else on the ship.

Sam sat alone in the crow's nest while the men below resumed their work. Sam was tired of being spoken of like an irrelevance. And the woman... Sam had to admit to himself that her skills were more than impressive. The way she moved, and fought – he wanted to be like that, more so than the flamboyant buccaneer with the whip-thin blade. But to confess such a thing? No, it was a step too far. Perhaps he could learn by watching her, so that one day he might kill her.

He pushed that thought aside. He didn't even truly believe he had it in him to take a life. Not even the life of a thrice-cursed hunter.

An hour or so passed. Sam nibbled upon a hard ship's biscuit, which he had to confess wasn't the worst thing he'd ever eaten, even if the thought of the weevils he had had to brush off it was dispiriting. Besides, plain biscuits were about the only thing he could keep down. He shivered. It was growing later than he'd thought. But that was impossible – it was late afternoon, and the climes would surely only get warmer the further south they sailed.

He stood, hanging onto to the signal-rope for balance. The sky was darkening ahead, while the skies behind were clear and blue. There was a shimmer on the southern horizon, a dark indigo haze moving unevenly beneath a grey sky. And then in that greyness, a black needle thrust upwards, parting the clouds like curtains. There were flashes of light, just pinpricks, like tiny stars appearing for the briefest moment behind the silvery veil. And slowly, Sam realised what he was looking at was a storm. That dark, blue-grey tumult was the waves, peaking and troughing far in the distance. But it could not remain distant, for they were sailing straight for it.

'Captain,' Sam shouted down. 'Captain Dagomir.'

'What is it, lad?'

'Storm ahead!'

Beneath the fluttering sail, which was turned to catch an easterly wind, Sam watched Dagomir race to the bow, whereupon he climbed the figurehead and peered out intently to sea. Even as he did, Sam saw the black pillar grow and shimmer, and join with the clouds. The pinpricks of light became jagged streaks. The storm was violent, turning day to night, and it was coming upon them so rapidly it did not seem natural.

'Storm!' Dagomir shouted. 'Helm, ten degrees east. All hands, batten down the hatches!' He ran back to the mainmast. 'Get down, lad,' he called up to Sam. 'We need all hands on deck.'

By the time Sam had touched down on the deck, every man was busy at his station. Anything that could not be nailed down was taken below, along with the cages of poultry and barrels of fresh water. Hatches were fastened down tight, the ballistae secured with ropes, block and tackle, and the sail was reefed.

'Get to my cabin,' Dagomir ordered Sam. 'Landsmen are no good in a storm.'

Sam did not want to get in the way, but nor did he like feeling useless. As it transpired, he barely had time to follow orders before the storm, as if from nowhere, was upon them. Sam grabbed a rope as the ship lifted high, as though in flight, tilting forward. For a moment, the sea twisted into a fantastical landscape of grey mountains and frothing white peaks, and the *Vanya's Wrath* began to slide down one such mountainside, into a deep valley of midnight blue. Sam was too awed, too frightened, even to cry out; he simply clung to the rope for dear life as freezing water lapped over the bulwarks, and rain the likes of which he had never seen pounded from roiling black clouds.

Down went the ship, gathering speed, until it spun about, slipping down sideways, vast waves towering over them fore and aft. Sam felt sure the ship would be engulfed at any moment.

The waves collided, and instead of pounding onto the ship and crushing it beneath a vast volume of water, the swell from below carried the vessel high once more, spinning it further, so the bows pointed up to the sky as the ship slipped backwards. Lightning flashed in jagged streaks. Sam squinted. There, at the bow, was Makeno. He stood by the figurehead, not even braced, waving his staff in the air. As the man's arms stretched outwards, lightning seemed to arc horizontally, scarring the clouds.

'Vanya tests us!' roared Dagomir. He slipped across the deck, grabbing a rope near to Sam, and laughed with such mirth that Sam thought him mad. 'She will not sink us, lad. Not today. I am destined for more than this!'

The ship pitched violently to starboard, and Sam lost his grip on the slick rope. He felt empty space beneath his feet; he knew beneath him was the fathomless sea, and he felt his stomach rise up as he fell.

Dagomir's hand was on his arm in an instant, and as the ship bobbed the other way like a cork, Sam clattered to the deck.

'Like I said, lad, get to my cabin. You're no good to us dead.'

The ship plunged downwards more rapidly. A great wave swept over the stern, and Sam found himself with no choice but to obey Dagomir as he slid along the deck towards the cabin. He clattered into a wooden wall, and the door flew open, only for Yana Selishe to appear, looking rather less immaculate than usual as rain and saltwater pummelled at her. She grabbed Sam and helped him inside, as the ship lurched violently upwards. Sam finally got to his feet, and tried to pull away from the woman, when he saw something in her eyes that filled him with dread.

For a moment, her face was lit by a flash of lightning. And following that flash came a great *crack*, and the cries of panicking men.

'Oh no…' Selishe muttered.

Sam turned around; the woman's hand still firmly gripped his arm. The mast was aflame, and worse, it was sundered. A black rent opened up near its base. Ropes snapped and whipped about, striking one man and sending him flying backwards. The mast creaked and groaned even louder than the roaring wind, and finally it toppled. It smashed into the starboard bulwarks before tearing fully free of the ship, and Sam's eyes widened in horror as he saw two men taken overboard with it.

Dagomir fumbled his way to starboard as the ship leaned heavily, pulled by the trailing ropes and rigging. 'Man overboard!' he shouted, his booming voice travelling but weakly over the torrent.

Three or four men struggled to join Dagomir, and Sam wrenched free of the huntress's grip and went too. He took a deep breath, drawing upon his powers. Even he wasn't quite equipped for keeping his footing on a ship in this storm, but he was determined to try. When he reached the men, he heard one cry, 'There, look! That's Torvus. He's clinging to the mast.'

The ship leaned further starboard, so that the tumultuous sea was lapping over the bulwarks.

Dagomir cried, 'Vanya claim him! The mast will sink us. Axes and swords – cut the ropes, or we're done for.'

There was no resistance; the fear in the eyes of the men far outweighed any sense of fellowship with poor Torvus, and so at once they set about hacking at the tarred ropes, sending each thick cord whipping out to sea. Dagomir held out an axe to Sam. 'Make yourself useful.'

Sam looked out at the crashing waves, at the tiny white speck that was Torvus's face, bobbing about with the remnants of the mast. Sam looked to Dagomir, and shook his head dumbly.

'Then away with you!' snapped the captain. 'There's men's work to be done.'

Dagomir himself pitched an axe-blade through the final rope, and with an abrupt groan the ship righted itself, sending Sam toppling once more to the deck, landing hard on his backside. The ship sat low in the sea, so much water had it taken.

Sam slipped and slid back towards the cabin. There came a guttural cry from the foredeck. Sam looked back to see Makeno standing at the dragon figurehead, arms held up to the heavens, an aura of light around him. Then Sam realised it was not an aura, but a sliver of sunlight ahead, breaking the storm clouds. The pitching of the ship became less violent. The light brought with it an inexplicable feeling of hope; it would be over soon.

But too late for the men who had fallen.

CHAPTER 8

In the days that followed, the crew became increasingly dissatisfied. The loss of the two hands wore heavily on the survivors. Sam felt it keenly; every time he was served a meal, he remembered how, were it not for those deaths, the rations would be even poorer. For with a jury-rigged sail, the journey became ponderously slow. Dagomir predicted it would take at least three extra days to reach Caldega, perhaps more if the winds weren't fair. There, they would have to stop an extra day to recruit two more hands and find a new mast. That would come at a cost – Dagomir said the self-proclaimed governor of Caldega claimed ownership of the scant forests, particularly those trees suitable for ships' masts. It was a commodity on an island ruled by pirates, and thus commanded a heavy price.

The fat Dar'Shuri, Ranbhir, made no bones about his discontentment, nor about the cause of it. 'Mark my words,' he would say when the captain was out of earshot, 'that woman is to blame. Bad luck, that one. She has the blood of innocents on her hands. She draws power from the very demons of the underworld. They give her protection in Yad-Sha'Rib, but here, on the ocean, the gods of the sea show their displeasure. And we'll be the ones to pay the price for bringing her into their dominion. She'll be the death of us if we're not careful.'

It seemed to Sam that the more Ranbhir made this point, the more the men began to nod along with him. It was as though simply repeating the thing was enough to make it true. And he began to wonder himself if there was something in it. After all, she *did* have blood on her hands.

Whenever Emilio heard the grumbling, he was quick to silence it with a curt word or stern glare. Dagomir, on the other hand, became increasingly aloof from the men, and spent much time shut away in his cabin. Shut away with the woman. Sam did not think her the type for romancing a pirate captain. Instead, his mind wandered onto the subject of dark plots and treachery.

The only good thing that had come out of the storm was that Sam's sea-sickness had finally lessened to the point that he no longer really noticed it. When he looked at the horizon, it didn't seem to bob about quite so much, and when he walked across the deck he did so with nary a stumble. With Yana Selishe making herself scarce, Sam chanced to ask Emilio for more sword training, and although the first mate was not in his usual high spirits, he seemed to relish the chance to duel at every opportunity.

'You learn fast, lad,' Emilio said after training. 'Just remember your footwork and we'll make a swordsman of you yet.'

Sam took a tentative swig from his water ration, and wiped beads of sweat from his brow. The training seemed to get harder each time. 'How did you learn to fight?' Sam asked.

Emilio frowned, such that Sam almost regretted the question at once.

'I was instructed by the swordmasters of Tareta, from an early age.'

'Where is Tareta?'

'Far from here. Far from anywhere, I suppose. It was home.'

'Do you not miss it?' Sam knew he was intruding, but he was already missing his mother, and Hassan, and the firm ground of home.

'Of course. Every day I miss it. But I can never go back.'

Sam said nothing, for Emilio now looked wistfully out to sea.

The buccaneer sighed. 'You are too young to understand. But... where I am from, honour is more important than life itself. To dishonour one's family is the worst sin of all. And that is what I did.'

'How?'

'By falling in love. It sounds strange, I know, but let me tell you, lad, there is such a thing as falling in love with the wrong person. For me, it was with a woman so beautiful it was like she had been blessed by the gods. Camila was her name. But she was promised to another.'

'I see...' Sam knew something of this. The girls of Yad-Sha'Rib were often promised to eligible men who might offer them better status, although they rarely seemed happy about it, and Sam had come to see it as immensely unfair. 'Did she love this other man?'

'I don't think she did. Unfortunately, the other man was my older brother, Santo. He was a strong man – a good man, if a little sour. And he was a soldier: a hero. He had already seen two wars when his marriage to Camila was arranged, and he was called away to another soon after. During that time, I saw Camila every day, and in foolishness born of youth, I declared my true feelings for her. She denied me, of course, for she was virtuous and true. But soon after, she told me that although she was sworn to Santo, her heart belonged to me.

'What could I do with such knowledge? It turned my world upside down. She begged me to elope with her, to run far away, but my honour made me stay. I would confront Santo and tell him how we felt, and we would settle the matter like gentlemen. Well, Samir, I got what I wished for, but not how I imagined it.

'Santo returned from battle in a wretched mood, for it had been hard-won. I chose my timing poorly, and when I told him that Camila and I were in love, he flew into a violent rage and beat me. We were separated by our father, and the truth came out. Before I could be punished, I grasped at my only chance: I challenged Santo to a duel. In Tareta, the winner of a duel is granted legal privilege in any quarrel – that means Santo would lose the right to marry Camila if I beat him. But he was a soldier, and well trained. He was also in the blackest of moods, and ordered the duel to take place the very next morning at dawn.

'If I have taught you, Samir, to remember your footing in a duel, then a better lesson still is to never fight angry. That morning, Santo came at me like a bull, and even though the duel was not to the death, he wanted nothing more than to kill me. I had not thought him capable of such passion, and soon I was fighting for my life. He slashed me across the chest, deep – I still bear the scar – and kicked me to the ground. I dropped my sword. I heard my mother wailing, and my father ordering him to stop, but he would not. He raised his sword, ready to run me through. In desperation I took a handful of dry earth and threw it into his eyes. He spluttered, and dropped his guard. And in that moment I grabbed my sword and ran him through.

'You must understand, it was instinct in the heat of the moment. I had never meant to harm my brother, and had he not tried so hard to kill me, I don't think I ever would have. But nonetheless it was done. He fell to the ground dead.'

Sam had no siblings – Hassan was the closest he had to a brother, and he could not imagine them fighting so. 'But… you won the duel. You could marry Camila?'

'No, Samir. It was bad enough that Santo was dead at my hand. But for that I could have been forgiven, for in his rage he had clearly tried to kill me, and would have. But when I threw dirt in his eyes to blind him, I breached the code of single combat, and thus my own life was forfeit. My father could not bring himself to lose two sons that day, but nor could he allow the family name to be sullied. And so I was banished, never to return on pain of death. Camila, of course, was not allowed to come with me. I don't know what became of her. I took very little with me, save two swords. This one,' and at this he held up his sword, with its long, thin blade, 'was Santo's. I admit I stole it to remember him by. The smaller one, the one you hold, was mine, for when all this happened I was not much older than you are now. It has killed several times, both in honourable duels and in desperate battle, but no life was more bitterly taken than that of my brother.'

Emilio fell into a melancholy silence. Sam looked at the sword in his own hand in a very different light.

The moment was interrupted by a shadow passing over them: the shadow of a bird.

Emilio leapt to his feet, and looked around at the sky. 'Did you see that?' he demanded.

'Yes... what is the matter?'

'There can be no birds here. We are too far out to sea. Unless there is an uncharted island nearby or... another ship.'

'There is no sign of it now,' Sam shrugged.

Ranbhir called over, 'What are you looking at?'

'I thought I saw a bird. Or the shadow of one.'

'A bird?' the big man laughed. 'That's ridiculous...'

Ranbhir stopped, and looked up, an expression of great concern on his podgy face. It was no bird that had caught his attention, and it took Sam a moment to work out the problem. The makeshift sail had stopped fluttering, and now sank, perfectly limp and still. Every breath of wind had gone, and the ship began to slow.

'No,' said Emilio. 'No, no, no. Captain!' he strode aft, calling for Dagomir, who appeared at once. 'We are becalmed,' Emilio explained.

'Impossible. First a storm and now this. Where is Makeno?'

The wild man was already making his way along the deck, staff rapping upon the boards, bones and trinkets jangling.

'Makeno, what devilry is this?' the captain asked.

'Devilry indeed, Captain. I sense dark forces working against us.'

This caused murmurs and whispers to circle around the crew.

'Then do your job,' Dagomir snapped. 'Summon the wind. Get us to Caldega before anything else goes wrong.'

As Makeno considered this, Ranbhir shouted, 'There are your dark forces.' He pointed behind Dagomir, towards the cabin door, where Yana Selishe now stood.

'Get inside,' Dagomir ordered her, but not before more calls and insults, and angry grumbles swept through the press of men.

'No!' shouted Ranbhir. 'It's time to put an end to this. She has brought a curse on us. Throw her into the sea and have done with it.'

Dagomir stepped forward, drawing himself to his full height. He placed a hand on the pommel of the broadsword at his belt deliberately, as if to remind everyone that he was armed. 'Listen to me,' he boomed. 'That woman is a passenger on this ship. *My* ship. And what's more, she's paid her way. When any of you can fill the coffers with your personal fortunes, maybe then you can give the orders.'

'Haven't we filled the coffers thrice over, with sweat and blood?' a gap-toothed man called out.

'Aye,' shouted another. 'Didn't you empty the coffers at Yad-Sha'Rib to bribe the city guards? And a fine plan that turned out to be.'

'Because I can see the greater prize,' Dagomir said angrily. 'A chest of gold today for a lifetime of wealth tomorrow. That's why I'm captain of this ship.'

'Perhaps we'd rather have food in our bellies and a warm bed tonight,' sneered Ranbhir, 'and a new captain tomorrow.'

'Why, you dog…' Dagomir made to draw his sword, but everything happened too fast.

Someone circled behind him and struck him over the head with a piece of wood. Dagomir fell to the deck with a great thud. Emilio dashed forward, but only as far as the points of three cutlasses. The first mate narrowed his eyes, weighing up the opposition.

Yana Selishe drew her own sword, but the men turned to face her. Ranbhir had an arrow nocked and aimed at her, and Yana checked her advance.

No one paid Sam any heed at all. He looked to Makeno, who leaned on his staff, watching events unfold impassively.

'This is mutiny, Ranbhir,' Emilio said. 'You'll hang from the rigging for this.'

'What rigging?' Ranbhir laughed. 'Thanks to this witch we have none. And no wind. How long this delay? How long before we're down to half rations? Then one-third rations?'

As Ranbhir spoke, Sam removed his amulet, and slowly placed it on the deck, sliding it away from him with his foot. He felt power surge through him, filling him with warmth. His fingertips tingled. He remembered the sensation of the dream, in which the Crystal Pool had flooded his body with nurturing light. It had not occurred to him before, but now he realised the truth of it. The source of his power, or, at least, that of his forefathers. He glanced surreptitiously to Selishe, who gave an almost imperceptible nod.

'It won't come to that,' Ranbhir went on, drawing more shouts of approval from the hungry and thirsty men. 'She dies now, and if the captain doesn't have the guts to do it, then it falls to me.'

He loosed the arrow.

Sam could almost see the air ripple around the fletching. He could hear the arrowhead singing. There was nothing else; the men stood like statues, their voices muffled to him, slow and deep. Only the arrow moved, pushing its way inexorably towards its target, only an arm's length away from him. Pushing its way towards Yana Selishe, the Manhunter he so despised. Her fate was in his hands, and, knowing that, could Sam allow her to die? Wasn't that just as bad as killing her himself? And what then? Would Ranbhir stop at one death? Or would he go on to take the ship by force?

All these questions crowded Sam's mind in an instant. And by sheer instinct, he reached out, and plucked the arrow from the air.

Everything returned to normal all at once. Men gasped in astonishment at what they had witnessed. Sam's heart pounded. He looked down at the arrow in his hand. His palm burned where the wooden shaft had scraped his skin. The pirates were agog. Sam couldn't believe it himself. He dropped the arrow on the deck.

There was a moment of pure awe, and nervousness. Ranbhir cracked first.

'Maybe she's not the only curse aboard,' he snarled. 'Best kill them both and have done with it.'

The fat Dar'Shuri drew his scimitar, and pushed towards Sam, whose legs felt leaden as he found himself in the sights of a killer.

Ranbhir never reached his target. There was a gleam of sunlight from steel, and a broad, heavy blade swung over and down in a great arc. Ranbhir screamed. His arm fell to the deck, still holding his sword. Dagomir stood before him, a bestial snarl on his lips. One hand was pressed to the back of his head, the other held the broadsword like it weighed nothing. Sam had never seen anyone look so dangerous – not even the huntress.

Emilio spied his chance. With one deft move he drew his sword and lashed out, rattling the cutlasses of the men who confronted him, before adopting his fighting stance. They looked nervously to one another, and dropped their swords.

Over Ranbhir's high-pitched screams, Dagomir shouted, 'Should any man raise a hand against me again, on my own ship, they will lose that hand, if not their life. You!' He pointed his sword to the man who had struck him. 'You're a useful man, and I would not have you crippled while our ship is in these doldrums. So Ranbhir shall take your punishment this time. There will be no second chance.'

Without another word, Dagomir plunged his blade downwards, through the heart of the stricken Dar'Shuri, into the deck beneath him. The fat man's screams ceased at once. Sam looked away from the blood that spread across the limewashed planks.

'Blood magic...' Makeno muttered, breaking the silence. He spat upon the deck.

'What?' Dagomir asked.

But it became evident what the Storm-Caller meant. A soft breeze touched Sam's cheek. He looked to the sail, which fluttered again, if only softly.

'Makeno, this is your doing?' said Dagomir.

The wild man shook his head. 'No, Captain, it is yours. Our predicament was caused by blood magic. And the spilling of blood on this ship has dispelled it. Dark forces really are at work against us, but not aboard the *Vanya's Wrath*. Someone is out there, pitting their will against ours.' He nodded to stern, out to sea.

'Zhar-Mharrad,' Sam said. All eyes turned to him. 'You said before that Zhar-Mharrad uses blood magic. It is he who pursues us. He who wishes to reach the Lost Isles before us.'

'Aye.' Dagomir nodded. 'And if we delay any longer, he'll succeed.' He turned to the men, who were still in two minds about their mutinous intentions, and frightened of talk of dark sorcery. 'Don't just stand their gawping. Get to work! Harness the wind. Hang your underclothes over the side for all I care, but get us under sail. We'll reach Caldega or die trying.'

'Aye!' the pirates shouted as one, and scattered, glad to be under orders at least.

Dagomir clapped a firm hand on the slowest of the crewmen, stopping him in his tracks. 'You. Throw this mutinous dog's body overboard, and swab the deck of his traitorous blood. I want none to remember the name of Ranbhir on this vessel.'

With the tension broken, and the ship already creaking forward, Sam stopped to pick up his amulet. When he stood, Yana Selishe was before him.

'I do not think you will need that any more, young one.'

Sam recoiled, holding the amulet away from the woman warily.

'I don't mean to take it,' she said, her voice a soft purr. There was something strangely unruffled about her; given her brush with death moments earlier, she of all the crew seemed singularly calm. 'I simply mean that you will need your wits about you if you are to endure this voyage. Who knows from where the next attack will spring? And besides, I might need you to save my life again before we're through.'

'How do you know what this amulet is for?' Sam asked, feeling himself grow flustered beneath the gaze of her beautiful eyes.

'Because I told her,' Dagomir interrupted. He placed a hand on Sam's shoulder, and guided him to the cabin. Emilio, Makeno and Selishe followed. Once the door was closed, Dagomir stumbled his way to a chair, clutching a hand to the back of his head.

'Captain, you're hurt,' Emilio said.

'It's nothing. But I cannot show weakness in front of the others. You've seen this before, Emilio. This is the most dangerous time for us. The men are a superstitious lot, and once pressed to the brink of mutiny it will take all our efforts to satisfy them. Ranbhir's death will frighten them into obedience for now, but for how long? And if we have an enemy on our tail, will these curs fight for us?'

'We've sailed with some of these men for a year or more,' Emilio said. 'They followed Ranbhir out of fear, but they'll come good.'

'Will they? I trust Bardo, certainly, and one or two of the others who did not raise arms just now. But the others… we're pirates, Emilio. Do not fool yourself into thinking that they are honourable. You left all that behind long ago.'

Emilio looked down at his feet. 'So what do we do?'

'Pray to Vanya for better luck. But more than that, you four are my lieutenants now. I need your help to keep the peace.'

'I'd rather just be a passenger, if it's all the same,' said Yana Selishe. 'When I have to discipline men, they usually end up dead.'

Sam glared at her, though she paid no heed. Dagomir looked at her with admiration.

'If you please, Captain,' Sam said. 'I am no lieutenant. I don't know how I can help.'

'Ha! It is you we need most of all, lad. When you snatched that arrow from the air, you turned the tide in our favour. If any man doubted your power, they doubt no more. I need you to be more confident. Act as though you have every faith in your own abilities, even if you do not. Learn some swagger, lad, like Emilio here. And after Caldega, guide us true to the Lost Isles.'

'But I still don't know how.'

'You will,' Makeno said. 'As we sail south and draw near to the island, you will see the way forward as clear as day. The islands will call, and you will answer.'

'There, you see?' Dagomir beamed. 'But first we must reach Caldega. Keep your eyes and ears open. If any man so much as looks sideways at this woman, or me for that matter, I want his name. When we get to Caldega, we'll offload those with mutinous tendencies, and use what's left of our gold to recruit new hands. In my experience, men recently paid are far more loyal than those who've had a hard voyage.'

There was some brief discussion before all assembled agreed to Dagomir's request, though Sam still felt uneasy about spying on the crew.

'Oh, and Samir,' Dagomir said as they were about to leave the cabin. 'Best leave that amulet with me, like our guest suggested. I want you at your best in the days to come.'

Sam looked to Emilio and Makeno for support, but none was forthcoming. And so, with the utmost reluctance, he pressed the amulet into Dagomir's hand, and followed the others out onto the deck, where the wind blew strong from the north.

CHAPTER 9

Zhar-Mharrad looked over his shoulder, down to the deck of the twin-masted dhow, *Devourer*, where his Bidajah laboured relentlessly. Scarred flesh rippled with exertion, but each moved with mechanical purpose and practised efficiency. He had achieved much over the long years, but Zhar-Mharrad was most proud of his faithful servants, these tireless automata, blessed of Birrahd.

He smiled to himself, and turned his gaze once more out to sea, where the waves gleamed with red rind under the sinking sun.

'I promised I would finish my story,' he said. 'It pleases me to confide in someone. There are so few whom I can trust these days. Now, where was I? Ah, yes, I had just slain my master, the Thaumaturge, Alam'Vir. He had unearthed a relic of singular power in the ruins of the frozen city that men call "Frostgrave". That place is a world apart from Yad-Sha'Rib, so far from my humble birthplace that it might as well be upon the moon. But there I learned much of man's frailty, his failings. It is why I created the Bidajah, you know. How much more than men they are now, without pity, or pain, or misplaced trust. Without avarice, or fear. Only devotion to their master. It is a life free of worry and doubt; a blissful existence they would never have experienced without me. But again, I digress.

'Alam'Vir had found a relic of extraordinary value: the Periapt of Souls, written of in ancient scrolls, thought to have been a myth. Its workings were a mystery to all but my master and, by extension, me. I had studied the books he had given me, and more. I had long taken to stealing into his library of a night, devouring forbidden texts, and learning magics that he himself would never dare use. He was a fine sorcerer, have no doubt; but he lacked ambition. Under his tutelage, I would have been destined for little more than the role of librarian, tending books of powerful lore that would ever go unread, and unused. And so, I changed my fate.

'That the great Alam'Vir could be dispatched with a knife in the back was unthinkable. And so I used the blade not on him, but on myself. I stole the periapt from his desk as he slept, sliced open my own hand, and clutched the periapt tight. In a moment of pure exhilaration and terror that I shall never forget, I saw what lay within the periapt, and what it could do. You see, it is a gateway to another place, a dark dimension that I call the Rift, in which myriad demons vie for dominance. They will do anything to gain ingress to the mortal realm, even if only for a few fleeting moments, for they desire nothing more than to feast on the souls of men. My blood attracted the attention of the demons – the Riftborn – and quickly I recited the spell that had not been uttered in a thousand years or more, ending with the name of a great demon – a lord of murder and war. Once the name was spoken, that creature came forth, bound by all the laws of magic to do my bidding. And my bidding was simple: kill my master.

'It was over quickly. All the wards of preservation in the world could not stop a thing so powerful, and I knew I had found the key to fulfilling my own ambitions. The Riftborn are fickle. They must have a soul as payment for their services, or else they will swiftly turn on those who summon them. Thankfully, the mighty wizard Alam'Vir was more than a sufficient prize for the demon I had called. My old master's soul was absorbed into the periapt, adding its cries of torment to the ceaseless throng already within. The demon bowed to me, and vanished whence it had come.'

At this, Zhar-Mharrad took the chain from beneath his collar, upon which hung a tiny sphere of black glass, held in a silver setting shaped like a skeletal hand. The vizier gazed into the orb's surface, at the roiling, inky dark within it, the red light of dusk giving it an almost liquid appearance. Like blood.

'The Periapt of Souls is home to many demons,' he went on. 'They feed on souls, and on torture. The souls dragged into the Rift are subjected to an eternity of pain, the likes of which we could not possibly imagine. Well, you perhaps. I have an excellent imagination these days. But in return for these souls, ah! What treasures lie in store for the man who controls the demons. He who sates their thirst may be granted certain… boons. The people of Dar'Shur might call these creatures 'djinn', but they would be very wrong. I suppose in practice, the results of communing with such entities are much the same. They do my bidding. They grant what lesser men might call "wishes", in exchange for the blood price.'

Zhar-Mharrad paused. He had taken so many lives to get to where he now stood. But more than that, he thought of the price he himself had paid over the years, and would continue to pay willingly.

'I fled the Frozen City,' said Zhar-Mharrad. 'After a long and arduous journey I returned to my master's keep, whereupon I used the periapt to take control of all that the old sorcerer had. I steeped myself in ancient knowledge, and hired mercenaries to scour the world for more artefacts. Soon, I was unrivalled in power, and I looked to the southern deserts, to the place where I had been born a slave. Yad-Sha'Rib. Slowly, I made my way to the Golden City. Everywhere I stopped, I became known and feared. Noblemen would bow and scrape at my feet. Caliphs would wonder at my power, not knowing that I bore for them a hatred unrivalled. These were the very people who had beggared my family and forced me to scrape an existence in the streets. Had I not been found by Alam'Vir... no. I owed him nothing. I found him, and he taught me little, guarding so jealously his own power until I was forced to take it.

'In each city I sowed the seeds of dissent. I gained allies, and destroyed rivals. I could still not act openly, for my studies were not complete, and I was but one man, despite my magical prowess. And so, when at last I reached Yad-Sha'Rib, I had only to find a suitable pawn. Someone with sufficient influence and ambition to rid the city of the Caliph, and rule anew, under my counsel.

'So'Kurrah, a powerful merchant whose wealth was fed upon by the corrupt Caliphate, was that man. I confess that, although it took little enough to encourage him to seize the crown, it has taken much, much longer than expected to bring him fully under my sway. He was once a courageous man, but finally he has succumbed to my will. And as he has grown weaker, I have grown stronger. I have studied much in order to gain total mastery of the periapt. The Riftborn bring to me great luck, wealth and knowledge. They kill at my behest. They bewitch weak-minded men to do my bidding. They allow me to inhabit the minds of my enemies to see their plans, or to exert influence over their thoughts, even their dreams... All it requires is that I know the correct name of the demon best suited to the task. And believe me, after half a lifetime of wandering and study, I know many of their names. I have experimented with new sciences and long-forgotten magic. I have built a small army – sufficient for the task of keeping So'Kurrah in check, but not yet powerful enough to spread outwards from Yad-Sha'Rib. For that, I will need more than just the Bidajah. For that, I will need the Crystal Pool. Then, my enemies will truly know what power is, and I will have protection enough to ride personally at the head of Yad-Sha'Rib's armies, as its king. As a conqueror.'

The man made some small grunt, as if in protest. It was the first sound he had made in many an hour on this voyage. Zhar-Mharrad raised an eyebrow in surprise.

'Something troubles you? Ah, it is not the thought of me overthrowing the Caliphate. No one, not even you, would miss them. You are thinking of the boy, are you not? Best put him out of your mind now, for it shall only cause you distress. He will not find the Crystal Pool. Already, my agent watches him closely, and when his usefulness is exhausted, he will be killed. Do not fret so! What else can I do? I have enough enemies without encouraging new ones to come seeking revenge.'

With a sudden thud, the vizier's two-headed raven landed upon the wooden rail of the forecastle. The creature cawed softly, and Zhar-Mharrad smiled.

'And there we have it,' Zhar-Mharrad beamed. 'We have reached Caldega.' On the horizon, five degrees from the port bow, the silhouette of a jagged mountain seemed to rise from the sea, and hundreds of tiny lights glinted like stars. If it weren't renowned as a haven for every murderer and thief with a boat, it would almost appear welcoming. 'Now we wait, and see what our quarry does next.'

Zhar-Mharrad looked to the blind Heritor, who was lashed securely to the bowsprit of the *Devourer*. The man tried to say something, but since the vizier had removed his tongue as punishment for his escape attempt, that was not possible. His sinewy muscles strained against the silvery ropes, but even the Heritor's prodigious strength could do nothing against the enchanted bonds.

'I admire your spirit, old man,' said Zhar-Mharrad. 'But I would appreciate it if you would save your strength for the Lost Isles.'

With that, the vizier turned and swept down the steps and along the deck, his raven gliding overhead, and the Bidajah saluting his passing. The blind and mute Heritor who now served as the *Devourer*'s figurehead tried to call out, but the sound was lost on the wind.

CHAPTER 10

From the very moment Sam laid eyes on the island of Caldega, he felt a sense of trepidation and unease about the place. It was dark when the *Vanya's Wrath* limped into port, steering carefully between a haphazard shoal of vessels from every part of the world, all of which had seen better days.

The docks were nothing like the large, industrious landings of Yad-Sha'Rib; instead, rickety wooden jetties led away to cobbled narrows, winding their way between hovels and seedy taverns, and twisting halfway up the single, forested mountain that dominated the island. From the lofty heights of that natural fortification, the self-made governor of the island took stock of his assets, surrounded by mercenary soldiers whose reputation for brutality and corruption had reached even Sam's ears. The governor's villainous dominion was a near-vertical conglomeration of trading posts, smiths, shipwrights, taverns, inns, rickety verandas and bawdy-houses, all huddling precariously together against the side of the mountain as though clinging to each other for support.

'Have your wits about you here, lad,' Emilio had advised. 'Caldega is a pirate-town. A capable man can buy anything here, and take his pleasure in ways beyond counting. A careless man will find himself face-down in the water, with an empty purse and a knife in his back. Never trust a pirate.'

'But… you're a pirate,' Sam had said.

'That's a matter of opinion,' Emilio had laughed, leaping from the ship, into the arms of two rouge-cheeked women who seemed to know him by name.

Dagomir came up beside Sam next, stepping onto the gangplank. 'Don't stray far from the ship,' he advised. 'I have business to attend to, and with any luck we'll start repairs at first light. Until then, we need to take care. There'll be a man on watch at all times – if you get into trouble, come back here and you'll be all right.'

'Trouble?' Sam said. 'Why would I…'

Dagomir patted Sam on the head like he was a toddler. 'Good lad,' he said. He turned to his men and said, 'Right, lads. Business first, and then the night's your own. Just don't come back dead!' And to the sounds of laughter, Dagomir walked down the gangplank in great strides, a whistle on his lips. He exchanged words with a shifty looking man who seemed to hold some position of authority at the dockside, pressing a coin purse into his hand, before striding away purposefully.

Most of the crew followed suit, separating into small groups and heading off into the night. They all seemed to know their jobs, and set about them automatically. Makeno was somewhere below deck, although when Sam had last seen the warden he had been meditating. He could sit for hours, still as stone, and there was no interrupting him.

And so Sam sighed and took his first tentative step onto the docks of Caldega.

He had not been ready for the sensation of solid ground beneath his feet after so long at sea. The ground itself seemed to rise up beneath him; he felt dizzy for a moment.

'You found your sea legs,' a woman's voice purred close by.

Sam suppressed a shudder as he realised Yana Selishe was standing beside him. He hadn't seen her before, and had heard nothing. The woman was like a ghost.

'I think I need to lose them again.' Sam paused. 'You don't go with the others?'

'No. I have business of my own to attend to.'

Sam was about to ask what kind of business a Manhunter of Yad-Sha'Rib could have on the pirate isle, but the woman did not give him a chance. She was already striding away, silently. Sam looked about. Every time he looked up, he felt that men were watching him intently, but as soon as he cast a glance their way they turned back to their fellows. Perhaps Emilio and Dagomir had simply made him feel paranoid. Or perhaps everyone on Caldega was ready to rob or murder him.

Yana Selishe had almost vanished into the shadows, when Sam made his decision. He, too, was stealthy, and fast. And whatever business the woman had, it could not be anything good. If she was working against the crew of *Vanya's Wrath*, and Sam could prove it, he might yet be rid of her. And with that thought in mind, he took a deep breath and followed.

The woman took a circuitous path, through alleys barely wide enough for two men to walk abreast, along cobbled streets strung overhead with eerie red lanterns, up winding stairs and down dirt slopes. Sam padded along, keeping to the shadows where he could, doing his best not only to avoid detection, but also to escape the attentions of the many pirates who staggered drunkenly about the narrow streets, and the cutpurses who followed in their meandering wake in the hope of relieving them of a few pieces of silver. Sam had, of course, long navigated such paths through dangerous quarters of Yad-Sha'Rib; but this was not the Golden City. There were no armed guards ready to keep the peace if things went ill. There was no familiar marketplace to evade capture. There was no Sivita's Bakery where Sam could hide and maybe scrounge some leftover flatbread. Most of all, there was no home to return to at the end of the day – no sanctuary or respite from the many perils of the city.

Yana Selishe, Sam determined, knew where she was going. Her step was steady and purposeful, her course unfaltering. Once, two men stepped from the shadows in front of her, one making some lewd remark in a barely intelligible dialect. The huntress flashed steel their way, and the men retreated. At last she ascended a tall flight of wooden stairs, which clung precariously to the side of a rocky redoubt. Sam was forced to hide in a goat-pen, for the stairs were open-sided, and as Selishe climbed higher her view of the street below was unobstructed. He wondered if he could even risk pursuit any further; one look over her shoulder and he would be discovered. He heard loud, slurred voices further down the sloping street, and saw shadows shift as a group of pirates wended their way from the nearby tavern. He could not stay hidden forever. Sam looked to the spindly wooden struts that towered from the rocks far below up to the precipice. Most people would baulk at the thought of climbing the dilapidated frame, but, Sam mused, Dagomir had been quick to remind him of late that he was not ordinary.

Sam waited until the woman had rounded the bend of the cliff stair, and the men in the street were looking the other way, and nimbly leapt over the fence of the goat-pen, darting low and quiet to the foot of the stair, and leaping over the edge of the cliff. His fingers closed around rough wood, splinters digging into his lubberly skin more painfully than he'd expected. He looked down, and the air rushed from his lungs as he saw a much steeper drop than he'd imagined, terminating at jagged rocks at a narrow defile, into which waves crashed far below, their white peaks gleaming by moonlight. He took a breath, and clambered onto the first crossbeam, before hopping to the next strut. Again, he felt a warm glow flow through him; but this time he checked himself. He did not want to experience the pain of Blood Burn again in a hurry – certainly not here – and so he tried not to exert himself unless absolutely necessary, taking the easier footholds and spars wherever possible. Even without his uncanny balance and agility he would have been a good climber. He and Hassan had once scaled the abandoned guard tower at Khar-Khaf. It was taller, but not quite so tumbledown as this wooden frame.

Nevertheless, it took mere minutes for Sam to reach a flat landing, which curved around the rock face, leading to a sheltered bluff. Here, Sam risked hoisting himself over the rail. His hands were chafed, and his lungs ached, like the act of breathing was just one more exertion. He tried to quieten his own ragged breaths for fear that the expert huntress might hear him even above the night breeze that whistled through the gaps in the weathered planks. But there was neither sight nor sound of the woman.

Sam moved close to the rock face, hugging the shadows. He tiptoed along the platform. It sloped upwards, and Sam hunkered low as the rocky outcrop above him gave way to a wooden wall. It looked like some kind of defensive position, or a lookout post perhaps. The platform ahead terminated at a small set of steps, leading to a grassy plateau. Sam paused; firelight danced on the ground.

He listened hard. There were voices, low and indistinct over the wind. Sam knew he had to risk a closer look, or his climb would be for nothing. He cast a look about, and felt very alone. Ahead lay possible danger. Behind was a den of thieves and cutthroats; and facing him across the platform were the crashing waves of the endless sea, under a strange sky.

Sam clenched his fists and set his jaw. 'What are you doing, Samir?' he whispered to himself. But he was already moving, skirting the wooden wall, until he reached the end. He steeled himself, and peeked around the edge.

A burning brazier stood in the middle of a circular space, half enclosed by the palisade wall that faced the sea, and half by the mountain that continued up to dizzying heights, trees jutting from rock at curious angles, covering the slopes in dark foliage. In the rock face was a small cave mouth, in which torches hung on sconces. In the open air, however, stood two figures. One was unmistakeably Yana Selishe. She stood with her back to Sam. On the other side of the flames was a man, a black hood almost fully covering his face. Sam could not make out any features through guttering firelight and acrid smoke. Was that a beard at the man's chin, or just a twist of shadow? For all Sam knew, it could have been Zhar-Mharrad himself. The man was speaking, but most of his words were snatched by the wind before they reached Sam's ears.

'The plan… be unwise… failure.' The voice was a low growl, forced and unnatural.

Sam contemplated moving closer, but it would mean crossing open ground, and even though the two figures weren't looking his way, it seemed a risk too far. Now Selishe spoke, angrily.

'…Ever failed? You… the greater plan.'

It seemed hopeless. Sam had risked much to find some crucial evidence with which to incriminate the woman, and now he could not even eavesdrop successfully. He leaned forward, and as he did a chunk of rock beneath his hand dislodged, tumbling onto the platform and over the side. The two figures looked in his direction, and Sam sprang back behind the wall, pressing himself against it, praying that Selishe did not come to investigate.

A black shadow swept overhead. An avian cry squawked into the night, and Sam fair jumped from his skin. He heard low voices again, but no one came to investigate. Instead, he heard a word. A name.

'Zhar-Mharrad.'

Summoning all his courage, Sam peered again around the corner, breathing a small sigh as he realised that no one was searching for him. But what he saw instead froze the blood in his veins. The two figures were no longer standing by the brazier, but were instead further away, by a section of palisade upon which sat perched a gigantic black bird: a raven – with two heads.

Sam had never seen such a creature, but he'd heard of it. It was whispered in the dark alleys of Yad-Sha'Rib that the two-headed raven was a servant of Zhar-Mharrad – a familiar. Some even said it was a demon, bound to the vizier's service. Sam could well believe it, for Selishe and the man in black now huddled together, seemingly talking to the bird as it cocked its head and scrutinised the pair intently with its four beady black eyes. After a short time, the bird flew away. The man in black bowed and marched swiftly away to the cave, taking down a torch at the cave-mouth, and quickly vanishing from sight. Yana Selishe paused, staring into the flames for a moment, then made her way back towards Sam.

Sam had anticipated this. He tiptoed out of sight, and quickly slid beneath the rail, swinging underneath the walkway, hanging on to a wooden beam for dear life. Again, he accidentally looked down at the crashing waves beneath him, and struggled manfully to keep his last meal in his stomach.

Footsteps tapped on the platform overhead. A shadow passed over the gaps in the boards, blocking out the silver strands of moonlight, and then they stopped. Yana Selishe was standing directly over Sam. Why had she paused? Sam considered climbing lower, but the chances of doing so quietly seemed slim indeed, and so he waited where he was, hardly daring to breathe.

He started to lose feeling in his fingers. His feet felt like lead weights at the ends of his ankles. The seconds dragged, until Sam wondered if he could hold on any longer. And then the shadow passed. Yana Selishe's footsteps faded away, and when he could not hear them at all, he hoisted himself up with all his might, crawling under the rail and collapsing on his back on the platform. He lay there for a moment, watching the slow circling of the stars overhead, and then forced himself to his feet lest the hooded man or, worse, Yana Selishe return.

Sam made his way carefully down the winding stair, scouring the paths below for any sign of the woman, and seeing none. Once he reached the cobbled street, he threw caution to the wind. As one-eyed thugs and bawdy harlots leered and pawed at him, Sam raced through the streets and alleys, back to the dock. He saw a familiar face from the ship, and made straight for the man. 'Where is Captain Dagomir?' he panted. The man, already drunk, pointed vaguely along a dark street.

Sam took it. Hawkers tried to sell him potions; gamblers invited him into unlit hovels. Sam ignored them all. At last, he came to a tall house, lights aglow within, men huddled in the doorway, craning their necks to see inside.

'Captain!' Sam shouted. 'Captain Dagomir?'

Some of the men in the doorway turned to look at Sam. One tried to cuff him round the ear, but Sam darted out of reach, much to the man's chagrin. Sam tried to push past them, but was shoved away.

'Get out of here, whelp,' growled a man with a red bandana. 'This is a place of business.'

'Is Captain Dagomir in there? I must speak to him,' Sam insisted.

The man raised his arm again to swat Sam away like a troublesome bug, but this time the brute's wrist was caught by a much larger hand, with thick, strong fingers and hairy knuckles. The man with the bandana turned to see who had dared accost him, and seemed to thinktwice when he saw the imposing bulk of Bardo the carpenter.

'This lad is one of Dagomir's crew,' Bardo said. 'If anyone is to teach him manners, it's the captain.'

The man in the bandana grumbled. Bardo put a paw-like hand on his shoulder and pushed him aside, before beckoning Sam into the house.

Sam followed Bardo, squeezing through a press of men who all seemed to be waiting in line for something. There were too many people in the entryway, and the air was thick with sweat, and so ripe that Sam had to pull his shirt up over his nose and mouth. At last Bardo entered a larger room, explaining to a man on the door that Sam was with Dagomir's crew, and pulled Sam to one side. A few armed men prevented the bustling throng from getting too close to the people in the centre of the room. The line of sailors that began outside the building threaded around this large chamber, each seaman waiting their turn. In the middle of the room was a row of four great desks, each laden with a huge pair of scales, a fat ledger, and bags of gold. Behind each desk sat some kind of administrator or clerk, finely dressed, faces impassive, their mean eyes full of cunning. Behind each man stood a burly guard, well protected by mismatched armour doubtless scavenged from the ships of far-flung realms. Sam could make out Dagomir's broad shoulders and golden hair, and the captain now leaned over one of the desks, remonstrating earnestly with the stone-faced clerk behind it.

'Stay quiet, lad,' the carpenter muttered in a low voice. 'This is the counting house, where captains make deals with the governor's agents. The captain is haggling over the price of tall trees for our mast and spars, and supplies for our voyage. The agent is driving a hard bargain: he wants a cut of the spoils from the Lost Isles.'

'He knows about the Lost Isles?' Sam said. Several men nearby turned to look at Sam at once.

'Shh!' Bardo hissed. 'Yes, they know. Every man-jack on Caldega is here for the same purpose. It seems this is not just an island of pirates at present – we have mercenaries, guild-men and adventurers from all over the world. For some, their voyage ends here, for they lack one vital component of their crew.' He nodded knowingly.

'A Heritor?' Sam whispered.

Bardo winked acknowledgement.

'Bardo... I have to speak to the captain.'

'It'll have to wait, lad.'

'It cannot wait.' Sam pushed forward, shrugging off Bardo's clumsy attempt to stop him, and ducked and wove his way through to the desks. For once his lack of stature and age worked in his favour; the guards made no move to stop him, perhaps assuming he was just some curious serving-lad come to get a closer look at the very serious business of Caldega's inner sanctum.

Dagomir was leaning over one of the desks now, speaking quietly but forcefully, punctuating his words by slapping his fist into his palm. The man behind the desk seemed singularly unmoved. A guard stood behind each desk, arms folded. The one nearest Dagomir eyed him suspiciously. Sam hovered indecisively for a moment, and then tugged at Dagomir's tunic.

'Captain Dagomir,' he ventured.

Dagomir cast Sam a sideways glance. He gave the slightest shake of his head to discourage Sam, before turning back to the agent, saying, 'We can give no more than a one-tenth share. But I'm willing to increase payment for the supplies up front. Two hundred gold, and that's twice what it's…'

'Captain!' Samir snapped, more forcefully. The strength of his own voice surprised even him, and everyone in the immediate vicinity stopped their bartering to stare at him, or mutter some jest about the audacious lad interrupting serious business.

Dagomir looked as though he was grinding his teeth. He glared fixedly at Sam, before turning back to the agent, who now wore a smirk. 'So two hundred. And for that I want four good men. Hand-picked men. And…'

Sam yanked hard at Dagomir's tunic. 'Captain, this is important. If you do not act now, there is no point to the voyage at all. We are betrayed! The woman has…'

So intent was he on attracting Dagomir's attention, and so worn out from the evening's exertions, that Sam did not see the backhand blow coming. Dagomir struck Sam so hard across the face he spun about, staggering back into the arms of Bardo, as men jeered and laughed raucously.

'What's this about a woman? And betrayal?' the agent was asking. 'I thought we could depend on you.'

'The boy is addled from too long at sea,' Dagomir said. 'I took him in, but it seems he is unsuited to life on the ocean. Maybe I'm too soft-hearted, eh?'

'Heh! That's not the Dagomir we know,' the agent smirked. 'Maybe we should say two-hundred-and-fifty, as you're in a generous mood.'

'Two-twenty, and not one copper more.'

Samir didn't hear any more. Bardo was already dragging him away, pushing through the throng, and out into the cold night air. Sam's face thrummed, and tears stung his eyes. He railed and cursed, but only half-heartedly, and not sufficiently to wrench himself from Bardo's strong arms.

'Easy, lad. Whatever it is, it's not worth getting on the captain's bad side over, mark my words.'

Sam could not reply. He looked at Bardo, mouth working noiselessly, then backed away. He bumped into a scrawny man, causing him to spill drink from a flagon. The man uttered some protest, and raised a hand to clout this impudent whelp, but Sam was already staggering away in a daze. He considered abandoning the *Vanya's Wrath*, with its mutinous crew and mean captain. He could stay on Caldega, take his chances on his own, as he so often had. But it was a small island, and hardly the kind of place where he could hide for long. There was no home to which he could retreat, no friend on whom to depend, no mother to comfort him when things got bad. He had no choice but to return to the ship. Maybe he could find Emilio. But what then? Emilio was loyal to Dagomir, and Dagomir was in thrall to that witch… Sam felt that he might as well be locked in Zhar-Mharrad's dungeons, for he was surely a prisoner here.

*　*　*

The men, at least, were in fine spirits the next morning. A train of mules arrived at the dockside, dragging behind them a newly felled tree, purchased by Dagomir, which must have been the height of ten men, and poker straight. Bardo organised some men to help hoist the tree onto some thick blocks, and then at once set every man to work, stripping bark, sawing, planing and carving. Bardo was a true craftsman, and would never be satisfied with an ordinary, plain mast. Instead, he monitored every man's work, and throughout the course of the day he chiselled intricate, swirling forms into the wood, following the grain, and uttering dedications to virtually every sea-god of every people in the world.

Sam wondered that they had time to take such care, but Emilio explained it so: 'The common sailor is superstitious – you have seen for yourself what they can be driven to by their fears. Bardo is revered by the common sailor, because he is not only an artist, but a devout man, who has spent his life appeasing the gods. Every sigil that he carves protects the ship, and he will not be hurried. He believes, Samir, and therefore the men believe in him. Dagomir would rather delay an extra day than displease Bardo. You see?'

'It is like when my mother makes eel stew,' he said. 'Everything is ready to eat in an hour, but she leaves it bubbling away all day, adding spice every hour, tasting, and stirring. By the time she serves the stew, everyone is starving, but she tells us it's worth the wait.'

Emilio laughed. 'And is she right?'

'I don't know,' Sam said. 'I have never dared try it before she's finished.'

'She sounds like a wise and formidable woman. I think I'd like to try this stew.' He paused for a moment, his face taking on an uncharacteristically serious caste. 'Samir, do not fret about last night. I spoke with the captain, and he says he will keep a close eye on the woman. Dagomir is a hard man, but he is not a bad man. He is used to dealing with the worst scum the world can dredge up. He has no idea how to handle decent folk.'

Sam frowned. His cheek still ached from the blow. 'That doesn't mean he has to side with the bad against the good.'

'No. But it does mean he's used to seeing more than just black and white – there is always more than one side to every story. Perhaps he knows something about Yana Selishe that we do not, and if he chooses not to share what he knows, that is his business. The world is complicated for men like him, and like me. We tread a fine line between good and bad. We just have to be careful that we maintain a balance, or we lose everything. Does that make sense?'

'Not really,' Sam said. 'How can being good... be bad?'

Emilio's expression brightened again, the familiar twinkle returning to his eye. 'Let's hope you don't have to find out, eh? Otherwise you'll be a pirate, too, and we can't have that. What would your mother say?'

* * *

Yana Selishe sat cross-legged at the stern of the *Vanya's Wrath*, looking into the middle-distance, her breathing slow and steady. She tried not to concern herself with the rueful glares of Samir; the boy was everything to her mission, and yet he was inconsequential. A conundrum best not dwelt on, for it clouded her thoughts and presented a distraction she could ill afford. Still, his friendship with Emilio could yet be a problem, and she had not yet decided how best to deal with it. Or, rather, she knew what she should do, but did not think it yet prudent.

Of more pressing concern was Captain Dagomir. He had been strangely quiet and thoughtful since returning to the ship late last night. He had barely spoken a word to her. Now, he stood behind her at the tiller, and she could feel his eyes burning a hole in the back of her head. Did he suspect something? He was a simple creature, like most men; she had twisted him round her little finger so far with little more than a flutter of her eyelashes and a sway of her hips. But now, he was suspicious, and that posed the greatest problem of all.

She took a deeper breath, and cleared her thoughts. She needed to be at her best for the trials ahead.

It was a relief to leave the island. Even though the sun was low, and the sky was already reddening, it felt warmer, and the wind smelled fair once more. As the cries of hungry gulls finally receded, Sam stood at the bows of the *Vanya's Wrath,* savouring the last of the sun on his face and the sound of the sea. It reminded him a little of home.

There were four new crewmen now, and they set to work with the others as though they had always been aboard. Of their predecessors who had been deemed too untrustworthy to stay, and of the slain Ranbhir, there was not a word uttered. Sam wondered how many times crewmen on ships such as this had been so utterly and seamlessly replaced because their faces no longer fitted, or they were deemed mutinous. He did not ask; it seemed not the done thing even to mention their names.

Every so often Sam would hear Dagomir shouting some command, or become aware of Yana Selishe prowling about the deck. He sometimes glared daggers at them both, his heart full of anger, not just at them for what they had done, but at the situation he had allowed himself to fall into. He'd let his wanderlust get the better of him. He had listened to Dagomir's promises, and gone too willingly aboard a ship destined for parts unknown. In doing so he had broken a promise to his mother only recently made. He missed her, and his friend, Hassan. He had been promised an adventure that might see him liberate his city from tyranny. Now, he wondered if he would ever see Yad-Sha'Rib again.

CHAPTER 11

Days became weeks. The *Vanya's Wrath* cut through the Southern Ocean with renewed vigour, faring rapidly though a seemingly endless sea. At the start, Sam spent most of his waking hours at work, or practising his swordsmanship with Emilio – anything to keep his mind from dark thoughts of vengeance. And yet, as time passed, Sam found not only that he was increasingly pressed by Dagomir to help navigate the waves, but also that he *wanted* to. He was compelled to do so, as if some external force eroded his free will, and spoke directly to his heart.

Sam had never truly believed he could do it. He had never thought for a moment that he could find the Lost Isles. But now each day he stood upon the deck, with the wind in his hair, and he knew where they had to go. He could sense if the ship was straying from its course by even a few degrees. He stopped offering to help the crew. He took fewer turns on watch, and never swabbed the decks. He spoke less with Bardo. Instead, he stood at the bow, alongside Dagomir – the man he had hated so much only weeks ago – and gave himself over to the call of the Ghost Archipelago. Only when he was certain in his heart that the ship sailed true would he leave his post. Sometimes,

Makeno would be waiting nearby, and would nod approvingly at him.

Dagomir had tried to apologise for striking Sam on Caldega. 'You know, when I left my homeland, I was no older than you,' he'd said. 'I had a boat, provisions for a few weeks, and a sword. That was all. I was sent out across an ocean grey and pale, under unforgiving skies. I sailed through islands of ice, and faced storms and sea-serpents, and nearly died a hundred times. When finally I reached lands far to the south, where the sun always shines warm and golden and the seas are blue and clear, I realised I had sailed farther than any of my people ever had before. In these new, strange lands there was nothing but danger, and I had no one to teach me the ways of these foreigners. I had to learn, alone, and make for myself a new kingdom, with wooden walls and sails. What I'm trying to say, lad… back on Caldega… I had to keep up appearances. A man cannot show any sign of weakness in front of the governor's agents, or he'll look like an easy mark. You understand?'

Sam had almost stopped caring. Exasperated, the captain waved his hand and left Sam to his thoughts. Sam had found that Dagomir would not hear a word against Yana Selishe, and so there was no discussion worth having. Dagomir said he'd learned the ways of foreigners and pirates on his own, and maybe that was what Sam had to do, too.

As the days drew on, Sam felt more powerful, more confident. He knew it was the island calling to him, singing a tune that only he could hear. Sam felt increasingly certain that all he needed to do was reach the Lost Isles, and everything else would fall into place. Dagomir, Yana…

they were of no consequence. This was Sam's destiny, not theirs; they would not – could not – stop him achieving it.

* * *

Sam had lost count of how many days had passed. He woke early, with the sun only starting to rise. Something stirred within him. His skin became gooseflesh; his fingertips tingled. His heart pumped blood through his body in oceanic swells. They were close, he knew it.

He hurried to the deck, where a skeleton crew had set them on course through the night. Makeno was already fore, leaning on his staff as fine sea spray misted his wrinkled face.

'You sense it,' said the warden.

'I sense... *something*.' Samir looked out to sea. The sky lightened slowly, and Sam orientated himself so the sliver of golden sun that poked over the horizon was to his left. He peered south. 'I see nothing,' he said.

'Not yet. So you must listen,' said Makeno.

Sam frowned, but listened intently all the same. He heard the waves, and the wind, and creaking ropes, and footsteps on deck-planks, and the fluttering sail. And then a soft cry, far away, that could almost have been a baby crying. But when it came again, Sam recognised it, and it filled him with hope. 'Was that... a gull?'

Makeno nodded, and looked south-east, where specks of shadow took flight into a pale yellow sky.

More footsteps approached, heavy and purposeful. 'Was that a gull I heard?' Dagomir's voice boomed. He must have had the ears of a wolf. He strode past Sam, and put one foot on the fore bulwark. The captain took a spyglass from his belt, and peered through it.

'We've strayed two degrees off course during the night," Sam said. He pointed to the gulls that now swept and glided over the surface of the water, plunging downwards periodically to catch a fish. 'The islands lie that way.'

Dagomir lowered the spyglass, turned about, and bellowed 'Helm! Two degrees to port! Everyone to your posts. Awake! Awake, you swabs!'

The stamping of feet shook the timbers of the ship. The men rushed onto the deck to the heed the captain's orders, and as they did there came a stuttering cry, and a large black gull swept gracefully over the port side, hanging in the air for a moment, before rising up and backwards on the wind. This brought laughter and a great cheer from the men, who now shook sleep from their eyes. It had been nigh on a month of tasteless rations, and all they had spoken about each night in their bunks had been hunting parties and roasting meat, and a return to normal rations of grog. The promise of land, even a potentially remote and hostile one, brought with it hope of those simple wishes being fulfilled.

Dagomir again put the spyglass to his eye and scanned the horizon. Sam knew what he'd see before the captain could shout out, 'Land ahoy!'

Emilio was beside Sam now, his hand on Sam's shoulder. 'Well done, lad.'

Sam squinted. He didn't need a spyglass to see the tiny peaks of dark land appear above the waterline. Three at first, then a fourth, then a fifth. More behind, lost to mists and shadow. Sam could almost envisage the islands ahead, like a memory from another time, or a dream. Mountains and hills, forests and jungles, grassy plains and vast lakes. And, more than anything, adventure. Nothing else seemed to matter any more.

Dagomir unfurled a roll of beaten leather, and studied it, checking again through his spyglass, then consulting the hide once more.

'You have a chart?' Sam asked in disbelief. 'How?'

'I bartered it from a merchant years ago. Said it belonged to a Heritor. Supposed to be drawn on the hide of some sea monster, from the Lost Isles.'

Sam craned his neck to see. The drawing on the hide was singularly unimpressive and crude. 'It doesn't look very accurate,' Sam said, doubtfully.

'It's not. But the position of these three large islands here, see – Makeno says that's right. So maybe the merchant wasn't entirely full of wind.'

'But how would Makeno…?'

'Sails! Ship ahoy!'

The shout came from the crow's nest. Sam, Dagomir and Emilio turned as one. The lookout was pointing aft.

The three of them raced astern, passing Yana Selishe on the way, who at once strode after them. Sure enough, a vessel had appeared on the horizon behind them, following the same course as the *Vanya's Wrath*. A vessel with fanned lateen sails. Black sails.

Dagomir looked through his glass, cursed under his breath, and passed the instrument to Emilio. The first mate looked at the ship, gave an accusing glare at the Selishe woman, and passed the glass to Sam.

The strange ship pulled into view. It was a Dar'Shuri dhow, without doubt. Its twin black sails turned to catch every breath of wind. The sails were adorned with a great golden insignia, depicting a two-headed bird outlined in gold. A raven. A crimson flag fluttered from the top of the mainmast, bearing the twin golden sun ensign of Yad-Sha'Rib. The ship's deck slowly came into view over the horizon, though Sam struggled to see it in much detail, until at last the rising sun gleamed brightly from many points of polished gold. Sam's blood iced in that instant, for he saw the uniform ranks of the Bidajah arrayed upon the deck of the vessel – the faceless army of Zhar-Mharrad. And as he trained the spyglass on the front of the ship, he saw something else, and could look no more. He handed the spyglass back to Dagomir.

'What is it, lad?' the captain asked. Frowning, he looked for himself. 'By all the gods…' he muttered.

What he saw – what Sam had seen – explained much. At the ship's prow, lashed to a bowsprit in place of a figurehead, was a man. A bedraggled, blind man. The Heritor who had fought alongside Sam back in Yad-Sha'Rib.

'Makeno,' Dagomir said, 'it is your turn. Grant us a fair wind, or grant them a foul one. Either way, I want us out of their reach.'

Makeno nodded, and knelt down, his staff laid out before him. He closed his eyes, and began to chant.

'This is the fastest ship in the world, isn't it?' Sam asked. 'We can outrun them.'

Dagomir looked a little less sure of himself than he had at the start of the voyage. 'We will need all the help we can get. Our one chance is to reach shallower waters and hope they cannot follow.'

The captain marched off to organise the crew. Sam looked to Yana Selishe, who acted as though he wasn't there – a skill she had perfected these past weeks. Then he looked back out to sea, to the dhow that pursued them. And as he looked, dark clouds gathered aft, heavy with storm, and travelling against the wind, which now blew coolly against Sam's cheek. Makeno's magic was taking hold.

* * *

Zhar-Mharrad marched between the ranks of his warriors, up to the foredeck. The clouds overhead blackened. The wind behind began to drop, and cross-winds blew, causing the *Devourer* to slow and list, first to starboard then to port. The blind, mute Heritor, tied fast to the bowsprit, moaned something unintelligible. Zhar-Mharrad laughed.

A hunter was there to greet the vizier. The jemadar, Faizil, Yana Selishe's lieutenant. The black-clad assassin saluted his master. 'My lord vizier,' he said. 'They use sorcery against us. This must be their "storm warden". What must we do?'

'Do?' Zhar-Mharrad chuckled. 'My loyal jemadar, you need do nothing. The pirates have a storm warden, true. But we need no warden. Behold!'

Zhar-Mharrad held his staff aloft, and in the other

hand he clutched the periapt. Thunder rumbled overhead. Lightning flickered about the ship, and then in one great bolt, struck downwards, alighting upon the tip of the vizier's staff, wreathing Zhar-Mharrad in coruscating bands of power. The jemadar stepped away, shielding his eyes from the dancing white light before him.

Coils of black smoke belched from the periapt, and spiralled about Zhar-Mharrad, merging with the lightning until it seemed the vizier himself was a storm cloud. The smoke began to shrink, and coalesce into a baleful form. The lightning moved with it, until energy and smoke took the semblance of a large, hulking figure, with glowing eyes, looming over Zhar-Mharrad. It growled menacingly, smoke-jaws snapping, great claws crackling with the power of the storm.

'O demon of the underworld,' Zhar-Mharrad intoned. 'Mighty lord of magic, whose name is Ziriz, hear me and obey!'

At this, the demon roared in anger, but its rage was impotent against Zhar-Mharrad. He knew its name, and he held the periapt.

'I command thee, demon: turn away this storm. Bring fair weather to aid our quest. Do this, and I shall meet your blood price. Go!'

With a great bellow, the demon shook, and two vast, bat-like wings sprouted from its back. It leapt into the air, and spun upwards, into the thickening storm clouds.

Zhar-Mharrad turned to his jemadar. 'Go below immediately, and bring me a galley slave. Do it quickly, man! The blood price must be paid when the demon returns, one way or another.'

Jemadar Faizil gulped, saluted, and raced away like his life depended on it. Even as he went, there came a break in the black clouds, and crepuscular rays of sunlight shone upon the Devourer's sails, which had already begun to flutter once more in the wind.

Zhar-Mharrad needed no storm warden.

* * *

Sam shouldered Makeno's weight as best he could. The warden's legs shook, and his breathing was laboured. The storm he had summoned dissipated almost as soon as it had appeared, and the winds that had momentarily propelled the *Vanya's Wrath* to great speed already subsided. Sam helped Makeno hobble along the deck, where Dagomir paced and gnashed his teeth.

The islands drew nearer, but so did the enemy.

'How is this possible?' Dagomir growled. 'That dhow should be no match for us.'

'That dhow,' said Yana Selishe, 'is the *Devourer*. Captained by a black sorcerer, and crewed by the damned. Magic alone will not slow it.'

'What then?'

The woman shrugged. 'I suppose you must use the one thing you have that Zhar-Mharrad does not. Seamanship.'

Dagomir nodded, and his stern expression slowly broke into a grin. He ran to the bulwarks and looked towards the islands with his spyglass.

'There,' he said, pointing. He handed Emilio the glass so that the first mate might see his intent. 'Where the chain of rocks almost meets. Zhar-Mharrad's ship is too big and too deep to get through there. But we might.'

'Might,' said Emilio. 'Captain, it is a risk indeed to take that course. We should sail around, and find one of the landings written of in lore.'

'To do that, we would have to tack, and then we would lose speed. Look at the size of the dhow behind us. If we slow for a moment, it will be alongside. How many Bidajah did you count? Thirty? More? And a dark wizard who can best even Makeno? No, Emilio – the woman is right. We pit our seamanship against his, and see who comes out laughing.'

Emilio looked unconvinced, but Yana Selishe nodded sagely. This alone was enough to make Sam mistrust the plan.

Makeno shook free of Sam, using his staff to support him instead. 'Captain Dagomir,' he said. 'To my eye, they look like the Widowing Rocks, told of in legend. If that is so, you take the most dangerous path imaginable.'

'Aye, I've heard of them. But only in stories. You aren't afraid of stories are you, Makeno?'

'No. But of the Lost Isles, stories are all we have. Nothing here is as it seems. And those rocks were given their name for the men they have claimed, and the widows left behind in distant lands.'

'Ha! Then it is a good job none of us is married. Helm!' Dagomir shouted, requiring no further discussion. 'Take us three degrees port. Make for those rocks. I want six men aloft, and eight below. When we get within three lengths we must take up the sail, and push through with oars.'

'Let me go up,' Sam pleaded. 'I'm your best climber. I know what to do.'

Dagomir nodded. 'That you are, lad.' He snapped his fingers, and a man who was about to climb the rigging stopped in his tracks.

Sam at once took the man's place, climbing the ratlines like he was born to it, beating every other man to his position despite their head-start. From his vantage point in the rigging, Sam saw that the captain was right to be worried – the *Devourer* was so close now that Sam could see the Bidajah standing unmoving as toy soldiers, swords and shields held parade-ground straight. Other figures scurried back and forth across the deck – slaves, little more than children, performing the work of grown men. And at the prow was the Heritor, and that frightened Sam more than anything. If he'd stayed in Yad-Sha'Rib, that could have been his fate. If Zhar-Mharrad were to capture him now, it could yet be.

Looking fore, Sam saw the islands more clearly as the sun rose higher. It was a chain of islets and larger masses, much bigger than he'd imagined, and more numerous. Some appeared from this distance as low mounds of mossy hills, while others were dominated by mountains so tall their peaks were hidden by clouds. The lower portions of the island were surrounded by silvery mist that drifted up from the sea's surface in the shimmering morning heat. The ship was already touching this strange mist, parting it like a grey veil. It seemed to thicken at the touch of the *Vanya's Wrath*, until the way ahead was obscured entirely, and the island chain was almost lost to sight once more, save for a few ghostly shadows of conical mountains. All that Sam could see now, even from his vantage point, were the jagged rocks, more numerous and harder to spot than it had appeared from a distance.

Dagomir called up, and Sam and the others at once took up the sail halfway, and waited, poised for further direction. The men below struck out the oars, pushing them up near-vertically, ready to use them should the ship steer to close to the Widowing Rocks.

Dagomir called instructions to his men. He ran along the bulwarks, looking over the edge, and other crewmen did the same, shouting out the positions of the smaller rocks for the tiller-man. Emilio supervised two men to take soundings, checking the depth at intervals.

Sam looked back; the *Devourer* was a dark smudge now in a mist that had not been there just moments ago. He looked down to see tendrils of shimmering fog coiling across the deck, until he could recognise the men below only by the tops of their heads, making them look like islands themselves in a grey sea. The captain's cries became muffled; even the sound of the waves was muted, until almost total silence fell over the ship. Sam had seen many strange phenomena in his relatively short time at sea, but even he knew this could not be natural.

A great black rock swept across the starboard side, just yards from Sam's position, so unexpectedly that he almost let go of the ropes in fright. Cries of alarm echoed dully upwards. The starboard spar scraped rock; the sail snagged and frayed at the edges. They were sailing blind.

'Take up the sail!' the captain ordered, his voice hollow and distant. Sam worked with the other men, and secured the sail entirely, before shimmying down the ratlines and back to deck. As soon as he set foot on the boards, a hand clasped upon his shoulder. Makeno pulled him close.

'Have your wits about you, boy,' he said in a low voice. 'There is sorcery against us that I cannot counter.'

'Zhar-Mharrad…' Sam whispered with trepidation.

'No. Something older and deadlier than that. Something that does not want us here.'

The ship groaned, and shuddered. A terrible scraping sound reverberated through the timbers, and the vessel leaned awkwardly to starboard.

'Oars!' Dagomir shouted down the deck hatch. 'Push us off!'

The oars lowered as one, clacking on rocks, pushing the ship slowly away from the obstacle.

A man appeared from below deck. He stood almost within arm's reach of Sam, but was indistinguishable in the fog. 'Captain, we are breached,' he gasped.

Dagomir cursed loudly. 'Get below and bail. Tell the men to row.' He grabbed two of the crewmen who had climbed down from the rigging after Sam. 'You two, get below and help. Find Bardo and tell him to patch the hole.'

They had no sooner gone below than the ship began to rumble again, but this time the sound was deeper, and the *Vanya's Wrath* grumbled like a wounded beast.

'Shallows,' Dagomir said. He marched off into the fog, shouting curses at the men taking the soundings.

Another sound came from the fog. A clicking and scraping, almost as if dozens of large birds had alighted the deck, claws scratching and tapping on wood. This was accompanied by altogether stranger noises – a soft, high-pitched trilling sound, and a rapid, wet snapping, like the frantic gnashing of jaws.

'What was that?' Sam hissed.

'Nothing good,' said Makeno, gripping Sam's shoulder more tightly. He held his staff before him, charms and trinkets jingling softly in the dead silence of the mist. 'Be ready.'

The clicking, rapping sound drew louder and more rapid, and a shadow passed inches in front of Sam's face. He felt the rush of air as it went, and the smoking mist parted for just a fraction, leaving Sam with the impression of something large and hideous, with a segmented shell glistening in the wan light. And he had no time to dwell on what he had seen, for a moment later a man's terrified scream shattered the eerie calm, and the sound of wet snapping became more fevered and rapid.

'We're under attack!' Dagomir was nowhere to be seen, but his deep voice carried on the dull air. 'Repel boarders. Fight!'

More scuttling sounds echoed all around. The deck vibrated beneath Sam's feet. Makeno shoved Sam forward as another black, slug-like form scurried between them. Sam spun around as the thing rose up. Still he could not get a clear look at it as the fog wisped thick all around. But it was some kind of enormous insect with a broad, segmented body, hauling itself upright. Left and right of its bulk, Sam saw to his horror hundreds of spindly legs lashing and flicking, and great antennae whipping ferociously atop what he supposed was its head.

It was facing Makeno, and the warden struck at the creature with his staff, desperately fending off the creature as it threw itself towards him, slashing relentlessly with its many spindly, sharp arms.

Sam drew the sword Emilio had given him, and sprang forward with it as he had been taught, thrusting at the back of the creature. The point struck some kind of thick, hard shell, and the blade flexed, but did not pierce the beast's flesh. Sam stumbled as the sword-point slipped from the beast's armoured hide. The monster twisted and writhed once more, and Sam found himself sprawled on the deck, Makeno's battle-cries ringing in his ears.

Another scurrying noise drew Sam's attention from the warden's struggle. He looked up at the bulwark beside him, and saw another wet, black shape haul itself over the wooden wall, directly above him. It paused, looking about, though it had no eyes that Sam could tell. The creature launched itself at him, great mandibles snapping beneath a domed, armoured head.

It hung for a moment in the air, and its descent became a slow arc, as Sam drew upon his power. He rolled out of the way, and sprang to his feet as the creature crashed to the deck, screeching in frustration that its prey had escaped. He heard cries of alarm and more screams all around. He saw Makeno shove a creature away with his staff, and the beast vanished into the enfolding mist. The thing on the floor writhed, and turned at once to Sam, raising itself up to its full height. It was much larger than a man, resembling some gigantic louse. Beneath its armoured hide was a many-segmented, fleshy body, grey as stone and encrusted with mineral deposits that shimmered as it moved. Its many hundreds of thin, bony arms whipped and flicked all about, and at the head, a great circular maw opened up, thousands of tiny teeth snapping and whirring in concentric rows, while hideous, clawed appendages flailed at the air, as if trying to grab anything that moved into that hungry mouth.

For a moment, Sam was rooted to the spot, his limbs unusually leaden. He had faced danger many times, true enough, but never something like this. And as the sounds of fighting echoed all around him, he knew that this could be his undoing. He could die here, without ever setting foot on the Lost Isles.

The creature lunged, countless legs lashing outwards, ready to enfold Sam in a deathly embrace. He thrust his foil forwards, acting on instinct, and this time the blade found purchase in soft flesh between rib-like crenellations. So heavy was the creature that its own momentum helped push the blade fully into its body, until the sword hit thick chitin on the other side, and Sam staggered backwards, the beast upon him. Teeth and claws snapped at Sam's face. He twisted the sword, thick, oozing ichor flowing from the wound, over his hand. The creature screeched, an ear-piercing cry, ending in an ululating trill. Foul breath blasted from its maw, and Sam staggered further, as those many insectoid arms now closed around him, like long, spindly fingers.

The mists parted as another black shadow burst from the mist, colliding with the creature, pulling it off Sam. He wrenched his blade free as the monster was yanked away by this new combatant. With one sweep of her curved blade, Yana Selishe sliced dozens of the beast's appendages from its body. It screeched again, and lurched awkwardly at her; she crouched low, then sprang upwards, slashing outwards with her scimitar. The monster opened up like a fresh lobster, spilling steaming black guts across the deck that smelled of rancid fish. It toppled backwards, hitting the timbers hard, rocking upon its armoured shell.

'Are you all right, boy?' the woman asked. She was injured, one sleeve torn open, blood seeping from a deep cut. She was covered in the foul, pinkish blood of the strange creatures – how many she had slain, Sam could not tell.

It was all he could do to nod. 'Makeno,' he said, feebly.

A roar of anger – Makeno's roar. There was a flash of light, the crackling of lightning in charged air. Another creature ripped its way through the mist, past Selishe, past Sam, energy rippling all around it. It landed in a heap, smouldering. Makeno stood in the fog now, chanting in some unknown tongue. Thunder rumbled overhead. More lightning crackled, striking down towards the ship – down towards the enemy.

There came a multitude of shrill screams as the beasts were struck by bolts of energy. The mists began to fizz and clear, swirling tendrils pulling away from the ship, revealing the battle all around. Dagomir was near the prow, stamping down upon one of the creatures, carving it in two with his mighty blade. Lightning struck another creature, charring it instantly; as it fell away, Sam saw with dismay that it had been feasting on a crewman, who was now stripped almost to his skeleton. The bones blackened as energy wreathed about monster and corpse both.

All around, the creatures were driven back, dropping onto their bellies, scuttling away over the bulwarks and back into the sea. But the carnage they had left behind turned Sam's stomach. Men lay dead and dying. The deck was awash with blood.

A great flash of lightning struck a retreating creature, burning it to a cinder before it could wriggle from the ship. At this, Dagomir looked about, and saw that victory had come, if at a cost. He raised his sword to the air and cried, 'Vanya's wrath! They flee Vanya's wrath!'

And from the mist, dead ahead, came the largest of the Widowing Rocks. The figurehead drove into it like a battering ram, splintering upon impact. The ship buckled with a deafening crack, and rocked this way and that as it split along the keel. Sam was thrown to the blood-soaked deck again, and others with him. The deck opened up, seawater bursting upwards in great fountains. Ropes snapped, whipping dangerously about the deck, biting deep into a man's face and sending him spinning overboard.

Sam struggled to his feet, looking for Makeno, taking the warden's arm. He met his eyes for just a moment.

'The islands protect their secrets,' Makeno said.

'Abandon ship!' Dagomir cried. 'To the boats if you can, or swim for your lives!'

Makeno and Yana Selishe shepherded Sam aft, where inadequate boats waited. Emilio was there already, lowering one of the boats into the water.

'There aren't enough boats,' Sam groaned.

'Then best make sure you get in one, and quick,' said Emilio. He grabbed Sam's arm, and swung him over the side.

Sam dropped into the boat, consumed by guilt. There were two men already waiting at the oars. Makeno came next, then Emilio. Selishe sprang lightly down last of all.

Dagomir appeared at the bulwark, and threw three sacks of supplies down to Emilio. 'Go!' he shouted. 'Emilio, protect the boy.'

'Don't go down with the ship,' Emilio said.

Dagomir found it within himself to grin. 'I'll take the next one. Now go.'

At Emilio's word, the two sailors pulled on the oars, and the boat glided past the stricken ship.

'How did you ready the boat so quickly?' the huntress said, casting a strange look at Emilio.

'Experience. That's why I'm first mate, and you're just a passenger.'

The mists thinned slowly. As they parted, Sam saw men swimming towards the island, and clinging to wreckage. One man saw them, and began to swim for the boat. Sam and Makeno held their hands out, calling him to swim faster. Something moved beneath the surface of the water; a dark, bulbous shape, and then a segmented body broke the waves, and with a scream cut prematurely short, the man was gone.

'By the gods,' Emilio hissed. 'Row faster. Go! We can wait for no one.'

The men redoubled their efforts, and the boat picked up speed, navigating through the rocks far more nimbly than the *Vanya's Wrath* ever could. Screams echoed through the mists, and then ceased, until soon there was no sound at all but the dipping of the oars and the swish of the water.

CHAPTER 12

Sam jumped from the boat, and helped drag it through the foaming shallows onto a beach of white sand, bounded by a thick tangle of tall, old trees. Sam had never seen their like. He'd walked sometimes in the public gardens of Yad-Sha'Rib, until the guards had sent him on his way, but those manicured groves were nothing like this. These trees were ancient beyond measure, taller than the temples of the Golden City, and full of shadows and mystery.

Beyond the jungle, great cliffs presented a formidable wall of craggy, yellowish rock, here and there seemingly carved with vast, leering faces. Or, rather, skulls. Beyond them, almost lost to a distant haze, was a vast purple mountain, its single, sharp peak piercing the clouds. High overhead, strange birds of prodigious size circled and called to each other. The sounds echoing from the jungle ahead were equally strange, and ominous. This was Sam's first impression of the Lost Isles, but for all he had longed to be here, he could barely take it in. Instead, he turned back to the sea, where the rolling mists had begun to shrink away, revealing a maze of razor-sharp rocks.

The *Vanya's Wrath* was almost sunk, its infamous figurehead and meticulously carved mast jutting from the water in one last act of desperation.

The boat securely on dry land, Emilio came to stand beside Sam, and wiped his brow.

'Three boats,' Sam said. 'Not everyone will fit on three boats.'

'Two,' said Emilio.

Sam shot him a confused look. 'Two?'

'One was holed in the collision.'

'So… we took the place of other men. They could die while we live.'

'Captain's orders,' Emilio shrugged. 'And let us hope he made it.'

'Ahoy there!' a cry came from the retreating mist. A rowboat pulled towards the beach, a shadow at first, but coalescing as it shook off the last of the silver shroud. It was Dagomir.

Sam and the others helped bring the boat ashore. Despite himself, Sam threw his arms around Bardo – or as best he could, given the carpenter's great bulk. Only three other men occupied the boat, and one of them was badly wounded, his shoulder mangled by dozens of punctures made by the teeth of the creatures.

'Pulled this one from the water,' Dagomir said. 'Maybe Makeno can do something about these wounds. We couldn't wait to get anyone else off the ship. She went down too fast.' He hung his head sorrowfully. 'Best ship I ever sailed in. Vanya truly is a fickle mistress.'

'Mayhap you courted her attention one too many times, old friend,' Emilio said.

'Eleven of us,' said Yana. 'And one in no fit state to fight. Hardly any supplies to speak of… a sorry expedition this has turned out to be.'

'We have the boy,' Dagomir said, defiantly. 'And we don't need to fight, not yet. Zhar-Mharrad cannot navigate those rocks in his dhow – he'll have to sail the coast and look for a landing, and by then we'll be well away from here.'

As if in answer, there came a piercing *caw*, and all turned to see a great black bird arrow through the mist. Zhar-Mharrad's two-headed raven swept over the heads of the assembled crew, circling up and around, squawking all the while as if raising an alarm.

'That cursed bird!' Dagomir spat. 'What is it, a spy?'

'A herald,' Yana Selishe replied, and pointed out to sea.

Sam's heart sank. The last of the mists now dissipated, and three longboats swept between the Widowing Rocks, past the wreckage of the *Vanya's Wrath*. They were much larger than the simple rowboats employed by Dagomir's crew, each propelled by five pairs of oars, pulled by ten golden-masked Bidajah, whose prodigious strength lent the boats uncanny speed. At the head of each boat stood a commander. Two were Manhunters, swords in hand, faces masked. At the head of the centre boat stood an altogether more fearsome figure, swathed in loose robes of black, a great turban upon his head, and a cloak of red and gold billowing out behind him. This was a man whom Sam had never seen so close, but whose long shadow loomed large over the citizens of Yad-Sha'Rib.

Zhar-Mharrad himself had come to the Lost Isles.

'Take everything you can carry,' Dagomir cried. 'And run.'

Sam grabbed a heavy sack from the boat, and the others did likewise. Dagomir had a look in his eyes that Sam had not seen before. He had lost his ship, and a goodly part of his crew, and now he was forced to run from the very man who had visited this ignominy upon him. Sam saw hatred for Zhar-Mharrad in his eyes, and bitterness that he could not exact revenge at once. This alone made Sam see the captain in a different light. He recognised the emotion he saw; had he not felt it himself enough times over the years, living in fear of one day meeting the same fate as his father? Dagomir hated Zhar-Mharrad; therefore, Dagomir could perhaps be trusted after all.

The men ran up the beach as fast as they could, struggling with heavy loads, feet sinking into soft sand. Sam made to follow, but stopped, as the strangest sensation overcame him. A voice carried towards him on the wind.

'Samir! Wait!'

Sam recognised the voice. The hair on the back of his neck prickled. He turned slowly.

The boats were almost at the beach. Upon the lead boat, behind the imposing form of Zhar-Mharrad, stood a familiar figure, arms outstretched, a forlorn look in his eyes, calling to his friend.

'Hassan…' Sam gasped.

'Samir, help me!' Hassan called. His eyes were sad and pleading, but there was something strange in his voice. Some listless, melancholy lilt that did not sound at all like the boy Sam knew.

'Come on, lad!' Dagomir snarled. He grabbed Sam by the arm and pulled him away from the water's edge.

'That's Hassan!' Sam protested. 'My friend.'

Dagomir took one look back, but it only spurred him

to yank Sam's arm harder. 'There's nothing we can do for him. Save yourself, and think about him later.'

Sam knew the captain was right, but leaving Hassan in the clutches of the dark sorcerer seemed unforgiveable. His legs moved, but he felt like his shoes were filled with lead weights.

The cry of the raven came again, closer. Sam looked up in time to see a black shape dart downwards, and a flurry of claws and feathers struck Dagomir in the face. Dagomir staggered, flailing at the bird. The huge raven flapping and screeching, claws gouging at the captain's cheek, its two hooked beaks pecking towards his eyes.

Everyone else was further up the beach, in no position to help. Sam leapt forward, his reflexes quicker even than the hateful bird's. He snatched at its wing, and it shifted, pecking his arm with such force that it tore his tunic and drew blood. The distraction was enough for Dagomir to recover his wits, grabbing the bird and flinging it from them both. The side of Dagomir's face bled profusely; more scars to add to his collection.

The raven hit the sand in an undignified tumble, yet at a command from Zhar-Mharrad, in his booming tones, the creature righted itself in a flurry, and at once took to the air again. It soared high, before angling downwards, swooping at Dagomir once more, intent on its target.

Dagomir held up one hand to protect his eyes, and tried to shake loose his broadsword with the other. Sam raced towards him, but was too far out of reach to lend aid, even for one with his prodigious reflexes.

Beak and claws poised to strike, and were but inches from Dagomir's face, when the creature was shot from the sky. A crossbow bolt, aimed expertly, narrowly missing Dagomir and striking the bird. Blue-black feathers flew in all direction. The bird dropped to the sand once more, and this time it moved only to twitch feebly, and caw weakly.

Further up the dunes, Yana Selishe stood, reloading her crossbow. Her face was wrapped again in scarves, only her keen, dark eyes visible, testament to her hawkish accuracy.

'No!' Zhar-Mharrad's cry seemed to shake the very ground. Sam saw the vizier wade from the shallows, and sink to his knees, clutching at his head as though the quarrel had struck him, and not his pet. He cried out in anguish. And that cry turned to a chant; a malevolent string of indecipherable words in some black tongue. The spell cut the air as clearly as if Zhar-Mharrad was standing beside Sam and Dagomir. Though the sun was high, it reddened, and the sky grew dark.

'I won't tell you again, boy,' Dagomir muttered in Sam's ear. 'We must go.'

'I think you're right,' Sam gulped. An unnatural cold breeze had begun to sweep around the beach, causing Sam to shiver. He backed away, up the sandy slope, somehow unable to tear his eyes from the vizier.

Twelve of the Bidajah marched from the boats, forming six pairs of warriors, each pair carrying some large bundle. Rolled carpets. Sam frowned. The warriors unfurled the six carpets onto the sand, and in unison, like clockwork soldiers, stepped upon them. One warrior knelt at the front, and drew a scimitar. The other stood behind, taking up a gold-tipped spear.

And then Zhar-Mharrad's chanting ceased. The vizier

stood slowly, arms raised. And as he reached his full height, the carpets rose into the air, stiff as boards, their riders carried aloft upon them.

'What devilry…?' Dagomir said.

There was utter silence, as Dagomir's rag-tag crew gaped in awe, not believing their own eyes. Zhar-Mharrad smiled wickedly. Then he roared, at the top of his lungs: 'Kill them!'

The carpets moved, as though controlled by the will of the masked warriors upon them. They came slowly at first, but then gathered pace, sweeping through the air like parchment caught on the wind. Dagomir slapped Sam on the shoulder, and ran towards his fellows, who now shouted to their captain to hurry. Sam ran, as fast as his legs would carry him. Far ahead, half of the men were gathered at the treeline, where they had set down their supplies and taken up bows and slings to cover the retreat of the others. Emilio, Yana and Bardo had stayed further down the beach, beckoning urgently to Dagomir and Sam to hurry.

Something hit Sam hard in the back. He fell face-first into the sand as a shadow swept over him. Sam rolled over to see one of the flying carpets circling awkwardly above. The standing Bidajah spun his spear around, and thrust it downwards. Sam acted on instinct, his perception speeding up, muscles working to push him out of the way of the spear-tip even as it struck the sand. Sam scrabbled to his feet. The carpet was directly above him, and a scimitar slashed at him. To Sam's eye the blow was clumsy and slow, and he spun aside as the blade flashed harmlessly through the air.

'Get down, boy!' Yana Selishe shouted.

Sam obeyed, ducking low and scurrying out of the shadow of the carpet on all fours, kicking up sand as he went. Selishe fired her crossbow, striking the kneeling Bidajah. The masked soldier fell sideways onto the ground, and the carpet spiralled away, the spearman atop it struggling to keep his balance.

Sam could only watch in horror as the wounded Bidajah sat upright, snapped the quarrel protruding from his ribs, and lumbered slowly to his feet. Blood pumped from the wound, but the brute did not flinch. Instead, he turned his golden face to Samir, picked up his scimitar, and lurched forwards.

The sounds of battle grew louder. Steel rang upon steel, crewmen shouted in fear for their lives, carpets swooped overhead in a dance of death. Samir scrabbled away from his pursuer, unable to take advantage of his speed for once, so gripped was he by fear. As the eye-slits of the golden mask fixed him with a soulless gaze, everything seemed all too real, and all too dangerous. Sam thought of Hassan, down there in the grip of Zhar-Mharrad. Captured doubtless because of him. He thought of the *Vanya's Wrath*, the famous ship lost to the Widowing Rocks, and the men who were lost with her. And he thought also of the remaining crew, who would surely follow the fate of their brethren – how could they fight against these numbers? Against foes who could not be stopped by a crossbow bolt to the ribs?

The Bidajah was almost upon Sam, blotting out the sun, casting over him the shadow of death.

'For Vanya!' Dagomir roared, launching himself shoulder-first into the side of the Bidajah, into those wounded ribs.

Both men fell to the ground with a dull thud and a plume of sand. Dagomir was first to his feet, swinging his massive sword high over his head, down towards the Bidajah in a deadly arc. Yet somehow the masked man thrust out his scimitar with an arm strong as iron, parrying the blow, and once more climbing to his feet. Dagomir, almost as tall as the Bidajah, pounded at the cursed soldier with his blade, a relentless barrage that forced the Bidajah back, inch by inch. The captain unleashed all of his rage at the brute, all of his frustrations at the loss of his ship and crew. His muscles rippled with exertion, his flesh slick with blood and sweat. He cursed, he spat, and his blows battered at his enemy, whose scimitar buckled and bent, and finally the Northman's broadsword bit into the Bidajah's shoulder. The blade jerked free with a shower of blood, but Dagomir did not think it enough. He struck once more, sword ringing against the golden mask. The fastening cracked loudly, the mask flew off into the sand, and only the shock of what lay beneath gave Dagomir pause.

Sam knew he had almost died because of his hesitation, and he jumped to his feet now, determined not to take his life for granted. He stared for a moment at the creature before him, as did Dagomir, but then urged himself to act, to overcome his fear. He darted forward as another carpet swooped low towards him. He grabbed Dagomir's arm, and shouted the captain to flee. Dagomir retreated, not taking his eyes from the lumbering brute before him, who flailed and fumbled like a blind man. Sam and Dagomir turned and ran as one. Sam knew he would never sleep soundly again. He would never forget that blank face, featureless save for the patchwork of stitched flesh. No eyes, nose, ears or mouth. Just a jumble of old skin concealed beneath a mask of polished gold.

The carpet flew low. Sam didn't need to see it to know where it was. He felt the presence of the enemy; could see where they would strike even before they did.

'Down!' Sam cried, and pulled Dagomir to the ground as hard as he could.

The captain resisted, doubtless not knowing why the troublesome boy again hindered their escape. This resistance vanished in a heartbeat, as a scimitar arced downwards, slicing Dagomir's arm. He dropped low as the shadow passed overhead and the carpet began to turn again. Blood oozed onto white sand.

'If you hadn't…' he began, but thought better of it. Instead, he stood at once, glancing back to the sea. 'Come on.'

Sam dared a look back, too, and wished he had not. All the guards were assembled now, in serried ranks. Zhar-Mharrad and two Manhunters led their Bidajah up the beach, while the vanguard upon the flying carpets harried the scant survivors of the *Vanya's Wrath*.

The carpet came back towards Sam and Dagomir, gathering speed. Yana Selishe was too busy defending herself to save them this time. Sam drew his sword, and for the first time felt that the fine blade was wholly inadequate for the fight. Dagomir, still clutching his bleeding shoulder, drew himself up to his full height. He planted his feet far apart, his sword dragging limply by his side. Yet, at the last moment, as a slashing scimitar and jabbing spear came so close Sam could feel them part the air, Dagomir stepped sideways, hoisting his sword up with all his strength, slashing it beneath their attackers.

The blade cut the carpet in twain with a loud tear. The Bidajah kneeling at the front spun around wildly, the carpet taking him off into the distance like a leaf tossed on the wind. The man behind him fell crashing to the sand, the sorcery that had elevated him into the air now vanquished, and his half of the magic carpet now nothing more than a torn rug.

The Bidajah flailed in the sand, grasping for his spear, trying to pull himself up to his feet. Dagomir took no chances this time. The captain pushed the man down with his boot-heel, and thrust the tip of his sword into the brute's throat. The Bidajah struggled for the briefest moment, and then died, silently. Dagomir freed his blade, and looked down the beach, to where Zhar-Mharrad drew closer still, malevolence gleaming in his dark eyes. And though it must have pained him, given the depth of his wound and the weight of his Northman's blade, Dagomir raised his sword and pointed to the approaching vizier, in part as salute, in part as a warning. He held the vizier's gaze for a fraction longer than Sam thought advisable, and only when he appeared satisfied that his honour was assured did he allow Sam to help him up the sloping dunes to the others.

'Captain, we cannot win this fight,' Emilio shouted, glancing nervously at another carpet that circled overhead. Beside the mate, Yana Selishe squinted along the haft of her crossbow, searching for a target, while Bardo stood ready with a billhook in one hand and an axe in the other.

'Where is Makeno?' Dagomir panted. 'We need his magic!'

'He ran into the jungle,' Emilio said. 'He's mad. Says he's talking to the island.'

'Better hope it answers him quick. Look out!'

Two flying carpets swooped down upon the group in a pincer movement. Dagomir pushed Emilio to the ground as a spear thrust at his head. Yana Selishe fended off a scimitar-stroke with her crossbow. Bardo thrust upwards with the billhook, finding a fleshy target, but only succeeding in being dragged from his feet by the momentum, losing his weapon and his dignity as he was dumped into the sand.

And then Sam felt a large, strong hand upon his shoulder, and before he knew it his feet left the ground, and he was carried slowly aloft. He looked up in blind panic, slashing with his sword. The thin blade bounced from the mask of the Bidajah who had seized him, and the brute threw aside his scimitar in order to grab Sam's sword-arm and hoist him onto the carpet as though he weighed nothing. He was placed across the Bidajah's knee like a petulant child. Sam held onto his blade for all he was worth, in the hope that he might be able to fight his way free, though his captor's strength was so immense he could not see how. As he looked down at his comrades, and the carpet gained height, he saw Yana Selishe swinging a rope about her head. A grapple.

She loosed the rope, sending the small iron hook flying towards the carpet, where it wrapped thrice about the neck of the Bidajah standing at the rear. The brute almost toppled over, but somehow managed to stoop low, grabbing at the carpet and hanging on with immense strength. Instead of bringing the Bidajah down, Yana Selishe was carried upwards as the carpet gained height more rapidly. The Bidajah grunted and fumbled at the rope about his neck, but remarkably did not move, his feet remaining planted firm upon the carpet. From his prostrate position, Sam could only watch from the corner of his eye as Yana Selishe climbed the rope almost as effortlessly as Sam had traversed the rigging of the *Vanya's Wrath*. If Sam had not been so concerned with the possibility of imminent death, he would have begrudgingly admitted his growing admiration for the hateful woman.

In a flash, Yana Selishe was aboard, and the carpet lost altitude, as if it were a living creature overburdened by the weight of its riders. The front-most Bidajah relinquished one hand from Sam to flail backwards at the woman, but she slipped out of reach, taking the rope and pulling the standing Bidajah down as hard as she could. The brute now buckled at the knees, which Yana promptly kicked from under him, throwing him from the carpet.

Sam's captor began to thrash and look about as though panicked, if panic he could even feel. The woman coolly drew a pair of daggers from her belt, and thrust both of them deep into the Bidajah's back, above each shoulder blade. Now it let go of Sam completely, and he almost rolled from the carpet, but somehow managed to grab it, hanging for dear life from its edge by one hand, his sword still in the other.

'Get aboard, boy!' Yana Selishe cried.

Sam wasn't entirely sure what the woman's intention was, but she was in no position to help him, and so he swung himself upwards, trying not to think of the drop beneath him. He swung up, stabbing the point of the foil into the carpet, using it to gain some purchase. Finally he heaved himself up, panting, and utterly nauseous when he saw the horizon veering and lurching in all directions.

'Men were not meant to fly!' Sam cried. 'That is why the gods did not give us wings.'

'Then lucky neither of us are men,' Selishe snapped. 'Let me concentrate.'

Sam looked on in awe as he realised what the woman was doing. The Bidajah below her seemed transfixed, flinching and jerking occasionally, but otherwise unable to move. Yana Selishe held tight to the hilts of her daggers, using them like a coachman used reins to steer the carpet through the air.

'How...?' Sam gasped.

'Zhar-Mharrad's sorcery makes the carpet fly, but the carpet itself is bound to the will of the Bidajah at its head. And the will of a Bidajah is weak. A blade pressed against the right nerve can pacify them well enough. That's what I was aiming for with the crossbow earlier.'

'So... you missed.'

Selishe shot an annoyed glare Sam's way. 'I'm trying to concentrate, lad. They're weak-willed, but Zhar-Mharrad still controls them. He's trying to pull us towards him.'

Sam had been so preoccupied with keeping his balance and trying not to vomit, he'd not considered the direction they were heading. He dared to look over the tasselled edge of the carpet, and sure enough, the vizier was not far below, arms outstretched, chanting some foul spell. Hassan knelt behind the billowing cloak of Zhar-Mharrad, like a cowering pet.

'Don't get any ideas,' Selishe snapped, as if reading Sam's mind. 'That boy is not our concern. And besides, he's the one who gave you up. He doesn't deserve your loyalty.'

'He would never do that!'

'You would be surprised what people will do with the right kind of persuasion. Ha! I have the brute now. Hang on!'

The carpet pitched lower, veering away from the approaching soldiers, and towards the jungle. The pirates cheered. Dagomir saluted. No – not a salute. He was waving urgently. Pointing behind them...

Sam turned to see another carpet coming alongside, like a ship making a boarding action.

'By the Seven Serpents!' Yana Selishe snarled. 'Fight them, lad. Do your best!'

Sam had no idea what to do, and had no time to think. A spear thrust towards him, and in his haste to dodge it, he almost stepped off the side of the carpet. His stomach lurched; his head swam.

'Just buy us some time,' the woman shouted. 'You're a Heritor aren't you? Use your power!'

Sam didn't want to admit he'd been using his power just to stay alive, but as he side-stepped another spear-thrust, he knew it fell to him to take action. He concentrated. Breathed in through his nose, out through his mouth. And the world slowed down.

He heard the crashing waves as if he were standing amidst them. He heard the wind weave through the tasselled fringes of the carpets. He heard the cry of distant birds, and the rumble of volcanic mountains far away. He saw the spear come at him again, slowly, inch by inch, like the Bidajah who wielded it was trapped in ice, struggling to break free.

Sam stepped aside, thrust his blade beneath the armpit of the brute, aiming true for the gaps in his armour.

Time sped up, all at once. Sam's sword pierced the Bidajah's flesh, and thrust out of the brute's back. The Bidajah toppled forwards, and almost dragged Sam with him. But at last, Yana Selishe managed to control the carpet; she let go of one of her daggers, and grabbed Sam firmly by his sleeve, so the Bidajah slid free of his blade and fell to the ground far below.

Something struck the carpet, and it flexed upwards. Branches scratched at Sam's face. The other carpet careened into a tree-trunk, and was immediately lost to sight as Sam and Yana's own carpet crunched through foliage. They were crashing into the jungle.

'Abandon ship!' Selishe shouted, and shoved Sam in the back.

He felt for a moment as though he were hanging in mid-air, and then he fell. Thick branches rose up to meet him. He summoned every drop of power within him, grabbing at foliage, slowing his fall as best he could. He sprang from one bough to another, and finally caught side of a tangle of creepers. He snatched at it, caught it with a sigh of relief, and swung himself to the ground.

As soon as his feet touched soft earth, Sam convulsed. Agony overcame him. His veins burned, his skin felt like it was set on fire. He screamed in agony, falling to the ground in a fit.

'Get him up!' Dagomir's voice sounded distant, dreamlike. Sam was vaguely aware of feet marching all around him, then of the canopy of the jungle spinning into view as he was hoisted upwards by his arms. He could barely move; every action brought with it more pain.

'All of you, behind me!'

Was that Makeno? Sam felt himself dragged along, feet snagged on undergrowth.

'The island has spoken to me. It has shown me the way.' It *was* Makeno. 'I will teach this Zhar-Mharrad what it means to threaten one such as me!'

'Taken your time…' someone muttered. Emilio?

Makeno began to chant, and then shout, his foreign tongue spitting nigh-unpronounceable words in swift succession. Where Zhar-Mharrad's spells had sounded evil, blasphemous, like they had spoken to the very demons of the nine hells, Makeno's words were primal and raw.

Images of trees, and birds, and mountain-tops and roiling storms flashed into Sam's mind. He pulled himself free of the men who held him, the pain at last subsiding. Sam staggered forward, squinting to clear his vision.

Zhar-Mharrad was close now, his slow and purposeful advance calculated to strike awe and fear into the hearts of his enemies. The Bidajah marched alongside him, clashing scimitars and spears against shields ferociously. The remaining three carpets circled overhead, unable to broach the treeline. As Makeno chanted, the wind whipped harder, causing the vizier's cloak to billow fully outwards like smoke, and blowing clouds of white sand across the beach. Dark clouds gathered overhead, until the entire beach was cast into deep shadow.

'You dare challenge me?' Zhar-Mharrad shouted over the wind.

At that, the vizier drew a dagger, and made a dramatic, diagonal slash in the air. Makeno grunted in pain, taking a step backwards. Sam saw a precise cut open up across the warden's chest, oozing blood. But Makeno barely stopped his chants, which grew louder once more as a flash of anger changed his dark features. He stepped forward again, ignoring the wound, staring directly at his adversary. Makeno rubbed his hand across his chest, covering it in his own blood, and then dropped to one knee, plunging the bloodied palm of his hand into the sandy ground where the beach and jungle met.

Now it was Zhar-Mharrad's turn to be surprised. The vizier sensed something at his back, and turned about, his men almost knocking him over in their relentless march. Behind the soldiers, a great plume of sand rose up from the beach, growing and changing like a swarm of white insects. It towered over the golden-masked soldiers. Finally, the vast cloud came together in an undulating mass that resembled a face. Makeno's face. The mouth opened, wider and wider, and the gigantic head lolled forwards. The mouth engulfed the flying carpets, swallowing them whole, before tilting downwards. The last Sam saw of Zhar-Mharrad was of him crouching to the ground, covering his head with his arms, as the gigantic sand-effigy of Makeno crashed into the ranks of the Bidajah.

Lightning crackled overhead. The wind erupted into a fierce gale that bent the trees and blew up an impenetrable wall of sand.

Sam ignored all shouts to flee. He looked into the whirling sandstorm for a moment longer than was safe. He had to know if Hassan was all right.

Then he saw it. A shadow staggering in the cloud. A slight figure, fleeing the storm – fleeing Zhar-Mharrad. Hassan stumbled into view, coughing up sand. He got to his feet with a great effort, saw Sam, and ran towards his friend.

'Samir, no!' someone shouted from the treeline.

But Sam was already running to Hassan. He put an arm around his friend, and half ran with him half dragged him back to the treeline, where Dagomir and Emilio pulled them both to cover, scolding Sam severely.

'We must leave here now!' Makeno shouted. 'Follow me!'

CHAPTER 13

'It won't hold him for long,' Makeno said, as the party climbed a steep trail. 'But Zhar-Mharrad has learned the first lesson of the Lost Isles.'

'What lesson?' Sam asked.

'That these islands look after their own.'

Makeno smiled sagely, and picked up the pace, marching swiftly and surefootedly up the line. Sam could ask nothing more; he was still weak from his second encounter with the Blood Burn. The battle had exhausted him, and now it was all he could do to stumble his way up the ill-marked track with the others. At least he had Hassan. His friend was not himself – he had hardly said a word, and wore a vacant expression as a result of his ordeal at Zhar-Mharrad's hands. But he was safe now, and that was all that mattered to Sam. Hassan was safe, and in the Lost Isles, and they could share their greatest adventure together.

The trail, if it could be called such, rose up through the steaming jungle, towards a towering rocky outcrop. The vegetation was thick and lush, and the conditions so hot and humid it reminded Sam of the Caldega counting-house, though it did not smell half so bad. His torn tunic stuck to him; his sore feet caught on every barbed briar and jutting rock. The sounds of birdsong and chittering creatures were deafening, and sometimes they were joined by the distant roar of something larger and deadlier, which always made Sam flinch even though it had to be far away. Of more immediate concern, certainly to the scrawny crewmen who toiled nearby, were the huge spiders – some as big as water-flasks and red and shiny as rubies – not to mention the large green insects that looked like leaves or twigs at a distance, but reared up and hissed menacingly when anyone strayed too close. Then there were the frogs – tiny things, of every colour under the sun, which Makeno said were the most venomous creatures on the Lost Isles. Every so often, Sam would see the thick zig-zag bands of a snake's scaly hide unfurl and slither out of sight. He thought it was worse when you knew the creatures were there, but weren't sure where exactly.

The men at the front of the column hacked at recalcitrant undergrowth with cutlasses and axes, but still only forged a path wide enough for two abreast when the going was good. Dagomir stayed close to the vanguard, his hand never straying far from the dragon-carved pommel of his sword, almost sniffing out danger. Behind him was Yana Selishe, who sometimes, Sam noted, showed signs of discomfort – a stiff shoulder, a mild limp. The fall through the trees had taken a toll on her. By all accounts she had crashed the carpet into the tree canopy, and half-climbed, half-fallen to the ground in much the same way as Sam. The men had remarked how she and Samir were like 'peas in a pod', which did not sit at all well with Sam. Yet neither of them had escaped unscathed.

Those men who marched in the middle of the column, alongside Sam and Hassan, carried the supplies. Bardo shouldered the greatest burden thanks to his size and strength. The wounded man, Akho, was not fit to march, and was carried by two men, on a plank to which he had been lashed hastily. Emilio had expressed concern about bringing along such a burden, but Dagomir had insisted that no man would be left behind to suffer an inhuman fate at Zhar-Mharrad's hands. Sam shuddered again when he thought about what that meant. What had befallen the Bidajah in Zhar-Mharrad's black temple? What had become of those 'faithful of Birrahd', who had volunteered willingly to join the vizier's guard?

'They're still following,' Emilio called up from the rear-guard. 'And they're gaining.'

Dagomir looked down into the vast gloom of the jungle. Sam followed his gaze, but there was little to see but the thick trunks of towering trees and the multi-coloured foliage of gigantic, exotic plants. 'There.' Dagomir pointed.

The foliage some distance away, near the foot of the sloping trail, shook briefly, followed by the startled cry of disturbed birds. Was that the sound of iron-shod boots marching in unison? Sam wondered how they'd got so close.

Emilio pushed his way up the line, and Sam followed him to where Dagomir, Yana Selishe and Makeno stood. Dagomir signalled for the crew to keep moving up the trail while the leaders spoke.

'We must leave Akho,' Emilio whispered. 'He is slowing us down. We should leave him, and divide the supplies into lighter loads.'

'No,' Dagomir replied.

'No? Is that all you have to say? What about you, woman?' He looked to Yana Selishe. 'The captain listens to you more than to his first mate these days, eh? What do you say?'

The woman shrugged. 'I'm better at doing the chasing than the running. Dagomir is in charge, not me.'

Emilio appeared exasperated. He turned again to the captain. 'Look how quickly they've gained on us. They are following the trail that we ourselves are making. They will catch us, and soon.'

'We are heading further up the trail,' Dagomir replied. 'Soon, there will be a sheer precipice to one side, and hard rock to the other. If they catch us, they will have to fight in pairs at the very most, and we shall have the high ground. That's why you're in the rear-guard. You're still my best fighter, aren't you?'

Emilio exchanged an awkward glance with Yana Selishe. The woman's face was covered by her headscarf, concealing her opinion on that matter. 'And what of the sorcerer?' Emilio said at last.

'Tell him, Makeno.'

The warden leaned on his staff and smiled again, in that way that made him seem very wise, but that often infuriated the men. 'Fear not the sorcerer. Here, in this place, he is not the ultimate power. We do not need to escape Zhar-Mharrad. We only need to reach our destination before he does.'

'What does that even mean?' Emilio snapped.

'Have faith,' Makeno said, nodding. 'The island has spoken to me.'

* * *

'Pick up the pace!' Dagomir roared.

The men did their best, stepping faster as the slope grew steeper. The vegetation ahead had at least thinned, and now only the tallest trees poked above the trail to their right, a sea of green canopies falling away, stretching out towards the ocean. To their left, mossy rocks thrust upwards to the sky.

Sam stumbled faster, parched and weary, but too scared to look back. He took Hassan's arm, helping his friend as best he could, as Hassan could barely help himself. The older boy moved in whatever direction he was instructed to, his legs working almost mechanically. There seemed little spark in him.

The Bidajah were close at hand, always just around the bend, always gaining. The sound of their heavy boots was like a drum-beat. But now there was another sound, almost drowning out the percussive marching on the tails of the beleaguered crew.

Water. Loud, rushing, water.

Dagomir and Makeno appeared up ahead from around the bend.

'Everyone, hurry, this way!' Dagomir urged the men on, slapping each on the shoulder as they passed him, pushing them up the slope. 'Go with them, boy! We can't lose you. Makeno, lead them on. Emilio, with me.'

Dagomir drew his sword. He and Emilio took up the rear-guard position, hanging back just a little to put distance between themselves and the crew.

Sam felt a hand on his shoulder, and looked up into the eyes of Yana Selishe.

'Stay close to me,' she said.

The first Bidajah rounded the bend further down the slope. It was the first time the enemy had been seen clearly. The brute did not check his stride, but marched onwards, tireless. His scimitar was held before him, stock-straight. Another appeared behind him, then another, identical, marching like automata.

'You're first, Emilio,' Dagomir said. 'No mistake this time – aim for the head or the heart. We must conserve our strength.'

Emilio nodded, and took a step forward, adopting the fighting stance of his people; feet far apart, blade outstretched, left hand raised behind him. As soon as the lead Bidajah came within arm's length of his sword, Emilio lunged forward, the point of his blade finding the brute's heart with unerring accuracy, punching through the golden breastplate as powerfully as an arrow. The Bidajah froze and clutched at the wound, and as Emilio withdrew the blade, the Bidajah fell over the edge of the precipice, accompanied by the sounds of snapping branches. Emilio sprang back, and as the next Bidajah advanced, Dagomir took the first mate's place.

The Bidajah swung his scimitar. Dagomir knocked it aside with the flat of his broadsword. The scimitar struck rock. Dagomir seemed to think just for a moment, and instead of following his own advice he swept his sword low, taking the brute at the knee. It did not sever the limb, but Dagomir withdrew the blade roughly, slicing the back of the Bidajah's leg so that the golden warrior collapsed in a heap. At this, the captain kicked the soldier down the track. He rolled into his fellows, causing one to fall, and the one behind him to stumble to keep his balance.

'Go!' Dagomir said.

Yana Selishe nodded approval, and dragged Sam up the track, while Sam in turn dragged Hassan.

'I thought we were making a stand,' Sam said, breathlessly.

'No, we were buying time,' the woman replied. 'The captain is expending the least energy to do the most damage. A cunning strategy worthy of a Manhunter. Speaking of which, they will be upon us soon, and I do not relish the thought of facing my old lieutenants – and neither should you. Come on, faster, no slacking!'

Sam did not think he was slacking at all; his legs were barely functioning, and as the trail grew even steeper, he felt as though they might buckle beneath him at any moment, leaving him as prostrate as the hamstrung Bidajah behind him.

Yet soon enough they rounded the bend at the top of the slope, and Sam was partially refreshed by a cool vapour upon his face. Before him, the track levelled out, and passed into – or rather, behind – a large waterfall. Torrents of foaming water fell from on high in three great plumes, like the tails of gigantic white horses, disappearing into the jungle far below, the river obscured by their dark canopies. Sam looked up to the dizzying heights from which the falls came, and shuddered as he saw the water tumbling from a gigantic maw, carved from the rock, sitting beneath two huge eye-sockets.

'Behold, the Mouth of Savaishe!' Makeno emerged from the spray, looking like a ghost within the embrace of the swirling mist. 'Quickly. Come, come!'

Yana led Samir along the track past Makeno, into the mist, and onto a precariously narrow ledge. Sam sidled along it in near-darkness, legs shaking like jelly, keeping the slick wall to his back, while the torrent of water fell relentlessly before him in a deafening roar. Yana Selishe shouted something to him, but Sam could not hear her for the raging falls. As he moved along the ledge, he felt the strangest sensation: a warm glow in his fingers and toes, spreading all over his body. He felt his strength returning, as the cool water sprayed his face and the mist soaked him through. And just for a moment, within the raging power of the waterfall, he thought he heard distant whispers in a tongue he could not understand. Or perhaps they were echoes, but not, Sam somehow knew, of any living voice.

Hassan stopped. Sam turned to his friend, to see what the matter was. Hassan blinked and looked around the eerie cavern as though seeing it for the first time. Then he threw his arms around his friend and held Sam tight.

Sam was overcome. It was the first sign of lucidity his friend had shown since his rescue, but there was no time for celebration. Sam pulled away, patted Hassan on the shoulder and said, 'We have to hurry. You understand?'

Hassan smiled, and Sam led him on.

At last, they reached daylight on the other side. Sam grabbed Bardo's hand, gasping as he left behind the soaking mists and its strange whispers. Bardo grinned, like he understood what Sam was feeling. Perhaps he, too, had been replenished by the strange properties of the 'Mouth of Savaishe'.

Sam turned to Hassan, and his heart sank. His friend stared blankly at the rock, all personality drained from him once more.

'What's wrong, Samir?' Bardo asked.

'I… I thought… It's nothing.'

The burly carpenter helped the boys onto the track, which broadened out now into a rugged trail some four men broad. Ropes had been lashed around jutting trees, whose gnarled roots clung to the rock for dear life. Two crewmen manned the ropes, which trailed over the edge of the path. Sam saw that the supplies had been lowered down the cliff face, into the jungle, and that most of the men had gone too. He looked over the ledge just in time to see Akho, on his makeshift stretcher, disappearing beneath the leafy canopy.

Yana Selishe emerged from the falls, Makeno close behind.

'You have all felt it now, yes?' Makeno said. 'The power of the island gods? Zhar-Mharrad's magic cannot touch us while we are in the embrace of Savaishe.'

'Looks like we have another climb,' the woman said. 'You first, Samir. Do as you're told this time, or we're as good as captured.'

Sam frowned. He did not relish taking orders from the woman, but he could see little choice in the matter. The trail wound upwards further, broader and flatter, and would make a poor position for a battle. A purple mountain range sprawled beyond it, vast and jagged.

They had made this climb purely to cross the river, Sam guessed, and to give Zhar-Mharrad the slip. Far be it for a mere street urchin to jeopardise the plan for which much had been risked.

He nodded, and grabbed the rope.

'They're almost here!' Dagomir shouted, bursting from the waterfall, his blond mane wet and tousled. 'They threw their own men over the edge and carried on. Hurry: the path is narrow, and they are clumsy, but it won't stop them forever.'

Sam began the descent, and everyone else followed, shimmying down the ropes like ship's rigging. Makeno came alongside Sam on the second rope, wincing as his injured hand took the strain. His staff was lashed across his back, the many charms, bones and trinkets jingling as he climbed.

'They will follow us,' Sam said.

'They will. But I think the golden warriors are not built for climbing. They will be slow, or they will have to find a longer way around.'

'The carpets?'

'As I said, Zhar-Mharrad's magic is weaker here. And how many infernal carpets does he have now? Two? Three? Not enough to transport an army.'

'I should have worn the amulet. Perhaps he tracks me with his magic.'

'No, Samir. The power of the amulet to shield you from his magic is a natural phenomenon, because that amulet is of these islands. While you are here, everything, from the rocks to the birds, masks your power, because you are also of these islands. Understand?'

'Not really. How can I be...?'

'This is a time for climbing, not talking,' Makeno said, puffing out a breath as he struggled down the rope. 'Now come, concentrate.'

Sam afforded himself a laugh. 'I don't need to concentrate, old man. I'm a Heritor.' And with that, Sam threw caution to the wind, and scurried down the rope swiftly, using the rocks themselves to help him descend, until he was through the trees, and back into the dark embrace of the humid jungle.

He emerged into a clearing at the base of the rock, where the spray of the churning waterfall created a low-hanging mist around the banks of a turquoise river. The sun penetrated the tree canopy over the water only in thin, crepuscular rays, in which flying insects danced and swirled.

Most of the men had set about finding a new trail already, and soon Makeno was in the clearing, and at once began to direct them. Sam had guided the ship to the island, true enough, but now that they were here he was lost. Makeno acted as though he had been here before. The island, it seemed, really did speak to him.

Bardo was next down the rope, Hassan clinging to his back. The big carpenter landed clumsily, looking somewhat shaken and red in the face after the trial of lowering his large frame down a thin rope. Emilio came close behind, slapped Bardo on the back, mussed Sam's hair, and went after the others. Dagomir and Yana Selishe came next. Some distance from the ground, the woman stopped, and signalled Dagomir to go on. Once Dagomir was safely on the ground, Yana cut his rope, so that anyone using it to climb down would have to face a drop of thirty feet or more. The woman then shimmied quickly down her own rope, and when she reached the bottom she turned back, took up her crossbow and aimed upwards. With unerring accuracy, she fired, the quarrel tearing the second rope before it broke against the rocks.

'They can find their own way down,' she said.

Sam saw the admiration in Dagomir's eyes, and turned away before he was forced to express some similar sentiment.

* * *

Sam did not know how long they trekked through the boiling heat and claustrophobic confines of the jungle. It felt like days. Sam had always imagined the archipelago to be small; yet this was not the case. And this island was but one in the chain that made up the Lost Isles. Makeno would only say that they were going to a 'sacred place', where they could rest, safe from Zhar-Mharrad's magic.

'When we set out on our voyage,' Sam asked Makeno, 'you said that blood magic was bad. But did you not use blood magic before? Back on the beach, when you summoned the sandstorm?'

Makeno nodded gravely. 'Of a kind,' he said. 'The difference is, it was my blood, spilled by my enemy. And I knew that it was the only way to combat Zhar-Mharrad's spells. Blood follows blood, they say. Zhar-Mharrad's magic relies on the spilling of innocent blood, and that is why it is a vile form of sorcery, second only to the black art of necromancy.'

'Necromancy... you mean, raising the dead?'

'I do. Remember, Samir: any branch of sorcery can be used for good, or for ill, if the circumstances require it. But once you dabble in the dark arts, no matter how justified, you take the first steps on a dangerous path.'

'We're already on a dangerous path...' Emilio had been listening nearby, and now interrupted with a grumble.

'But we have our lives, and our souls, intact,' Makeno countered. 'We have not yet allowed darkness to corrupt our hearts. The island will know that, and it shall judge us accordingly.'

Emilio looked worried. 'Really? I wish you'd mentioned that before you led a band of reavers and plunderers on this expedition.'

Makeno merely chuckled to himself, and walked on.

The party wound through the immense green, climbing ponderously down awkward slopes, and sluggishly up steep banks. They took much-needed refreshment by a freshwater stream, half-hidden by enormous ferns. They stepped gingerly around a tangle of vast, purple-spotted plants, each taller than a man, with bulbous flowers that moved when anyone drew near, opening their petals to reveal rows of pin-sharp teeth.

'Carnivorous plants,' Makeno whispered. 'I never dreamed I would finally see one. My people call them "*ya'kudla*", the Devouring Rose. Venture too close and it ensnares you with its roots. See!' Makeno pointed to the base of the plants, where thorny, vine-like roots writhed and coiled slowly like snakes. 'Once it has you in its grip, the flower envelops you, and slowly digests you over the course of many weeks. Be careful – this one looks as though it has not eaten in a while.'

'A real man-eater,' Emilio whispered, leaning in close to Sam. 'Like our friend, eh?' He nodded back along the line, towards Yana Selishe, who even now walked close to Dagomir, sharing some private word in his ear.

Sam frowned. 'What do you mean?'

Emilio put a finger to his lips, and lowered his voice further. 'I mean, lad, she's got her thorny vines well and truly into the captain.'

'But she saved our skins back on the beach. Maybe we were wrong about her.'

'Have you already forgotten what you saw in Caldega? She may have fooled the captain, but she'll not fool me. Keep your wits about you, lad. Trust no one.'

Sam nodded, and felt very foolish that he had allowed himself even a measure of respect for the woman. He had to harden himself, he knew. The Manhunters of Yad-Sha'Rib had killed his father. He must not forget it. Not ever.

They pressed on for hours more, until they reached a clearing lit dimly by the reddening of the setting sun. Crickets struck up their chirruping, and Dagomir instructed some of the men to light torches. Here, Makeno signalled that they could rest for a moment, and the crew all but collapsed into the grass.

Dagomir distributed hard ship's biscuits to everyone, and then told two of the men to go and hunt game for the pot. 'We must save the rations as best we can,' he explained.

Sam sat on the ground, sinking into the soft, mossy floor of the forest, and imagined for a moment that it was a soft feather bed with plump cushions. He bit into the stale biscuit, and willed it to taste like some of Sivita's flatbread. But that memory only reminded him sharply of happier times shared with Hassan, the friend who might never be the same again. The biscuit tasted like ashes in Sam's mouth.

Makeno warned the men to tread lightly, explaining that they'd be most likely to catch a snake or lizard rather than anything they'd normally call food. 'That's all right,' one of them, an archer named Vatus, said. 'We've had worse, and doubtless will again.' With that, the two men departed into the jungle.

For a while, everyone sat in silence, doubtless contemplating their fortunes after a disastrous start to the expedition. It was Yana who broke the silence.

'Samir,' she said. 'Ask your friend about Zhar-Mharrad's ship. How many crew? How many Bidajah?'

'He can't remember,' Sam said. He'd tried to speak to Hassan during the hike, but had received barely anything but uncommunicative grunts.

'He can remember. I've seen this before. Zhar-Mharrad's methods can take a toll on a person's mind, but he's still in there, somewhere.'

Sam looked at Hassan, who stared blankly at the trees, and hoped the woman was right.

Yana moved across the clearing, and crouched in front of Hassan. She waved a hand in front of his face, snapped her fingers. There was no response.

'Hassan,' she said. 'Listen to me. You have to tell us about Zhar-Mharrad's forces. How many men were on his ship?'

Nothing.

Yana put her hands on Hassan's chin, and turned his face to hers. 'I know you're in there. Think hard. How many?'

Hassan began to tremble. A single tear rolled down his cheek.

'Stop it!' Sam snapped, jumping to his feet. 'You're scaring him.'

'I doubt I'll scare him more than Zhar-Mharrad already has.' She stared into Hassan's eyes. 'Answer me, boy, or maybe I'll send you back to the vizier. How would you like that?'

Sam grabbed Yana's shoulder, and she shoved him away. Hassan began to whimper like a frightened puppy.

'That's enough!' Emilio shouted, also jumping up. 'You're not in Yad-Sha'Rib now, woman. You don't get to…'

'Quiet!' Makeno said, standing suddenly.

Everyone turned to the warden, whose eyes darted about the clearing, head inclined, listening intently.

'I hear nothing,' Yana Selishe said at last, stepping away from Hassan.

'Exactly. No crickets, no birds. Not a…'

Makeno was cut short by a piercing, throaty scream. Everyone leapt to their feet, weapons drawn; all but Akho, who tried in vain to pull himself from his stretcher. The man's fumbling and grunting was the only sound in the clearing.

The undergrowth exploded, and a breathless Vatus emerged, his eyes wide, face purple. Everyone looked at him, he looked at everyone else, and then hissed, 'Run. By all the gods, run!'

A great roar sounded in the jungle behind Vatus. The ground shook as something very large approached, the percussive beat of gigantic footfalls.

'Run!' Vatus shouted, and fled, tripping over poor Akho in his terror, scrambling to his feet, and racing from the clearing before anyone could react.

The creature erupted into the clearing as violently as a volcano. A reptilian beast, its bright red, scaly head bigger than Bardo, its gleaming yellow eyes fixing the astonished party as its new prey. It opened a vast mouth, with teeth as long as scimitars, and unleashed a roar like the blast of a war-horn, sending a powerful gust of spittle-flecked air into the clearing that smelt of rancid meat. Sam darted away from the creature instinctively. One man dropped his axe and fled after Vatus. Everyone else backed away, weapons ready.

Everyone but Akho.

The creature strode from the undergrowth, now fully in view, its patterned scales glistening by torchlight. It carried itself on huge, muscled legs. Jagged spines protruded from its back like the battlements of some great castle. Its head swept around at the end of its serpentine neck, great nostrils flaring as it sniffed the air. And then it looked down upon Akho, who quailed in fear, and snapped him up, stretcher and all. With one jerk of its massive head, Akho was gone, swallowed whole.

'Vanya's wrath!' Dagomir roared, leaping towards the creature without hesitation, swinging his sword.

Steel met claw, as the beast lurched forwards, swiping one of its small arms at the captain. Dagomir spun backwards, jarred by the impact. The great head turned, the jaws snapped, and the captain barely had time to leap aside as the creature's huge teeth slashed thin air.

'Charge!' Bardo cried at the top of his lungs. 'With the captain!'

Sam saw Emilio take a step backwards, shaking his head in disbelief. And fear. Bardo, on the other hand lumbered forth, billhook aimed down like a lance at the monster's underbelly. Only one man went with him: Toldar, who back on the *Vanya's Wrath* had been a cook, and now ran at the monster like a hardened warrior.

A crossbow bolt struck the beast near the throat, prompting a terrible roar. Yana Selishe reloaded quickly.

Bardo reached the monster, but it turned aside at the last, and the billhook scraped against thick scales. The second man thrust at the monster's jaws with a spear, and it recoiled for a second, before striding forward, a vast foot crashing down upon the man, hammering him into the ground. Bardo struck at it again, and it swiped a claw, swatting the big carpenter aside like a bug. He dropped the billhook and landed heavily, the spongy ground barely cushioning his fall.

The monster bent down and ripped Toldar in half. His blood sprayed across the clearing in a gruesome arc. The man's torrid, gurgling scream shook Sam from uncertainty. He ran towards Bardo as the monster turned towards the prone carpenter. Sam was vaguely aware of Yana Selishe calling him back, but her cries fell on deaf ears. Sam had seen too much death today. He would not lose Bardo as well.

Dagomir was on his feet, hacking at the beast's hide, unable to get anywhere near its softer underbelly. Sam ran past him, and the monster seemed to sense his approach, swinging its long, fat tail in a violent lash towards him. Sam leapt over the sweeping tail, landed on his feet and kept moving. He didn't bother to draw his sword – it might as well have been a needle against this hulking reptile. And so he instead snatched up the billhook as he ran.

The monster snapped at his back. He felt its hot breath at his neck, smelled its foul stink. He kept running, the sound of thundering footfalls signalling that it was following still. Another snap of those massive jaws. This time Sam afforded a glance over his shoulder, and saw the beast lunge forward, all of its weight bearing down upon him, its mouth open wide.

'Bardo, help!' Sam shouted.

The carpenter was still trying to stand, and he looked up now with astonishment and terror writ upon his broad features as Sam – and the monster – bore down upon him.

Sam skidded to a halt, sliding low beneath the monster's jaws. He planted the shaft of the billhook in the ground, and tipped the point upwards.

The beast ran onto the billhook, its own weight pushing the metal point deep into its flesh. The shaft bent, and creaked like it might snap. The monster roared, and reared upwards as it regained its balance, pulling Sam off the ground as it went. The hook caught fast within its thick hide. For a moment, Sam was dangling in the air, his face inches away from flailing claws. Then he felt a weight about his ankles, and Bardo was with him, pulling Sam back to earth, grabbing the billhook in his strong hands. Bardo planted his feet, and pushed the weapon harder into the creature's flesh.

The great tail lashed about again, cracking the trunk of a tree on the edge of the clearing. In its wake, Dagomir ducked forward, driving his sword upwards into the monster's flesh, until its blood bathed his arms. Another crossbow bolt thudded into the beast's throat. Makeno was amongst them, hacking at it with a dagger. The beast screamed now, a shrill, ear-piercing roar of agony and hate, and it pulled away with all of its awesome might. The billhook at last wrenched free, Dagomir pulled away his blade, and the monster staggered to the edge of the clearing. With one last roar, it thundered away as fast as its enormous legs would carry it, trees cracking and toppling in its wake. Soon, the heavy tread of the monster subsided entirely.

Dagomir collapsed on the ground, and Sam beside him. For a moment, all was quiet, the only sound their own ragged breaths. Sam felt Bardo's hand on his shoulder.

'You saved my life, lad,' Bardo panted. 'I'll not forget that.'

Sam could only nod. He wiped thick, blackish blood from his face with a shaking hand.

'We've lost two men to that thing.' Emilio approached now. 'And who knows where Vatus has gone, the coward. We carried Akho here for no reason.'

Dagomir glared up at his first mate. 'I did not see you helping, Emilio. Perhaps if you had acted a little quicker, like Samir, we could at least have saved Toldar.'

Samir tried not to show how proud he felt at Dagomir's praise.

'I think none of us can act as quickly as Samir,' Emilio replied bitterly. 'All I know is, we'd have done better to abandon Akho and follow Vatus. At least he's…'

'Quiet, all of you!' Yana Selishe hissed. All turned to her. She held up a hand to silence the ragged remnants of the crew, her dark eyes scanning the treeline warily.

A cascade of leaves drifted dreamily into the clearing from above. Sam looked up, while everyone else seemed rooted to the spot, moving painfully slowly. A black shadow fell from above, a man, swinging from the trees. A blade flashed red in the last light of dusk.

And then everything sped up.

The black figure landed noiselessly in the centre of the clearing, lashing out with a blade at Yana. The woman leant backwards, almost impossibly far, the assassin's scimitar sweeping past her by a hair's breadth. She levered upwards swiftly, drawing two scimitars of her own from her back, smaller and lighter than her attacker's. She slashed downwards with both in the form of an 'X', the assassin parrying one and leaping out of the way of the other.

Finally, everyone was on their feet, though confusion reigned. Sam's eyes adjusted fastest: the black shadow was a Manhunter.

The two black-clad assassins slashed and parried at each other, blades flashing in dizzying arcs. Dagomir ran forward to assist the woman. As he drew close, the enemy darted aside, so that Yana Selishe had to pull her blow to avoid hitting the captain. Dagomir jerked his blade up instinctively as the enemy thrust a scimitar at him, almost blindsiding him. The blade nicked Dagomir's cheek, and the captain leapt back as Yana Selishe stepped forward.

Emilio now joined the fray, his sword dancing elegantly and swiftly towards the new Manhunter. With a scimitar in one hand and a dagger in the other, the enemy was forced slowly back, parrying furiously as two skilled warriors hacked and slashed and thrust at him. He saw an opening, and kicked out, catching Emilio hard in the midriff, sending him to the ground. But this was enough for Yana Selishe to press home an advantage. She slashed outwards with both blades, opening up the assassin's defences, then planted a balletic kick to the man's face. The enemy staggered away, parrying blindly as Yana attacked again, this time cutting him deep on the arm. He dropped his dagger, and skipped away swiftly.

A crossbow bolt whistled through the air. Sam wondered if only he could hear it, and see it, but Yana Selishe's reflexes were swift indeed. She cut it from the air with her blade, and scoured the treeline for its source.

Sam ran to her side, and Dagomir, too. The bushes shook, twigs snapped, birds fluttered skyward in panic.

Vatus stumbled from the undergrowth, gasping for breath, dropping to his knees beside the Manhunter. The hunter turned to face Yana Selishe once more. Two Bidajah strode from the jungle. Others appeared behind them. Golden masks appeared all around as Zhar-Mharrad's soldiers cut their way through the brush.

'I… I'm sorry, Captain,' Vatus croaked.

Dagomir looked about. Sam could see his desire to fight, but also his exhaustion. They all felt it. There were so few left now, and the enemy so strong, what could be gained by making a stand?

'This way!' It was Makeno who shouted. They turned to see the warden pointing to a spindly trail, and as one they ran to him.

More Bidajah entered the clearing. Hassan hadn't moved a muscle during the fighting, but now Sam hauled him up by his arm and dragged him away from the enemy. Makeno's trail was the only way out, and the beleaguered crew ran to it, into the jungle, as fast as their tired legs would carry them. Crossbow bolts thudded into the trees beside them. A war-horn sounded, calling reinforcements to the fray.

'They found us faster than I'd hoped,' Makeno said, his wiry legs carrying him with surprising speed for an old man. 'But fear not – the island shall deliver us!'

Bardo picked up Hassan and threw the boy over his shoulder. The group slowed for nothing, and nor did their pursuers. The Bidajah were silent, and their advance was marked only by the heavy stomping of mail-shod boots and the violent parting of undergrowth. Sam dared not look back.

Makeno led on, twisting and turning through the jungle's hidden ways as though he'd been born to it. Darkness fell rapidly, and the crimson light gave way to the bluish hue of night, the tracks visible only by the merest hint of a moon through the trees. They scrambled up a steep rise, and then onwards across a shallow stream, which signalled the start of a marshy expanse. Sam's feet sank into squelchy earth, and water rose up above his shoes.

'Makeno, this is unwise,' Dagomir hissed, as the crew slowed to wade through the marsh. 'They are nearly upon us!'

'And we are nearly there,' Makeno said. 'Look!' He pointed with his staff. Hanging from a nearby branch was a long rope, tied about with bones, painted stones and gruesome, leather-skinned shrunken heads.

'What is that?' Sam asked, apprehension in his voice.

'A marker. A warning.'

'A warning against what?'

'You don't want to know. Now, everyone follow me. There is a path here, but it is hidden. Step off it, and you are doomed. Tread only where I tread.'

With that, Makeno strode on, tapping his staff into the water ahead of him, placing his feet carefully. As he walked, he began to mutter words in his rolling, clicking language. And as he spoke, a greenish mist began to rise from the marshland, accompanied by a chill on the air that would have been welcome, were it not so laden with inexplicable dread. Sam fancied that, beneath the murky, waterlogged ground on either side of what Makeno called a path, something shone, bright green, with a strange luminescence. Whatever it was, Sam had an intense feeling that he should not stop to find out.

They passed another marker, hanging between two vast trees, whose gnarled roots protruded over the surface of the marsh, and whose branches formed a sort of archway over the path, like an entrance to an even darker part of the jungle. This marker was strung with more gruesome trophies: a monkey's paw, a human skull daubed with tribal sigils; some tangle of desiccated, greyish matter that

Sam felt sure was entrails. Makeno paused to offer some prayer, before waving the others on.

There came the sound of splashing footsteps behind them, dull and muffled in the eerie confines of the shadowy marsh. Sam looked back, and saw the glint of moonlight from golden masks, and readied scimitars. The Bidajah cared not about picking their way along a narrow, ill-marked path, and now gained on the crew with alarming rapidity. Though half concealed by the mist, Sam began to make out the shapes of at least a dozen hulking soldiers, and a black form amongst them, with a tall turban. It was Zhar-Mharrad himself.

Dagomir gave Sam a shove. 'Keep moving, lad. There's nothing for you back there but death.'

'I'm not so sure it's any better up ahead,' Sam muttered, but moved along all the same.

Yana's crossbow clicked and fired. There was a loud splash as whatever she'd hit fell into the marsh. The enemy were close.

'Past this marker!' Makeno said, and stood beside a tall, wooden pole that jutted from the mud, carved with leering skull faces and painted in garish colours. 'Hurry!'

He beckoned them on. Emilio dashed past Makeno, through the strange mist, and into a sheltered copse of trees that was so dark Sam lost sight of him at once. Sam went next, surprised when his feet found solid ground at last, but fumbling in the pitch dark. Emilio grabbed him by the arm and pulled him close. Next came Dagomir, then Yana, then Bardo with Hassan. Finally, Makeno hopped onto the bank of the marsh.

As soon as Makeno left the soggy path, a change came about the entire marsh. The chill breeze blew more strongly. Tiny orbs of green light flickered in the water, then rose through the mist, dancing upon silvery tendrils and bathing every tree and bush in a sickly glow. Makeno held out an arm, drawing the company back into the shadows, from where they watched the advance of their enemies.

The Bidajah came on, the first of them fully in view now, Zhar-Mharrad striding confidently behind them.

'Say nothing; do nothing,' Makeno whispered. 'Just watch.'

One of the Bidajah stopped, so abruptly that the one behind him walked into his comrade. The first soldier seemed to have his foot stuck. He pulled, but was rooted to the spot. The Bidajah behind him simply stepped around the first and continued. The others came on, too, spread out across the marsh, emerging from the mist like ghosts. Some waded waist-deep through the marsh. Only Zhar-Mharrad advanced cautiously, feeling for the path ahead, leaving his freakish warriors to labour.

The Bidajah whose leg was stuck struggled harder now.

'Help him!' Zhar-Mharrad shouted to a nearby warrior.

The soldier obeyed his master, and turned ponderously to help his fellow. As he did, the water erupted behind him, and some grotesque, skeletal form rose from the muck, covered in slime, rotten flesh sloughing from its body. It seized the Bidajah with bony fingers. The gold-masked warrior pulled away, slashing clumsily with his scimitar with a heavy blow that should by rights have smashed the walking corpse asunder. And yet the scimitar cleaved only mist, which parted before its arc, and then reformed, the corpse-creature appearing once more to continue its attack.

Another figure rose up beside the first, then another. All around the marsh, the Bidajah were stopped in their tracks as animated corpses rose up in great numbers. Some of them were armed, carrying large axes of discoloured bronze, and the weaker ones seemed to mob the Bidajah, while these grim executioners bore down upon them, and went about their bloody work.

Sam turned away as the blood began to flow, bile rising in his throat.

'We have passed through the Hall of Bones,' Makeno said. 'Here lie the remnants of a once-great people, who sought to tame the jungle. And yet they were brought to ruin by the god, Savaishe. Their temples fell, and the jungle reclaimed the land. The graves of the dead, of kings and slaves both, lie beneath the water. Only my ancestors, the Savaisal, know the safe trails through these cursed lands. And we do not share that knowledge with anyone.'

Zhar-Mharrad was shouting now, his voice rising in pitch as the Bidajah were overcome. Those who did not succumb were driven back by the relentless assault of the vengeful dead. Sometimes a scimitar would find its mark, and a skeletal head would fly off into the marsh. Other times, the Bidajahs' weapons would pass harmlessly though their attackers as though they were not there.

The vizier spoke some fell incantation, and black smoke swept around him in snake-like coils. Each time a shambling corpse tried to touch Zhar-Mharrad, it fell away at the touch of the smoke, bones cracking, flesh turning to powder. It was not enough; Zhar-Mharrad retreated, and his remaining warriors closed ranks around him, backing away through the mist. The shambling dead followed, clawing at the Bidajah, or hacking with weapons of bronze. Before long, the sounds of battle began to recede, and Sam could barely see anything, save for dancing marshlights.

Dagomir breathed a sigh of relief. 'Well done, Makeno. Well done indeed.'

'Save your praise, Captain,' the warden replied. 'We have far to travel still. But for now we should be safe from Zhar-Mharrad. He knows the island works against him, and that will make him cautious. By the time we reach our destination, Zhar-Mharrad will still be fumbling his way through the jungle, uncertain and afraid.'

'And… where is our destination?' Sam asked.

'Is it not obvious, Samir?' Makeno smiled. 'We are going to find my people. I am taking you home.'

CHAPTER 14

The moon was at its height when the exhausted travellers staggered down the hillside into the village. Ahead of them was a large clearing, in which perhaps twenty squat, round huts of mud and coarse stone were huddled in a broad circle. Around them, smaller huts jutted from the surrounding trees, growing almost organically from the jungle, connected by walkways of wood and vines. In the centre of the village, a large fire-pit glowed deep red, the embers sending a plume of grey smoke drifting lazily into the indigo sky.

Makeno had advised caution on the approach. The Savaisal had ever been a peaceful tribe, Makeno had said. They had lived in this place, in the same way, for many hundreds of years, and it seemed reasonable to assume that little had changed since the Lost Isles had last appeared. And yet the tribe were not without warriors, and magical protection. It was well past midnight now, and most of the Savaisal would be asleep in their huts – Makeno had instructed everyone to walk slowly, with weapons away, out into the open, so that the lookouts would see them and know that they were no threat.

'And what if they don't like the look of us?' Emilio had asked.

'Then we shall probably fall prey to a poison dart before we even see who fired it,' Makeno had replied, and that had ended the conversation abruptly.

Now they drew near to the village, walking in single file beside a narrow, burbling stream, towards the smouldering fire. The jungle rose up high on three sides, forming dark, natural walls, and sheltering the little village from the elements so that there was barely a breath of wind to be felt.

A distant, shrill whistle sounded. Perhaps the call of some foreign night-bird. Seconds later, it was answered by another call, nearer.

Yana Selishe reached for her crossbow, but Makeno sensed her intent and signalled for her to stop. She slowly, reluctantly, pulled her hand away, and carried on walking.

A final shrill whistle sounded, and it was clear now that it was no bird, or any other creature but a man. The shadows moved all around. Sam turned to whisper something to Dagomir, and found himself staring into a dark face, with unfamiliar eyes. He jumped out of his skin, and the party came to a halt.

Five men stood around them, impossibly close, brandishing spears threateningly. They were dark-skinned, like Makeno, wearing scraps of hide, fur and makeshift metal armour doubtless salvaged from some vanquished enemy. Each man was lean and muscular, faces dotted with paint, hair tousled and threaded with feathers and small bones. They had approached without a sound, across almost open ground, as if they were one with the landscape. Even Yana Selishe had been surprised, and Sam had always thought that no one could creep up on her.

Makeno said something in his own tongue, with its strange clicks and throaty, rolling verbs that sounded like thunder over the mountains. Whatever message he conveyed caused the five warriors to look at each other uncertainly. The one directly ahead then pointed his spear at Makeno's chest, jabbing it towards the warden, barking some demand that Sam could not decipher.

Makeno replied, his tone growing defiant, and then he held aloft his staff, shaking it so that the charms rattled. The lead warrior at once took two steps backwards. One of the others said something to him, which made him pause. Finally, he straightened, looked Makeno in the eye, and jerked his head towards the village.

Flanked by the guards, the ragged crew were led to the village of the Savaisal. More whistles heralded their approach. From the tree-huts, drums began to beat. A shout rang out on the night air. Torches were lit. A great fire was lit, and the whole village at once came alive. Men, women and children ran from their huts, chattering excitedly. The warriors who walked alongside the party eyed the strangers warily – whatever reception awaited, it was by no means guaranteed to be a friendly one.

Warriors raced towards them, dancing around the travellers with an energy that Sam, utterly exhausted, could only envy. They whooped and hollered, brandishing clubs and spears. Some bore painted hide shields, adorned with crude sigils of strange creatures. They darted ever closer as they danced, as if daring each other to confront the new arrivals. One threw himself within an inch of Dagomir, who gave the warrior a shove so hard he flew some yards away, striving comically to keep his feet. The others lowered their spears at once, their dance becoming more threatening.

'No!' Makeno hissed. 'Do not take the bait. They are testing you. They are daring you to attack. If you draw a weapon they will kill you.'

'They can try,' Yana Selishe muttered.

Sam looked ahead, at the shadowy figures gathering in the village, silhouetted by firelight. There were scores of them, shadows flickering. As much as he was impressed by the woman's confidence, Sam knew the odds were stacked against them. He felt very afraid, and entirely uncertain of Makeno's plan.

Soon they were amidst the throng of dancing, singing, shouting villagers. Wide-eyed children ran alongside to tug at the strange clothes of the foreigners, or to stare in awe at the gigantic frame of Bardo. Drums pounded all around. Masked dancers leapt at Sam, their great headdresses of grass and coloured feathers lending them a leering, demonic appearance. They carried rattles made of bone, strung about with charms not unlike the ones on Makeno's staff. Not in his wildest story-books of far-off voyages had Sam heard of such sights. He drew himself nearer to the warden, hoping that he would offer some protection. Perhaps sensing Sam's unease, Hassan shuffled closer too, though his eyes remained wide and unblinking even when the dancers drew within a hair's breadth of his face.

A tall man in a long, wooden mask leapt in front of Makeno, blocking the advance of the crew. He shouted something in the tribal tongue. Makeno replied, but quietly and calmly, and at his words a sudden hush descended on the village. Even the drums stopped, as if those distant drummers had heard Makeno's words plain as day. The man froze, examining Makeno through the carved eye-holes of his mask. Then, finally, he held aloft his arms, and shouted something indecipherable. A great roar erupted, as every villager shouted in unison. The throng parted, stepping aside one by one, forming a corridor of bodies leading all the way to a large hut, whose door was formed from a pair of gigantic, criss-crossing tusks, bigger than those of any elephant Sam had ever seen back home. A hide curtain was pulled aside, and a man stepped out of the hut, flanked by two tall warriors, each bearing torches. The man carried a staff, which jangled as he made his way slowly towards the crew.

'What's happening?' Sam whispered.

'I told them who I am,' Makeno replied. 'And I asked to see their chief.'

The chief approached in deathly silence. And as he drew close, Sam's eye was drawn to the man's staff, and his heart raced just a little faster. It was much like Makeno's, carved and adorned with trinkets in near-identical fashion; save for one prominent detail.

Atop the staff was a small, bronze tablet, roughly triangular, with one rounded edge, and inscribed with myriad strange symbols. It was almost exactly like Sam's amulet. The amulet now possessed by Dagomir.

Sam looked to the captain, who steadfastly stared ahead, not meeting Sam's look. An accusing look, for this was too much of a coincidence.

The chief stopped, and met Makeno's gaze haughtily. Finally, he spoke in his own language, his voice deep and rumbling, drawing nods and mutters from the crowd.

'What's he saying?' Dagomir whispered to Makeno.

The chief held up a hand to silence them, and then spoke in the trader's tongue. 'I will speak so that you all might understand,' he said, speaking slowly, his accent thick. 'I am Noaka, chief of the Savaisal.'

'You speak our language?' Dagomir said.

'Many of us do,' Noaka said. 'You are not the first outsiders to set foot in our lands, and you will not be the last. Many moons ago, during the Time of Revelation, our ancestors traded with outsiders like you, and fought with them, too. Not all of the outsiders were honourable. Some came seeking wisdom, yes, but others came to steal our sacred treasures. Some were slavers, come to take our people captive, and those men almost destroyed us. When the Time of Revelation ended, we reclaimed our land, and rebuilt our tribe, and now the Savaisal are stronger than ever before. The paths to our island have opened once more, and again outsiders come. This time, they will not find the Savaisal so easy to prey upon.'

'We do not seek to prey upon anyone,' Dagomir said. 'We are here to return Makeno to his people.'

'That is not the only reason you have come, Yellow-hair,' Noaka said. 'I see it in your eyes. My people have long learned that men such as you cannot speak the full truth. Do you know that not all of the outsiders left these islands after the paths were closed long ago? Some were trapped here, and their descendants live here still. Some say there is a village of your kind, a place of villainy and lies, built upon the shores of one of the northern islands from the carcasses of your strange ships.'

'We should have made landing there,' Emilio grumbled, half to himself.

'Emissaries from that place sometimes visit our island,' Noaka went on, 'to trade with the plains tribes who know no better. And yet none of them dare trespass on our land, let alone disturb the Hall of Bones!'

This drew some consternation from the crowd, and some angry shouts.

'Please,' Makeno said. 'It is true that my friend here has business of his own on the island, but it is not with the Savaisal.'

'Pah! He seeks the Forbidden Pool, as do they all. This boy…' he nodded to Sam. 'His ancestor drank from the pool, no? I see it in his eyes. I sense his power. You used him to bring you home, did you not? Clever.'

'If they seek the pool it is nothing to us. What matters is that they have returned me to my people. Many generations may have passed, but the blood of Makawenu flows through my veins, and none here has the right to keep me from my destiny.' With that,

Makeno held aloft his carved staff, drawing gasps from the villagers.

Noaka glowered. 'This man claims to be the descendant of Makawenu, who was chief of our people long ago, when the last outsiders came. But it is a lie. Makawenu was killed in a battle with slavers, and his staff was stolen! You are not of his blood.'

'Makawenu was not killed, he was captured, and taken from the island, along with his pregnant wife, Naekuru. The slavers sought to profit from him, and a hundred others, all taken from their tribes. But that ship never landed at its destination. Instead, it was wrecked in a great storm, sent by Savaishe himself!' This drew more gasps. 'Makawenu fought to overthrow the slavers even as the ship sank, and retrieved his staff that he might use his magic to save the captives. Later, a handful of survivors were washed ashore in a far-off land. The ordeal brought Naekuru early into labour, and she gave birth to a son. Naekuru did not survive. Makawenu, heartbroken, took his infant child and struck out into that strange world. He became a wanderer, a beggar, knowing that the Time of Revelation was over, and that he could not return home. But he passed down all the knowledge of his tribe, of our ways and magic, to his son; and he to his son. And now I stand here, the last of the line, the one chosen to return home at the Opening of the Pathways.'

'Your words are as pretty as they are false. It was my ancestors who rebuilt our village, and made us strong after yours were defeated. It is I who am chosen. Look!' He held up his own staff. 'The Fragment of Sav'Eq-Tul. I carry it, as only the chosen one can. It has protected our people from dark magic since the earliest times.'

'It can do more than that,' Makeno said. 'My forefathers have wandered far and wide, and learned secrets that you could not imagine. I have seen drawings in great books, written by the wisest outsiders. Drawings of the fragment, and the other pieces that once made up the whole – a great bronze tablet, a disc of bronze forged here, on this island, by the Temple Priests who now guard the Halls of the Dead. It was broken into three by dark sorcery during a terrible battle between rival outsiders who searched for the Crystal Pool. One fragment was lost in the marshes, and found by Makawenu. The others were stolen away by the outsiders, because even in pieces, the power of the bronze Tablet of Sav'Eq-Tul was undeniable.'

'A fanciful tale,' Noaka spat. 'Even if this story is true, what difference does it make?'

'Because,' Makeno said, drawing himself up to his full height, 'if it were not my destiny to return here, and to reclaim my birthright, how could I have found this boy, and another of the fragments?'

Makeno held out his hand, and Dagomir passed to him Sam's amulet. Sam scowled – was any of this true? And if it were, why not just tell him from the start? His head swam. He had not been plucked from the streets of Yad-Sha'Rib at random. Dagomir had been there looking for him specifically. He must have been. He had been courting Makeno to join his crew, and Makeno's price was the amulet. Sam's amulet, given to him by his father.

'That's mine!' Sam said, unable to stop himself. He lunged forward, but Dagomir held him back.

'Not now, boy,' Dagomir hissed. 'Besides, you're better off without it.'

Sam felt anger rise within. Dagomir spoke the truth, he knew – without the amulet, had he not felt stronger every day? But the amulet was still his: a piece of his father's legacy. It was not Makeno's birthright, but Sam's.

Sam had been so caught up in his own frustrations that he had barely noticed what was happening around him. Some of the villagers had taken a knee before Makeno. Some were shouting angrily. Noaka glowered, and finally held up a hand.

'Have I not guided you well, my people?' he shouted. 'As my father did, and his father before him? We have grown strong. No one dares challenge us, and we remain content. This stranger wishes to usurp me! He wishes to return us to dark times, when we were ravaged by war.'

'No!' Makeno cried. 'I see what has happened here. We were once a great warrior nation, who looked outwards for our hunting lands. We traded with the plains tribes. We trekked the mountains, unearthing precious metals and magical crystals. You have closed off the Savaisal. You have reduced this tribe to prisoners in their own land, guarded by the dead, and you have done this out of fear.'

'You dare call me coward?' Noaka's guards lowered their spear-points to Makeno's chest.

'I do! I am not here to bring back dark times. I am here to remind these people what they have lost. I am here to restore the glory of the Savaisal – to bring us from the darkness, into the light.'

'You will do nothing. For it is I, Noaka, who am chief of the Savaisal, not Makeno. You will not leave here alive.' Noaka turned away, and waved to his guards, who made to seize Makeno.

'Wait!' Makeno roared at the top of his lungs, and his shout was met by a peal of thunder so loud it felt as though the entire village shook, and the distant mountains echoed it in reply. Every man, woman and child cowered, covering their heads with their hands as though Makeno's wrath might bring the sky down upon them. The guards took a few steps back, looking to Noaka for guidance. Noaka turned to face Makeno.

Makeno met the chief's gaze and said, 'You might not believe my claim to the throne of the Savaisal, but it is not your place to refuse a challenge from a storm-caller. If you still hold true to the old ways in this village, you will grant me the Test of Blood, and my heritage shall be in doubt no longer. If I lie, kill me. If I speak truth, you will accept my challenge. Is this not the law?'

Noaka looked uncertain. A man from the crowd called out, 'It is the law!' Another voice joined his, then another, until all were clamouring in several languages at once.

'Silence!' Noaka shouted, raising aloft his staff. And silence fell. He paused, visibly shaking with anger.

Finally, he growled, 'Bring forth the Ancient One.'

He said these words quietly, but they caused a sudden rush of industry and excitement. The drums sounded once more, and the masked dancers leapt out of the crowd and resumed their frenzied display. The warriors at the backs of Sam and the crew urged them onwards, towards the blazing bonfire. Ahead, six warrior-women, shaven-headed and adorned with armour made of interlinked bones, marched forward, leading a shuffling old woman into the village centre. The woman was clothed plainly in a black shawl, and was so short and wizened she resembled the shrunken heads Sam had seen back in the marshes. They called her the 'Ancient One', and Sam could well believe she had seen more than a hundred summers.

When Makeno reached the fire-pit, all the villagers fanned out, and then formed concentric rings around the bonfire. Those at the front knelt so those behind could see. Noaka stepped aside, and the warriors indicated that Sam and the others should do the same, so that Makeno stood alone before the Ancient One and her fierce-looking guards.

'Who is it that comes before me?' the old woman asked, her voice a papery rasp.

'My name is Makeno, son of Makutu. I am the last living descendant of Makawenu the Storm-Caller.'

The old woman chuckled. 'A storm-caller, indeed? My grandmother spoke to me of Makawenu, who was chief of our people when she was a girl. Yes, Makeno Storm-Caller, I am very old. It is my duty to remember the history of our people. For the Ancient Ones, the span of years is as nothing. You have his staff?'

'I do.' Makeno held it out to the old woman, who traced her gnarled, thin fingers along the carvings, squinting to decipher its many runes by firelight.

'Only those who have lived among our people could create such a staff. But Chief Noaka believes it to be stolen, yes?'

'I do, Ancient One,' Noaka said. 'And the punishment for such a deception is death.'

'That is not my concern,' the old woman croaked. 'All that matters to me is the truth, and in this case the truth is beyond even my memory. This man, Makeno, has features not unlike my grandmother's description of Chief Makawenu – but so have many others I have met over these long years. The staff is authentic, I am certain, but as you say, Noaka, if Makawenu Storm-Caller was taken prisoner by outsiders, it could have been stolen. He speaks our language, but a language can be learned, just as our forebears learned the trader's tongue. There is something more, however. A second Fragment of Sav'Eq-Tul.'

Makeno handed it to the woman, who chuckled throatily once more.

'One of the fragments, long thought lost to the world of men. How came you by this?'

'Among the secrets passed to me by my father was the power of attunement, the harnessing of the great elemental song that is carried upon the four winds. The Tablet of Sav'Eq-Tul resonates with a song of its own, which can be heard only when the paths to these islands are open. When the paths are closed, the tablet lies dormant, and when it is dormant, it is anathema to magic. It hides, with a will of its own, and no sorcery can find it. But when the paths open – when the tablet is attuned to the song of the Lost Isles, it calls to those who know how to listen – those whose destiny lies here. People like me, and this boy. He is what the outsiders call a "Heritor". His ancestor was here, on this very island, perhaps in this very spot where we now stand. His ancestor drank from the Crystal Pool, and passed his powers through his bloodline, as my ancestors passed theirs through mine. My search for the fragment took me to a great golden city – a city of tyrants – where this poor boy lived, his power hidden from his enemies by the fragment given him by his father. It cannot be pure chance that my search for the fragment also led me to this boy; that when the Lost Isles called him across the sea, he provided the means for my return. The great song of the heavens, sung by Savaishe, brought us together, and I am certain the gods have not finished with us yet.'

Sam stood open-mouthed. If all of this was true, it changed much. Why had no one told him sooner?

The old woman nodded sagely. 'You would appear to speak wisdom, Makeno Storm-Caller. But if you know all of these things about our people, then you must also know our laws. Words alone are not proof of your heritage. Do you submit freely to the Test of Blood?'

'I do.'

'Then hold out your hand.'

Makeno did as he was bid, and a deathly hush descended on the village.

The guard to the Ancient One's left handed her a small, polished stone. The guard to her immediate right handed her a dagger. Without further ado, the Ancient One drew the dagger across Makeno's palm, and pressed the stone into his bleeding hand.

'Squeeze it tight,' she said, 'and cast it into the fire.'

Makeno held up his hand so the crowd could see, bunching his fist around the stone. Blood dripped from his hand. Without a word, he threw the stone into the heart of the fire.

Nothing happened. Noaka, standing near to Sam, breathed a sigh. His relief was short-lived.

The bonfire crackled and hissed. Sparks flew, dancing into the night sky like fireflies. The fire-logs popped and fizzed faster and louder. The air was filled with shining yellow sparks, increasing in number, swirling upwards into a spiralling funnel, before arcing back around on themselves, forming a circle of fire in the air. The bonfire flared for a moment, the flames rushing upwards, taking on a green hue that caused those at the front of the congregation to shuffle backwards in fear. The fire calmed, the flames returned to their normal colour, and the sparks dissipated.

'The gods have spoken,' the Ancient One said, her voice sounding now stronger. 'Makeno Storm-Caller has returned home. His line was broken, but he is heir to the throne of our people.'

'He is not!' Noaka said angrily. 'As Ancient One, you must know the law. I, too, am from a line of shamans. My forebears have sat upon the throne while these "storm-callers" have been in exile. I do not have to give it up now, and I defy anyone here to challenge me.'

'None can challenge you, Chief Noaka,' said the Ancient One. And then her wrinkled lips curled into a smile. 'Except for Makeno.'

Noaka turned to Makeno, his eyes full of venom. 'And do you, Makeno? Do you, a stranger to our land, seek to challenge me?'

For once, Makeno looked unsure of himself. He looked to Dagomir and the others, then around at the villagers, who waited on his words with bated breath. He appeared exhausted. His eyes bore the weight of the world. In that moment Makeno truly did look kingly.

At last, with a deep breath, he said, 'I do. I challenge you for the right to rule the Savaisal.'

Noaka snarled, and stalked away to his hut, his warriors scurrying after him. The drums began. Villagers rushed forward to paw at Makeno and speak with him. Children came to gawp at Dagomir, with his pale skin and golden hair. Women surrounded Yana Selishe, offering her beaded necklaces and flowers.

Makeno struggled to re-join his friends, and when he did he said, 'The duel is set for moonrise tomorrow. Captain Dagomir, I would give you this for safekeeping.' He handed the amulet to Dagomir, who immediately hung it about it his neck, and tucked it beneath his tunic. Makeno must have seen the look Sam gave him, because his tone softened immeasurably. 'I am grateful to you all for what you have done – especially you, Samir. More than you could know. I will explain more tomorrow, but for now you should rest – if you can. These people have not seen this much excitement for a long time, and they will make festivities all the night through. But I have explained that we are weary, and these good folk here will show you to a hut where you might try to sleep.'

Sam wanted to ask Makeno more, but the warden had already turned back to the throng, where he tiredly and patiently answered the many questions of the villagers. His people, Sam reminded himself. He could not deny Makeno this reunion, several lifetimes in the making, and so he followed the others to a small hut on the edge of the village, the sound of drums pounding in his ears.

CHAPTER 15

'Why didn't you tell me?' Sam demanded.

'Tell you what?' Dagomir replied, stretching out and yawning.

'That you only chose me because of the amulet? That you planned to steal it from me all along?'

'Go to sleep, lad.' Dagomir rolled over on his pile of hides. Bardo, Yana and Emilio were already fast asleep on the floor of the hut, or at least making a show of sleeping. It wasn't easy with the chanting and drumming outside.

'How can I sleep?' Sam looked to Hassan, who appeared to have no such difficulty drifting off. 'Look at what's become of my friend. And for all I know my mother is in Zhar-Mharrad's dungeons back home. *And* it is all your fault.'

Dagomir sat up. 'My fault?' he hissed. 'Were you not pining for adventure? Were you not already looking for a way to the Lost Isles? I needed a Heritor, and you needed a ship. It seems we have benefited mutually.'

'Benefited? Many have died to get us here, wherever "here" is. And if it were not for my amulet, you'd never have brought me along.'

'So you're saying I owe you a debt? I think not, boy. Freeing you of that amulet was the best thing I could have

done. If you truly want to fight Zhar-Mharrad, and free
your city, and be the hero, you need to be rid of that cursed
amulet. Cast off the shackles of your old life, and look to
the future.'

'My father…'

'Your father!' Dagomir spat. 'Let me tell you something,
lad: fathers don't always deserve the adulation of their sons.
Mine was a hero, too. His heroism got him killed, and me
exiled. Everything I have now, I have through my own
toil.'

'And what do you have?' Sam asked. 'A pirate prince
without a ship? Without a crew?' He regretted it at once.

Dagomir's eyes flashed with anger, then sorrow. 'You
understand nothing of life,' he said.

'I understand that Zhar-Mharrad will stop at nothing
to find us, and kill us,' Sam said. 'Do we tell the Savaisal
that we have brought terrible danger upon them?'

'To hear Makeno speak, the Savaisal can look after
themselves, as must we all. Besides, that's between them
and Makeno – it's not our place to interfere.'

Sam thought about this. 'What if Makeno loses
tomorrow? What happens to us?'

Dagomir shrugged. 'Better to think about what
happens when he wins. This is Makeno's plan, lad. When
he becomes chief of this tribe, we not only have a powerful
ally on our side, but he can restore two pieces of the tablet.'

Sam frowned. 'And?'

'Makeno searched far and wide for your amulet. His
journey brought him to Yad-Sha'Rib, and to you. He hopes
that the third piece is somewhere on the island, and that he

can persuade his people to help find it. The completed tablet holds a clue to the location of the Crystal Pool. That's why the first explorers fought over it; it provides one of the few ways to find the pool again. They all wanted to pass that knowledge down to their progeny – their "Heritors" – so that their line would be the most influential the next time the Lost Isles appeared. Maybe your ancestors took that fragment fair and square. Maybe they stole it, or killed for it. Who knows? Who cares? They're long gone now. But if the fragments can be combined, we will have the greatest treasure on this archipelago. That was my price for helping Makeno. And that is the prize that you will share.'

'So… it was all a bargain? I help you get here; you steal my amulet for Makeno; Makeno restores the tablet and gives it to you… and then you drink from the pool.'

'*We* drink from the pool. I don't know what it'll do for me, but based on the legends it'll be doubly powerful for you. You can go home with the keys to the kingdom. The power to destroy Zhar-Mharrad, free the slaves, become king… whatever you can dream. And I can be the greatest pirate who ever lived.'

'You won't go home? To restore your own kingdom?'

'There's nothing for me in that frozen wasteland,' Dagomir said, bitterly. He paused, and looked as though he might say something more, but stopped. Finally he said, 'It'll be light soon. Get some sleep.' He turned over once more, and that was the end of it.

* * *

Yana kept her eyes closed, and her breathing rhythmic, pretending to be asleep as Sam and Dagomir argued. They thought the tablet would guide them to the Crystal Pool ahead of Zhar-Mharrad. What they didn't know was that Zhar-Mharrad had the other fragment, and shared the same goal. Part of her wanted to warn Dagomir. But if they realised just how dangerous acquiring the third piece would be, they might well give up – and that wouldn't serve her purpose at all…

Sam could not sleep, as Dagomir had instructed. How could he? Fatigued as he was, his thoughts buzzed around his head like angry hornets about a disturbed nest. The noise outside had quietened a little. Even some of the drummers had stopped playing.

Sam waited until Dagomir had begun snoring, looked about to be sure no one else was awake, and slipped from the hut. Two guards stood nearby, doubtless sent to keep an eye on the visitors, but they leant torpidly on their spears, gazing towards the dying bonfire. A few revellers still danced and sang around the fire, but it seemed that many of the villagers had succumbed to the lateness of the hour and taken to their huts. Avoiding the guards, Sam crept around to the far side of the tent, and stole away into the night, circumventing the huts as best he could. He wondered if it was safe to walk about the village alone, especially with the incumbent chief being so openly hostile to their presence. That was not a comforting thought, and rather than feeling as though he were an honoured guest taking a late night stroll, Sam suddenly felt like a fugitive. He cast his eyes about furtively, and moved as quietly as possible, hoping that none of the Savaisal would spot him.

Sam was surprised at the extent of the village. It stretched back away from the stream, and beyond the tree-huts. He picked his way carefully through the undergrowth, freezing every time he heard a strange noise from the trees, or thought he saw the shadow of a tribesman move on the walkways overhead. He skirted past boundary-markers strung with carved bones, until the sounds of the dwindling revelry could barely be heard at all. Sam saw ahead another small clearing, in which torches burned weakly atop large stakes. As he drew near the treeline, he heard voices. Cautiously, Sam moved forward, and peered through the bushes.

Two boys, no older than Sam, were arguing in the Savaisal tongue. Beside them was a large, dark pit, covered in a lattice of thick wooden poles, bound together with rope and staked to the ground. One boy pointed to the pit, and jabbed the other boy in the ribs. The second boy looked uncertain, but then stooped to pick up a long stick from the ground. The first boy laughed as the second thrust the stick down into the pit three times, the third jab prompting a rumbling, mournful wail, like that of a wounded beast. He jabbed a fourth time, and this time there came a roar, which to Sam's ears sounded almost human. So abrupt and full of menace was the sound, that the boy dropped the stick and ran towards the village, his friend doubling over with laughter. When the boy stopped laughing, he looked around the clearing, and his face became less certain, as though he had only just realised he was all alone.

The thing in the pit snorted. The boy backed away, then turned, and ran.

Sam waited a while, until there was no sound at all but for the chirrups of crickets in the undergrowth, and only then did he creep into the clearing. He scoured every shadow for signs of guards, but saw no one. Maybe the thing in the pit didn't require guarding. But those boys had known they should not be here – Sam knew that look about them from personal experience. Maybe the guards had joined the festivities and had too much to drink. Did the Savaisal drink alcohol? Sam had never known a warrior who didn't.

He could not contain his morbid curiosity. He picked up one of the torches on its long pole, and walked very slowly to the edge of the pit. He leaned over cautiously, but saw nothing but darkness. He took a deep breath, and then held out the torch, moving it closer to the mouth of the pit. This elicited a low, wearisome groan, and Sam saw something move. A gigantic, lolling head. Pale, wrinkled skin. Something malformed and monstrous in proportion, and yet not entirely a beast.

He almost dropped the torch in surprise, and took several steps back. When no further noise came from the pit, he tightened his grip on the torch and stepped forward again, muttering to himself, 'What are you doing, Samir? Why do you put yourself in this position time and time again, Samir?'

He looked again, lowering the torch just a little further. And this time the creature in the pit looked back up at him, with small round eyes set within that massive skull. Sam was staring at what first appeared to be some kind of elephant, but now he knew it could not be. It had a trunk, large tusks – although one was broken – and huge ears that flapped feebly. But that elephantine head was supported by the body of a man, albeit a massively tall and broad one. Large manacles were locked about its wrists, with long chains fastened to rusting iron rings in the floor. Its stubby legs ended in broad, elephant-like feet. The eyes still beheld him, and behind those eyes was a keen intelligence. Sam felt it.

Heritor.

Sam gasped. The word came from the creature, he was sure, but it had not spoken. Instead, it had entered his head, a thought transferred from one mind to another.

'What *are* you?' Sam asked.

I am Ashtzaph, of the Erithereans. I need not ask who you are, Samir Lahij. Your coming was foreseen, and your thoughts are as a gate unbarred and unguarded.

'Foretold…' Sam shuddered. 'How… can you speak to me so?'

It is a gift of my people, to use if we so choose, on those with the wit to listen. You should not be seen with me, young Heritor. If you are caught treating with Noaka's prize, the consequences will be severe.

'Chief Noaka? Why has he imprisoned you? Are you… dangerous?'

Of course I am dangerous. That is why I am shackled by enchanted iron. Noaka believes he can sacrifice me to his gods, and through this ritual gain some of my power for himself.

'And… can he?'

Perhaps. He is a fool, but a powerful fool.

Sam thought about that. Powerful? Did Makeno know what he was letting himself in for?

Who is Makeno? Ashtzaph's voice vibrated in Sam's head.

Sam frowned. The sensation of receiving the creature's thoughts made his skull ache. 'He is a friend; I think. His great, great, great — something-or-other — grandfather was chief of the tribe once. He's challenging Noaka for leadership at tomorrow's moonrise.'

Ah, a descendant of Makawenu. I knew him, in my youth. I can only hope that, if your friend wins, he is more just than Noaka, and honours the old ways like his more illustrious forefather.

'Old ways?'

The Savaisal and the Erithereans have long lived in peace. Few of my kind have cause to venture into these lands, and it has been perhaps a century since we last did. In that time, things, it would appear, have changed. Not expecting hostility, I blundered into a trap, and now I wait here to die. Noaka is a cruel man... he will not make it an easy death.

'Makeno is a good man,' Sam said, setting aside his bitterness over Makeno and Dagomir's secrecy. 'He will set you free.'

Perhaps. Or perhaps Noaka shall kill your friend, and nothing will change.

Sam looked about the clearing. There was still no sign of any guards. He looked at the cage-like construction that covered the pit, and the stakes that pegged it deep into the ground. He looked again at the chains that bound the creature. He had no real reason to trust the Eritherean, but something made him feel a deep obligation to help it. He shook his head. For all he knew, the Eritherean could be manipulating his thoughts as easily as it entered them to speak.

You are clever, young Heritor, it thought. *No, I am not bending your actions to my own will. It is not our way. If you trust me, it is because you are guided by the spirits of your ancestors, who themselves traded with the Erithereans long ago, during what the Savaisal call the Time of Revelation. You know me not, but your blood does.*

'A lot is said of my blood,' Samir said. 'And it's brought me naught but trouble.'

That is because you do not understand the extent of your ability. And you do not realise that a Heritor's power can grow, and change, throughout his lifetime. There is more in you than cat-like agility and swift perception, young Heritor. I could teach you, were I not a prisoner.

Sam narrowed his eyes. Again he wondered if this was a trick – whether this offer was some means by which to tempt him – but again the sad nobility in the eyes of Ashtzaph seemed anything but duplicitous.

'I would set you free,' Sam said. 'But I would need something to prise this cage open, and something to unlock your manacles. I… I don't know what to do.'

You do not have to do anything. I can accept whatever fate the gods have in store for me. If you are discovered even talking to me, your friend Makeno will be unable to help you. You are breaking one of Noaka's laws, and Noaka is still chief.

Something flared within Sam's breast, some spark of defiance, of rebellion. 'No,' he said. 'Maybe I don't understand anything, but I am a Heritor, aren't I? Maybe it's time I started acting like one. The very reason I came to the Lost Isles was to find a way to free my people from an evil sorcerer. He keeps people enslaved, too. Only his prisoners are Heritors. If I do not succeed in my quest, I'll be in a pit like this, waiting for my end to come – do you understand? If my being here is fate, and if it means anything it all, then I shall help you; because if I cannot fight tyranny here, on this small island, then what hope do I have of defeating Zhar-Mharrad back home?'

Ashtzaph raised his trunk somewhat weakly. Was that a wan smile on his face? It was hard to tell.

'I shall return before moonrise, when Noaka and Makeno meet for their challenge.'

Very well. Thank you, young Heritor. Your kindness shall not be forgotten.

'Don't thank me yet. Wait! Someone's coming. I'll be back, I promise.'

Sam retreated back to the undergrowth quickly. He picked his way through the bushes, circling back towards his hut, already formulating his plan to rescue the strange prisoner.

* * *

Yana Selishe entered the clearing as Sam hurried away. There were two guards on their way, and so she'd made a little more noise than usual to give Sam a head-start. Still, she had to see what the boy had been up to.

She peered over the edge of the pit, and almost retreated when a great, elephantine head lolled back, and two bestial

eyes looked up at her. But they were eyes full of keen
intelligence. The creature made no sound, but moved its
huge hands slightly, so that Yana saw a pair of weighty
manacles at its wrists.

'Interesting...' she muttered.

She heard the two guards approach, and slipped from
the clearing like a shadow. From a safe distance, she saw
two Savaisal, with spears and tall shields, shuffle into the
clearing. One of them stretched and yawned, the other
took up position leaning against a tree by the pit, making
some show of guarding the prisoner despite his dereliction
of duty.

There was no more time to linger – Yana needed to get
back to the hut before Sam. Besides, now she really did
need some sleep.

CHAPTER 16

When morning came, Sam regretted his decision to explore rather than sleep. He had woken sluggishly, to find the hut empty save for Hassan, who sat cross-legged against a mud wall, staring into space.

'Hassan?'

There was at first no reply from Sam's friend. Then Hassan blinked, shook his head quickly from side to side, and offered Sam a weak smile.

Dagomir entered the hut before Sam could question his friend. The captain carried an armful of large, yellow fruits, one of which he threw to Sam.

'Breakfast,' he said, as Sam caught it. 'And one for you, Hassan.'

Hassan made no attempt to move, or even acknowledge Dagomir's charity.

The captain sighed. 'Still talkative as ever.' He placed the fruits on the floor. 'Look at this!' he beamed, pointing to his left arm, which was wrapped about with rags. 'The Savaisal treated my wound with some foul-smelling poultice. I had my doubts, but it already feels good as new. We need to get some of that stuff before we leave.'

'And when will that be?' Sam asked, through a mouthful of pulpy fruit.

'When Makeno wins his challenge. Then he'll give you your amulet back, and send some of his people with us as guides. We could have a small army at our disposal.'

'And what if he doesn't win?'

'Ah. Then we'd best leave sooner than planned, unless we want our shrunken heads hanging from the trees. Enough of this – eat up and come along. This place isn't so bad in daylight.'

'What about Hassan?' Sam asked, nodding to his friend.

Dagomir waved away the question. 'Let him stay and stare at the walls if he likes,' he said, and ducked out of the hut.

Things were very much changed in the village by day. It was a riot of colour, with flowers and feathers and painted banners adorning every hut. Every man, woman and child seemed to have a job in preparations for what was to come that night. The fire-pit was stacked high with wood, hunters mounted expeditions into the jungle to bring game for the night's feast. Past the bonfire in the village centre, near the western treeline, a good many young men prepared the arena for the so-called Trial of Champions, under the stern eye of the Ancient One. This involved a shallow trench being dug to mark the perimeter of a large circle. Strange powders were sprinkled into the trench, which Sam was told were to protect the onlookers from stray magic. Outside the trench, thick stakes were hammered into the ground, and ropes were stretched taut between them, forming a barrier between combatants and spectators. It seemed to Sam that some things were the same the world over – the stage was a little larger, and the setting more exotic, but it felt a lot like the wrestling arenas of Yad-Sha'Rib, on which nobles would bet vast sums of gold darics.

Sam was surprised to discover that the Savaisal were traders, too. Other tribespeople came from far afield throughout the day – bringing livestock, dyes, beaded fabric, fruit and seeds. Many of the new arrivals did not speak the language of the outsiders, but it had been explained to Makeno that the Savaisal maintained homesteads and smaller camps throughout their vast territory, who would bring their goods to exchange with the main tribe. Needless to say, many of the visitors hurried back to tell their people that a Trial of Champions was imminent.

Sam spent some time in the afternoon trying to coax Hassan out of his shell, but it proved somewhat fruitless. He managed to prompt yes or no answers to simple questions – whether he was hungry or thirsty, whether he needed some shade, or would like to see the preparations for the trial – but any mention of Zhar-Mharrad, the sea voyage, or even the Golden City paralysed Hassan once more. Eventually, Sam felt it a small mercy when his friend curled up to doze once more. Besides, Sam knew he had more immediate worries.

He began to gather things in secret, in preparation for the night's other business – the rescue of Ashtzaph. He would use all of his thieves' guile, loitering, making conversation, distracting. When the time was right, he would steal what he needed, and bring it back to the hut where he'd hidden a sack of supplies around the back, amidst a log-pile. A hatchet, a knife, some rope, and an armful of fruit for Ashtzaph's journey had seemed like a good start. He still wondered if he'd be able to break the Eritherean's chains. There must be a key to the manacles somewhere, but Sam didn't know where to look, and in broad daylight he found it hard to go anywhere in the settlement without attracting attention.

'Whatever you're planning, I'd advise against it.' Yana's voice startled Sam from his ponderings.

'Planning?' he laughed, too breezily.

'Given your thieving today, I'd say you intend to either run away, or help someone else run away. The former would be foolish. The latter would be… dangerously foolish.'

Sam jumped up, feigning indignation. 'Thieving? I never…'

He stopped. Yana's stern glare incredulous. It was like she was looking into his soul and examining the extent of his guilt.

'Samir, I have spent my entire life hunting fugitives, assassins, even magi. I have interrogated the most hardened criminals, and I always get results. But…' she sighed. 'I am not your mother. I am not here to tell you what you can and can't do. Just remember that we are strangers in a strange land, and if you were to upset the wrong person – say, by taking from them something that they prize – who knows what trouble you might bring on yourself. And us.'

Sam tried to think of something clever to say, but he felt sure that, somehow, Yana Selishe had discerned his intentions.

'You're right,' Sam said at last. Yana visibly relaxed, until Sam added, 'You're not my mother.' With that, he turned from her, and marched away, hoping that his plans would not be undone by the infernal woman.

* * *

The sky blushed pink in the west as the sun sank beneath the vast expanse of jungle. As the light faded, the mood in the village palpably changed. The bonfire was stacked high; torches were lit; warriors emerged from their huts in full ceremonial garb, their faces painted, headdresses of scarlet feathers donned, shields painted. Sam's pulse quickened. He felt like the air was thick with anticipation, and he had his own reason to be nervous.

Sam wanted to speak to Makeno, to offer some words of support, but the warden was surrounded by attendants, supporters and detractors, all vying for his attention. Instead, he stood beside Emilio, who watched the activity in the village with some bemusement.

'When does the challenge actually begin?' Sam asked.

Emilio pointed to a mountaintop to the north-east. 'When the moon is level with that summit, the Ancient One starts the proceedings,' Emilio said. 'Or so I was told. I received the impression that there will be much talking and posturing before any actual fighting is done.'

'I thought that was how you preferred it?' Yana Selishe said, arriving stealthily behind them.

Emilio shot her an annoyed glance. 'A little showmanship never hurt anyone,' he said. 'But in a duel, too much talk can get you killed.'

Sam looked to the mountain. The moon was already rising, and the sky darkening.

'I... um... have to check on Hassan,' Sam said, needing an excuse to leave.

'Stay, boy,' said Emilio, perhaps not wishing to be left alone with Yana. 'Your friend is in a world of his own.'

Sam shrugged, and retreated, under the reproachful stare of Yana Selishe. He felt her eyes burning into him even as the crowd gathered, and he did his best to push through the villagers and get out of sight.

By the time he reached his hut, Sam was riddled with guilt. Not at defying Yana – if anything disobeying her still gave him a small thrill. No; it was more that he wanted to lend his support to Makeno. By helping Ashtzaph, there was every chance he'd miss the challenge, and if Makeno were to lose... there seemed little point in returning.

He entered the hut, finding Hassan asleep, and no one else around. He gathered up the items he'd spent all day collecting, and heaved them onto his back. He grabbed Bardo's trusty billhook, in case he had to rely on brute force to break the Eritherean's chains. Sam took a last look at Hassan. How he longed to have his friend back to his old self – to bring him along on this adventure. But this was not the Hassan he had thought left behind in Yad-Sha'Rib. This was a ghost of his old friend, weak and withdrawn. Sam could only hope that he would recover. He thought again of the consequences of Makeno failing the trial. If that happened, Sam would do whatever it took to lead Hassan from the village of the Savaisal, and together perhaps they would brave the island. Just the two of them against all odds, like it used to be.

A gaggle of villagers tramped past the hut, and Sam waited for their voices to fade away entirely before he crept outside. The shadows had already lengthened, the moon rising quickly towards the pinnacle of the distant mountain. Checking the coast was clear perhaps more times than was necessary, Sam stole away to the treeline once more, only this time laden down with supplies.

Sam retraced his steps from the previous night as best he could, taking a circuitous route around the perimeter of the Savaisal territory, until he recognised at last the edge of the clearing where Ashtzaph was held. Above, Sam could make out the outlines of high-up walkways and guard platforms, which he had not seen the previous night in the darkness. He thanked his lucky stars that they had been abandoned, and now was extra careful, scouring the trees as well as the undergrowth for any sign of movement. As he neared the clearing, he heard a shout nearby, and saw it answered by a guard, who ran across the clearing, hastily affixing his headdress. He dropped his shield and almost tripped over it, picking it up clumsily and running off to the path on the far side of the clearing, from where another man beckoned him. Both of them vanished in the direction of the village centre, leaving the clearing quiet and dark. Sam had no idea whether the Savaisal were always so lax in their guard duty, or whether it was simply Makeno's arrival that had caused such sloppiness. Perhaps Noaka, for all his supposed strength, was a poor leader. Sam hoped for Makeno's sake he was also a poor sorcerer.

The clearing was dark, being shrouded from moonlight and the setting sun by tall trees. Sam scurried to the edge of the pit, and whispered into the gloom, 'Ashtzaph. Are you there?'

I am here. The voice penetrated Sam's thoughts, though the words were faint and hollow, like an echo.

'Is something wrong?'

I am... weak. Noaka has taken of my blood today, to... aid him in... battle.

'Oh no...' Sam muttered. 'Will it help him win?'

No. He is a fool. His beliefs are... misplaced. Only the... gods... can decide his fate. And that... of your friend.

'Are you strong enough to escape, if I help you?' Sam asked, not relishing the thought of trying to lift the hulking creature from the pit.

I will... try.

That would have to do. Sam fumbled in his sack, taking out a ship's hatchet, and set about quickly chopping the thick ropes that tied the trapdoor to four deep stakes. They were unforgiving, and took more effort than he'd expected, but eventually they were all loose. Sam heaved at the trapdoor, and found it was heavy indeed – it would have to be to guard against a creature the size of the Eritherean. It was not hinged, and must have needed four men to lift and carry it into position. He pushed the billhook underneath it, and levered it with all his strength, managing to move it perhaps half a yard before he began puffing and panting with the exertion. Realising this method would take him all night, Sam examined the latticed construction of the trapdoor. The thick wooden poles were bent in on each other so that they were interwoven, and then tied with thin ropes. It wouldn't be easy to dismantle, even if he cut all the ropes, but Sam thought he could at least remove a few of the poles and make the whole thing lighter.

He reached into the sack again, and this time pulled out a short-bladed cutlass, which the men – the now-deceased men, Sam reminded himself – had used to clear a path through the jungle. With that sombre thought, he began to hack and saw at the ropes, managing eventually to remove one of the poles, although it sprang back into shape so violently when the tension released that it almost took his eye out.

Sam levered the trapdoor a little further, now drenched with sweat. Back in the village, the drums began to pound again. Was that the start of the trial? Or was it merely the opening of the prolonged festivities, like Emilio had suggested? He looked at the trapdoor ruefully. He'd never be able to move it in time.

Can you… climb down? Ashtzaph's voice came into Sam's thoughts. *If you can free me… I can… do the rest.*

'Yes,' Sam said. 'I think I can fit through the gap. Hold on.'

Sam emptied the sack onto the grass. He took up a coil of ropes and tied one end to one of the wooden stakes in the ground, and cast the other end into the pit. He took up two small knives with which he hoped to prise open Ashtzaph's manacles, and tucked them into his boot. He hung the hatchet from his belt, and squeezed through the gap he'd made in the trapdoor, climbing down into the pit.

It was almost too dark to see the Eritherean, but as Sam's eyes adjusted, he found himself face to face with the creature. He felt suddenly afraid – Ashtzaph was even bigger than he'd looked from above. Though he was hunched and huddled upon the dirt floor of the pit, he was perhaps fifteen feet tall, his head alone as broad as the barrel-chested Bardo. His one intact tusk was almost as long and thick as Sam's arm, coming to a point that could easily impale a man.

'Do not be afraid,' Ashtzaph said.

Sam flinched at the sound, so surprised was he that Ashtzaph used his real voice instead of his strange mental powers. The voice was low and rumpling, quiet and pained.

'Yes, I can speak, when I wish. Listen to me, young Heritor: I will not hurt you. You are the only human to show me any kindness at all for several moons. But I am weak – these manacles are made of ensorcelled iron, created by an ancient race of men who once ruled this province a millennium ago. Men who were enemies of the Erithereans.'

'These are the same men who now haunt the Halls of the Dead?' Sam asked, remembering too well the grotesque, rotting corpses who had driven off the Bidajah in the marshes.

'You have seen much for one so young. I sense you have seen… much death, too.'

Sam nodded.

'These manacles,' Ashtzaph went on. 'They rob me of my strength, and my magic. If they were ordinary shackles I would have broken free myself.'

Sam took out his knives. 'I can try to pick the locks, but… well, I'm not very good at it. I'll do my best.'

'I can ask no more than that.'

Sam poked the blades into the first keyhole, feeling about for the mechanism. He'd done this once or twice before, though never with much success. But he had no way of knowing who had the keys to the manacles, and no one he could trust to help. And so he poked and pried with the knives, until finally he felt something move. A tumbler, perhaps? He slid the second knife in, wiggling it gently until he heard a faint click. The manacles remained resolutely locked. Ashtzaph let out a small sigh. Sam pretended not to notice, and tried again. This time he felt the blade of his knife bend, and there came a bright, metallic ping. The knife popped out of the manacle, as did its point. Sam examined the broken blade, face reddening.

He looked about the pit, and caught sight of the chains embedded into blocks of stone set into the walls.

'They look a bit rusty,' Sam said, hopefully. 'Maybe if I climb up and get the billhook, I can prise them loose…'

'With the manacles fastened, I will still be too weak to climb out,' Ashtzaph said. His voice was surprisingly free of judgement, though Sam felt his attempts at a rescue were doomed to fail.

'Well, it's a start,' Sam argued. He grabbed the rope and made to climb up, but froze.

Above him, staring down into the pit, was a Savaisal guard. The same man he'd seen running from the clearing just minutes earlier. They stared at each other in disbelief for a moment, and then the man shouted something in a language Sam couldn't understand, took his spear, and made to jab it downwards into the pit.

A shadow passed over the mouth of the pit. There came a dull thud. The guard grunted, and fell to the ground, out of sight. A figure in black peered down into the pit, and by moonlight Yana Selishe pulled down her mask to reveal her face.

'Having trouble?' she asked.

Sam breathed a sigh of relief. 'I suppose you've come to stop me,' he said.

'Samir… If you must disobey every instruction you're given, at least come better prepared.'

The woman squeezed through the gap that Sam had made in the trapdoor, and climbed nimbly into the pit. 'You've been sweating,' she said. 'You smell like a camel.'

Sam sniffed at himself, frowning.

The Eritherean looked at the woman knowingly, saying nothing. Or was he communicating with her as he had with Sam?

'You're unusual, I'll give you that,' Yana Selishe said to Ashtzaph. 'Sam seems to trusts you though, so I'll do the same. I'm going to set you free, and I'll thank you not to kill us when I'm done.'

Ashtzaph nodded his great head.

'These manacles are enchanted,' Sam said. 'They make him weak. But I can't get them off. Maybe the locks are magical.'

'It doesn't matter, if you have the key,' Yana said, taking a large iron key from her pocket.

'How?'

'I slipped into Chief Noaka's hut when he left for the trial. I guessed if the prisoner was so important, Noaka would trust no one else with the key. You forget that I have dealt with worse than him.'

'Makeno…' Sam hissed. The mention of Noaka brought home the guilt he felt about missing Makeno's trial of magic.

'Don't worry – Emilio was right. There is much ceremony to go before the combat begins. Now, let's release your friend and get out of here before more guards notice the mess you made up there.'

Ashtzaph held up his manacles for Yana. The woman unlocked them, and they fell to the ground. Ashtzaph tried to stand, and at first looked as though he might collapse with the effort. Yana stepped out of the way in case he crushed her. Presently, however, the Eritherean straightened, pressing his massive hands to the wall to steady himself.

'Thank you, Yana Selishe, and you, Samir Lahij. Already I feel some of my old strength returning. Aye, and anger, too! My kind are not used to such treatment, and used less to letting such an insult go unpunished.'

Ashtzaph's voice was much stronger now, and his tone much changed. Sam wondered if he had made a mistake. What if the Erithereans were a war-like race, and in freeing Ashtzaph he and Yana had merely paved the way for bloodshed.

Perhaps reading Sam's thoughts again, Ashtzaph fixed him with a look of steel and, more so, empathy. 'Fear not, young Heritor. My powers are returning. I have something in the way of foresight, and I see that Noaka will not wait long for his comeuppance – and it shall not be at my hand. His end will come soon enough.'

'So… Makeno will kill him?' Sam asked.

'No, Samir Lahij. But Noaka shall die all the same. Come now, let us delay no longer. I have spent too long in this pit!'

Ashtzaph turned, grabbed Sam's rope with one hand, and kicked one massive foot into the soft wall of the pit. With one mighty pull on the rope, and a push with his powerful legs, he was at the opening. He shoved it aside as though it weighed nothing, and heaved himself up and over into the clearing. Sam followed, and Ashtzaph held out a rough, grey hand to help him up. Yana came next, though she refused assistance.

By moonlight, Sam saw the Eritherean fully. With great pity he saw that Ashtzaph was covered in scars – he had seen the whip more than once.

'Yes,' Ashtzaph said, answering a question unasked. 'I have been treated to the greatest ignominy. But no more.'

Yana looked to the unconscious guard. 'He didn't see me. If it's all the same to you, if they come for Samir I shall tell them that you bewitched him, and used your powers to strike the guard unconscious.'

'I will happily shoulder the blame. The Savaisal can do nothing more to me.'

'Where will you go?' Sam asked.

'We Erithereans are a solitary people, but now I desire more than anything to be amongst my own kind. I will go south, to our old hunting grounds, and seek them out. But first, I will help you, Samir Lahij. I shall give you a gift that would otherwise be years in the earning, but which you will need more than you can know in the days to come.'

Sam frowned in puzzlement. 'What gift? And how do you know what…?'

Ashtzaph reached out with a gigantic, three-fingered hand, and rested it gently on Sam's head. Sam felt the fingers close around the back of his skull. From the corner of his eye he thought he saw Yana Selishe move a hand to the hilt of her scimitar, and perhaps with good reason – if he so desired, Ashtzaph could have snapped Sam's neck like a twig.

Open your mind to me, Ashtzaph said in Sam's head. *Let me in, that I might see your very soul. There is power within you, Heritor – power that remains locked away. Who knows what form it might take?*

Sam felt the strangest sensation. His vision swam and his head clouded. The sounds of distant drums and jungle creatures faded away to nothing. The ever-present heat and the smell of fetid earth were no more. He felt as though he were floating.

All around him, dark water. Above, light danced on its surface. Shadowy figures peered down at him, refracted on the rippling pool. He reached up slowly. His hand shone. A white light glowed beneath his skin. He breathed out, sending bubbles cascading upwards. He thought he might drown. But here, in this place, that didn't seem so bad.

He realised he was not alone. There was a creature here, floating in the dark water beside him. Sam thought he had known it once. Ashtzaph? Was this its name? It reached out to him, and he touched his glowing fingers to its wrinkled flesh.

Everything went white. Sam was wracked with pain. Every vein in his body burned, like his blood was boiling. He thought lava might ooze from his pores. He thought he might boil away the Crystal Pool to nothing, and lose it forever.

He screamed.

'Samir. Sam!' Someone shook him hard.

Sam opened his eyes. He was lying in thick undergrowth. He was back in the jungle. But he must have been dragged from the clearing. Yana Selishe was bent over him, her hands on his shoulders, and where she touched him his skin burned. He grunted in pain. He felt as though he had a million needles sticking in his flesh.

'Samir, snap out of it. You'll bring every guard in the village.' Yana looked to a large, shadowy figure that stood behind her. Ashtzaph. 'What have you done to him?' she snarled.

'I do not know, not yet,' Ashtzaph said, his voice like an earthquake. 'He stepped forward into the moonlight, brushing Yana aside and lifting Sam gently from the ground. 'You have experienced the Blood Burn, or at least a form of it,' he said to Sam. 'It will pass quickly. As I told you before, Samir Lahij, you have abilities beyond those you know. I have merely delved into your future, and unlocked its secrets.'

'But… what secrets are they?' Sam asked.

Ashtzaph set Sam on his own two feet. 'That is for you to discover. When you need your power, it will make itself known to you. But I sense that you have become accustomed to suppressing your abilities. Hark my words, young Heritor, you must free yourself from earthly shackles if you are to fulfil your destiny.'

'People talk a lot of destiny,' Sam said. 'But… what is mine?'

'That is for every man to find out for himself. You need only follow your heart, and your fate shall reveal itself. I will say only one thing more, one final gift. For I have seen fleeting glimpses of your future, and your fate, it seems, hangs on a knife-edge. You will be betrayed, Samir Lahij. And that betrayal could yet destroy you.'

Sam could not help but glance sideways at Yana Selishe. Even after this, he still thought her a viper in the nest.

Distant thunder rumbled, and then in a heartbeat it was closer, booming overhead deafeningly. Sam looked up. Dark clouds churned in the sky, and blacked out the moon. A flash of jagged lightning illuminated the glade for a moment.

'The Trial of Magic has begun,' Ashtzaph said. 'You should go to your friend, and pray for his victory.'

Thunder boomed again, so loud it shook the earth. The first raindrops fell onto Sam's face, washing away the last vestiges of his ordeal.

'But how will I…?' Sam began. But his question went unfinished and unanswered. Ashtzaph was gone.

CHAPTER 17

Sam went with Yana back to the centre of the village, attracting a few odd looks from those at the back of the crowd, but as the rain fell upon them, and the Trial of Champions raged, no one bothered to hinder or question them. Sam guessed he looked a poor state, dirty from his struggle to free Ashtzaph, and somewhat bewildered and drained from what had followed.

They made their way through the excited throng, the cheers, jeers, singing and drumming a relentless, cacophonous din. Something about the scene reminded Sam of Yad-Sha'Rib, and he slipped effortlessly through the crowd, as he so often did in the markets back home. Soon he had overtaken Yana, moving past the great bonfire, past the Ancient One's hut, and up to the great Ring of Champions. There, Sam's path was blocked by two surly warriors, who crossed their spears to prevent him reaching the ropes that bounded the large circle.

Makeno was on his knees in the centre of the circle, coughing fitfully. He struggled against a tangle of roots, which coiled about his wrists, protruding from the dirt now slick with mud from the torrent of rain. Just a few yards away stood Noaka, chanting rapidly, a look of triumph on his features. He leaned on his staff heavily, and Sam saw blood flow down the chief's arm.

Another thick root shot from the sodden ground with a wet snap, lashing at Makeno, wrapping about his neck.

'Makeno!' Sam cried, and darted forward, only to have a warrior shove him back hard, snarling some command at him.

Sam felt a hand tug at his arm, and turned to see Dagomir, with Bardo behind him.

'Don't do anything foolish, lad,' the captain said. 'Makeno knows what he's doing.'

'Noaka's killing him!' Sam protested.

'He's not. This battle is not to the death – the Ancient One forbade it. Don't count Makeno out yet.'

Sam could hardly bear to watch.

Slowly, with great effort, Makeno tilted his staff upwards, pointing the top towards the sky. There came another great peal of thunder, and lightning zig-zagged down from the heavens, striking the staff and enveloping Makeno in coruscating arcs of dancing energy. The crowd shrank back as the sudden light dazzled them. Sam blinked away spots before his eyes, and his spirits rose as he saw Makeno stagger to his feet, shrugging away the last wriggling tendrils, now blackened from the electrical assault.

'What did I say?' Dagomir cheered. Then he pulled close to Sam and said, 'Are you going to tell me where you were just now?'

'What do you mean?'

'I mean, what was so important that you had to miss the start of the trial? And why was Yana with you? I thought you hated her.'

'I just lost track of time, that's all.'

'Lost track of time, eh? I don't suppose you saw Emilio on your travels?'

'Emilio? Why?'

'Because he's nowhere to be seen, and I thought he was with you.'

'I... Wait, look!' Sam pointed to the ring, where the two combatants now fought staff-to-staff.

Noaka gave Makeno a shove, sending him stumbling backwards, and then stooped, thrusting his fingers into the earth. Almost in answer to his call, the trees around the edge of the village seemed to bend inwards towards the circle. There came a whipping, cracking sound, and dozens of thick vines shot from the undergrowth like huge, striking snakes.

Makeno rolled out of the way of the first, then leapt to his feet, dodging each strike, but being driven back all the time by lashing tendrils. He stretched out a hand, and wind whistled through the trees. The wind became a gale, blowing out the torches around the circle, knocking people off their feet, roaring so loud that the noise of the crowd could no longer be heard.

Sam braced himself behind Dagomir, holding up a hand to protect his face from the debris that blew through the village.

'Ha!' Dagomir shouted. 'Makeno is truly blessed of Vanya!'

The trees bent away from the circle. The vines swung about feebly in the wind, their unnatural animus unable to flourish against the onslaught of the elements. But Makeno was not done; to Sam's astonishment, the winds began to whip around the circle, sending the rain and mud spiralling about like a tornado, which tightened around Makeno. The warden was lifted from his feet, high into the air, towering above his enemy. Noaka planted his feet firmly, leaning into the wind, shielding his eyes with a forearm.

Dozens of rocks, small and large, were torn from the ground, and joined the circling torrent around Makeno. And finally, with a shout like thunder itself, Makeno unleashed the full force of the elements upon Noaka. The rocks flew at the chief as surely as if they had been flung by a trebuchet.

Quick as a flash, Noaka twisted and changed before Sam's eyes, transforming himself into a creature of bark and vines, more tree than man. The rocks crashed against him, and drove him backwards, but he did not fall. His gnarled, woody flesh shielded him from harm; his bulky form gave him the strength and weight to withstand the barrage. When the winds ceased, and Makeno floated to the ground, Noaka was still standing, facing his enemy once more.

Noaka's transformation was not complete. His bark-skin thickened; he grew taller, and great thorns sprouted from his arms. His face resembled now the wooden masks worn by the tribal dancers of the Savaisal. His hair had become a mane of vines and leaves, which cascaded down his back, lending him an almost regal appearance.

At a sweep of Noaka's arm, the ground all about Makeno erupted, spraying Sam and the front row of the crowd with dirt. A thick tangle of black brambles grew rapidly from the muddy earth, encircling Makeno before he could chant a counter-spell. In an instant, the warden was engulfed in a dome of thorny vegetation, and Noaka's croaking laughter rang upon the night air.

The mass of thorns expanded further, the black dome growing taller and broader. Sam feared that it was crushing Makeno, tearing at him with vicious barbs. He realised he was shaking when Dagomir squeezed his shoulder to steady him.

With a sound like crashing waves, the dome exploded outwards, a concentrated gust of wind tearing it apart, sending branches and roots blasting across the circle. Makeno stepped from the sundered remains of his bramble prison, his skin a patchwork of scratches, but a look of utter defiance on his face. He glowered at Noaka, and Sam saw rage in Makeno's eyes that he had never seen before.

Chief Noaka stood tall, like a knight armoured in thick bark. If he even noticed the severe change in Makeno's demeanour, he did not show it. Perhaps it was sheer rage that drove Noaka on, but he charged at Makeno, his bark-shod feet shaking the ground. He struck down at his enemy with a spiked fist, despite the agreement not to kill. Makeno ducked under the blow, and Noaka struck the ground, pounding a small crater in the sodden earth. He freed himself quickly, and swung wildly at Makeno, who leapt out of range of Noaka's blind flailing.

Makeno held his staff aloft to the tumultuous sky, and uttered a strange incantation, quietly and firmly, with all the menace of a man now determined to end the fight.

Noaka wheeled upon his opponent once more. There were no more spells to come, no twisting vines and lashing thorns. The chief wanted nothing more than to pummel Makeno with his fists.

Thunder rumbled, a long and ominous reverberation. The clouds overhead thickened and rolled like noxious smoke. A streak of lightning tore the sky, striking Makeno's staff, sending a shower of sparks cascading all around him. He struggled with the energy, pulling it to earth like he was landing a gigantic fish with a rod and line. The lightning hung in the air, a moment too long to be anything but sorcerous, and then it leapt from Makeno's staff in an incandescent lash, striking Noaka in the chest with the full fury of the heavens.

Sparks, wood and bark flew in all directions. Noaka staggered, his tree-like form in tatters, revealing at least some of the man within. What remained of his wooden armour ignited, tongues of orange flame licking all around him as he sank to his knees. Noaka let out a torrid scream, and collapsed to the ground in a broken heap.

The crowd was silent, holding its collective breath. Makeno paused for just a moment, hands trembling, jaw set firm. And then his expression softened, and with one last incantation, the clouds unleashed a heavy torrent of rain. The great bonfire, which had so far survived Makeno's storms, now flickered and hissed as the rain pummelled down. When at last the rain subsided, and every onlooker was thoroughly drenched, Makeno stood over the groaning, wheezing form of Noaka, returned to his human form, steam drifting off him. Makeno bent and picked up Noaka's staff, and an eerie silence fell over the village once more.

The silence was broken by the voice of the Ancient One, who alone crossed the boundary and entered the circle. 'The Trial of Champions is over!' she called. 'All hail Makeno Storm-Caller, chief of the Savaisal!'

The raging winds and rain were replaced by cheers of jubilation. The drummers struck up again, redoubling their efforts. The ropes bounding the circle were cut, and the villagers surged forward, all eager to be the first to declare their loyalty to the new chief; to kneel at his feet; to proclaim his divine right to rule the Savaisal to the heavens. The bonfire, almost extinguished by Makeno's storm, flared up once more as men threw kindling and logs onto it, piling it high again.

Sam pushed forward, almost in a daze. He followed Dagomir's lead, the tall Northman shoving his way easily through the crowd. It had been so long since Sam had had any cause to celebrate that he almost did not recognise what he was feeling. It was relief, and elation. Now, perhaps, he could find some semblance of security, here amidst the Savaisal. Now there would be no danger of repercussions for freeing Ashtzaph. He wished Hassan were not so out of sorts. He wished his friend were able to enjoy this fleeting moment of triumph with him.

With Dagomir paving the way, Sam finally managed to reach Makeno. There were many warriors now kneeling before him, offering up their spears, pledging their allegiance to the 'storm-caller'. Makeno bade them all stand, accepting their oaths, then he turned to Sam.

'Thank you, Samir,' he said. Though he bore himself now like a king, Sam saw Makeno was much weakened.

'For what?' Sam asked.

'For trusting me. For helping me. You did not have to, and I know it has been hard for you. I apologise for keeping secrets from you, but that time has now passed. If you will permit me, I wish to put your amulet to use once more, and then our real task begins. The task of helping you and Captain Dagomir fulfil your own destinies, as you helped me fulfil mine.'

Sam nodded.

Dagomir took out Sam's bronze amulet and handed it to Makeno. The warden nodded thanks, and passed his staff to Dagomir to hold for him. He turned to the crowd, holding up Noaka's staff triumphantly, and then with an effort that was all too plain to see, broke it over his knee. Makeno took the upper portion of the staff, and broke the bronze fragment away from its fixings. Now he held up both fragments to the expectant onlookers.

'Behold, two pieces of the Tablet of Sav'Eq-Tul,' he said. 'It has not been seen in this land since before the time of the Ancient One. Now, I unite these pieces, as I shall unite our people. We shall prosper through unity, and wisdom, as we did in the time of Makawenu.'

With that, Makeno clashed the two fragments together with a flourish. To Sam's amazement, there was a flash of green light, and the two pieces were as one in Makeno's hands, forming a rough crescent-shape. One part of the tablet was missing still, but already Sam could see patterns in the strange sigils of the tablet's surface that he had never before noticed.

'Before the festivities begin, I must make my first decree,' Makeno said. This drew the excited throng into a hush. 'Captain Dagomir and his crew are no longer to be viewed with suspicion. They have upheld their part of the bargain, and returned me to you, my people. They are trusted and honoured friends – my debt to them knows no bounds.' This brought a great cheer, and a few of the nearby villagers patted Dagomir and Sam on their backs and offered words of praise that Sam didn't entirely follow.

'And now,' Makeno went on, holding up a hand to restore order, 'bring forth Noaka.'

The atmosphere became more serious. Noaka had managed to drag himself to his feet, and now sat far away from the others, with several of his trusted servants and warriors about. At Makeno's order, a strong contingent of tribesmen approached Noaka's group, and for a tense moment it looked as though they might come to blows. Dagomir drew a little nearer to Makeno, hand on the hilt of his sword lest a coup be attempted. The two groups exchanged angry words, but eventually, despite Noaka's protests, his warriors stepped aside, and allowed their former chief to be dragged before Makeno.

Noaka looked up at the new chief with sheer resentment blazing in his eyes.

'Noaka, I would ask you to cast aside bitterness from your heart,' Makeno said. 'You know the laws of our tribe as well as any. You offered me the chance to face you in an honourable trial, in the sight of the gods. My family name is restored, but it does not have to be at the expense of yours. Your line has guided the Savaisal for two hundred years, and we must all be thankful for it. The tribe has endured because of you. It is said that in ages past, when a Trial of Champions has been completed, the victor has banished his rival from our ancestral lands. I would not have it so! I would rather we were allies. I would offer you a position of honour in the tribe. I would have you be my lawmaker, if you would accept me as your chief.'

Sam wondered why Makeno would make any sort of offer to Noaka. The former chief had tried to kill him in the trial, and was set to give up much wealth and status to make way for Makeno. Even as he weighed up Makeno's offer, Noaka's eyes shifted slyly. Sam could not see how or why the old chief would swear fealty to the new.

At last, Noaka shrugged off the men who held him, glaring at them defiantly each in turn. He raised his chin, looking down his nose at Makeno, and said 'I... will... *never...*'

'The prisoner has escaped!' The cry came from the rear of the crowd, and cut short whatever foolish words Noaka was about to speak.

Sam looked about in panic for Yana Selishe, who stood some distance away. She gave the most minute shake of her head when Sam met her gaze, indicating that he should hold his tongue, and his nerve.

'What prisoner?' Makeno demanded.

'The Eritherean...' the guard stopped, realising that Makeno was now in charge, and that the new chief had no idea what he was babbling about.

'Chief Noaka's prize,' the Ancient One croaked. 'A creature of immense power.'

'I have heard of Erithereans only in stories,' said Makeno. 'Noaka, why would you have one prisoner? Were they not once our allies?'

'Pah!' Noaka barked. 'We have had no dealings with them for the longest time.'

'Since you made our people inward-looking and territorial,' Makeno said, accusingly. 'And yet now this situation must be addressed. The Erithereans are powerful – I would not risk war with them. We should find this creature and persuade it that we mean it no harm.'

Noaka scoffed. Sam wanted to tell Makeno that it was too late for all that – that Noaka had already harmed Ashtzaph – but he said nothing.

'There is something else,' the guard said, hesitantly. 'One of our warriors was found in the pit where the prisoner was kept. He cannot say much yet, but he must have been attacked. Someone must have helped the creature escape.'

Makeno allowed his eyes to scan his friends for the briefest moment – Dagomir, Sam and Yana Selishe. 'The Erithereans were once our friends,' he said at last. 'I will not brook any hostility against them until such time that I can speak with them and make things right between our people. But if, as you say, this creature was freed by force, from an intruder in our village, then this intruder must be found.'

'Yes, Oh Anointed One,' the guard said.

'But not now,' Makeno added hastily, before anyone could act on his order. 'Now, this is a time of celebration. Thoughts of hostility can wait.'

'You would be foolish to allow the Eritherean to remain loose,' Noaka said. 'In our possession it is a valuable resource. But out there in the jungle it may yet prove to be a dangerous enemy.'

'And you, Noaka, would be wise to hold your tongue. You have not yet accepted my offer of a place among my inner circle, and I sense that you will not. This saddens me. But it also removes any right you have to offer me counsel.'

Noaka only glowered at the new chief.

'Come now, everyone,' Makeno said, forcing a smile through his exhaustion and raising his voice so all could hear. 'Feast! Dance! Let us make this a night of entertainment.' He clapped his hands together, nodded to Dagomir, and swept away to speak with the Ancient One.

The guard who had interrupted proceedings looked utterly confused, and then turned his eye rather suspiciously towards Sam and the others, before leaving. Noaka, now entirely snubbed by the new chief, also looked to Sam, but with a glare of pure malice. Yana Selishe was by Sam's side in an instant, her large, dark eyes burning towards Noaka. Dagomir noticed it too, and pulled Sam closer, returning Noaka's look with an altogether more intimidating one. As the only man in the village with skin of palest white, hair like spun gold, and a prodigious height that saw him tower over everyone – his own crew included – Dagomir had a considerable presence. A large, meaty hand slapped on Sam's shoulder, and he looked up to see Bardo at his back – not as tall as Dagomir, but almost twice as broad. The big carpenter winked.

With such a display of force before him, Noaka could only give one last growl of frustration, before slinking away through the dancing crowd. But not alone: he was accompanied by several of his trusted guards – those who had not sworn fealty to Makeno.

'They'll be trouble, mark my words,' said Dagomir.

Sam nodded. 'The last time I saw that look in a man's eye, it was Ranbhir.'

'You learn fast, lad. When you see a man look like that, it's because he feels backed into a corner. He's been slighted and embarrassed. He's cunning and dangerous, and is looking for a way to get even, regardless of the cost. It won't be tonight, but it will come.'

'Captain.' Sam, Dagomir and Yana turned as one, to see Emilio. There was something about the mate that gave Sam cause for concern. He looked deflated, serious – lacking a certain braggadocio that so characterised him.

'Where the devil have you been?' Dagomir frowned.

'Captain, might we speak in private?'

'Tell me it wasn't you who set that prisoner free,' Dagomir groaned. 'I'll be honest, I thought it was the boy… but you?'

'I…' Emilio looked puzzled. 'No, Captain. This is something else.'

'I think you can say whatever it is in front of these three,' Dagomir said. 'After everything we've been through; there are but five of us left now, and…'

'Captain Dagomir!' Emilio snapped. 'I will speak only to you, and it must be now.'

Dagomir frowned. 'Very well, if you must be so mysterious about it. Bardo, save me some haunch of whatever it is they're roasting over there. I'll return presently.'

* * *

There was something about Emilio's manner that troubled Yana. And worse than that, there was something familiar about it, that she had not previously noticed in him. She cursed. While she had been away helping Sam on his fool's errand to free Ashtzaph – an errand that now was entirely pointless given Makeno's victory – she had allowed her guard to slip. The party was not yet free of Zhar-Mharrad. He would not give up easily, and now she turned over several unpalatable possibilities in her mind. The vizier was wily indeed. What if Yana was not the only agent on the island?

'What's wrong?' Sam asked. The boy was also better disposed towards Yana. Perhaps he was finally starting to trust her.

'Nothing,' she said. 'Why don't you go with Bardo and get some food. And take some to Hassan – he must be awake by now.'

Sam looked at her suspiciously – that was more like the boy she'd come to know. He nodded anyway, and trailed after Bardo.

Yana slipped through the crowd, taking a circuitous path away from the torchlight and tribal dancers. She pulled her scarf over her face, and darted into the shadows, doubling back around the huts and through the undergrowth, to where Emilio and Dagomir were huddled in a severe conversation. Yana Selishe was the best of Yad-Sha'Rib's Manhunters, well-practised in all the arts of subterfuge, and few could see her if she did not wish to be seen.

She drew as near as she dared, climbing into the branches of a large, black-barked tree, where she crouched like a panther, straining to hear the two men.

'If I didn't know better, I'd say you've had your head turned just a little too far by that woman,' Emilio said.

'Meaning what?' Dagomir growled.

'Meaning, *Captain,* that you never could resist a

pretty face, and perhaps keeping her in your trust for so long has jeopardised everything.'

'You know something, don't you? Out with it, Emilio.'

Emilio paused. 'Even now the enemy closes in on us. I've... seen them.'

'*What?* Where? How close are they?'

'Too close for us to do anything about it. Listen to me, Captain – we need to leave. Get the amulet from Makeno any way you can. Bring the boy if you like, though we don't need him any longer. The two of us, maybe Bardo, can slip away. But if we raise the alarm, it will only end badly for everyone.'

'How can you possibly know this, Emilio? We must tell Makeno and prepare ourselves.'

'You aren't paying attention. We have one chance to save our skins – that's always been our way, right? Put the crew first?'

'Ha! What crew?' Dagomir said, bitterly.

'I know, I know.... But if we try to raise the alarm, we'll end up like the rest of them. I expect that Selishe woman will slit our throats – she's one of them, mark my words. Whatever is between the two of you has clouded your judgement. I think Samir was telling the truth back on Caldega. I think she was meeting with Zhar-Mharrad's spies, and you wouldn't hear it.'

Dagomir was hunched and tense, balling his fists. Was he considering running away with Emilio, even after everything? Maybe she was losing her edge, but she could not countenance Emilio's lies any longer. She dropped noiselessly from the tree, and stalked from the undergrowth. Emilio saw her first, and his expression became one of fear.

'What I did on Caldega,' she said, 'was keep up appearances to buy us some time, as well the captain knows.' Dagomir spun around at the interruption. 'Do you think your captain is such a weak-willed fool that he never questioned me?' Yana went on. 'You do your old friend a disservice, Emilio.'

'Perhaps,' Emilio snarled. 'Or perhaps he has believed your lies for too long.'

'I'm standing right here,' Dagomir snapped. 'You will both do me the courtesy of addressing me directly.'

'Very well,' said Emilio. 'There's an attack coming, and it's coming now. Where was this woman earlier? She wasn't around when the trial began. She wasn't at the hut. So where?'

Yana seethed. 'Where were you, Emilio? You seem awfully well-informed about Zhar-Mharrad's movements. And I hear you were not at the trial either. In fact, I returned before you did – and I have a witness as to my whereabouts.'

'What witness?' Dagomir demanded, his tone harsh towards them both. Maybe he had grown weary of the conflict; Yana couldn't blame him for that. But she had to keep him on side.

'Samir. As you know, the boy is no friend of mine, and would not lie to protect me. Ask him yourself if you don't believe me.' Yana saw a flicker of doubt cross Emilio's face; he hadn't counted on that. Only a few days ago, she wouldn't have been able to count on Samir either. Their fool's errand now seemed a little less foolish.

'Samir?' Emilio said. 'You have dragged the boy into your schemes, have you?'

Yana's hand went to the hilt of her sword, and Emilio's to his.

'You would do well to hold your tongue,' Yana purred, coolly, 'lest I cut it from your head.'

'I would welcome another chance to duel with you,' Emilio said, 'but alas, time is short, and you have already kept us here longer than is prudent. Was that your plan?'

'Will somebody please explain…' Dagomir began.

Then the scream came. The unmistakeable sound of a man dying in agony. Angry roars followed. The drums stopped, the ringing of steel and the shouts of warriors filled the night air.

'It has begun,' Emilio said. 'I tried to warn you.'

Dagomir looked to his first mate, then to Yana, then he was gone, ploughing through the undergrowth, broadsword drawn.

Yana glared at Emilio. For a split second, she considered running him through on principle. He held her gaze with an infuriating look, half resentment and half mockery. He made no attempt to follow his friend.

'Fine, stay here, or flee into the night, coward,' she said. 'I am done with you.' Yana rushed after Dagomir, towards the sound of battle.

CHAPTER 18

Sam did not see the first man die, but he heard the scream over the din of drums and the raucous singing. He saw the second, though. The Savaisal tribesman fell into him, clawing at Sam as he dropped to the ground, a black-fletched quarrel jutting from his shaven temple.

The tribespeople scattered like a flock of ground-birds before the hounds. Sam wrenched his arm from the vice-like claw of the dying man. Bardo grabbed him, and pulled him away to the cover of the nearest hut. The big man was surprisingly swift to act, though he had not yet seen fit to drop his haunch of roasted lizard.

From the shadows, Sam crouched, and watched. Half-a-dozen bodies lay strewn upon the ground, the bonfire illuminating their tribal garb and garish paint. The unseen enemy had driven the Savaisal from the village, but only as far as the treeline around the village centre. Sam saw the dark figures of the Savaisal warriors gather in the undergrowth, spears readied, shields up. The tree-huts shook with activity, as warriors armed with blowpipes raced to their positions along the rope-bridge walkways.

When Sam saw the flicker of firelight reflecting from

gold helmets, however, he knew the Savaisal were done for. Zhar-Mharrad had come.

For a moment, there was silence. Then the ground began to shake as Bidajah filed into the village.

A baby screamed. It came not from the jungle, but from the heart of the village. Sam risked poking his head out of the shadows, ignoring Bardo's hissed protests. Squinting against the glare of firelight, with the oncoming soldiers marching closer, Sam saw a swaddled bundle twitch upon the sodden ground, wriggling beside the prone, still body of a tribeswoman. A baby, left behind in the confusion, crying in the night from the hastily formed no-man's land.

'Don't!' Bardo urged.

Sam was already urging his limbs to action, breaking from cover, every step a challenge to the fear that gripped his heart. And from the shadows all around, he sensed the regrouped Savaisal surging forward, silently.

He knew not how, but he heard the crossbow-string twang, and the flight of the quarrel sing in the air. Sam checked his step just a fraction, enough to see the bolt sweep before his eyes and thud into the fire-logs, sending a shower of sparks cascading from the bonfire onto the ground. He stumbled onwards, ducking a slashing scimitar, hopping over a thrusting spear, running as fast as he could. Someone was shouting in the language of the nobles of Yad-Sha'Rib. They were commanding the Bidajah to kill him.

Sam sensed the next quarrel, diving to the ground as it sailed harmlessly over him. He rolled in the dirt, scooping up the babe in one hand, scuffing the palm of the other. He scrabbled between the legs of a Bidajah before the brute could bring a sword down upon his head. Sam scrambled to his feet, ran around the other side of the fire.

The Savaisal charged towards the Bidajah, towards Sam, wild rage in their eyes. Their advance had been deathly quiet, but now they roared their battle-cries as they closed with the enemy. Sam clutched the wailing babe close, using every ounce of his preternatural skill to weave in and out of the charging mass of warriors. He flinched as he heard spears punch armour. He tried to block out the phlegmy cries of dying men as the heaving Savaisal waves broke upon the wall of gold.

Sam passed the last of the charging warriors, and reached the treeline, gasping for breath. He passed the baby to a stricken-looking tribeswoman. He felt a hand upon his back, and wheeled around, fumbling for his little sword, sighing with relief when he saw only Bardo.

'That was foolish,' Bardo said. His tone softened almost immediately. 'But brave. By the gods, that was brave, lad.'

'Look out!' Sam cried.

A Bidajah had somehow made it all the way to the clearing's edge, and strode towards them, looming behind Bardo with scimitar readied. At Sam's warning, Bardo swung about instinctively, breaking his haunch of meat across the Bidajah's golden face, sending the brute staggering. Bardo unhooked an axe from his belt, and hacked into the Bidajah's neck, felling the hulking warrior in one stroke.

'We can't win this fight, Samir,' Bardo said.

'We... we can't just leave them. This is all our fault.' Sam looked back to the fighting, and already the ranks of the Savaisal were thinning. The Bidajah towered over the tribal warriors, hacking down double-handed at their foes, golden masks reddening with spilt blood.

From the jungle came the sounds of war-horns and battle-cries. Makeno stepped forth, dozens of warriors at his back, including many muscular guards with feathered headdresses – the elite warriors of the Savaisal.

'I have given everything to return to my people,' Makeno said, half to Sam, and half as if in entreaty to the gods. 'I will not shirk my duty; I will not let them fall. Warriors of Savaishe! Repel the intruders. Charge!'

Bardo pulled Sam aside as the jungle erupted in a mass of warpaint and coloured feathers. Ear-piercing battle-cries filled the air, as scores of warriors raced from their position, swarming into the village. Makeno stood resolute as his people surged about him, parting them into two charging files like a rock parts the crashing waves. Thunder rumbled in the sky overhead.

Sam felt breathless. His blood pumped harder than ever before. He felt the rage and indignation of the Savaisal in his bones. He wanted to join them, to run alongside them, and smash into the ranks of Zhar-Mharrad's soldiers himself. It was easy to see how men could be carried along with the tide of battle-lust.

Yet Sam checked himself, and it was the sight of Makeno that gave him pause. The warden gave his people the appearance that he was strong still, but Sam knew him better. Makeno was much weakened. He didn't have it in him to surrender, or to flee, but nor could he fight. The Trial of Champions had taken much out of Makeno. That was why the warden was not at the frontline. That was why he did not attack now; and that was why the grumbling of the storm above was just that – a growl, not a roar. Something felt wrong.

The warriors sprinted around the bonfire, where the enemy waited for them. Sam saw the Bidajah standing in serried ranks, scimitars and spears readied to receive the charge. And something more. Behind them, more golden-masked soldiers stood, levelling crossbows through the ranks.

Crossbows...

'Makeno!' Sam shouted. 'Call them back. Call them...'

Sam's voice was lost in the echoed cries of the Savaisal. A dozen or more fell to the ground as the quarrels loosed. More still fell as the long-hafted spears of the Bidajah thrust forward in unison, presenting a wall of jutting steel. Less than half the warriors reached the Bidajah line, crashing into the brutish foe with diminished belief. Tripping over the bodies of their fallen comrades.

Makeno had been shouting encouragement to his warriors, and even he now stopped. Uncertainty flickered in his eyes.

Sam rushed to him. 'Makeno. Call a retreat.'

'I...' Makeno looked lost.

'Vanya's wrath!' Dagomir's shout seemed far away, but sang over the noise of battle.

Sam ran forward as far as he dared, and there, on the east flank of the enemy, the yellow-haired Northman flung himself into the Bidajah. His attack was so forceful that he made an opening, and the fanatical vanguard of the Savaisal breached the Bidajah line, swirling about with spear and axe, attacking the soldiers of Yad-Sha'Rib from behind. Sam squinted. Beside Dagomir was a black shape; a shadow, sweeping between the Bidajah, blades finding weak points in armour with expert precision. Yana Selishe was helping.

Sam stood a moment, open-mouthed. Yana Selishe was fighting Zhar-Mharrad's forces. This was the moment when surely the vizier stood on the edge of victory. If the woman was going to betray Sam and his friends, now would be the time. Sam drew his sword.

'Don't do it, lad,' Bardo growled, sensing Sam's desire.

Sam looked around to Bardo, then to Makeno. The warden was slumped over his staff, shaking his head, muttering something in the native tongue. Sam knew there would be no magic to help this time. He looked back to the fighting. He couldn't see Dagomir any longer; just a messy, visceral melee.

'Vanya's wrath,' Sam whispered. He ran forward, as fast as his legs would carry him, towards the battle. 'Vanya's wrath!' he shouted, as loudly as he could, but his words were already lost in the noise of clashing swords and the roars of enraged warriors.

* * *

'The boy comes to me…' Zhar-Mharrad stared in disbelief at the scene unfolding before him. 'This urchin dares defy my will. This will be a delight indeed.'

'Lord Vizier,' Faizil said. 'The Bidajah are having trouble with that pirate scum. Shall I dispatch him?'

Zhar-Mharrad looked to the east flank, where Dagomir the 'Pirate Prince' hacked away at his warriors. And where Yana Selishe was making rather too effective a show of unity with the Northman.

'No,' he said. 'Have your hunters subdue him. And signal Selishe to stop her act. The time is nigh.'

There came a grumble of thunder overhead. The trees all about began to shake, against the wind, bringing about a strange aura of foreboding.

'Their warden,' the jemadar said. 'More of his sorcery?'

'Perhaps.' Zhar-Mharrad rubbed his fingers against the cold, smooth surface of his periapt, and smiled. 'You have your orders, Jemadar Faizil. I shall take care of the rest.'

* * *

Sam ducked beneath a scimitar, jabbing his blade upwards into the armpit of the Bidajah, who spun away clumsily. Sam almost fell to the ground as a spear thrust hard towards him, striking bare earth, missing his foot by inches. He righted himself, only to feel a stinging pain in the back of his head as another Bidajah struck him a mighty blow with a mailed fist. Sam fell, skull ringing. He rolled aside, instinct driving him as a scimitar swept past his face, slicing an inch from his fringe. He slithered away on his elbows, dodging spear and sword from all sides, as the Bidajah began to close on him. He rolled over, willing himself to his feet, scrambling between the legs of his assailants on all fours.

Someone rushed between Sam and the Bidajah, shoving the hulking brutes away. Steel clashed upon steel, with a sound that chimed on the blood-scented air like a tolling bell. Dagomir was beside Sam now, thrusting his broadsword into the belly of the nearest foe, and shoving Sam out of the press of fighting men with his free hand.

'Get behind me, boy!' he commanded.

Sam didn't need telling twice. He staggered backwards, looking dumbly to his slender sword, the blade bent in two places.

Dagomir swung the broadsword about in a shimmering arc, even the insensate Bidajah seeming reluctant to come within range. One took up a spear, and thrust it at Dagomir. The captain knocked it aside. Another came, stinging across Dagomir's ribs. Now the Northman cursed, and backed away as the Bidajah seized their opening. He parried a scimitar, then a second.

Sam swallowed hard. Whatever had possessed him to charge into the fray? The ground was littered with dead, mostly Savaisal. Their blood stained the earth. Sam fancied it stained his hands, too. They had brought death to this village, and now the Bidajah bore down on him and Dagomir. Sam turned to the jungle, looking for an escape. There was none. The darkness of the undergrowth was broken by the gleaming of golden masks, and the shadows of hunters.

Dagomir saw it too. He pulled Sam close against his back, and swept his sword all about as the circle of foes moved in, slowly, inexorably. Was that a falter in Dagomir's stance? Did he, too, sense the end was nigh? It was hard to imagine another outcome, for the screams of the Savaisal were even now fading, as their number thinned and the remaining warriors lost heart. Sam didn't know where Bardo was, or Emilio, or Yana. All he could see was the hulking forms of the Bidajah closing in, impassive even in their moment of triumph.

Something snapped past Sam's face. Whip-like, barbed. It struck the closest Bidajah in the chest. Sam gawped for a moment, then realised it was a plant. A thorny, supple branch. The Bidajah looked down, barely registering what was happening. The branch hooked onto the brute's armour, and bloomed at once into a hundred tendrils, which snaked and coiled all about the Bidajah's body. He struggled against it for a moment, and then was jerked bodily into the air, whipping silently into the jungle where he was lost to shadow.

Sam pulled Dagomir's tunic, and the captain heeded the warning, dropping low as another great tendril snapped from the treeline, ensnaring another Bidajah. The trees themselves began to groan, and lean in. All around the village, the low, keening noise of the wind through the trees sounded like a droning war-horn.

The other Bidajah stepped towards Sam and Dagomir, as if in haste before they, too, were snatched. But too late – roots erupted from the earth in a shower of dirt, entangling their feet. Tendrils grasped at their arms.

'Come on, lad!' Dagomir said. He seized the moment, leading Sam between the Bidajah, who struggled impotently against the living plants.

The remnants of the Savaisal warriors staggered away from the Bidajah, and now Sam and Dagomir stood with the tribesfolk, who looked on astonished at the scene before them. Some of the Bidajah had pulled free, and were hacking at the roots, branches and vines that extended from all sides, like some vast spider web centring upon the village. Many, however, were stuck fast, their bulging muscles straining against the very force of nature.

The Savaisal continued their retreat, to the dying bonfire. The ground began to rumble, and then burst open, sending Sam toppling backwards and the tribesfolk scattering. Thick, thorny brambles sprouted from the mud, rising upwards in a heaving torrent, forming before Sam's astonished eyes a great, barbed throne some ten feet off the ground. And upon that throne, impossibly, sat Noaka.

'Hear me, my people!' Noaka shouted, his voice powerful upon the night air. 'Have I not always been your protector? Have I not always steered you to victory? Tonight, you have embraced a pretender to my throne: an exile; a traitor! But I forgive you, for I have love in my heart for the Savaisal, always. The outsiders have brought with them aggressors to our village. They have brought death to our people! But listen to me now! Makeno Storm-Caller is no leader. Look at him!'

Sam looked to where Noaka now pointed.

'Makeno!' Sam shouted.

Makeno was kneeling on the ground, beaten and bloodied. Noaka's faithful warriors stood around him, holding him roughly by the arms as he spat blood into the dirt.

'He is nothing!' Noaka shouted. 'I will destroy these warriors of gold: these invaders! And when I am done, I will restore our village as my forefathers did. I, Noaka, am the protector ruler of the Savaisal. I, Noaka, am the ruler of the Savaisal!'

Something changed in the village even as Noaka spoke. Sam's flesh goosed. His breath misted on the air, which was no longer warm and humid, but colder than anything Sam had ever felt before. Overhead, black clouds gathered. No... not clouds. A shadow on the sky, blotting out the stars and moon. Sam sensed in his bones that this was not Noaka's magic, nor Makeno's. Noaka sensed it too, for he stood tentatively upon his dais of brambles, looking around in confusion.

'Thank you, Noaka, for your proclamation.' The whisper was little more than a murmur on the breeze, but it was clear that all in the village heard it. Was that fear now in Noaka's eyes? The thin, papery voice continued, 'As the king of this pitiful tribe, perhaps your death will serve as an example. Let none defy the will of Zhar-Mharrad, lest they share this fate.'

A pall of black smoke rose from behind the struggling Bidajah. It swirled in great coils towards Noaka, thickening, coalescing, until finally a gigantic form of smoke and shadow hung in the air before the former chief. Some of the Savaisal fled the demon. Others fell to their knees and cowered. Sam could not move. The smoke-creature was almost the semblance of a man, featureless and black. Fiery, red pits opened in its incorporeal head – baleful eyes that blazed with the fires of hell. And then it opened a mouth, revealing a black, starlit void. Wider and wider it grew, impossibly wide. Noaka looked into that maw, into a realm beyond the real world, and something changed in his eyes. He looked mad for a moment, before he screamed – a noise unlike any Sam had ever heard from human lips before.

The great mouth closed around Noaka, snapping shut with a deafening *boom*. The smoke dissipated in an instant, and when it had gone, so had Noaka. To where, who could tell?

All around, the sounds of struggling ceased. Vines fell to the ground, inert once more. The trees creaked back to their old places, and for a moment all was still.

The Bidajah straightened themselves, and picked up their weapons. They took a few steps forward, forming up into ranks once again. At this, most of the Savaisal – at least, those who were not paralysed with fear – threw down their weapons and fled. Sam would gladly have joined them, but several Bidajah stepped from the treeline, barring his path.

He turned back to the wall of golden warriors. From the centre of the line, a figure emerged. A tall man, in robes of black and crimson, adorned with gold and jewels, untouched and unsullied by the trials of the jungle island.

Zhar-Mharrad himself.

CHAPTER 19

The vizier looked around at the dishevelled opposition before him. For a moment, his eyes met Sam's, and Zhar-Mharrad flashed a wicked grin, his eyes sparkling with cruel intent.

Sam felt the point of a spear at his back, and Dagomir turned angrily as he received the same treatment. Several Bidajah stepped forward, and ushered them closer to the vizier. From the other side of Noaka's great thorny dais, more Bidajah brought forth Bardo and Makeno. Another Bidajah wrestled Emilio from the treeline. Sam hadn't seen the buccaneer during the battle – he must have been lost in the confusion, or fighting within the jungle. He certainly looked dismayed at having been captured.

Finally, Yana Selishe arrived, her hands bound with rope. She shrugged away the two Manhunters who escorted her. She stood beside Makeno, her dark eyes burning with indignation.

'You have led me a merry dance,' the vizier said at last. His voice was sharp and clear, with a slyness and cruelty that clipped every syllable. 'And yet you were not so very hard to find. Not when you have my servant amongst you, drawing me to you every step of the way.

Sam glared at Yana. Yana glared at Emilio.

Zhar-Mharrad laughed, and clapped his hands together. 'You poor fools. Not an ounce of trust amongst you – but what does one expect from pirates?' He glanced over his shoulder and said, 'Bring forth the boy.'

Even as the two Bidajah behind Zhar-Mharrad stood aside, Sam realised what was happening. When Hassan took his place beside the vizier, Sam was not surprised. But he felt like a dagger had twisted in his heart all the same. He felt also the accusing looks of Dagomir and Emilio burning holes in his skull. He dared not meet their eyes.

Hassan looked at Sam and his friends with glassy eyes. Sam had mistaken that look for sickness, or some product of Zhar-Mharrad's vile torture. Maybe that was indeed the case. But it was something more than that. It was an enchantment. There was nothing behind Hassan's eyes. He was no more in command of his faculties than the Bidajah themselves.

'What a sweet boy,' the vizier said, patting a hand on Hassan's shoulder. A hand, Sam noticed, with fingers tipped with golden claws. 'Now, Northman,' Zhar-Mharrad looked to Dagomir. 'The legendary "Pirate Prince", I'm told. Although I dare say your fellow pirates owe you no fealty. You have something I want. Two things, actually. First, you have my tablet.' He pointed to Makeno. The tablet was now too large to sit atop the warden's staff, and instead hung about his neck.

'It's not mine to give,' Dagomir growled.

'Indeed. But you are the commander of this pathetic group, and so it is you I ask, purely out of courtesy, you understand. The other thing I want is the boy. I have a

Heritor of my own, of course, but he is blind and somewhat… eccentric in his ways. This one has a little more life in him, wouldn't you say?'

'He is not mine to give, either,' Dagomir said. 'In fact, I don't think I'll let you take him, if it's all the same to you.' The captain met the vizier's astonished glare with cold fury.

'I said I was doing you a courtesy,' Zhar-Mharrad snapped. 'I see now that was a mistake – manners are wasted on the likes of you. Very well: you and your men shall drop your weapons and surrender at once.'

Sam saw Dagomir's jaw tense. The captain's hand squeezed the grip of his broadsword until the leather strapping squeaked. Sam had never seen such simmering rage encapsulated in one man. Dagomir looked like a tiger, ready to pounce. He shifted his weight, looking as though he might charge at the vizier and try his luck.

'Do you… seek to fight me?' Zhar-Mharrad laughed, with affected mockery. 'Oh dear, oh dear. By all means, Captain Dagomir, have at me! I am sure all of these crossbows trained upon you will miss. I am sure you will not run onto one of these spears.' His eyes narrowed, and his tone grew more pointed. 'And I am sure my magic will not transport you away to a realm of eternal torment. Perhaps you wish to send your regards to Chief… Noaka, was it?'

'Captain,' Emilio said. 'Listen to me. I've known you a long time, longer than anyone else here, and I know that you'd fight to your last breath to avenge the merest slight. But look around you. We cannot win this fight. And what is it for? This lump of metal? This boy? These things are nothing to men like us. Hand them over, and maybe

Zhar-Mharrad will let us walk out of this village with our lives intact. Maybe we can find someone on this accursed island who'll lend us a boat. I say we leave here and never look back.'

Sam looked to Emilio open-mouthed. He didn't meet Sam's gaze, but he seemed sincere. Sam couldn't believe that his friend – the one man on the *Vanya's Wrath* who'd supported him on the voyage – would forsake him so completely.

'You could live with yourself, Emilio?' Dagomir asked. 'If you abandoned Samir to his fate, you'd live with that?'

'We've both lived with worse,' Emilio shrugged. 'There are men like us who refuse to call themselves what they are. Pirates. That's all we are. That's all we'll ever be. To hell with this island and everyone on it. Let the fates decide where the boy goes next; our part in the story is done.'

Dagomir hung his head, and squeezed his eyes shut. When he opened them, he was changed. He threw his sword to the ground. He strode past Sam, to Makeno, and took the warden's amulet from him.

'No!' Sam shouted, and made to rush at Dagomir, but a Bidajah pulled him back.

Dagomir held out the tablet towards Zhar-Mharrad, who brandished a self-satisfied smirk.

'Very good, Captain Dagomir. I am glad you listened to your shipmate. I was beginning to think I'd have to slaughter you all. Yana – be a good soldier and bring me the tablet, would you?'

Sam looked uncertainly to Yana, and Dagomir wore a surprised expression too.

Yana Selishe straightened, stretched out her neck, and pulled her hands apart. The rope that had supposedly tied her wrists fell to the ground. Without a word, and with no expression on her smooth features, she stalked towards Dagomir, snatched the tablet from his hand, and took her place at Zhar-Mharrad's side.

'Ah, my dear,' Zhar-Mharrad said. 'It is good to have you back. I must say, you played your part so well you almost had me fooled.'

'That is why you chose me, is it not, my master?' Yana said.

Dagomir's shoulders sagged. He looked crestfallen; like the strength had drained from him. He might have been willing to betray Sam, but perhaps he cared more for Yana than he'd admit.

'And my raven?' the vizier purred coldly.

'Regrettable. I had intended only to clip its wing,' Yana replied.

Zhar-Mharrad sighed. 'Regrettable indeed. Almost as regrettable as having you sail with this... barbarian... for these past months. I shudder to think what uncivilised practices you were subjected to. Still, all of that will be as nothing when we return home. When you take your place by my side, you will never know hardship again.'

'What?' Sam blurted.

'Not that it's anything to you, boy, but Ku Selishe is to be inducted into the mysteries of Birrahd; to protect my temple, and enforce my rule.'

'So 'Kurrah is the ruler of Yad-Sha'Rib!' Sam shouted. He felt stupid saying it; he had no love of the Merchant-King, but even less for Zhar-Mharrad.

'If you say so,' Zhar-Mharrad said, waving a hand dismissively.

Was that a flicker of animosity in Yana's eyes? The Manhunters were famously loyal to So'Kurrah. They were the means of the first Merchant-King's ascension, and had served every one since, striking from the shadows to remove the enemies of the throne, often before guilt was even determined. Were these hunters the first to serve a new master? Was Yana willing to set aside her oaths after all?

'Enough talk,' Zhar-Mharrad said. 'Seize them. Take their weapons. Clap them in irons. We'll decide what to do with them back at the camp. No, not that one,' he pointed at Emilio. 'He has a sound head on his shoulders, and an admirable sense of self-preservation. I might have use for him.'

Emilio nodded humbly. Sam felt sick to his stomach.

Two Manhunters stepped forth with manacles. They locked them around Dagomir's wrists, then Makeno's. The manacles were not large enough for Bardo's massive wrists, and so they bound him with rope instead.

It came to Sam's turn. He looked around, for a way out, for any sign that resistance would not be met with a swift death. He looked to Yana Selishe, who stared right back at him with expressionless eyes. He looked to Dagomir, who was already being shoved away between the ranks of the Bidajah, shuffling, head bowed in defeat. Finally, he looked to Hassan. His best friend, the older boy he'd always looked up to for his daring, now a mind-addled slave. Sam thought of similar slaves confined beneath the black Temple of Birrahd. He thought of the city gaols filled with people whose only crime was trying to feed their families in a city under rule of tyranny. He thought of his mother, who for all he knew could be among those poor souls even now. Sam's dream of liberating Yad-Sha'Rib seemed so very far away.

He thought all of this and more as the first Manhunter approached because, Sam now realised, everyone was moving considerably slower than he. Time itself had become a crawl; even Zhar-Mharrad was not immune to this effect, his long face, skeletal arms and spindle-fingers lending him the appearance of a bug trapped in tree-sap. Sam's instincts, it seemed, had made the decision for him.

The Manhunter reached out with the iron manacles. Sam moved aside, reached to the assassin's belt, and pulled free a dagger.

Everything seemed to happen at once; time rushing in at Sam like the first breath after emerging from deep water. The Manhunter fumbled forwards at the space Sam had previously occupied. Sam shoved him in the back while he was off-balance, sending him crashing headfirst into the nearest Bidajah. Sam spun away from the second Manhunter, slashing Bardo's ropes with one swift strike.

'Run!' Sam said. The big man didn't seem to realise what was happening.

The hairs on the back of Sam's neck stood on end; he sensed incoming danger, and whirled away as a scimitar struck down at him, raking the ground where he'd been standing. He ducked under a second clumsy strike. Sam knew that everyone around him was trying to capture or kill him, but to him they appeared rooted to the spot, faces contorting slowly as they shouted and snarled. The words of his enemies reached his ears like low moans.

Sam darted past Emilio, who had barely moved a muscle, but beheld unfolding events with a look of contempt. What game was he playing? Maybe it was a ruse; maybe Emilio would help Sam. But Sam could depend on no one right now.

He saw an opening through the press of bodies, into the jungle, to the clearing where he had first found Ashtzaph. Sam thought to run as fast as he could, to sprint away into the night alone. He ducked beneath a spear-thrust. He wouldn't last much longer. The Blood Burn would take him soon enough. But what if he could end it all before then? What if he took this one chance, and slew Zhar-Mharrad?

The thought of it made Sam's pulse race even faster, so that he thought his heart would pound right out of his chest. The indecision slowed him for a fraction of a second, enough for a Manhunter to land a sharp, open-palmed strike to his chest. In that moment, time seemed to flow normally, and Sam found himself lying in the dirt. The Manhunter was standing over him in an instant, grabbing Sam's tunic with one hand, readying his other hand to punch again.

End it.

Sam summoned his strength. The Manhunter punched downwards as though he were swimming in tar. Sam flicked out the dagger, slicing the inside of the man's thigh. There was a cry. Sam shimmied along the ground like a snake, and leapt to his feet as the hunter fell forwards, clutching his leg. Sam looked up. Two Bidajah had lumbered before their master. More closed in behind Sam. They could not stop him. In this one moment, Samir would have to kill. He would have to become an assassin himself. Maybe he'd die in the attempt, but would it not be worth it? Would not Zhar-Mharrad's death make the world a better place?

Sam dug his heels in, and darted forward; one last push, one last fight. He held the dagger tight. He jerked out of reach of the Bidajahs' flailing hands. He rolled around the nearest, using the brute's own body to shield himself from the others. Sam slipped within the circle of golden armour, to where Zhar-Mharrad stood, surrounded by guards. And he stopped.

Zhar-Mharrad faced Sam, grinning wickedly. His left hand was cupped beneath Hassan's chin, golden claws raking the boy's flesh. In his right hand, he held a large black gem, from which smoke seemed to emanate unnaturally. Wisps of black smoke coiled around the vizier's robes, like a cloak of shadows. It snaked and curled around Hassan, contrails probing his nose and mouth. Yana Selishe stood behind the vizier, making no effort either to stop Sam, or to help him. Zhar-Mharrad nodded to his soldiers.

Sam let them seize him.

'I am uncertain whether or not to kill you,' Zhar-Mharrad said. 'But know this: if you do not surrender fully to my men, I *will* kill this one.'

Sam only nodded sullenly. He had not felt the Blood Burn – perhaps he was growing accustomed to his powers, as Makeno had foretold – but it was scant consolation. The strange magic that Zhar-Mharrad wielded would kill Hassan before Sam could reach him. Sam let the dagger fall from his hands.

'Very good,' said Zhar-Mharrad.

He relinquished his grip on Hassan, and the smoke withdrew into the gemstone. Hassan gasped and gulped at the air as the foggy black tendrils left his lungs.

There were two Bidajah flanking Sam now, their large, strong hands pinning his arms to his sides.

Zhar-Mharrad turned about, and waved a hand in the air to several small groups of Bidajah. 'You, and you,' he called. 'Search the village for stragglers, and put them to the sword. Burn every hut.'

'No!' Sam shouted,

'No?' Zhar-Mharrad laughed. 'Do you think I have become powerful by virtue of forgiving my enemies? No, boy. Come to think of it, I am not sure one as impudent as you will prove useful at all. The blind one shall have to do.' He looked to the nearest Manhunter. 'Kill him,' he commanded.

The Manhunter drew a curved blade, and stalked towards Samir.

Sam struggled, but it was too late. He had allowed the Bidajah to seize him, and now he would die, and Makeno's people with him. Dagomir had already been taken away. Makeno, too. Emilio made no move to help. Yana Selishe stood behind Zhar-Mharrad, though now she turned her eyes away in shame.

Sam was jolted hard from behind. He fell to the

ground, one of the Bidajah with him. The second Bidajah released him, and staggered away as it received a stinging blow to the side of the head. Sam scrambled to his feet.

Bardo. The ship's carpenter had come to Sam's rescue. In the confusion, everyone had overlooked him.

The Manhunter leapt forward, planting his dagger in Bardo's shoulder. The big man swatted the hunter aside, the knife still protruding from his flesh. He roared with rage, like a huge bull, and swung his billhook hard. The barb caught in the Manhunter's back. Bardo swung the assassin about, driving back every guard in the circle, and sending Zhar-Mharrad himself cowering for cover behind Yana Selishe.

'Run, Sam!' Bardo shouted. 'Run far away, and don't look back.'

Sam paused. Bardo was one against many. Leaving him was almost unthinkable. And yet Sam knew if he stayed they would both die.

'Run! Fight another day! Live now, and save your friend later.'

Sam felt hot tears sting his face. He staggered away, unable to take his eyes off Bardo, who swung the billhook about with great fury, holding a horde of soldiers at bay. As Bardo turned to slash the weapon at an onrushing Bidajah, Sam could only watch as a man stepped out behind him, with a sword pointed to Bardo's unprotected back.

'Bardo, behind you!' Sam yelled.

Bardo only half-turned as the sword pierced his ribs. A slender, flexible blade, punching deep into the big man's lungs. As he spat blood, Bardo's eyes told the whole story.

The last thing he saw was Emilio, his crewmate, his comrade, withdrawing the blade that had killed him.

Sam backed away, even as Emilio turned to face him, flicking Bardo's blood from his sword.

'No…' Sam gasped, unable to believe what he was seeing.

'Kill him!' Zhar-Mharrad shrieked, sheer outrage and hysteria entering his sharp voice.

'No…' Sam said again, stumbling backwards, tripping over the trailing leg of a dead tribesman.

Sam landed hard in the mud. Emilio marched towards him, two Bidajah by his side. His sword was held outwards, ready to run Sam through. Sam scrambled away on his elbows, unable to find the strength to stand and run. The three foes were almost upon him.

Then all three stopped. The Bidajah looked all around, almost comically. Emilio frowned in confusion, his eyes darting left and right.

They… can't see me.

Sam held his breath, in case even the slightest sound might alert Emilio to his presence. He looked down at himself, and stifled a gasp. He couldn't see his own body. He held up a hand. Or, at least, he thought he did. There – he saw the shimmering outline of his arm, but he could see the ground through it. Distorted, like looking through aged glass. He knew instinctively that he was not truly invisible, but his body, clothes and all, was changing to match his surroundings. He felt it, as though the ground was somehow being absorbed into him, and he was reflecting its image to Emilio and the Bidajah. He was a chameleon. This was the power that Ashtzaph had unlocked within him.

'Where is he?' Zhar-Mharrad shouted.

'He... he's gone!' Emilio called back. 'Vanished into thin air.'

And as Emilio turned to his new master, Sam seized his moment, and ran.

He heard some slight commotion behind him as the sound of his sudden flight alerted Emilio to his position. But Sam did not stop. He ran to the treeline, slipping undetected past a Bidajah patrol, who were busy setting light to the Savaisal huts. He plunged into the jungle, and had a mind to run and run, and never stop. But stop he did. He needed to see what was happening, to formulate a plan.

Sam darted to one of the larger trees, and used the creepers to climb effortlessly up into its boughs. He reached one of the Savaisal walkways, and sped along to the next tree, and then the next, until he was close enough to the village to see Zhar-Mharrad. Only when he had concealed himself well within the tree canopy did he urge himself to become visible, and as soon as he did he felt pain well up within him. Sam's vision blurred. His blood fair boiled, his skin grew hot, like a thousand needles pushing their way out of him from the inside. He felt it in his limbs, behind his eyes, in his skull. He wanted to curl up, to scream in pain and anger, but he could not. Sam gritted his teeth, trying as hard as he could to resist, to make not a sound.

When finally Sam was able to look down upon the village centre, he saw Zhar-Mharrad's forces dividing. Small patrols had been formed, the Bidajah spreading out across the village. They set light to every hut as they went, and then progressed into the jungle in search of survivors.

Some passed directly beneath Sam's position – one even looked up at the walkway, but perhaps thought better of trying to haul his great bulk up the creepers, and finally passed by.

The largest party of Bidajah, led by two Manhunters, headed south out of the village, past the hut that Sam had once shared with the crew, which now burned, acrid smoke streaming into the night sky. Sam thought he caught a glimpse of Dagomir's yellow hair amongst the group, and wondered where they might be taking their prisoner.

Below him, a few guards, Manhunters, and Yana Selishe stood beside Zhar-Mharrad. Yana appeared to be remonstrating with the vizier. Sam strained his ears, trying to make out their words. They spoke in the Dar'Shuri tongue, and Sam realised that Emilio was nearby – perhaps they sought to hide their plans from the pirate. Sam could hardly blame them. Once a traitor, always a traitor.

'The whelp... alone...' Zhar-Mharrad was saying. '... Won't last...'

'...Underestimate the boy...' Yana replied. And then something about being 'too conspicuous.'

'If he is so powerful,' Zhar-Mharrad argued, 'Why should I risk my most valuable servant?'

That was clear enough, and Sam's anger grew sufficiently to mask his pain.

Something more was said that he could not make out, although he was certain Yana spoke of Makeno at one point. In the end Yana bowed to Zhar-Mharrad, gathered her things, and struck out alone, while Zhar-Mharrad summoned the rest of his warriors to him, and strode away to the south. Emilio, Sam noted with some disgust, walked after Zhar-Mharrad without protest. He was still armed, treated more like a trusted follower than a prisoner.

And so Sam hid among the trees, until the last of the soldiers had gone; until the fires had died, the sky began to pale in the east, and birdsong returned to the jungle. Only then did Sam descend from the tree-platform. He scouted the village swiftly, picking up any scraps of food he could find. He found a fur pelt that was sodden with mud, but he bundled it up for the journey ahead anyway, because he knew not where he would go, or what conditions he might face. Last of all, he went to Bardo, who lay cold and half-sunken in the mudpool that had formed in the aftermath of battle. Sam closed Bardo's eyes. He fumbled for some words to speak, because Bardo had been a devout man.

'Dorak, I don't know if you can hear us here, so far away from Bardo's home. But know that he was a faithful follower of your ways. Whatever he may have been, whatever he may have done, Bardo was a good man, and he died selflessly. He died for me.' Sam sniffed, and rubbed his sleeve across his face. 'He wanted to wipe his slate clean before he met you, so that you'd let him enter the Dreamlands. Maybe I have no right to speak for him, but I think he's earned his place. Please, Dorak... please let him in.'

Sam fought unsuccessfully to hold back his tears. Bardo had been perhaps his one true friend of all the crew. Who else among them could he really trust? Makeno and Dagomir had played him false. But the burly carpenter – he'd been an honest man amongst a ship of thieves.

Sam gritted his teeth and pulled the Manhunter's dagger from Bardo's shoulder. He wiped it clean on the tunic of a fallen Bidajah.

'I don't think I'm strong enough to fight Zhar-Mharrad,' Sam said, quietly; to Bardo. To the gods. 'I'm just a boy. A stupid boy who should have stayed home with his mother.'

He held the dagger out in front of him. A curved, Dar'Shuri weapon. Familiar, in a way. He would not use Emilio's sword again, it was the weapon of a coward and traitor. This dagger was the weapon of a hunter. Sam narrowed his eyes, and tried his best to summon his strength.

'Maybe I won't ever find the Crystal Pool,' he said, with as much steel as he could conjure. 'Maybe I won't save my city. Maybe I won't ever see home again. But if I can, my friend, I will avenge you. Before my time on these cursed islands is through, I will try my best to avenge you. Because you were the only friend I had here, and that has to count for something.'

With that, Sam turned and marched through the boggy ground, and left the sundered village behind him.

CHAPTER 20

'Where is your friend today?' Sivita asked.

Sam shrugged. His eyes were fixed on the row of flatbreads that steamed on the counter, their oven-charred dimples glistening with melted butter. With his belly grumbling, Hassan's whereabouts were far from Sam's mind.

Sivita shook her head reproachfully, but her smile was kind. 'Well,' she said, 'I can spare just one today. If you're a good friend you will save some for him. Here.'

She took a strip of banana leaf and wrapped it around an oval-shaped flatbread, before handing the treat to Sam.

'There you go,' she said. 'Now go on your way, and don't tell anyone. If all the urchins come to my door, I'll have nothing left!'

Sam nodded, almost too distracted by the smell of the bread to say thank you, but he managed to mutter it before running off through the marketplace, where the traders were setting up their gaily coloured stalls. Sam felt a tang of guilt that he was begging for food. His mother would be ashamed. But he did it for her; she could afford so little, and so Sam, just ten years old, rose early each morning and went adventuring with Hassan, to fend for himself. One less meal for his mother to find was one less worry for her, he thought.

They'd had money once, though so long ago Sam could barely remember. That was when his father was alive. He couldn't even picture his father's face any more. He was strong, and bearded, but otherwise he was a faceless man in Sam's mind. He remembered the voice though – the deep voice, which used to tell Sam stories from picture-books, before Sam even really knew the meaning of all the words. But it was a nice memory regardless. He'd kept the books. It was the only thing they hadn't sold to survive. And even though Sam's mother hated him reading of adventures in far-off lands, she couldn't bear to part her son from those relics of past happiness. And so they remained.

Sam drifted through the streets in a daydream. He wondered where Hassan had got to. He headed through their usual haunts in the winding alleys and backstreets that made up the shadowy, pungent seam of the city, where the slums, the market district and the docklands met. Sam had learned to keep his head down in this part of the city. Look small, innocuous. Don't let anyone think you have something they might want. He kept a brisk pace, occasionally pausing to take a bite of bread that melted in his mouth, buttery and herby. It was so good, he'd eaten half of it by the time he reached Talao Hill, a notorious haven for corrupt moneylenders and robber barons. It was rare for anyone to pay much mind to a young boy – the men of this area were normally too busy sleeping off the previous night's excesses, or stalking unwary travellers for their purses.

'Ho! Look who it is!'

Sam stopped when he heard the voice. The flatbread turned to dry, claggy dough in his mouth. He turned slowly, knowing who it was he'd see.

Sure enough, there was Abib. He was a year older than Sam, rough and wiry, with long hair and mean eyes. He lived on the east side of the slum district, with a brute of a father who worked as an 'enforcer' for one of Talao's crime bosses. Behind Abib, a motley assembly of boys stood, smirking through dirt-smeared faces.

'What're you doing here, Orphan? This isn't your street.'

Sam looked around cautiously. He'd taken a shortcut, but hadn't been paying attention. Normally he saw Abib well before the other boy saw him.

'I'm not an orphan,' Sam said, indignantly.

Abib stepped forward. 'Then you're a mummy's boy.'

Sam turned to run, but bumped into another boy, a fat tub named Vadi. The boy shoved Sam hard in the chest. Sam fell backwards, landed on his behind, and dropped his bread into a gutter swimming with filth. Sam sniffed back tears, scrambled quickly to his feet, and backed up against the nearest wall, looking for a way out. The boys approached from left and right.

'Gonna cry?' Abib said. 'Bet you cry all the time, mummy's boy. 'Cos your dad was a criminal.'

'He wasn't!' Sam said, and he felt tears warm his cheek, even though he was trying so hard not to cry.

Abib laughed. 'Your dad was killed by the Shadow-Viper. Do you think the best Manhunter in all of Yad-Sha'Rib kills people for nothing? I bet he was a thief, or a murderer!'

'No! He was…' Sam bit his lip to stop himself blurting anything out.

'What? What was he?' Abib asked, in arm's reach now.

Sam was shaking all over, but he wondered, what if…?

'He was a warrior,' Sam said. And with that, he lashed out, punching Abib square on the nose.

Abib spun away, clutching his nose. Sam didn't wait to see what would happen next. He bolted forward, but again the blubbery wall of Vadi blocked his path. Sam almost bounced off the boy, right back into the reach of Abib.

Sam spun about as Abib swung a blow at him. Something strange happened; Sam felt as though he was outside his own body, looking at the fight from elsewhere. And everything was so slow. Sam moved aside as Abib's fist inched towards him, puzzled. The punch sailed past Sam's face. He felt the air part in front of his nose; saw Abib's cruel expression turning to one of befuddlement.

Everything sped up again, time flooding back around Sam with a crash. The jeers and insults from Abib's crew were deafening. Abib cursed as his own momentum almost toppled him.

'Why, you…' he growled, angry at having to save face.

'Wait!' Sam protested feebly. 'I didn't mean…'

Abib's follow-up buried deep in Sam's gut, sending the air rushing out of his lungs. Another blow hit Sam's cheek, sending him reeling across the alley, into the other wall. Abib pressed home the advantage, his eyes blazing triumphantly, his features twisted in a snarl. He punched Sam in the chest, and recoiled immediately as his knuckles pranged on something hard and metallic. Sam's amulet.

Abib threw Sam roughly to the ground, and fumbled for the leather thong around Sam's neck. He pulled the bronze amulet from under Sam's tunic.

'What's this? You can't afford something like this. You're a thief, like your father!'

'No, no!' Sam shouted, now terrified not at the beating he was going to get, but at the loss of the amulet. The one thing his mother had told to him always to look after. He fumbled to keep it from Abib's grasp, and received a stinging slap across the face for his trouble.

'Give it here!' Abib snarled. 'Give it here, now, or...'

A pained cry interrupted Abib's threat. He and Sam turned together, to see Vadi clutching the back of his head, bawling like a baby.

'What?' Abib snapped.

Another cry, this time from one of the crew. Abib spun around in confusion, finally letting go of the amulet.

From his position on the ground, Sam saw Hassan on the roof of the shack opposite him. Hassan lobbed a third stone, this time cracking Abib on the side of the head with pinpoint accuracy, drawing a bead of blood.

Abib's friends began to back away in a huddle, looking around for the source of their attacker. At this opening, Hassan dropped down from the rooftop, and rushed across the alley, barrelling into Abib so hard the older boy was launched into the wall, hitting his head as he went.

'Come on!' Hassan said, holding out a hand.

Sam took it, and let his friend hoist him upwards. A shout came from behind them, and Abib's crew regrouped, building the courage to chase Sam and Hassan down.

Hassan only laughed, and thumbed his nose at them, before dragging Sam away into the crowded streets of Talao.

* * *

Sam woke cold, and hungry. The fire had gone out hours ago, although he could still smell the cloying smoke from the burning of damp wood. For a moment, he thought he was in the Savaisal hut. He thought he could hear Dagomir's snoring, and Bardo stomping about outside. But there was no one there.

The memory of Bardo seemed to swell up from Sam's belly, catching in his throat, causing him a single sob to escape him involuntarily. He squeezed his eyes shut for a second to stop the tears returning. He'd already decided that crying about it would do no good. It wouldn't bring Bardo back; it wouldn't save Makeno's people. It wouldn't make him feel any less alone.

Sam hauled himself up from the dirt floor of the cave, squinting as grey light streamed in at him. Sam couldn't see anything of the hills beyond; only an endless haze of drizzle that had poured relentlessly since he'd left the Savaisal village. He stretched his aching muscles, feeling a hundred summers older than his fifteen years, and threw his fur cloak about his shoulders. It still smelled of dirt, smoke and blood, but it was better than nothing.

Sam made his way from the cave, onto a craggy hillside overlooking a wide valley, where the rain almost drifted down, settling on his shoulders in filmy sheets. On his side was little more than bare rock, which stretched down to a fast-flowing river, coloured grey-brown from constant mudslides. On the other side of the river, the jungle rose upwards, covering the rolling hills in a sea of swaying emerald. The rain and mist blotted out the farthest hills, but the impression Sam had received the previous day was that the jungle extended as far as the sea, and it was many miles away.

That was where Zhar-Mharrad was heading. Sam had followed them for a day and a half, once getting so close he had almost stumbled across the rear-guard, and had had to use his newfound powers to avoid detection. He wished he could remain invisible, and then he could have followed Zhar-Mharrad all the way to the coast, and perhaps mounted a rescue attempt for Hassan and Dagomir. But it was not to be. Sam had fled to the foothills, hoping to watch from a vantage point, only for the vizier's forces to strike suddenly into the jungle, and become lost from sight. Then another tropical storm had driven him to seek shelter, and dashed his hopes of catching up with his enemy that night. Sam had decided to seek shelter in the caves, hoping that he could find a trail south and pick up the scent once more. How big could the island be, after all?

A rumble of thunder answered his musing.

Sam sighed, and went back to the cave to gather his things.

It took him some time to find a safe place to cross the river. The rain had swelled it beyond its banks, all save one stretch where a sandy island had risen in the centre of the riverbed, and tough foliage had conspired to grow, choking the river and slowing its flow sufficiently for Sam to wade across. Sam had rolled up his fur and slung it over his back, but had resigned himself to getting them drenched once more.

He clung to hardy reeds, and did his best to feel about beneath the muddy water for firm ground, but still he managed to plunge into the water three times. The third time, he went so deep that he panicked, swallowing a mouthful of silty water, before bursting upwards into fresh air once more. By the time he clambered out onto the other side, he was thoroughly wet and miserable, and coughing up dirt.

Sam rued his own cowardice. If he'd simply lain low and followed Zhar-Mharrad's force a little more closely, he'd have made the river crossing earlier, and he'd have more of an idea exactly where he was headed. Now, Sam looked up at the jungle before him, which rose up over the tall hills. He didn't relish one bit the prospect of hacking through it alone, aimlessly. He didn't have Dagomir's unerring sense of direction. He'd have to try to march straight, and not get turned around, which he knew was easier said than done.

At least the mist was lifting. The morning sun rose higher, and with it the warmth returned to the island. Steam began to drift lazily from the jungle, bringing with it the thick scent of exotic blooms, sap, and an underlying odour of decay. The whooping call of a monkey echoed into the valley, signifying that the jungle was coming to life again. Sam would just as rather it had remained dormant, but he saw no other option than to press on. He hoisted his bundle of meagre possessions higher onto his shoulder, and marched into the forbidding undergrowth.

On this side of the river, the jungle felt very different. Sam had noticed immediately that it was darker, thicker; the noises somehow more sinister. Whereas previously he'd seen a few large spiders and snakes, and given them a wide berth, this place was teeming with life, and of a less familiar sort. Centipedes of prodigious size entwined themselves around the boughs of smooth-barked trees. Something many-legged and bloated leapt overhead, its shadowy form vanishing into the dark canopy before Sam could get a clear look. Sam had a very real sense that hundreds of pairs of eyes watched him, hungrily, from every shadow.

He did not veer from his course, but strode blade-straight to what he believed was the south. Before long he felt the incline steepen, his legs working harder to clamber through thick undergrowth. Sam took out his Dar'Shuri dagger to hack at the most obstinate tangles, though it was barely sufficient for the task. Progress became slower as he became increasingly mired in bush and root and soft earth. Sam's breaths grew heavier, his muscles more tired. He could use his gifts, he thought. He could take to the trees, and leap effortlessly from one to the other, like the spider-monkeys that inhabited the city walls of Yad-Sha'Rib. But how far would he get before the Blood Burn overwhelmed him? It wasn't a sensation he welcomed, and he had little sense of just how far he could exert himself before the curse of his bloodline struck.

Again, he wished he'd stayed closer on the tracks of Zhar-Mharrad… he doubted very much that the vizier of the Golden City would be perspiring and toiling at this moment.

Sam stubbed his toe against a rock, cursed, hopped a little, then looked down. It was not just some rough stone, but a large, square block, half-buried in the hillside and covered by foliage. Sam scoured the ground ahead. There were more such blocks – large, yellow stones that looked like parts of some ancient structure long since toppled and consumed by the jungle. Sam picked his way a little further through the brush, where the ruins became eventually more prominent, until he came to what from a distance he had thought was just another massive tree. But instead he stood now before a towering pillar, still standing by virtue of the many vines that clung to it. It was ten times Sam's height, and broad. Sam gazed up at it in awe, because the outward face of the pillar was carved with a strange figure. A tall, humanoid body reached upwards to carved relief stars and a moon. The figure had large feet and three-fingered hands, and great wings that sprouted from its back. But its head was like that of an elephant, with great flapping ears, large tusks, and a long serpentine trunk. It looked like Ashtzaph.

Sam heard a noise – something animal, and threatening. He looked left and right, but saw nothing but thick shadows.

It came again, more distinct. A low, rumbling growl. Not a snake or a spider, nor even a centipede.

Sam turned his head slowly to the source of the noise. He squinted at a copse of tall, striped grasses, and the darkness that flickered beyond them. And in that darkness, a pair of yellow eyes, gleaming like polished amber. They inched closer, and a shaft of weak light sketched in a vague feline form. Black fur like velvet; a large, powerful head; teeth as long as Sam's fingers. He stared at the creature for seconds, which felt like hours. He realised he was holding his breath. Not that it would do any good – it had seen him. It was stalking him.

He felt the creature tense. He saw its eyes narrow, just a fraction. That was enough.

Sam turned and ran. The second he moved, he heard the bushes behind him shake violently, followed by the thud of large paws hitting the ground. There was no time for caution now; Sam summoned every ounce of his power, leaping over rocks and trees and detritus, climbing up the hill more rapidly than ever. He skidded on loose rocks, leapt up to high branches, swung from creepers to cover more ground. With every obstacle, the sound of his pursuer grew louder. The snarls were close, claws swiped the air at Sam's heels. Sam knew he was faster than any human assailant, but this creature stuck with him no matter how fast he ran.

Sam gave one last effort, racing up onto firm ground, where the dirt gave way to a tall, rocky defile, leading to a shadowed ridge. He heard the skittering of rock behind him, and thought the creature had slipped back down the hill. He took a glance back over his shoulder, and realised too late his mistake.

By dappled light, Sam saw the beast plainly for the first time. It was a black cat, a panther, but larger than Sam had ever heard of back home. It had not slipped, but had merely gathered itself as Sam had slowed his pace, ready to pounce. Its sleek, powerful body sprang forward, massive claws outstretched, huge yellowing teeth bared.

Sam leapt aside as a set of black, shiny claws swept overhead. He clattered to the rock painfully, and rolled sideways towards a steep slope. Sam whipped out a hand to slow himself, but withdrew it at once as the hulking black form of the panther bounded at him once more. He tried to kick out at the rocks, to find some foothold, some ledge, but there was nothing beneath him.

Sam went weightless for a moment. He found himself looking up at the dappled light of the tree canopies; into the yellow eyes of the panther. He fell. His heightened senses slowed his perception. He saw everything, every detail, from the swaying of the trees above to the scurrying of ants along the rocks all around. That was strange, he thought. He was falling into some kind of hollow in the rocks; a pit.

His dreamlike state exploded away abruptly as Sam hit solid ground. The rolled furs on his back took some of the impact, but the jolt shook his every bone, and expelled the air from his lungs. For a moment his vision blurred, and he fought to stay conscious. The panther was above him, looking down into the hollow. What if it followed? Surely it could make the climb? If Sam blacked out, he would be dead.

Sam shook some of the grogginess away. The shock of the fall made him slow, his every movement painful. He frowned – the panther was not following. Why? It paced from side to side, paused to stare back at Sam one last time, and then padded away from the precipice, and out of sight.

A flicker of panic rose up in Sam's belly. What if there was another way down? What if the beast was making its way to him right now?

Spurred on by that thought, he urged himself to move, fighting the pain. Then he froze.

There was a loud hiss in his ear.

Sam sensed the strike even before it came. He rolled aside, fear and instinct overriding his injuries. The snake latched momentarily onto Sam's pack, greenish venom oozing from curved fangs, before letting go and slithering back to its friends. And it had plenty of those.

Hundreds of beady eyes stared at Sam. The ground beneath him writhed. Sam moved his hand gingerly and a snake wriggled away from him. He couldn't count them; they lay all around him, underneath him, slithering over him. Long, thin, mottled creatures of black and yellow, so numerous they reminded Sam of the ropes and fishing nets from the end of a day's toil aboard the *Vanya's Wrath*. What he wouldn't give for such labours now!

Sam gingerly slid his hands through the press of scaly bodies, feeling for solid ground. He began to push himself up, wincing all the time, but as soon as he moved another snake struck at him. He flinched, and that single motion saved him from a bite, as the snake bit the leather straps upon his shoulder. More snakes wriggled from beneath him. Others moved more rapidly now, agitated. The hissing grew louder – Sam was in their nest, and the snakes would not tolerate the intrusion.

A large specimen rose up in front of Sam's face. Its forked tongue flicked out, smelling for its prey. If Sam didn't know better, he'd have sworn that was a look of anger and malevolence in its eyes. But he knew it was worse than that: cold, reptilian indifference.

There was soft mulch beneath the snakes, pressing between Sam's fingers. The gruesome thought that other creatures might have met their end here, this same way, probed into Sam's mind and refused to leave. There might be decomposing animals under him, he thought. Creatures killed by the fall, or by poison, or both.

He weighed up his chances. Could he use his powers to avoid all of the snakes and reach the rocks? He knew that his strange new chameleonic abilities would not work against snakes – the cobras and shadow-vipers back home were half-blind, and relied on smell and taste more than sight. But his speed and reflexes gave him a small chance. He'd never tried anything quite so ambitious. One or two strikes, yes. But if he riled them all…

Sam knew he couldn't just lie there on his belly, with snakes sliding across his face. So he very slowly pushed himself up on his arms, tensing, ready to go. The very act of preparing himself seemed to invigorate the nest. The snakes moved faster, coiling and twining about each other in swirling patterns, almost hypnotic. They moved quickly around Sam's arms. He could feel one slithering over his leg. The prospect of running through the writhing pit seemed a grim one indeed. He bit his lip so as not to cry out.

'If you move, you'll die.'

The voice was so jarring, so incongruous, that Sam could barely believe anyone had spoken at all. But as his senses began to focus, and his brain caught up with what he was hearing, he recognised the voice. His blood froze in his veins. It was Yana Selishe.

'Don't say anything,' she called from above. 'Don't look at me, don't move at all. I'm coming down.'

Sam's heart began to pound; his mind raced with possibilities. She had tracked him. She was going to take him to Zhar-Mharrad. He wondered, to his shame, whether to wait until she reached him and then make a break for it. Perhaps the snakes would bite her instead of him. Perhaps they would both die. Part of Sam thought it was worth the risk, but another part of him at once rejected such a fatalist strategy. It would hardly honour Bardo's memory if he died here, with no chance of revenge upon Zhar-Mharrad. It would hardly do Hassan or Dagomir any good either. No: Sam could take some solace in the fact that the woman was coming to capture him. If she wanted him dead, she could just leave him in the pit. He'd find a way to escape later.

Sam's arms tired. He wished he hadn't pushed himself upright, because now he dared not move, and the effort was draining. He looked up, and saw a shadow drop silently into the pit, on the other side of the sea of snakes. Yana Selishe, the assassin, was here.

Sam could only see her feet; the black boots moved gracefully, smoothly, completely quietly. Inch by careful inch, Yana made her way through the snakes, careful not to disturb them. She calmly squeezed her feet between their bodies, seemingly ignoring any annoyed hiss that was directed at her. It took a long time for her to reach Sam, too long. His arms were shaking from the effort of holding himself still; his legs felt numb.

Yana's hand appeared in front of his face. She cupped it beneath a snake that had pressed its face uncomfortably close to Sam's nose, and gently took it away, whispering musically like she was singing a lullaby. She placed it harmlessly aside, and it slithered on its way, rejoining its brothers and sisters.

'A fine predicament you're in, Samir,' she said softly.

'What do you care?' Sam snapped.

'Shh!' she whispered, and the snakes echoed her sound. Only when they'd calmed again, did she speak. 'I am going to clear a path for you, as best I can. It won't be quick, so you need to be strong. When I'm done, you must run as fast as you can towards me, and I'll give you a leg up over those rocks.'

Sam strained his eyes to look at where Yana was pointing. There was a tiny ledge, perhaps twelve feet up a sheer outcrop. 'But…' he whispered, confused, 'how will you get out?'

'Don't worry about me, Samir,' she said. 'Do you understand the plan?'

He gave the smallest nod he could.

'Good. These snakes react only to immediate threats. As soon as you stand, the snakes will strike. They are a type of viper, and so their bite will be sudden, like a sharp stab, and there will be only a small amount of venom. One, maybe two bites will make you sick, but you'll survive. More than that – out here in the jungle – you'll die.'

'A real… comfort…' Sam said through gritted teeth, trying not to think of his shaking arms.

With no further word, Yana inched away, carefully – almost lovingly – moving each snake with her bare hands, feeding them through her fingers so they were directed away to the edges of the pit. She plucked one from Sam's back, and he did his best not to shudder as its tail brushed across his face while Yana moved it. She made her way slowly and methodically across the hollow, clearing the snakes as best she could. Some merely slithered back to where they began as soon as she'd released them; others went on their way, finding holes to hide in. Some reacted angrily, and several times Yana had to freeze, statue-still, until the creature had calmed a little and allowed itself to be moved. There was something unsettling about it – like Yana understood the snakes a little too well. The sinewy grace with which she moved had always struck Sam as feline, but now he changed his assessment: it was serpentine. She possessed certain characteristics that were wholly too snake-like for Sam's liking, her interaction with the creatures as tender as a mother soothing her babies.

When Sam thought he could stand it no longer, Yana hissed, like a snake herself, 'Samir! Now!'

He looked up. She stood before the rock face, no more than five yards away, hands cupped ready to hoist him up to the ledge. The path she had made was narrow, and only growing narrower as the snakes ebbed towards the centre of the pit like dark waves. Sam flexed his aching muscles as much as he dared, took a deep breath, and lurched forward. He almost fell immediately, his arms barely able to push himself upright, his legs so stiff they moved only reluctantly.

Sam stumbled in front of a rearing snake, and got to his feet as it struck, stepping quickly out of its way. He took another step, and the pit came alive with hisses and movement. He summoned all of his energy, reached out with his senses to detect incoming danger, and, finally, he ran. He skipped one strike, then another, seeing only peripherally the bared fangs and darting heads. He was halfway there. Sam jolted aside to avoid a third snake, but kicked a tangle of serpentine bodies in the process, upsetting a mass of vipers. He took a quick step away, but felt a sharp prang at his calf. The pain was sudden, and fleeting, but it brought with Sam such fear of death that he felt the hope drain from him.

'Run!' Yana urged, though to Sam's heightened senses it sounded more of a low drone than a shout.

Whether through bloody mindedness or sheer momentum, Sam didn't stop. But his rhythm was broken. He leapt forward, barely able to sense the danger. Two snakes converged on him, and collided with each other as their prey dived past. Sam reached Yana, and leapt upwards. He felt another stab of pain at his trailing ankle, but his other foot touched down upon Yana's hands, her interlocked fingers making a firm platform. She launched him upwards, and he reached out instinctively for the ledge, his vision blurring and his arms weak. Fingertips caught firm rock, and Sam at last scrambled feebly over the edge, onto a shallow platform, where he collapsed in a heap. He heard Yana below, gasping in pain. She was bitten.

Sam lost all sense of time. His mind was as clouded as his vision. He was vaguely aware of a black-clad figure standing over him, shaking him, saying indistinct words to him. He felt like he was being moved, but he could neither help nor resist. He could only close his eyes, and embrace oblivion.

✳ ✳ ✳

Sam woke with the sun on his face, and the smell of roasting meat drifting to his nostrils on smoky air. It made him nauseous. It overcame him in a sudden wave, and he rolled onto his side, retching violently.

'Good. Get the last of the poison out.' Yana Selishe crouched beside a small fire, cooking some kind of lizard on a makeshift spit. Beside her was a bundle of supplies – her pack, Sam's scant provisions. His knife.

With some embarrassment, Sam wiped his sleeve across his mouth.

'You won't want to eat,' Yana said, 'but you should.'

'What happened?' Sam asked.

'You were bitten. Seems even you are not faster than a snake. I managed to drag you up here, and suck out some of the poison. You'll be fine after some rest.'

Sam looked down at his wounded leg. It was wrapped tightly in strips of cloth. 'And… and you? You were bitten too. I heard you. At least, I think I did.'

'I'm used to it. Once I recognised that they were vipers, I knew I had a better than even chance of being immune to their venom. I was right.'

'Better than even…' Sam grimaced as he fought back another wave of nausea. 'Why would you risk your life for me? Am I worth that much to Zhar-Mharrad?'

Yana narrowed her eyes. 'I didn't do it for Zhar-Mharrad. I did it for… Never mind. You wouldn't understand.'

'But you're going to take me to him. I heard you, back at the village.'

Yana stood suddenly, slapping her arms at her sides in exasperation. 'Must you take everything at face value, Samir?' she asked.

'No,' Sam said. 'I've learned that people lie, all the time. You lied to us from the start, just as Emilio did. The only difference is, I expected it of you.'

Did Sam imagine it, or did the Manhunter look wounded by that? Part of the act, perhaps.

'I've never shown my full hand,' she said. 'I've withheld certain truths, in order to protect my own interests – as did Dagomir; as did Makeno. But I have not lied to you, Samir. I have, however, lied to Zhar-Mharrad, and even to myself.'

'What do you mean?'

Yana strode over to Sam, and knelt on the hard rock beside him. 'I mean, I hate the Heritors. Your kind… it was a Heritor who killed my father.'

'It was one of yours who killed mine!' Sam snapped, though he felt himself turn green with sickness as anger washed over him.

'And killing always begets killing. That's one thing I've learned after all these years in the service of the Merchant-King. You can never kill enough enemies, or rivals, or Heritors, or soldiers… there are always more. The friends of those who were slain then rise up against you, and then their friends, and so it goes on. That's why So'Kurrah is such a coward. He wielded power with an iron hand in the early days, but his methods only gave rise to rebellion and discontent, to attempts on his life, to challenges to his throne. And so when Zhar-Mharrad came along, with promises of unparalleled power and the protection of his dark magic, So'Kurrah struck the deal readily, as he had struck a thousand deals before. Only this time the price he paid was not gold, or ships, or camels; the price was his soul. Zhar-Mharrad is the real power in Yad-Sha'Rib. So'Kurrah is merely a puppet.'

'Do you not serve the ruler of Yad-Sha'Rib, whoever he may be?' Sam grumbled.

'I serve the Merchant-King!' Yana snapped, the flash of anger in her eyes giving Sam pause. 'Through oaths of blood, three generations of my family have served the king of Yad-Sha'Rib. When the merchant-kings bought our independence, they secured the loyalty of the hunters, who supported their claim to the throne. My father swore for So'Kurrah, and so did I. The ritual bonds of fealty are not easily severed, whatever the vizier may think.'

'The other Manhunters... will they not help you? Are their oaths not as strong?'

'I... I do not know,' Yana said. She looked sorrowful. 'I am their captain, but I fear Zhar-Mharrad is their master. I have noticed for a long time his influence working upon my men. And now... I suppose we will find out the hard way where their loyalties lie.

'Listen well, Samir. When Zhar-Mharrad returns from the Lost Isles, having drunk from the Crystal Pool, the pretence will be over. He will bring about an age of darkness like you cannot imagine. Everyone you know in the Golden City will be in danger. Zhar-Mharrad's servants, mortal and otherwise, will walk the streets unchecked. And So'Kurrah, having lived out his usefulness, will be killed. Do you think I, as a loyal huntress, could allow such a thing?'

'He said you were to rule beside him,' Sam said.

'One does not openly resist Zhar-Mharrad. Not in Yad-Sha'Rib, at any rate. But here... Let's just say things are different. If some ill were to befall the vizier here, the Golden City could be saved.'

'You think So'Kurrah would be a good king?' Sam spat. 'Everyone knows the merchant-kings only care for themselves. They sold their own people into slavery long before Zhar-Mharrad arrived. Only now they send them to the black temple instead...'

'You don't know So'Kurrah like I do,' Yana said, ruefully. 'Or, rather, like I thought I did. Perhaps he is not yet beyond redemption, if only he can be freed from the shackles of fear placed upon him by that blackguard vizier. Or perhaps he will turn out like all the others, but I'll cross that bridge when I come to it. Zhar-Mharrad is the more immediate threat, and believe me, failure is not an option. Once I make my true allegiance known, there will be no going back for me. Either he dies, or I do.'

'And what? You saved me from the snakes because you think I can help you?'

Yana stood, and paced back to the fire. She removed the lizard from the spit and slid it onto a battered metal plate. Then she turned and said, 'Yes, as it happens. I know my own capabilities. In a fair fight, there are few enough who can best me. But I am still a mortal. I have no defence against Zhar-Mharrad's magic. A Heritor, on the other hand...'

'And I know my own capabilities,' Sam snapped. 'I'm just a boy! I want revenge, yes. I want to free Hassan, and Dagomir… but I can barely control my power.' A hollow opened up inside Sam. He began to feel that it was hopeless. Even if he could trust Yana Selishe, what difference could it make? His dream of saving his friend, his city… it was just that. A dream. The snake-pit had brought home the reality of his situation, and the dangers presented by the island.

'You are more than that, Samir,' Yana said, more softly. 'You evaded Zhar-Mharrad back at the village. You vanished before our very eyes, and escaped. Do you have any idea how angry you made him? That's a good thing – it means you embarrassed him. There was nothing he could do to stop you, and there is nothing he can do to find you.'

'He can't find me? Why not? I thought he could sense the Heritors with his magic? I half expected his men to double back and kill me while I was following.'

'Your amulet – the tablet. You know that it masked your presence from Zhar-Mharrad's magic. Well, now he has the complete tablet in his possession. He keeps it close, and will not let it go. He may not even realise it, but the tablet clouds his magic. It stops him from seeing you, or any other Heritor, just as it stopped you from realising the full extent of your power. And there is our chance. If we can only reach him while his magical vision is clouded, we may be able to best him once and for all.'

'Best Zhar-Mharrad,' Sam muttered. 'I couldn't even escape from those stupid snakes.'

'Yes you could. You just needed a little help. We all need help, sometimes.'

'You didn't. And how are you immune to their poison, anyway?' Yana's blasé dismissal of her incredible feat had only made Sam more curious.

'I have trained as a Manhunter since I was a little girl. Longer and more rigorously than any of the others. My father saw to that – he taught me that, as a woman, men would underestimate me. But when I showed my hand, I would have to be better than them. Faster, more accurate, even stronger. He gave me every advantage. When I was eight years old, he took me into the desert and taught me how to survive. He found a pit of shadow-vipers, and taught me all about them – how they move, how they hunt, how they kill. And then he let one of them bite me, and make me very sick.'

'What? Why?'

'It was the first step on a long and difficult path. I have imbibed poisons from all over the world. I have been bitten by snakes of every type. And little by little, I built up a resistance to their venom. Soon, I was able to walk into a nest, like that one down there, and take barely a scratch. If they did bite me, it was nothing. But the point of it was for me to collect their venom, and use it to kill. It was always the shadow-vipers that I returned to. I heard it said that they'd bitten me so many times that I might as well be related to them. The city guards used to tell all manner of tall tales about me. "The Shadow-Viper struck again last night," they'd say. "I heard she…"'

She did not finish. Sam leapt to his feet, his legs shaking like jelly. But he fought the weakness, gritted his teeth so hard he thought they might break in his jaw.

'Murderess!' he roared.

Sam's legs could barely support his own weight. He felt so completely empty, his muscles so devoid of energy, that he moved in a ragged lurch, his athleticism abandoning him. But he dug deep, summoning his power, willing time to slow, willing Yana Selishe to become as a statue in his wake, so that he might kill her.

Yana Selishe: the Shadow-Viper. The killer of Sam's father.

She tried to grab him as he dived forwards, a look of surprise in her eyes. Sam wasn't trying to flee – he was going for his knife.

Sam wasn't himself. Even as he reached the blade, he felt Yana's breath at his neck. She kept pace with him, but he twisted away from her grasp, and shook the knife free of its binding. Sam spun around with all the speed and strength he could muster, blade extended.

It struck steel with a ring, and a jarring blow that vibrated through the bones in Sam's arm.

'What... are... you... doing...?' Her voice was slow and thick, yet somehow she fended Sam off, despite his speed.

Sam stabbed at her, and she stepped aside, but only just. Was that worry on her face now? He tried to throw a punch, but she grabbed his wrist, twisted hard, and Sam yowled in pain. He kicked her, connecting with her shin, and it gave him some respite to pull away. He slashed out again with the knife. He wasn't fast enough. Yana's blade was up again, but again she barely managed to see his attack coming. She stumbled backwards, grimacing.

Sam felt like he wanted to vomit, and cough, and collapse in a heap. He knew he didn't have much left in him. If he wanted revenge, he must seize it quickly. He only had a knife, but with his speed, perhaps he could put Emilio's training into practice. Sam shifted his weight to his back foot, sprang forward in a fencer's thrust, the knife stabbing outwards towards Yana's throat.

He over-extended. He felt his muscles pull, and his legs buckle. Worse, he felt a violent heat flare up inside him, and with it stabbing pricks of light clouded his vision.

In that moment, Yana Selishe was a blur. She dropped low as Sam faltered. She spun about, sweeping the back of Sam's leg with her own. He felt her boot crunch at the back of his swollen calf. He felt his legs fly up in front of him, and the ground rise up to meet his back with a painful thud.

He screamed with rage, and anguish, and pain. Half blind, weak as a kitten, he rolled over, coughing so violently he thought his ribs might crack. He staggered to his feet, and swung the knife about in wild arcs. He was half-blind. His powers failed him; the Blood Burn came upon him, though he fought to maintain some semblance of control.

'Stop it, Samir!' Yana snapped. 'I am not your enemy.'

'You killed my father!' he shouted, breathlessly, voice raw.

She stopped. He saw her only as a dark shadow. He felt her confusion.

Sam rushed at her with all the strength he could muster. She didn't move.

A great flash of light overwhelmed him. He slid to a halt as a pure white bolt of energy shot from the sky, striking the ground before him, scorching the air. Sam fell again, scrambling for cover. White afterglow danced before his eyes.

A growl of thunder crashed over the hills.

When Sam's vision finally cleared, he saw Makeno standing between him and Yana. The chief of the Savaisal leaned on his staff. From the shadowed treeline behind Makeno, dozens of pairs of eyes blinked. Dark figures stepped forward, Savaisal, to stand with their chief.

'If you have finished trying to kill this woman,' Makeno said, his eyes full of steel even though his body looked weak and weary, 'we have important matters to discuss.'

CHAPTER 21

They had returned to the river where Sam had begun his ill-fated contest against the jungle. A fire blazed – they could not risk lighting it on the crest of the hill – and Makeno now stood between Yana and Sam, firelight turning his broad features into a shifting, orange mask. That he had escaped the village seemed miraculous – Sam had felt certain that Makeno was dead. But the warden had been dragged from the mud during the confusion of Sam's escape, fleeing into the night in ignominy with the survivors. That the defeat weighed heavily on Makeno's brow was clear.

Sam was starting to feel better, at last. Makeno had made him drink some foul potion. He'd even managed to keep some food down, though nothing tasted as it should. But that was not down to his sickness. Everything was bitter in his mouth, now that he knew Yana's real identity. She was the instrument of his family's misfortune. She had killed his father. Makeno had offered counsel to them both all day, but it meant nothing. Sam would kill her.

'You must set aside this hate!' Makeno said, his exasperation plain. It was like he'd read Sam's mind. 'What is past is past. None of us can change it. But Yana Selishe can help us make the future right. Don't you see this, Samir?'

'It is not that simple,' Sam spat.

'It will change nothing, but I'll tell you one thing, Samir,' Yana said. 'I said before it was a Heritor who killed my father. Well, he is here, on this island. He is the blind man who led Zhar-Mharrad here. The vizier could have chosen any one of a dozen Heritors from his dungeons, but instead he used *him,* for some twisted purpose. To test me, perhaps.'

'And how many of those dozen other Heritors did you put there?' Sam asked, although he knew deep down he was speaking purely from spite. Yana's pain must run as deep as his own, though there could be no forgiveness. Not now.

The woman said nothing more.

'You must see that she has reason to hate Zhar-Mharrad as much as you,' Makeno said. 'If you cannot accept this woman as a friend, can you not accept her as an ally of convenience?'

'You mean a truce?'

Makeno nodded. Yana looked at Sam, her expression now the familiar, unreadable face of stone.

'And then... after?' Sam returned the woman's stare, summoning all his courage, and hatred, so that he would not look like a weak boy.

Makeno bowed his head, disappointed. 'Then after, perhaps you two must settle your differences in whatever way you see fit.'

'I agree,' Sam muttered.

Yana nodded.

'But,' Makeno added, 'at least try to conduct yourselves with honour in the meantime. There is a fight coming, and we are nothing if we cannot trust each other.'

No sooner had Makeno spoken, than Yana stood, her hand on her sword, looking north across the river. She relaxed almost at once, as more Savaisal appeared. Their leader, marked by the red feathers in his beaded headband, raised a hand in greeting. The warriors then set about looking for a place to cross.

'Where have they come from?' Sam asked. 'So many were killed at the village... I thought Zhar-Mharrad had done for your people.'

Makeno winced at the memory. 'Not quite. The Savaisal are one of the larger tribes on this island. Before Noaka's line shrank our territory, the Savaisal travelled in large groups, trading with other tribes, and even Erithereans. Our ancestral hunting grounds were vast. Those traditions may have ceased, but we still have smaller colonies out there in the jungle – pockets of our tribe that live independently of the main village. The Ancient One told me that this is how the Savaisal survived after the last storm-caller left. With no trade, they had to learn to produce all they needed for themselves. Those warriors across the river there – they are from a mountain settlement, who herd goats. The Savaisal of old were never farmers, but it seems that all things change.'

'The Ancient One!' Sam said, remembering suddenly. 'Is she...?'

'Dead? No. She is safe – her guards took her away when the fighting began. Without her, our history would be lost.

When this is over, we will return to her, and she will help us rebuild.'

Sam felt relief at that. It did not entirely compensate the guilt he felt over the loss of so many lives, but at least the tribe would endure.

'So what is the plan?' Sam asked. 'We don't have enough warriors to attack Zhar-Mharrad.'

'We know where his camp is,' Yana Selishe said, coming forward finally. 'He has sent scouts across the island – including me, admittedly – and we have a rendezvous point in a large clearing near the southern coastline. If we don't return by dusk tomorrow, Zhar-Mharrad will return to his ship without us.'

'The sun is already setting now. We have just one day to prepare, and launch an attack?' Sam looked around again at the Savaisal. There were fifteen warriors in fighting condition, a few walking wounded. Maybe ten more across the river. It would not be enough – at the last count, Zhar-Mharrad had more than twenty Bidajah, a handful of Yad-Sha'Rib soldiers, and three Manhunters that Sam knew of, not to mention the treacherous Emilio.

'Not unless we have no other choice,' Yana said. 'I believe our best hope is subterfuge – it is, after all, what you and I are both good at, Samir. I will return to the camp and tell Zhar-Mharrad that I was unable to find you. This will make him angry, and distract him. You will then use your powers to sneak into Zhar-Mharrad's tent and steal the tablet from him.'

'The tablet? Is that what this is about? What about Hassan? What about...'

'Samir!' Yana snapped. 'Focus on the bigger picture. First of all, we must ensure Zhar-Mharrad cannot find the Crystal Pool. His power will enable him to translate the writings on that tablet, and then he will locate the pool and destroy us all.'

'You forget that I cannot steal the tablet,' Sam said. 'It weakens my powers – I don't know if I can remain unseen in its presence.'

Yana considered this. 'Then we give the signal, and the Savaisal attack to cover your escape.'

'Against superior forces?' Sam asked. 'Against the Bidajah, who do not eat or sleep?'

'The Tablet of Sav'Eq-Tul is a legendary relic of this island,' Makeno interrupted. 'My people will fight hard for its return, you may count on that.'

'I do not doubt their bravery,' Sam said, 'just their numbers. Tell me, Yana, why can we not creep into the camp and kill Zhar-Mharrad? Are you not an assassin?'

'I am,' Yana replied. 'But Zhar-Mharrad is protected by sorceries beyond any of us. He is watched over by demons. It is said that the creatures are always looking for a way to usurp him, but that he has found a way to bind them to his service, and so they must obey his every command. Although there might be a way...'

'Yes?'

'Zhar-Mharrad draws his power from an amulet of his own – a black periapt, which he wears always. If we could take it, or destroy it... perhaps it would sufficiently weaken him. But the truth is, I don't know for certain. For all I know it could simply release the demons and drag us all to the underworld.'

'It would be worth it, if Zhar-Mharrad was dragged there with us,' Sam muttered.

'You are too eager to die,' Yana said, 'when too much rests upon your success.'

'There is another way,' Sam said, 'if only we have time.'

'What way?'

Sam turned to Makeno. 'When you found us at that hilltop clearing, near to the snakepit... you saw the fallen statues, yes?'

'I did,' Makeno said. 'That stretch of jungle would have been home to the Erithereans long ago, and maybe some dwell there still. Because of what Noaka did, I did not want to stay and find out.'

'But Ashtzaph said he was heading south to find his kin. If I could find Ashtzaph, then maybe he would help us. Zhar-Mharrad is in Eritherean territory, isn't he?'

'It is a bold idea, but we cannot count on the Erithereans. Any bonds of comradeship that once existed between our peoples are long severed.'

'Ashtzaph might not trust the Savaisal, but perhaps he will trust me. It is worth a try, isn't it?'

As Makeno pondered this, Sam clambered to his feet. 'There's no more time for talking. I'm going to find Ashtzaph.' He took a few steps towards the jungle, but stopped as cramps squeezed at his stomach. It took all of Sam's willpower not to double over in pain. 'I... I will need... a guide...' Sam said, through gritted teeth, and hobbled another couple of steps.

Yana placed a hand on Sam's shoulder, and stopped him in his tracks. Sam didn't even have the strength to push her away. 'You need to rest a while longer, and drink more of Makeno's medicine. I will find Ashtzaph.'

'You?'

'I helped save him. I think he trusted me – besides, I'm a better tracker. A hunter, if you recall.'

Sam glowered. 'I recall very well. No. I must do this. I…' he tried to pass by Yana, but the cramps bit more violently, and he sat down involuntarily on the soft ground.

'Makeno, you have to get Sam ready,' Yana said.

'I will.'

'I'll do my best to find the Eritherean, but who knows what that will achieve? Our window of opportunity narrows… you must go to Zhar-Mharrad's camp, as close as you dare. Watch out for his scouts – use your stealth to your advantage. If I am not with you, then you must stick to the original plan. Create a diversion and let Sam steal into the camp. Once Sam has the tablet, flee as fast and as far as you can, for otherwise Zhar-Mharrad will unleash upon you the very forces of hell.'

* * *

It was well past midnight. The jungle was pitch dark, and Sam couldn't risk a light, and so he crept slowly and carefully through the undergrowth. He stopped when he heard the crack of fallen branches. Sam flattened himself against the broad trunk of a tall tree and waited for the Bidajah to pass. The patrols were small and infrequent – Zhar-Mharrad must have been confident in his forces to post so few guards.

Once the clomping tread of the Bidajah had faded, Sam continued on his way, following Makeno's directions to the clearing, where the vizier was encamped. The Savaisal had spread out, their forces all-too thin around the enemy camp.

Of Yana Selishe there had been no sign. Part of Sam wished her dead – trampled to death by an angry Eritherean, perhaps. Another part of him wished she was with him, so he didn't have to undertake this fool's errand alone.

Soon, a glimmer of firelight led Sam to the edge of a large clearing. As soon as Sam reached it, he knew they were closer to the coast than he'd realised – a salt tang carried on the breeze, and the night-calls of gulls sounded in the distance.

Zhar-Mharrad's camp was impressive. Three large tents, bigger than the largest of the Savaisal huts, stood in the centre of the clearing, with lanterns swaying outside their entrances. The largest was black, while the other two were dirty white canvas – Sam assumed that the black tent was Zhar-Mharrad's own, and cursed that it was the furthest from his position, and the hardest to reach. Smaller tents, perhaps big enough to sleep three or four soldiers, were dotted all around. There was little enough movement in the camp. Two soldiers – human soldiers, not Bidajah, Sam noted – stood on watch near the largest tent, beside a crackling brazier. Lumbering, dark figures moved occasionally around the fringes of the camp – Bidajah, patrolling ceaselessly through the night. Sam wondered if the regular soldiers were more alert and trustworthy – perhaps, despite Zhar-Mharrad's magic, he still needed mere mortals to keep watch. But then, if none of the Bidajah had eyes, could they even see?

Sam shook that macabre thought from his head. He had to focus. It was bad enough that his temperature blew hot and cold, and that he periodically succumbed to involuntarily trembling. The after-effects of the poison were unpleasant, but thankfully his strength had returned, and he hadn't suffered the cramps since supper. Sam could only pray that he'd be up to the challenge ahead.

He waited until another slow-moving Bidajah walked by, and ran as quickly and quietly as he could into the clearing. He kept low, using the tents as cover, while hoping that the occupants were fast asleep. If, indeed, they slept at all.

Sam skirted the back of the first tent. He wondered what was inside. A barracks? Maybe Zhar-Mharrad's slaves… but would they not be back at the ship, ready to make way upon the vizier's return? But if the prisoners were in the camp at all, they would surely be in one of the large tents – Dagomir and Hassan perhaps? That gave Sam pause. Could he really leave the camp knowing that Hassan was here, in chains? And if Dagomir was alive, would he not prove a useful ally in the event of a fight?

Sam knew he had to stick to the plan. He would try to seize the tablet, and if he was not discovered, he would look for his friends.

He skulked around the side of the black tent, creeping up on the guards' position. He breathed in deeply, and out slowly, focussing. He willed himself to become one with his surroundings. He looked down at himself, concentrating as hard as he could, until his shoes reflected the grass beneath them, and his hands looked almost translucent, the black canvas of the tent visible beneath their vague outline. As quietly as he could, hoping that his camouflage would hold, he tiptoed around to the front of the tent, past the lollygagging guards, and through the flap.

The tent was almost entirely dark, save for a flickering green light coming from a golden lamp in the far corner. By that ghastly hue, Sam could only just make out the outlines of a clutter of furniture, chests, and piles of plump cushions. It looked like the room of a palace – it must have taken many slaves to carry the supplies from Zhar-Mharrad's ship, so that the vizier could sleep in the lap of luxury.

Sam squinted against the near-dark. He saw the outline of a bed, and heard the faint sounds of snoring. Sam skirted the edge of the chamber, past a table adorned with strange phials and a variety of animal skulls, past a rack hanging with sumptuous robes, and carefully past the sleeping form of Zhar-Mharrad.

Sam stopped, gasped, then covered his mouth lest his intake of breath give him away.

Zhar-Mharrad's eyes were wide open. He was staring directly at Sam.

Sam didn't move. He prayed his camouflage would hold. But slowly, he came to the realisation that the vizier was not awake. He was still snoring quietly, his chest rising and falling gently. He was asleep with his eyes open.

Sam studied the vizier for a moment longer. Without his robes, and painted eyes, and waxed moustaches, he looked almost harmless. Scrawny and elderly, with a balding pate atop long features, and a thin neck giving him an almost avian appearance, like a vulture.

Sam shuddered, and crept past the head of the bed. He saw his target now. Upright, upon a wooden stand, was the tablet. Zhar-Mharrad had replaced the thong that had held Sam's section about his neck with a larger leather strap. All the better for carrying it in its larger form.

Sam reached out and lifted it. Immediately, his hands came partially back into view, his chameleonic abilities struggling to match the strange, nullifying effect of the tablet. He slung the tablet over his shoulder, and went as quickly as he dared to the tent-flap, crawling low in case Zhar-Mharrad should stir and see the thief in his tent. Sam was partially disguised, but not enough to escape attention should someone look fully in his direction.

He peered out of the tent-flap at the two guards, waited what seemed like an age for them to look the other way, and slipped from the tent. Sam darted around the side of the tent, where the black canvas only helped disguise him, and when he was certain no alarm would be raised, he sneaked carefully around the back, between Zhar-Mharrad's tent and the smaller of the two white tents. Only then did he allow himself to breathe.

Sam crouched by the back of the tent, his heart pounding. He clutched the tablet tight in his arms. He tried to calm himself, to think rationally. No one would see him here in the shadows. Zhar-Mharrad could not detect him while he had the amulet. What matter, then, if he was no longer invisible?

He slung the tablet over his shoulder by its leather strap, and took out his knife. He'd promised himself that he'd look for Hassan, and so now he would. He very carefully worked the blade into the canvas of the tent, making enough of an opening to see through, and peered inside.

A glimmer of light shone into the tent from the lamps outside the entrance, but it was mostly in darkness. Sam could not make out any guards, and the lack of light within suggested that no one was awake. He squinted, and his eyes at last alighted on a silhouetted figure. In the centre of the tent was a man, slumped on the ground, his back leaning up against a thick wooden stake that protruded from floor to roof. He had his arms tied around the back of the stake. Even in the darkness, Sam would recognise the imposing figure of Dagomir anywhere.

Why were there no other guards? Sam looked around once more. The two men posted outside, and the occasional patrol of Bidajah seemed insufficient were Dagomir to attempt an escape. But then, where would he go? Zhar-Mharrad surely thought the Savaisal destroyed, along with Dagomir's crew. What would it matter if the captain fled into the jungle alone?

Certain now that the tent was otherwise unoccupied, Sam worked his dagger back into the hole he'd made, and sliced the canvas inch by inch down to the ground. He stopped now and then, paranoid that the tearing sound would wake half the camp, but his fears proved unfounded. Eventually, he stepped through the slit, into the tent.

Sam resisted the urge to rush straight to Dagomir, remembering that he was in the belly of the beast. Instead, he crept cautiously around the edge of the tent to get his bearings. There was a large, locked chest, a table on which was a pitcher of water and a ladle, two bedrolls, empty. There was nothing else, but for the captain, who seemed to be asleep. Everything had been too easy so far – Sam couldn't shake the feeling that this was some elaborate trap. No sooner had he thought that, than his mind raced to darker possibilities. What if Yana Selishe had engineered this to get Sam to come here of his own free will? What if she had never gone to find Ashtzaph at all, but had instead come straight here to alert Zhar-Mharrad? For all Sam knew, the Savaisal were being murdered silently in the jungle by Yana and her Manhunters even now.

'Stop torturing yourself, Samir,' he whispered to himself. He felt stupid that he had not considered the possibility sooner, but Makeno trusted Yana, so maybe Sam should, too. Besides, he was already past the point of no return. He had no choice now but to see it through.

Sam crept up to Dagomir, listening for sounds of breathing, and relieved when he heard it. He checked the captain's bonds – thick rope, fastened tight, cutting into Dagomir's wrists and forearms, and doubling back around his waist.

'Captain,' Sam hissed. 'Captain Dagomir!'

Dagomir stirred, and then his eyes snapped open, and he strained at his ropes. 'What! Come on, I'll...'

'Shh! Sam urged. 'Captain, it's me. Sam. Please be quiet.'

Dagomir shook his head as if to clear his mind. 'Sam? What the devil?'

'I came for the tablet,' Sam whispered. He tapped it.

Dagomir nodded. 'Clever. You should go before that wizard notices it's missing.'

'Have you seen Hassan?'

Dagomir jerked his head towards the tent-flaps. 'The other tent is where the rest of the prisoners are. I was put in here alone for head-butting a guard.' Dagomir smiled at the memory almost wistfully. 'Broke his nose. Aye, with my hands tied behind my back they couldn't tame me. Well, until now. The other tent, that's where your friend is, anyway. And the blind man, and a few others I didn't see properly. Slaves, I think, and some woman – I've heard her wailing oft-times.'

Dagomir had rarely been so talkative. It was like he'd been in solitary confinement for a week, not a day. Sam began working the ropes with his knife. 'Hold still.'

'What are you doing, lad? Get out of here.'

'I won't leave you, Captain,' Sam said. 'I'm not alone. Makeno is out there, with the Savaisal. And Yana... she's gone to fetch help.'

'That witch!' Dagomir snarled, then looked embarrassed at his outburst, and lowered his voice. 'You can't trust her, lad. I trusted her, and look where it got me.'

'Believe me, Captain, I have more reason to hate her than anyone.'

'Pah! I doubt that very…'

'She killed my father.'

'Oh.'

'I found out only today.'

All was quiet, but for the low rasp of Sam's knife travelling back and forth rapidly across the ropes.

'I understand why you came back, lad, I do,' Dagomir whispered. 'Your father gave you that amulet, right? Although it's not really an amulet any more, but that's beside the point. The only thing I have of my father's is his sword. When I was exiled, I was given food for perhaps a couple of days, and that sword. It was too heavy for me even to lift, I was such a stick of a boy. It saved my life more times than I can count, and I always thought it was my father, the rightful king of my land, guiding my arm, lending me strength. And now look at me. Betrayed and imprisoned. What did I expect after a life of piracy, eh, lad? I had hoped that when I died, I might take a place of honour in my father's hall, in the land of endless summer. But after the life I've led, what hope is there for honour even in death? Emilio took my sword. Emilio! That's what a life of piracy does for you, lad. My so-called friend… Zhar-Mharrad was going to throw the sword away, and Emilio asked if he could have it. When that black wizard asked why, Emilio said, "So that when I return to Caldega..."'

'I might show the pirates the legendary sword of Dagomir.' Emilio strode into the tent, and set down a lantern. Dagomir's sword was slung over Emilio's back – the captain strained at his bonds when he saw it. Emilio grinned, but his eyes were cold and mirthless. 'And prove to them that I slew the Pirate Prince,' he finished. 'Put the knife down, Samir.' Emilio drew his sword.

Sam was almost through one set of ropes. Dagomir might be able to break one arm free, but that would be all. Sam dropped the knife on the ground, deliberately within reach of Dagomir's fingertips. He stood warily.

'I see from your face you want this,' Emilio said to Dagomir. He unslung the sword from his back, and set it down atop the wooden chest. 'I carry it everywhere now. It is my ticket to fame and fortune – the bedrock of my own legend. As for you,' he turned to Sam. 'I'm glad you came back, Samir,' Emilio said. 'And I'm glad it was me who caught you. I'll doubtless get another reward for this.'

'You killed Bardo,' Sam said, simply.

Emilio shrugged. 'He was going to ruin things for all of us. If you'd just surrendered, Bardo would be alive now. So really, it's your fault he's dead.'

Sam shook with rage. He thought about rushing Emilio. He knew he had the speed, but unarmed, against a skilled fighter, Sam didn't think it wise.

'You can still put things right,' Sam said, edging away from Dagomir. He hoped the captain would take the hint and try to free himself. 'You can still restore your honour.'

'My honour?' Emilio laughed bitterly. 'Are you really such a fool? My honour was lost years ago. The things I've done since then… The things I've done on *his* orders.' He glared at Dagomir. 'I'm a pirate, lad, and so's he. And like all the best pirates, I've learned to pick a winning side.' Emilio darted forward, so fast even Sam didn't see it coming. Sam felt the sharp point of Emilio's sword at his throat.

'Come on, Emilio, he's just a boy,' Dagomir said.

'We both know he's more than that.'

'Curse you if your loyalty is so easily bought. So what if he's a Heritor? He sailed with us. He fought with us.'

'You've gone soft,' Emilio scoffed, never taking his eyes from Sam. 'You don't deserve my loyalty any longer. Samir is a prize, "Captain", just like all the others we've plundered over the years.'

Out of the corner of his eyes, Sam saw a shadow move across the back of the tent. Another figure was within, silent and indistinct. Sam's eyes followed the shape as it slipped noiselessly towards Emilio. For a moment, he thought the demon had followed him, and was about to exact a terrible revenge upon him. But he soon saw it was no demon.

'There's only one prize for traitors, Emilio,' said the shadow.

Emilio spun about quickly, shoving Sam away with one hand, slashing his sabre in the other. His blade met the enduring steel of a Dar'Shuri scimitar.

Yana's scimitar.

For a moment, the two glared at each other, swords crossed.

'Cat got your tongue, Emilio?' Yana purred.

'I'm trying to decide whose side you're on,' Emilio replied. 'You play every role most convincingly.'

'It does not matter whose side I'm on – killing you would be pleasure, not business.'

Emilio stepped back, scraping his blade along Yana's. He placed one hand behind the small of his back, in the fighter's stance. But Sam saw that hand curl around the hilt of a thin blade, tucked into Emilio's belt.

'I like to act on occasion, too,' Emilio said, his voice quiet and measured. 'Like the time I let you beat me in a duel.'

'Ah,' Yana smiled. 'So you think you are a match for me?'

'I've been relishing the opportunity to clash swords with you again, she-devil.'

Sam tensed. He was about to leap forward, to grab Emilio's knife, and help Yana kill him. But a great flash of light filled the tent, dazzling Sam instantly. The sound of gushing flames roared briefly, before normality returned. The gloom of the tent was lifted. Torches flickered in every corner, filling the chamber with warm light.

But in the entranceway of the tent stood Zhar-Mharrad, tall and gaunt, his high turban and flowing robes lending him a theatrical appearance. Behind the vizier stood two of his men – a Bidajah, even more imposing in the confines of the tent, and a Manhunter, arms folded, everything but his eyes shrouded in black cloth.

'Put your swords away,' Zhar-Mharrad commanded. 'While this petty rivalry is amusing, it does not become my most trusted spies to behave in such a manner.'

Yana and Emilio glared daggers at each other one last time before, to Sam's dismay, they both sheathed their swords.

'That's better,' said the vizier. 'I see the boy came of his own free will after all. You were right, Emilio – his loyalty to his little friend is far greater than his desire for self-preservation. How… noble?' He chuckled, then at a wave of his hand the Bidajah lurched forward, and grabbed Sam roughly by the arm.

Sam was too stunned to do anything. He knew he couldn't escape Zhar-Mharrad's magic, and if Yana was truly the vizier's servant after all, then it was all over.

'And you, Ku Selishe,' Zhar-Mharrad purred. 'You failed in your mission. This pirate knew the boy better than you, it seems.'

'Apparently so, my lord,' Yana said.

'Perhaps you are losing your touch. It had to happen sometime, but it does rather cast aspersions on your suitability to stand at my right hand.'

'I assure you, my lord, you will find no one more capable.'

'Ah, there's the old confidence. And I assume, of course, that you know where your loyalties lie?'

'My lord?'

'Emilio tells me that your act was so often too convincing. I must say there is something persuasive about that argument. You did kill my beloved pet, after all. You are surely not planning to betray me, Ku Selishe.' His words took on a sinister bent. Zhar-Mharrad was holding a black gemstone, fastened about his neck with a silver chain. As he spoke, he rubbed the gem between finger and thumb – the torches guttered, the shadows thickened unnaturally.

'You would believe this vagabond over me, my lord vizier?' Yana said, coolly.

'He is no mere vagabond,' Zhar-Mharrad replied. 'He has been in my employ since his ship came to Yad-Sha'Rib. He has proven himself many times since then.'

'What?' Dagomir cried. All turned to see the captain, still sitting on the dirt floor of the tent, bound with ropes. 'Emilio, you worm!'

Zhar-Mharrad clapped his hands together gleefully. 'He is almost as good as you, Ku Selishe! This "vagabond", as you put it, met with you on Caldega, in disguise – and you never suspected it was him.'

'You!' Sam and Yana said in unison.

'The same,' said Emilio. 'I know all the secret ways around Caldega. Zhar-Mharrad's raven brought me my instructions, and I passed them on to you.' He smirked at Yana. 'You thought the vizier had a spy on the island the whole time, while in truth I was travelling with you. When I learned the boy had seen us, I knew I could count on you to deny everything, while all I had to do was have a word in the captain's ear. Isn't that right,

Dagomir? You were ready enough to believe me when I told you the boy was making up a story – especially when this comely wench was on hand to persuade you.'

'Why, Emilio?' Dagomir growled. 'We could have found the Crystal Pool together. We could have had everything.'

Emilio shrugged. 'We'd all heard the legends of Zhar-Mharrad,' Emilio said. 'The vizier of Yad-Sha'Rib commands unimaginable forces. Forces capable of granting a man's every wish. Your dream, Captain, was to come here, to the Lost Isles, and find power, wealth and fame. To sail back to the Northlands and reclaim your father's throne, perhaps. But to do that, you first had to draw the wrath of Zhar-Mharrad by taking something he wanted from his city. That gave me an idea. Why chase your dream, when I could realise my own far more simply? By helping Zhar-Mharrad, I could secure a prize worth far more to me than travelling with you to the frozen north.'

'What prize?' Dagomir spat.

'I wish only to return to Tareta, and be welcomed back with open arms. And there to marry my dear Camila.'

'How can that happen?' Sam shouted. 'You killed your brother. You were disgraced.'

'Ah, I asked the same question of Zhar-Mharrad here. And do you know what he told me? He said that if I helped him, his demon would alter the very strands of time, so that none would remember Santo. It would be as if my brother never existed. So when I returned,

Camila would be waiting for me, and my parents would wish to know all about my adventures in the Lost Isles, and never again mention the name of my sainted brother. Gods know I heard his name often enough my whole life. Santo, the hero. Santo, the warrior. Santo, the…'

'He didn't cheat, did he?' Sam interrupted. Emilio shot him a fierce glare. 'You killed him in cold blood, because you wanted to steal his love from him. He never cheated you. He was twice the man you were and you couldn't stand it.'

Emilio took a stride towards Sam, and cracked him hard across the cheek with the back of his hand. The look he gave confirmed Sam's suspicions.

'Enough of this tedious nonsense,' Zhar-Mharrad snapped. 'Emilio, be so good as to bring me my tablet.' Emilio began to wrestle the tablet from Sam's shoulder, while the Bidajah yanked at his arm. 'As for you, Yana Selishe,' Zhar-Mharrad continued, 'perhaps we should speak in private, to put the question of your loyalty to rest once and for all.' As he said this, he held the periapt higher.

The shadows gathered in the corners of the tent like smoke. The scent of brimstone filled the air. Yana's eyes widened. Was that fear in her eyes?

'O demon of the underworld,' Zhar-Mharrad muttered. 'Mighty lord of magic, whose name is *Ziriz*…'

Thunder boomed so loud overhead, the canvas walls of the tent vibrated, and the ground shook. Zhar-Mharrad took a step backwards, his eyes darting about furtively. Emilio and the Bidajah stopped trying to wrestle the tablet away from Sam, and looked up to the roof instead, which billowed like rolling waves, wind whistling through every seam.

'Yes!' Dagomir roared. 'Vanya!'

'Not Vanya,' Emilio muttered. 'Makeno.'

'What?' Zhar-Mharrad said. 'The warden lives still? Then he shall meet his end at the hands of the Riftborn.' He held aloft the periapt once more. 'O demon of the underworld...' he began again.

Yana Selishe moved so fast Sam would have taken her for a Heritor like him. She drew a dagger from her belt, and slashed out as quickly and precisely as a striking viper. The blade slashed Zhar-Mharrad's hand. A finger flew away, separated from the hand. The periapt fell on its chain to Zhar-Mharrad's chest. The vizier screamed in a pitch so high he might have been whistling dogs.

Only the other Manhunter reacted, reaching for his sword, but too slowly to stop Yana. She levelled a kick into the vizier's gut, and he flew backwards, through the flap, out into the night.

The Bidajah holding Sam stopped. His grip was still firm, but he appeared rooted to the spot without his master's guidance. Emilio swung around behind Sam, putting the boy between himself and Yana.

Yana had her own problems to contend with first. The Manhunter had freed his sword, and unleashed a flurry of blows, so fast that his blade became a blur of reflected torchlight. Yana parried his strikes aside with her dagger, dodging backwards past Dagomir, before finally swinging her own scimitar from its scabbard. She crossed both her blades, trapping the Manhunter's sword, stopping him at last, then pushed him away.

The Manhunter crouched low, sword readied.

'Don't do this, Faizil,' Yana said. 'You swore the blood oath. You serve So'Kurrah, not Zhar-Mharrad.'

'You know the law,' the Manhunter snarled. 'The Grand Vizier speaks for the Merchant-King. Zhar-Mharrad's will is an extension of So'Kurrah's will. It is written.'

'You know what Zhar-Mharrad has planned. You know he will stop at nothing once he's found the pool. He will usurp our king!'

'And then he will be the new king, and I will have served both in accordance with the law.'

Disappointment was etched on Yana's face. Faizil sprang at her.

The Manhunter was snatched from the air by his neck. Dagomir had managed to free most of his bonds, all but one wrist. With speed belying his size, Dagomir had leapt up, grabbing the Manhunter with his free hand. He put one bear-like arm around the man's neck, and, with a mighty heave, wrenched him upwards so hard that the Manhunter's neck broke with a sickening snap.

Sam kicked and struggled against the Bidajah with renewed vigour. Emilio grabbed Sam by the scruff of the neck.

Yana's crossbow twanged. A quarrel thudded into the neck of the Bidajah, and at last the brute moved, clutching at the bolt, blood soaking his hand. The Bidajah's grip on Sam slackened, and the brute toppled backwards.

Emilio snarled, and gave Sam a stinging blow that sent him spinning away, crashing painfully into the wooden chest. As Sam fell, he felt the tablet wrench free, into Emilio's grasp.

'Cut this rope,' Dagomir called to Yana.

Sam looked up groggily as Emilio slung the tablet over his shoulder, and leapt towards Yana.

'Look out!' Sam called feebly. He tried to stand, but his head spun, and he fell back to his knees. On the floor of the tent before him, disturbed by the commotion, was Dagomir's sword.

* * *

Yana hadn't expected Emilio to attack – she'd thought him too cowardly for that. He struck with uncanny speed and precision, his sword stabbing forwards so quickly, with such unexpected reach, that Yana managed only to knock the blade aside with her crossbow before Emilio thrust again.

Yana ducked low, rolling past Emilio. If she could reach Dagomir, the two of them together could end this quickly. They could pursue Zhar-Mharrad. They could win.

Emilio's blade whistled towards Yana's head. She jerked away, felt the sharp sting of the sword-point bite into the skin above her eye. She threw the crossbow at Emilio, buying a second, and in that second she was on her feet, sword in hand.

Another rumble of thunder boomed outside. Lightning shone momentarily through the canvas.

Emilio grinned. 'Can you feel it, Selishe?' he said. 'Can you feel death calling?'

'I've felt it since the day I could walk,' Yana replied. 'And it will not come at your hand.'

She flicked her wrist. Three small, poisoned blades flew towards Emilio. He was already moving as the smile evaporated from his face. The knives flew past harmlessly, and Emilio sprang forward, sword glittering in torchlight.

Yana parried three swift strikes. Emilio drew in close. She drove her forehead into the bridge of his nose; felt the crack of bone. Hot, sticky blood splattered on her flesh. Emilio fell away, crying out in pain.

There could be no respite. Yana raised her scimitar to strike the killing blow.

'Yana, no! Behind you!'

Sam? Yana tried to turn, but the Bidajah was already upon her. The brute grabbed her wrist, twisting the sword from her hand. She pulled a curved dagger from her belt and pushed it under the Bidajah's armour, between the ribs. She thrust five times in swift succession, striking like a serpent, and finally the hulking soldier let go, and dropped to its knees.

'No!' Sam again. And Dagomir, together.

The long, red point licked outwards from beneath her ribcage like a long, flicking tongue. Yana looked down at it, confused. She felt so very cold, all at once. It was a blade, covered in blood. Her blood.

It withdrew, and pain overwhelmed her. Darkness shadowed her vision. She turned to see Emilio. He was still on his knees, sword in his hand. The blade was coated in dark red blood. Yana tried to raise her knife, to fight on, but she had no strength. It fell from her grasp, into the dirt.

Emilio stood too. He flicked Yana's blood from the blade.

'Don't be ashamed,' Emilio said. 'Death comes to us all.'

He pushed Yana. She was too weak to resist. She fell on her back, looking up at the point of Emilio's sword, her world already turning to black. She had failed.

* * *

Sam was on his feet at last. He drew on his power, sprinting across the tent towards Yana. He saw Emilio poised, and then start to strike. Sam was too far away. No matter how slow Emilio's sword-thrust appeared to Sam's preternatural eyes, it would be over in a heartbeat. Sam's mind raced with the horror of what he was witnessing. Yana had redeemed herself at the last, and Sam would have to watch her die.

There was movement at the periphery of Sam's vision. Dagomir had freed himself. Sam tumbled aside as Dagomir closed on Emilio; time sped up again.

Dagomir crashed into Emilio, roaring like a demon. Emilio was flung bodily into the canvas. He tried to get up, to thrust his blade into Dagomir's ribs as he had

Yana's, but Dagomir parried the blow with a bundle of his own ropes. He kicked Emilio in the head with sickening force, like a blow from a mule. Emilio scurried away on all fours like a dog. Dagomir shouted curses in a multitude of tongues.

Emilio leapt to his feet, sword in one hand, his dagger now in the other. He thrust towards Dagomir, who barely knocked aside the blade. He followed through with the dagger, coming in close, slashing Dagomir across the arm. The captain was driven back, his rage not enough to protect him from naked steel. Emilio slashed with the sword, a confident grin returning to his bloodied face as he opened up a thin wound in Dagomir's chest.

'Captain!' Sam shouted. And with all his strength, he took up Dagomir's hefty broadsword by the wide blade, and slung it over to the captain, hilt-first.

Dagomir caught the sword in one clean motion. For a moment, Sam felt that the sword had been guided to its owner by some invisible hand. As soon as he held the blade before him, everything about Dagomir's demeanour transformed. By the flickering orange torchlight he looked like a grim omen of death – a demigod, sent to the world to exact some terrible vengeance. Emilio sensed it too. He looked at Dagomir, glanced nervously at Sam, then turned and ran from the tent as fast as his legs would carry him.

Sam staggered to Yana. Dagomir knelt beside her.

'I'm sorry…' Sam began.

'Don't be,' she gasped, coughing up blood weakly.

'We are... even.'

'Yana,' Dagomir said. 'I must tell you. I...'

'I know,' she cut him short. 'No... time. The tablet... Zhar-Mharrad...'

Dagomir nodded, his eyes full of pain.

'Go!' she said. She collapsed, limp and lifeless.

Sam wanted to give up. He wanted to curl up next to Yana and weep.

There came a third peal of thunder, and this spurred Dagomir to his feet. The captain took a deep breath, and roared, 'Vanya's wrath!' With that, he ran from the tent, sword raised.

Sam took one last look at Yana. He picked up her dagger, and followed the captain.

CHAPTER 22

The camp was in disarray.

Soldiers and Bidajah ran in all directions, trying to find the source of the attack. The Savaisal, still few in number, used the jungle to their advantage, attacking from the treeline with blowpipes and javelins, then melding back into the shadows. All the while, a great storm raged, wind and rain lashing at the defenders, lightning flickering all around the camp. Zhar-Mharrad's great tent was aflame. Makeno had taken a very literal revenge for the razing of his village.

The vizier screamed like a harpy, wheeling about, screeching orders at his warriors. He was frantic with panic, and mad with pain and anger. Sam knew this was a man unused to such ignominy.

Ahead of him, in the centre of the camp, Dagomir fought like a man possessed. He raced between the tents in pursuit of Emilio. The former ship's mate fled wildly, pushing soldiers into Dagomir's path, only for the captain to slay them, his father's sword thirsting for blood. Half a dozen soldiers charged at Dagomir, and the captain cleaved through them all as if they weren't there. With every stroke of his sword, limbs were severed from bodies, heads from necks. With every kill, the darkness in Dagomir's eyes grew. He roared Emilio's name, daring his old friend to face him. But Sam saw now that Emilio was working his way back around to Zhar-Mharrad. He was leading Dagomir back to the vizier and his guards.

Sam raced to intercept Emilio, feet slapping muddy ground. He darted between two small tents as Emilio bore down on him, looking over his shoulder at the pursuing Dagomir. Emilio turned at the last moment, saw Sam before him, tried to dart aside. Sam was too quick – he stuck out his leg, and Emilio tripped, rolling head over heels in the mud, the tablet sliding away from him.

Dagomir roared a guttural battle cry, like a wild beast. He leapt from the darkness, jumping over Sam, bringing his sword down on Emilio with enough force to cleave a tree in half.

Emilio rolled aside, dirt flying as Dagomir crashed to the ground, and the mighty broadsword tore into the earth.

Sam leapt forwards, dagger bared. Emilio parried his blow aside with arrogant contempt.

'You shouldn't have followed Dagomir,' Emilio panted. He tried to act composed, but he was hurting. 'You should have stayed in the gutters of Yad-Sha'Rib, rather than die on this island.'

Dagomir was up, swinging his sword in a great arc. Emilio leapt aside. Sam sprang at him, but Emilio parried the blow more easily this time, and wheeled about with an acrobatic kick that took the knife from Sam's hand, and sent Sam sprawling into the mud.

Sam felt about for the dagger. By the time he found it, Dagomir and Emilio's duel had driven them further away. Sam leapt up, and ran to catch up with the captain.

Emilio had finally steadied himself, adopting the fighting stance of the Taretan swordsmen. Dagomir hacked and stabbed like a butcher, the weight of his sword tiring him, making him that much slower the harder he fought.

Sam was almost in reach of the captain when Emilio struck. The Taretan shifted his weight, as he had done so many times before, and darted forwards beneath Dagomir's sword stroke. The slender foil punched effortlessly through Dagomir's chest, and out through his broad back. The captain jolted and shook, then stopped. Emilio drew in close, allowing the captain to lean on him even as he twisted his sword up to the hilt. Emilio winked at Sam.

He winked.

'None of you could ever defeat me,' Emilio said. 'I'm sorry it had to end this way, Captain, truly I am.'

Sam stopped, numb. He stepped away, part in fear, part in disbelief. Behind Emilio, a shadow formed, and Zhar-Mharrad loomed from the rain.

The vizier laughed.

'Truly you are a fine addition to my army,' Zhar-Mharrad said. 'Your reward now barely seems enough!'

Emilio made to push Dagomir off him, to drop his lifeless corpse into the mud. But he could not.

Dagomir was not yet dead. He grabbed Emilio's hand, crushing it into the hilt of his own sword. Emilio's eyes widened in disbelief. Zhar-Mharrad echoed the sentiment, taking a step away from the Northman who refused to die.

Inch by inch, Dagomir pulled the sword from his own chest, Emilio's hand held firm. Emilio struggled, but against Dagomir's strength he was like a child. When at last Emilio was a full arm's length away from the captain, Dagomir, with a mighty effort, hoisted his broadsword aloft. Lightning flashed, reflecting white from the blade. Emilio looked at the sword, the grim terror of inevitability in his eyes.

'For… Yana,' Dagomir grunted. And he brought down the sword with such a terrible force, that it sliced through Emilio's collarbone, and split the treacherous mate in two from throat to navel.

Sam stood open-mouthed as Emilio sank to the ground. Dagomir threw Emilio's sword aside. He faltered. He looked at Sam once more and said, 'Get the tablet. Save your friend.' Then the captain turned to Zhar-Mharrad, who looked as though he had seen a ghost, and leapt at the vizier, sword aloft.

Sam saw Zhar-Mharrad sweep away as Dagomir tried to grapple him. The vizier called for his guards, and they came, marching from the darkness, golden masks glimmering in firelight. There was nothing Sam could do. Four Bidajah kicked Dagomir to the ground, stabbing down at him with spears. Sam knew in his heart that Dagomir was already dead before the Bidajah attacked him – the captain had just been too stubborn to realise it.

'The boy!' Zhar-Mharrad shouted. 'Kill the boy!'

The Bidajah turned at the order from their lord. Sam sprang forward, snatched up the tablet from the mud even as steel-shod boots shook the ground before him, and scrambled away.

Zhar-Mharrad began to chant. Sam turned back to see a roiling, smoke-like form spiral into the night sky. Two flaming red eyes opened in an indistinct serpentine head. Wings of pure darkness unfurled, raindrops hissing as they touched the smoky membrane. The vizier had at last summoned his demon.

The Bidajah gained on Sam as he stumbled before the horrifying sight of the 'Riftborn'. Zhar-Mharrad's power, it seemed, was absolute.

A large, mailed hand grabbed Sam's tunic. His tunic tore half off his back, but Sam did not stop. He held the tablet close, praying that it would protect him from Zhar-Mharrad's spells. An unearthly sound filled the air, the guttural moan of the demon. Sam did not look back again, but ran in blind panic away from Zhar-Mharrad, and the Bidajah.

He collided with someone. Sam sprawled in the mud once more, dropping the tablet. He looked up to see a familiar face, but an unexpected one. Hassan sat in the dirt, blinking with confusion.

'Hassan! You've escaped. Come on, let's get out of here!'

Sam's words fell on deaf ears. Hassan stood slowly, eyes staring into the middle distance, glazed and weak. He looked thin and pale, like a ghost of himself. From behind his back, he revealed a dagger.

'Hassan? What are you doing?'

A Bidajah came up behind Sam. Sam sensed the danger, and ducked aside, skipping away from a clumsy blow. Hassan turned, keeping Sam in sight, the dagger pointed at his friend. Sam eyed the tablet, now lying behind the towering Bidajah. To his right, the vast, smoking swirls of the demon ploughed into the jungle, then erupted upwards again, its baleful eyes looking for its next victim. From the sound of distant screams, Sam knew the Savaisal were losing.

Hassan strode towards Sam. Sam backed away, eyes fixed on the knife. Then he looked up, over Hassan's shoulder, and saw Zhar-Mharrad in the distance. He looked directly at Sam, hand outstretched, blood dripping from his missing finger. There was a hateful sneer on the vizier's face, and now that sneer was mirrored by Hassan.

'Kill him!' Zhar-Mharrad called, voice almost lost on the wind.

'Must... kill you...' Hassan murmured, staggering forward awkwardly, as though not in control of his own limbs.

The four Bidajah crowded in behind Hassan. Sam realised that Zhar-Mharrad wanted the cruellest of deaths for him. He wanted Hassan to be the one who killed Sam, and the Bidajah were there only to ensure the job was done.

Sam didn't have the strength. He'd been a bystander as his friends had died. And now his best friend in the world wanted to kill him. Sam knew he should just run into the jungle and never look back. But Hassan would die either way. If Sam couldn't find a way to defeat Zhar-Mharrad, the vizier would enslave the Golden City. And where next would Zhar-Mharrad's greedy eye fall?

Hassan fell upon Sam, stabbing down with the knife. Sam grabbed Hassan's wrists, wrestling with him. His friend was always bigger and stronger, and Sam strained to turn the knife away. He swerved his body, kicking at

Hassan's legs, sweeping his feet from under him. Both boys splashed into the mud. Hassan recovered quickly, both hands on the knife now, pushing with all his might against Sam. Sam tucked his legs up, feet against Hassan's belly, and kicked as hard as he could. Hassan flew backwards, slamming into the nearest Bidajah. He dropped the knife.

'Hassan, please! I know you don't want to do this. It's Zhar-Mharrad's magic making you do this. You have to fight him!'

Hassan paused, confusion clouding his features just for a moment. Then he looked at the knife. Sam's heart sank.

A Bidajah strode forward, spear readied. Clearly, Hassan was taking too long for Zhar-Mharrad's tastes. Sam backed away as the golden-masked warrior hoisted the spear, ready to strike.

Lightning streaked across the sky, hurtling from the heaven, blasting the Bidajah in a mighty, blinding bolt. The brute was reduced to a blackened, lurching mess in a heartbeat, and coruscating bands of energy danced from him, flashing out to his comrades and enveloping them too. Makeno leapt into their midst, staff whirling, forcing them back. Overhead, the demon roared, turning its gaze to the storm warden. Makeno raised a fist to the sky, and another flicker of light danced amongst the storm clouds for a split second, before striking down through the smoke-creature, igniting a tent in a shower of sparks and flame. The demon moaned, dissipating, and only slowly coalescing into its hideous form once more.

Sam rushed to Hassan, knocking his friend to the ground before he could find his knife.

'The tablet, Samir,' Makeno shouted. 'Use it to protect your friend, and get out of here.' He thrust his staff upwards. Another bolt of lightning struck it, wreathing Makeno in energy for a moment, before forking outwards towards both the demon and Zhar-Mharrad. The demon screamed and shrank back. The vizier seemed to catch the lightning bolt in his bare hand, twisting it, and casting the energy aside. A ball of green flame erupted in Zhar-Mharrad's hand, and he threw it at Makeno, who planted his staff firmly into the ground. Just as the fireball was about to engulf him, the pounding rain was drawn rapidly to Makeno, concentrating in front of him in a swirling shield of water. The flame ploughed into it, and evaporated in a plume of hissing steam.

Sam was already racing past Makeno, Hassan hot on his heels. He scooped up the tablet just as his friend tackled him, driving them both to the ground once more. Sam hardly had the energy to fight. He was soaked through, covered in mud, and his limbs felt leaden.

Hassan punched Sam hard in the face.

Sam felt blood in his mouth. The pain jolted him to action. He fumbled for the tablet again, grasped it firmly, and brought it upwards, hard. It cracked Hassan aside the head, knocking him off Sam and into the dirt. Sam scrambled up immediately, taking the leather strap and looping it around Hassan's neck. Hassan moaned groggily. Sam grabbed his friend by the wrists, and dragged him bodily though the mud, away from Makeno, who had now attracted the full attention of Zhar-Mharrad and his demon.

The Savaisal struck out further from the jungle now, inspired by their chief, but managing to do little more than distract the Bidajah, who lumbered after them single-mindedly. Sam remembered the behaviour of the Bidajah in the tent – just how much mental control did Zhar-Mharrad need to exert over his masked soldiers? Without his direct command, did they simply act on instinct? If so, Makeno's battle with the vizier could well save the lives of the Savaisal.

'Sam…' Hassan groaned.

'You're awake!' Sam helped him sit upright.

Hassan touched his face, swollen from the fight. 'Wh… what happened to me?'

'I'll tell you later, my friend. Hassan, do you know where you are? How much can you remember?'

Hassan wore a clouded expression, and his brow furrowed into a frown. Had his face always been so lined?

'Oh no… Samir, I am sorry. I didn't mean to betray you. It was… He…'

Tears welled in Hassan's eyes. Sam had never seen him cry in all the years he'd known Hassan. What must Zhar-Mharrad have done to him?

'It's alright, Hassan. I know it was Zhar-Mharrad. This tablet around your neck – it protects you from his sorcery. We must get far away from here, where his black magic cannot touch you.'

A flash of lightning lit the scene of battle all around the edge of the camp. For a moment, Sam saw the Savaisal fall. He winced. There would be none of the tribe left at this rate.

Sam tried to yank Hassan to his feet, urging him to flee.

'No!' Hassan said. He grabbed Sam's arm, squeezed so tight it hurt. His eyes were wide and pleading. 'Are you mad, Samir? We cannot leave him!'

'Who?'

'I'm sorry, Samir, truly I am. I knew all along. I wanted to tell you, back at the village, but I could not. I could not speak, for Zhar-Mharrad had bound me to silence. By the gods, how can you ever forgive me?'

'What are you talking about?' Sam wanted to shake Hassan, but he could see his friend's distress. 'You are making no sense, Hassan, and we have to leave before it's too late.'

'Your mother!' Hassan blurted. 'She was taken to the Temple of Birrahd, and she told Zhar-Mharrad a secret. A terrible secret. I heard it all, and I should have told you, but I could not.'

Sam pulled away from Hassan, and stepped back.

'And where is my mother now?'

'I don't know.' Tears streamed down Hassan's cheeks.

Sam's fists balled tight. 'And what is the secret. If you are my friend, tell me now.'

'The blind Heritor… he would not obey Zhar-Mharrad. Not until… until the vizier hurt your mother. And then it was revealed. Your father was never killed by the hunters. He was imprisoned, all these years. The blind Heritor is your father.'

Sam's heart beat faster. He couldn't breathe. Hassan's words were like a slap to the face. But how could he even believe it? What if Hassan was lying, even now? How deep did Zhar-Mharrad's magic flow?

'I'm telling the truth,' Hassan said, sensing Sam's mistrust. 'Zhar-Mharrad blinded him. He cut out his tongue so that he could not defy him. Even now, your father is shackled like a slave, and he is not alone. There are others in there, imprisoned. They were brought to the island as Zhar-Mharrad's porters.'

'When you were captured – did you tell him where to find my mother?' Sam snarled. 'Answer me, Hassan!'

'No. I swear it to all the gods. His spies found her. I never betrayed her. I would not do that to you.'

Sam rubbed at his face. He couldn't take it all in. And there was so little time.

'You don't know what he did…' Hassan sobbed. 'I'm sorry. So sorry…'

Sam realised his fists were clenched so tight he was drawing blood from his palms. 'It's all right, Hassan. I forgive you. But you must take me to him – to the Heritor.'

Fear filled Hassan's eyes.

'Be brave!' Sam snapped. 'I don't blame you for what you did, but I know you'll feel guilty for it anyway. But maybe you don't have to… Be brave, help me. Help us win.'

Hassan nodded. He held out a hand, and Sam took it. 'Follow me,' he said.

* * *

The low moans of the captives started up again. Hassan had managed to quieten them when they'd entered, but now they seemed agitated anew. They were mostly children, crowded together in small cages like animals, pushing their hands out through the bars in search of comfort.

The Heritor stirred, his head lolling. His eyes were covered in a dirty rag, the face beneath it bruised and swollen.

'Listen to me,' Sam whispered, 'I am here to rescue you.'

The old man groaned, and fumbled around. Chains rattled. His wrists were manacled.

'There's no time to explain. I have to get you out of this cage. We have to escape.'

Sam tried to force the cage lock with his dagger, but it would not budge. 'I'll find a way,' he said. He rattled the door ineffectually. He looked for the bindings on the cage bars, and wondered if he could cut through them, but they were many, and the construction was strong. Unnaturally so.

The Heritor seemed to come to his senses at last, and grasped the bars. He shook his head, grunting something unintelligible with his tongueless mouth. He tried to shoo Sam away.

'Don't worry,' Sam said. 'We have the tablet. Zhar-Mharrad cannot detect us now. And my friends are out there, fighting his army. Once we've escaped... Curse it! Why will these bars not budge?'

'They are enchanted,' Hassan said. 'Enchanted so that he cannot break them'

The man was standing now, hands around the bars of his cage.

'I know what Zhar-Mharrad has done to you,' Sam said. 'And I know that he imprisoned my mother. And I know I should not be here. But here I am, and all these things cannot be helped now. You know me, don't you?'

The Heritor's shoulders sank. His head slumped forward, mane of greying hair falling over his face. He nodded.

'Your name is… Asim Lahij?'

The Heritor nodded again.

Tears welled in Sam's eyes. He reached through the bars, fingers brushing aside the man's matted hair, touching the face of his father for the first time since he was a baby. The old man raised a filthy, rough hand, and wrapped his gnarled fingers around Sam's. He shook uncontrollably.

A spark passed between them. Warmth and light, quickening Sam's pulse, filling him with energy. The old man straightened – he felt it too.

'Father…' Sam choked. He knew in that moment it was all true, and that the Heritor knew it also. The world crashed in upon him, but he fought to maintain control of his conflicting emotions. Nothing could be helped now if he broke down here. He had to get his father away, and Hassan, and the tablet. He did not believe Makeno, for all his power, was enough. But here, there seemed to be a glimmer of hope: an ally. His father, long thought dead. Together, perhaps, they stood a chance. It felt like destiny.

'Father, I have seen your strength. You must help me. Break out of this cage.'

The old man shook his head ruefully.

'He has tried before,' Hassan said. 'Zhar-Mharrad strengthened the enchantment after the last time.'

'Please, I beg you. Stand with me, fight with me. I cannot do this alone. You know why Zhar-Mharrad is here. You know what will happen if he succeeds. I have the tablet – it is restored! But I cannot escape Zhar-Mharrad's forces alone. All of this will be for nothing if I am caught. Search your heart, father. You know what will happen next. You know that when he returns to Yad-Sha'Rib, he will make slaves of our people. How many more Bidajah will he create in his dungeons? How many more Heritors will be rounded up and tortured? And what will happen to mother? If ever there was a time to fight, it is now. What more is there to lose?'

The blind Heritor hung his head for just a moment. He seemed to gather himself, then wrapped one of his chains around both hands. He took one deep breath, and heaved. The chain groaned. Sam could almost see the links grinding against each other, bending. The Heritor's hands shook; the veins of his wiry arms bulged; his face purpled.

The chains did not break. He stopped, panting for breath.

'The cage, then!' Sam cried. 'Break the bars, then I can help you with the chains.'

The old man nodded. He placed his hands on the bars, and heaved with all his might. Again, it looked as though he might succeed, but again he stopped, this time collapsing to his knees, the effort too much for him. The bars were merely wooden poles – how great must the enchantment be to strengthen them so?

Sam considered using the tablet to weaken the sorcery, if such a thing could even work, but realised it would only weaken the Heritor, too.

He placed his own hands on the bars. 'Father,' he said, quietly. 'Your blood flows through my veins. I do not have your strength, but maybe I can help. Try once more. With me, together.'

The Heritor's gnarled hands reached up to the bars, and felt for Sam's hands. Sam felt his energy, warm, thrumming, flowing into him. Asim Lahij pulled himself up from the floor, and grasped the bars once more, his hands above Sam's. He nodded that he was ready.

Sam pulled with all his might, and his father pulled too. He felt his power grow, he saw his flesh turn slowly translucent, as it mimicked his surroundings, the power manifesting itself unbidden. His hands became like shadows, until he could barely see them at all. But something else came, a flicker of warmth that started in his chest, and spread like a swig of ship's rum, through his muscles, through his arms, into his hands. This was not the Blood Burn. It was something else, something new. This was his father's legacy, flowing through his veins in his time of need.

The Heritor's face was an agonised grimace. Sam thought his father might falter, but he did not. He felt the bars bend, and crack, just as Sam did. It gave him the will to carry on. Father and son pulled at the bars, until, with an enormous crack, they splintered. Asim Lahij tumbled from the open cage into his son's arms.

They held each other tightly, just for a moment. Sam sniffed away tears.

Sam helped his father stand, then frowned. He became aware of something... of silence. The storm had stopped raging. The battle-cried of the Savaisal had faded.

'Come, father,' he said. 'I think we're out of time. We must break your chains. Do you think we can?'

The blind Heritor patted Sam on the shoulder. Together, they took up Asim's chains, and pulled.

* * *

Zhar-Mharrad stood over the limp form of the warden they called Makeno. The tribesman lay half-buried in the mud, his power spent. The storm was already clearing – just the lightest haze of drizzle remained to show that the warden had ever dared challenge Zhar-Mharrad's might at all.

The Savaisal had fled – what was left of them, at least – leaving their leader to his fate. Perhaps that was the wisest thing the tribals had ever done, for Zhar-Mharrad was feeling anything but merciful. He looked at his hand, bleeding still, throbbing with pain. The missing finger could be mended with magic. Once he had regained his strength. The flow of blood had at least made the summoning of Ziriz that much quicker, more violent.

The demon had returned to the periapt now, taking with it the souls of two of Zhar-Mharrad's lackeys. He would have preferred to feed the Riftborn with his slaves, but Ziriz was an impatient creature, his hunger insatiable. There had been no time to bring forth a prisoner in the heat of battle. Makeno was to blame for this also – he would pay dearly when he awoke. Zhar-Mharrad wanted him to be fully aware of his fate. The vizier would savour every moment of the warden's punishment.

Of the boy, there was no sign. He had taken the tablet. He would have to be hunted down and put to death for his insolence. Zhar-Mharrad was thoroughly sick of this island, but he had no choice but to remain here even longer while the boy was found. And his pet, Hassan, was gone, too. There was no loyalty left in this accursed world, it seemed.

Zhar-Mharrad shouted to the last of his Manhunters. 'Find the boy. Kill him. Don't come back without my tablet.'

The hunter bowed, and ran at once into the night. Zhar-Mharrad wished the jemadar was still alive. Before his fatal error, Faizil had at least been dependable – more so than his accursed captain.

Yana Selishe. Zhar-Mharrad shook his head ruefully. How he'd looked forward to taming her. Alas! Some things were not meant to be.

The Bidajah had secured the perimeter of the camp. Come first light they would have to rebuild, but for now they presented a thin wall of steel and gold to the unforgiving forest. Zhar-Mharrad's forces had been depleted a little, but his Bidajah could be repaired with a little magic and ingenuity. He waved a hand, and four of his warriors drew in close, forming an inch-perfect line before him. What a joy it was to see such obedience.

'You!' Zhar-Mharrad pointed to the closest of the four. 'Seize this savage.'

The Bidajah stepped from the line, dragged Makeno up from the mud, and slung the Savaisal over his shoulder. Zhar-Mharrad was about to lead the Bidajah to the slave tent, to create for Makeno a new cage imbued with enchantments, when the Bidajah stopped. The other three drew their weapons, adopting a defensive posture.

Zhar-Mharrad whirled around on his heels, towards the slave tent, where the Bidajah now looked. The tent-flap had opened. Standing before him were three sorry-looking figures. The boy, Samir; Zhar-Mharrad's new pet, Hassan; and the blind Heritor last of all. A flicker of... something... crossed Zhar-Mharrad's heart. Not fear; no, never that. Not of these wretches.

But had they not caused for him nothing but trouble? Had they not now escaped him again?

He stepped backwards, towards his Bidajah. The blind Heritor stepped forward, almost as though he could see Zhar-Mharrad. The old man clenched his fists, and stretched out the muscles of his neck so that the bones cracked audibly. Then the boy, Samir – that thrice-cursed, meddlesome boy – stepped forth beside the old man, and fixed Zhar-Mharrad with such a glare of defiance that the vizier's heart did beat just that little faster. His brow prickled with cold sweat. Zhar-Mharrad swallowed, and gathered his composure. He squeezed the Periapt of Souls tight, the blood from his severed finger making the gem quiver in anticipation.

'How dare you face me?' he shouted. 'By the black fires of Birrahd, I command you to surrender, and perhaps I will let you keep your miserable lives.'

The boy muttered something to Hassan. For a second, Zhar-Mharrad thought they meant to obey him, and this tiresome business would at last be done. But Hassan simply shuffled backwards, while Samir and the blind man took another step forward. Could it really be? Did they really mean to fight?

Zhar-Mharrad held up his good hand, and focussed his energies. The veins in his wrists began to glow a sickly green, before a ball of green flame materialised in his palm. He revelled for a moment in its warmth.

'Very well,' Zhar-Mharrad said. 'I will burn you to ash. And know this, when you die, your idiot friends will be of no further use to me. I'll have their heads on pikes before sunup.'

'You have made a grave mistake, Zhar-Mharrad,' said the boy, the strength of his words surprising.

Zhar-Mharrad chuckled. 'Oh?'

'I came here as a thief. It's all I ever was. I came here to steal the Tablet of Sav'Eq-Tul, and end your chance of ever finding the Crystal Pool. But during the fight, my friends were killed, by treachery, and by magic. And then I entered this tent – a prison, here in the Lost Isles. And I found among your captives this man. My father.'

Zhar-Mharrad had at first narrowed his eyes, wondering whether or not to burn the boy to cinders as he spoke. But now he was glad he had not. Now that the boy knew the truth, it would make his suffering all the more sweet. What agony would now be wrought on these three insects for the misery they had brought to Zhar-Mharrad's door.

'And so you see, Zhar-Mharrad,' Samir continued, much to the vizier's annoyance, 'this is your mistake. You made things personal. I came here a simple thief, but I will leave a vanquisher.'

There was a moment of silence. Then Zhar-Mharrad laughed. He thought tears might actually roll down his cheeks. The boy didn't see the funny side, naturally. But to Zhar-Mharrad – one who had walked with the Riftborn, and seen into the hell-realms with his own eyes – the threat was utterly ridiculous.

'Forgive me,' Zhar-Mharrad said. 'But that was the funniest thing I've heard for a long time. Thank you for that, boy. But now it's time for you to die.'

Zhar-Mharrad drew back his hand, and felt the ball of flame grow hotter.

The ground beneath Zhar-Mharrad's feet began to tremble. An earthquake? No – this was something else. And the sound of a war-horn, low, and close, filled the night air.

CHAPTER 23

Sam had been about to give the signal, to put his plan into action and distract Zhar-Mharrad. But someone had beaten him to it.

The ground rumbled. The war-horn blared again, low and unearthly. Bidajah lumbered to the eastern treeline, where the ground sloped high and the trees towered in strange, conical spikes. Those trees now shook as something approached.

Zhar-Mharrad spun about in confusion. That would do. 'Now!' Sam shouted.

Hassan whipped back the tent-flap, and the slave-children poured outside, racing across the camp, diving between the legs of Bidajah, who tried to catch them with clumsy swipes. Something crashed out of the jungle, but Sam couldn't see what it was. All he knew was that this was his opportunity to stop Zhar-Mharrad.

Sam summoned all his concentration, and ran towards the vizier. A step or two behind him, his father did the same.

Zhar-Mharrad sensed the attack. He turned back, unleashing a ball of green flame in Sam's direction. Sam felt a hand on his shoulder – his father's hand – and a sharp shove. Sam hurtled sideways, turning in mid-air, watching the fireball travel in slow motion, inexorably towards his father.

Asim Lahij sprang in the opposite direction to Sam. The ball of flame impacted the ground, exploding in a dazzling flash of green light. The mud evaporated at its touch, the ground itself igniting. Sam saw his father roll on the ground, dousing flames from his arm. He saw Zhar-Mharrad intone an incantation to the little black orb about his neck.

Sam leapt to his feet immediately, sprinting at Zhar-Mharrad as fast as he could. A Bidajah stepped into his path, scimitar swinging. Sam slid beneath the arcing blade, slashing a dagger to the back of the brute's knee as he went. The Bidajah stumbled forwards as his leg buckled. Sam rolled, got back to his feet and kept on running. His preternatural senses reached out before him, alerting him to danger even before it came. He leapt over a spear as though it weren't there. He spun around a third Bidajah, rolling off its hulking body. He heard the name 'Ziriz' leave Zhar-Mharrad's lips, a slow drone to Sam's ears in his state of heightened awareness.

Sam launched himself through the air, connecting with Zhar-Mharrad's midriff with both feet. The incantation died on the wizard's lips, and he flew back into his Bidajah guard, who dropped Makeno unceremoniously into the mud as his master crumpled in a heap to the ground. Sam leapt up, pressing the advantage. The Bidajah moved to intercept him, bringing down his huge scimitar at Sam's head.

Sam's father leapt in front of Sam, catching the blade in his bare hand. He needed no eyes to see his foe. He bent the scimitar in half, pulled the Bidajah off balance, and delivered a blow to the brute's face so powerful that Sam winced as he heard the bones of its skull crack.

Asim Lahij fell to his knees, groaning in agony, clutching at his ribs.

'Father!' Sam knelt beside him, certain his father had been mortally wounded by Zhar-Mharrad's magic. He quickly recognised the symptoms of Blood Burn. The blind Heritor bent double, pressing his forehead into the mud, gritting his teeth against the pain.

Sam looked up. Zhar-Mharrad was on his feet, scrambling away from his attackers. Sam had no time to wait for his father. He went after Zhar-Mharrad, gaining rapidly on the vizier, whose heavy, flowing robes only slowed him down. Zhar-Mharrad was again chanting, rubbing the periapt with his bloody, stubby finger. Sam caught up with the vizier and grabbed his high collar, yanking him backwards. He snatched the periapt, wrestled it from Zhar-Mharrad's fingers, and flung it away into the mud.

Zhar-Mharrad screamed with rage. He touched a hand to Sam's chest. There was a flash of green light, followed by an intense pain in Sam's chest. Sam hurtled away from the vizier, cold air rushing past his ears, and crashed into a tent, the canvas folding in beneath him.

He shook his head groggily, feeling like there was naught but sawdust between his ears. He heard Zhar-Mharrad's voice shouting orders. He heard marching boots on the ground.

Sam rolled over as a Bidajah thrust a spear down at him. The spear tore through his tunic and ripped the collapsed tent. Head spinning, Sam wriggled away on his elbows, the Bidajah coming for him again. His ribs ached like he'd been kicked by a mule. He glanced towards Zhar-Mharrad, too far away to reach, already on all fours searching for the periapt.

The Bidajah came again, spear readied. Sam could barely find the strength to move.

A massive, dark shape charged from the shadows, ground trembling beneath its feet. The Bidajah turned at the last moment, but couldn't raise its spear in time to defend itself. The brute was lifted into the air on a pair of long tusks, and tossed aside like a rag-doll. The dark figure roared in triumph, with a noise like a trumpeting elephant. It stopped, breathing heavily, wearied by battle. It was Ashtzaph.

We meet again, Samir, Ashtzaph intoned in Sam's mind.

'How…?' Sam wheezed. 'How did you find me?'

Your friend, Yana Selishe, came to us. Where is she?

Sam shook his head sorrowfully. All he had blamed Yana for was a falsehood. She had died helping him, and had paid the ultimate price.

Ashtzaph's great shoulders sank. *We have failed her, but we can still help you. My people did not want to aid the Savaisal. I have treated with them all day, and, finally, I have gathered enough to see this wizard expelled from our lands. Where is this 'vizier'?*

Sam grimaced as he sat upright. He pointed in the direction of the large tents, where he'd last seen Zhar-Mharrad.

His warriors are almost spent. Do you have the strength to finish this?

Slowly, every movement an agony, Sam stood. 'I do,' he said.

* * *

Zhar-Mharrad was still scrabbling around on his knees as Sam approached, searching for the periapt. At the heavy stride of Ashtzaph, the vizier spun about, looking up in fear at the Eritherean, and then at Sam.

Behind Sam, Makeno stirred, pushing himself groggily to his knees. The blind Heritor staggered forth next, placing a hand on his son's shoulder, which was all the comfort Sam needed.

'My... my Bidajah. Save me, my warriors!' Zhar-Mharrad shrieked.

At these words a few bloodied and broken soldiers began to crawl and limp towards their master. Behind them, all around the camp, the hulking forms of the Erithereans watched, and followed, like huge shadows.

'Give me the tablet, little one,' Ashtzaph said out loud. He held out a hand to Hassan, who watched proceedings from the tent-flap.

Hassan scurried forward, and handed the tablet to Ashtzaph warily.

The Eritherean took it in a massive, three-fingered hand, and held it aloft. 'By the power of Sav'Eq-Tul,' he said, his voice shaking the earth, 'I undo the spells of binding on these cursed souls. Let them find peace at last.'

The wind whistled through the camp, strong, warm. It circled Ashtzaph, and from him blew outwards in all directions. Each Bidajah it touched fell motionless, their unnatural life taken from them. When it was done, Ashtzaph staggered a little, his massive ears drooping. The conjuration had taken a toll on the Eritherean.

Zhar-Mharrad now clasped his hands together, and shuffled on his knees a little closer to Sam. 'Please, I beg of you,' he said, black-lined eyes wide and fearful. 'Show mercy! You have taken away my soldiers, my power. I am no threat to you now. Show mercy!'

Sam looked to his father, who only nodded sagely. He looked to Makeno, who gave a like signal. Sam thought of Dagomir, and Yana, and Bardo. He pulled a dagger from his belt. Sam wanted to kill Zhar-Mharrad, but wanting it and doing it were not the same thing. He knew that now. He could not really comprehend what killing this man would feel like. And in that moment, Zhar-Mharrad looked very much like an ordinary man. A ridiculous man, in his high turban and muddy robes. His face was lined with the toll of years, but caked in powders to give the appearance of use. His waxed moustaches drooped from exposure to the elements. He begged for his life. So what was he now, if not just a man, old and weak and cowardly?

Sam stepped forward, so that Zhar-Mharrad was now at his feet.

'I will spare your life,' Sam said. 'You have nowhere to go, and no one to help you. Your sorcerous artefacts will be burned, your ship, too. You can take your chances in the jungle, and live out your days as a mere mortal.'

'Thank you! Oh, by the gods, thank you, kind boy,' Zhar-Mharrad said. He pawed at Sam, clambering up him, until his head rested near Sam's shoulder.

Sam sensed his friends step nearer. They didn't have to worry on his account. He knew Zhar-Mharrad was a spent force.

'I will tell you one thing before I go,' the former vizier whispered, his voice weak and rasping.

'What is that?' Sam asked.

'I found the periapt, and my invocation is all but complete.' A silver chain jangled quietly, slipping from Zhar-Mharrad's sleeve into his bony hand.

Sam tried to step away, his senses warning him of danger, but Zhar-Mharrad wrestled with him, with a strength Sam had not expected.

'I command thee, demon: kill my enemies,' Zhar-Mharrad shouted.

Thick black smoke rose all around the vizier. Sam struggled against Zhar-Mharrad's grasp. His friends rushed in, but too slow, too late.

'Do this,' Zhar-Mharrad roared, 'and I shall meet your blood price. Go!'

Zhar-Mharrad raked his golden talons across Sam's face. Sam cried out in agony. He felt his own blood upon his cheek, his vision clouded red. The vizier wheeled away, and the Riftborn exploded upwards from the very earth, showering Sam and his allies with dirt and rock. Ziriz roared with inhuman rage, angered by being once more the servant of Zhar-Mharrad. The demon's baleful eyes flicked open, alighting first on Sam. A great fist, formed of roiling smoke and blackest shadow, hurtled towards Sam, who could only look on in horror as his doom came.

Asim Lahij barrelled into his son, throwing him out of harm's way. The fist smashed into Sam's father, grinding him to the ground, ploughing a great furrow into the earth. Sam saw his father's bones snap like twigs.

'No!' Sam cried.

The demon reared skywards, horns of smoke sprouting from an indistinct head.

'I... will... feast...' it boomed.

Ashtzaph stepped forward, incanting a spell in an indecipherable tongue. Makeno, too, began his own chants, bringing forth his lightning once more. He was weak, and his storm lacked the power of his earlier efforts. But the other Erithereans came now, lending their might to their kin's. Blinding rays shot towards the creature, like sunlight.

Ziriz roared with pain, then with laughter. He took up the nearest Eritherean in his smoke-like tendrils, folding the mighty creature in on itself, so that it trumpeted in agony before falling dead to the ground.

'Yes, yes!' Zhar-Mharrad cried. He held the periapt aloft, swinging it on its silver chain. He laughed giddily.

Sam dived aside as a tendril lashed at him. The smoke lingered, cloying, finding its way into Sam's nostrils, down his throat; infecting him with its evil.

He looked to Zhar-Mharrad, who stood in victory, arms outstretched. They said he was the greatest sorcerer who ever lived; Sam had little reason to doubt it now.

Zhar-Mharrad's eyes widened, mouth gaping. He spun about, clutching at his back, and stumbled aside. The hilt of a dagger protruded from the small of his back. And kneeling in the dirt was Yana Selishe.

At once, the smoke withdrew from Sam's lungs. He coughed fitfully, gulping fresh air. He saw Yana raise her hand to him in salute, then fall face-first into the dirt.

Sam clambered to his feet, and backed away from the demon, which now swept left and right, as though uncertain of its next target. Zhar-Mharrad screeched maniacally.

'Kill them, demon. Kill them!'

But Ziriz did not move. It beheld Zhar-Mharrad questioningly. It beheld him as though he, too, were a potential morsel. It turned its head, its baleful eyes alighting on an object in the dirt.

The periapt. And beside it, dragging himself through the mud, was Asim Lahij. His body was twisted and broken, but his Heritor strength kept him alive. He reached out a trembling hand, and seized the periapt.

'Father!' Sam shouted.

The blind Heritor looked at his son with sightless eyes, and smiled.

He squeezed the periapt with all his might. He grunted in abject agony as the Blood Burn overcame him, but still he increased the pressure on the black gem.

When it shattered, Zhar-Mharrad's screams were drowned out only by the roar of infinite souls, crying out as their torment was ended after an eternity. A shimmering portal of pure black opened up around Sam's father, consuming the blind Heritor utterly, dragging him into some other realm. And in return, flickering ghost-lights of every hue crackled and shimmered in the air, shooting high into the sky that even now brightened with the rising sun.

'Demon!' Sam shouted.

The tumultuous form of Ziriz turned, its blazing eyes fixed on Sam.

'Zhar-Mharrad promised a blood price,' Sam said. 'And he can command you no more. Take your revenge upon him, claim your prize, and leave this place.'

The demon opened a mouth – which for a moment seemed solid, made of infinite black teeth set in a maw of endless night – and it laughed a booming laugh, which caused the air to shimmer and reality bend. At last it turned back to Zhar-Mharrad, and stalked towards him steadily, inexorably, its limbs taking shape, its form becoming like that of a man.

Zhar-Mharrad stumbled away, one hand fumbling for the dagger in his back, the other outstretched towards Ziriz. 'No! I command thee, demon!' he cried. 'Leave me be!'

The demon did not leave him be. Instead, it seized him in its talons of smoke and shadow, enveloping the vizier in darkness. It transformed into a shapeless mass of dark tendrils, which spiralled high into the air, amongst the shimmering light of departing souls, before plummeting back to earth. Ziriz plunged into the black portal, which immediately closed behind it. Of Asim Lahij, and of Zhar-Mharrad, there was no trace.

* * *

The funeral pyres burned bright, sending their smoke into a yellow sky, where they joined the flickering rainbow-lights which drifted still.

In the centre of the circle of dead, the tallest pyre was reserved for Dagomir, the Pirate Prince.

'Dagomir,' Sam said. 'You died with honour, and can go now to join your father in his great hall, in the land of eternal summer.'

He looked skyward, and choked back tears.

'Father... wherever you are... I wish things could have been different. I wish I'd known... You – you gave everything for me. And I will honour your memory.' Sam squeezed his eyes tight shut. 'I will return to Yad-Sha'Rib, to free our people. If the Merchant-King will not turn from his path of tyranny willingly, then I will defeat him. This I swear to you.'

THREE WEEKS LATER

Samir crested the ridge, his thighs stiffening after a long hike, but he grinned nonetheless. The air changed almost at once. A sea breeze caressed his face, mussing his hair that had grown long after all these weeks on the island. The cliffs ringed a broad bay, whence a tribe of fisher-folk plied their trade; here, Makeno said, they could secure passage across the bay, to the place the 'outsiders' called Vaaden's Isle. From here, it was a dark sliver of land, less mountainous than Makeno's island home, and somehow even less inviting.

Far below Sam's vantage point, waves crashed upon rocks, huge black sea-birds diving amidst their foamy white tips. On Vaaden's Isle, lights flickered to life against the encroaching darkness. Dozens, scores. A large settlement; a harbour. And more than that, there were lights out to sea; lots of them, twinkling like stars of every hue. Ship's lanterns.

'More are coming. We were not the first, and we will not be the last,' Makeno said, hauling himself to the top of the ridge. He leant on his staff, savouring the warm, fresh breeze, as Sam had done.

'Heritors?' Sam asked.

Makeno nodded. 'Heritors, and their crews. These are the lucky ones. They have found a safer passage than us. And there, that harbour. It is said that, in ancient days, it was a settlement ruled by a race of half-giants, but it had long fallen into ruin. Two centuries ago, it was established as a camp for the first explorers, and looks like it shall be again. You could find a ship here, I am certain. You could go home. But…'

'But what?'

'Vaaden's Isle is a place steeped in old magic. They say the wisest of the wise still reside there, hidden from the sight of outsiders. If anyone could decipher the Tablet of Sav'Eq-Tul, it is they. If they can be found.'

Sam reached into his knapsack and ran his fingers over the etched runes of the tablet. 'It's funny,' he said. 'All these years, my amulet protected me from my destiny. Now it could help me fulfil it.'

'Don't count your snakes before they hatch.'

Sam smiled as Yana Selishe reached the summit. She still leaned on a stick, her strength not yet fully restored. She stood beside Makeno, her dark eyes scanning the sea. She was almost unrecognisable from the Manhunter of Yad-Sha'Rib whom Sam had met so many months ago. She had shed her black assassin's garb, and dressed now in loose-fitting silks and a tribal shawl, looking more like a Corsair than a hardened killer. Yana gazed down at the incoming ships.

'Everything changes now,' she said. 'For us, for them. For the people of these islands most of all. I wonder how many Zhar-Mharrads are among those crews.'

'But how many Dagomirs also,' Sam said. His eyes met Yana's, and they shared another moment of sadness.

'I support whatever decision you make,' Yana said, as if reading Sam's thoughts. 'The merchant-kings have never ruled Yad-Sha'Rib fairly, you know this. The Cult of Birrahd will not give up its influence easily. And So'Kurrah is not going to find his strength overnight and suddenly become just and wise. What I am trying to say, Samir, is that the death of Zhar-Mharrad is not the end of the struggle, but the beginning. We could go back now, and see what lies in store for us. You could be reunited with your mother... Or we could go to that settlement and find these wise folk Makeno speaks of, and see just how far your destiny will take you.'

Sam looked across the bay, weighing his options. 'So... do we go now?' He asked finally. 'Or wait till morning?'

'You're the Heritor,' Yana smiled. 'What is your command?'

Sam puffed his chest out just a little, feeling several inches taller. 'I swore to return to Yad-Sha'Rib, to honour my father's memory. And I shall. But first, I must find the Crystal Pool. When I go home, it will be with the full power of the first Heritors in my veins. When I go home, all those tyrants of dark heart will know to fear the name Lahij.' Sam looked to Yana. Was that approval in her dark eyes? 'We should rest tonight,' he said, firmly. 'Tomorrow, our quest begins.'

ABOUT THE AUTHOR

Mark A. Latham is a writer, editor, history nerd, proud dogfather, frustrated grunge singer and amateur baker from Staffordshire, UK. An immigrant to rural Nottinghamshire, he lives in a very old house (sadly not haunted), and is still regarded in the village as a foreigner.

Formerly the editor of Games Workshop's *White Dwarf* magazine, Mark dabbled in tabletop games design before becoming a full-time author of strange, fantastical and macabre tales. His Victorian SF series, *The Apollonian Casefiles* (*The Lazarus Gate*, *The Iscariot Sanction* and *The Legion Prophecy*) is available now from Titan Books. Mark has also written two Sherlock Holmes novels – *A Betrayal in Blood* and *The Red Tower*. Mark's short fiction has been included in several anthologies, including *The Further Encounters of Sherlock Holmes*, *Frostgrave: Tales of the Frozen City*, *Angels of Death*, *A Clockwork Iris* and *Gaslight Gothic*.

Visit Mark's blog at thelostvictorian.blogspot.com or follow him on Twitter **@aLostVictorian**.

SCENARIO

We hope you have enjoyed *Destiny's Call* by Mark A. Latham. This book is the second novel based on the popular tabletop wargame, *Frostgrave: Ghost Archipelago* by Joseph A. McCullough. If you would like to learn more about the game, you can join the *Frostgrave: Ghost Archipelago* Facebook group or order the rulebook from www.ospreygames.co.uk.

For readers who are already fans of the game, we present this exclusive scenario, loosely based on events in the novel.

* * *

PIT OF VIPERS

By Joseph A. McCullough

After a long and arduous trek through the thick jungle, your crew finally came within sight of the ruins. There, standing amidst the broken and overgrown stones, were several statues holding weapons of pure gold. This vision of riches proved too much for some of your crew, who broke ranks and surged forward. Just as the first of your men got close to one of the statues, colourful snakes slithered out from every hole and crevice in the ruins…

SET-UP

The table should be dominated by the overgrown ruins of a city. Instead of treasure tokens, players should place statues on the table, following the same rules. Players should set up their crews as normal, but once this set-up is complete, each player is permitted to move up to four members of the opposing crew (excluding the Heritor and Warden) by up to 12" in any direction. This cannot move the figure off of the table, nor cause it to take any damage. Finally, each player should place three pit vipers on the table. These can be placed anywhere on the table, provided they are at least 3" from any crew member.

SPECIAL RULES

Whenever a figure is in base contact with one of the statues, that figure may spend an action and make a Fight Roll with a Target Number of 10. If successful, that figure is now carrying a treasure token. Only one treasure token may be recovered from each statue. The treasure token recovered from the central statue counts as the central treasure token.

At the end of every turn, each player is allowed to place one pit viper on the table, following the same rules as above.